REVELATION (ASCENDANCY: BOOK 1)

By

D. Ward Cornell

Dedicated to my sweet wife who's been very supportive through this adventure. Also to my son, Jonathan, who tells me that he can imagine me saying some of the lines in this book and it makes him laugh.

Thank you both for your support and encouragement.

Thanks to my early readers who had the courage to read the early manuscripts. Special thanks to Theresa Holmes whose feedback helped make this story come to life.

Table of Contents

PROLOG

GODDARD SPACE FLIGHT CENTER, BALTIMORE

"Hey, Mark. Anything to report?" John asked as he walked into the room.

Mark Jenkins was on duty this shift, managing the repositioning of the Hubble Space Telescope. He'd been on duty for the last four hours. John Brooks was his manager, the Hubble Space Telescope's Associate Program Manager. Hubble was in the process of a significant repositioning and recalibration, one that was scheduled to take five days. In the early days of the Hubble mission, this kind of recalibration hadn't been necessary. But by 2014, the Hubble's aging gyroscopes could no longer hold position for long periods without recalibration.

"An urgent request just came in from the Administrator," John said.

"I hope it's not too urgent. We're tied up in recalibration for the next three days," Mark replied.

"Well, that's the thing. He wants us to redirect to these coordinates."

"What do you mean by redirect? The gyros are out of alignment. Hubble doesn't know where those coordinates are," Mark complained.

"That's OK. Just move to these coordinates. Record whatever is there with the coordinates displayed on the recording, then continue the recalibration."

"John. If this is a joke, I'm not getting it."

"No joke. The request came from the President himself," John said.

"From the pres..." Mark broke out laughing. "The President." More laughing. "Dude, you had me going there for a minute. The President doesn't even know what coordinates are."

John just stared at Mark, and the laughing slowly turned into a look of incredulity. "You've got to be kidding me. The President gives NASA some coordinates in the middle of a recalibration, and we just drop everything and make recordings of some arbitrary location in space?"

"The Administrator thought this would be a good way to win some goodwill with the new President. He was just sworn in a little over a week ago and is already showing interest in NASA. It would be crazy to say no. The coordinates are just a fraction of a degree off our current course, if we do it now. So, let's get after it."

As they settled in on the coordinates, at least according to the uncalibrated gyros, Mark realized that the implied distance at these coordinates was well beyond Hubble's resolution. *Just keeps getting better!* Mark thought, at least until the images started coming in.

Mark could not believe his eyes. There were three stars in close proximity. One was a white dwarf, which had sucked huge mass from its binary companion, a red giant. It was clearly in the last stages before becoming a Class 1a supernova. Further away was a hydrogen-rich yellow dwarf, one much like the Sun. But the yellow dwarf had come close enough to the binary that mass had begun streaming away from it, heading toward the white dwarf.

"Dude. This is going to go super in a matter of days. Can we stay on station and watch it?" Mark asked his boss.

"No can do my friend." John said. "The experts say this baby is going to blow in three days, which is four hours after it falls below the horizon."

"What! What experts? Why were we asked to look at this if other 'experts' already knew what was here?"

"Above both our pay grades, my friend. Get the clearest, cleanest recordings you can, then let's continue to do the job we're paid for, recalibrating the gyros," John said.

Mark shook his head in disbelief. They were scientists. They did their best to find new phenomena, and when they did, even if by accident, they didn't just continue to recalibrate.

Mark groaned. "When did NASA get taken over by the DMV?"

THE EVENT

This was the day! As the gate closed behind him, Michael turned left onto Kohala Mountain Road from his home near the summit of Kohala Mountain. Despite his excitement, Michael couldn't help but smile as he drove along the narrow mountain road. There were cattle on a grassy knoll to the left; horses wandering in protected pastures to the right. As he came around a bend in the road, he pulled over and paused momentarily to take in the vista. The pass he'd just come through was at 3,500 ft. It offered a spectacular view of two of the Big Island's volcanic peaks, Mauna Loa on the left and Hualalai straight ahead. And on the right... The beautiful blue Pacific Ocean. He paused a moment to take in the peace and center himself. The next couple weeks were going to be crazy.

Michael was on his way to the WM Keck Observatory in Waimea. The Keck Observatory operated two giant telescopes that sat atop Mauna Kea, Hawaii's tallest mountain. Michael had been invited to participate in what promised to be one of the most groundbreaking observations in human history, a supernova in the Andromeda galaxy. This was groundbreaking because historically supernovae were only discovered by chance. Therefore, the vast majority were discovered by hobbyists, not by professional astronomers. The amateurs simply outnumbered the pros, with more eyes on the sky at any given time. Scientists were always quick to confirm observations and lead the investigations that followed. But no one had ever done a high-precision observation of the onset of a major supernova. At least not until recently.

Michael was a well-known inventor and entrepreneur. His innovations in natural gas recovery from exhausted oil wells were the basis of most of his wealth and notoriety. But he was also known as an amateur astronomer, philosopher and philanthropist.

Two years ago, Michael had made an uncharacteristically public announcement about a pending supernova in the Triangulum galaxy. In his announcement, he posted the time and location where

3

hobbyists and major observatories could look to find it. Of course, he was mocked by the scientific community for the preposterousness of his claim. No one knew enough about the stars at those coordinates, or even about the composition of that area of the Triangulum galaxy, to make any statement whatsoever about what was going on there or what events might occur. The only known precursors to supernova observations were gravitational waves, which were not guaranteed to precede the light and were mostly useless for pinpointing the source.

Not a single major observatory had attempted the viewing, but numerous amateurs targeted the coordinates in the hours ahead of the announced time. And within a few hours, pictures started popping up all over the internet with claims of the discovery. Most of the pictures were grainy with questionable coordinate validation and inconsistent timestamps. Nonetheless, it didn't take long for the major observatories to confirm Michael's prediction.

Michael had made his second announcement about three months ago. It was for a smaller nova that would be difficult to observe. Despite the on-going academic cynicism, a scientist with one of the major observatories in Australia re-tasked their main telescope and started a high-resolution recording an hour before the predicted time. They were rewarded with the first publishable observation of its type in history.

Michael's most recent prediction was for a major three-star collision and supernova that would be observable in the Andromeda galaxy. That prediction had been announced two weeks ago.

Where his previous predictions had been greeted with cynicism and downright hostility, the response to this announcement was quite warm. A re-tasking of the Hubble telescope three days ago gave results that were visually spectacular.

One of the stars was one that had been previously observed in Andromeda. Until about 10 years ago, it had a numeric designation. But it was now known as Lorexi, the naming rights having been purchased by someone named Michael Baker. Lorexi had become involved with an approaching binary star composed of a white dwarf and a red giant. The binary was well along the path to becoming a Class 1a supernova. The white dwarf was pulling massive amounts of gas from its shrinking companion and was now close enough to Lorexi that it was drawing mass from it as well. Although NASA could not confirm how close this forming trinary system might be to destruction, their initial mass measurements put the white dwarf at the Chandrasekhar limit, which implied that it would blow sometime soon.

The giant telescopes on the summit of Mauna Kea, operated by the WM Keck Observatory, would have the best and longest viewing from any location on planet Earth. Michael had made that determination many years earlier. It was one of the reasons Michael had placed his most important research laboratory on the Big Island. His research initiatives required him to spend a fair amount of his time on the island. But he spent a lot more time here than was needed for research so that he could develop connections with the observatory staff and with the local government authorities. Those connections were necessary for the events that would be set in motion tonight.

Because Michael had made the predictions leading up to NASA's recent discovery, the director of the Keck Observatory, a woman Michael had befriended shortly after moving to the Big Island, had invited Michael to what everyone now assumed would be one of the greatest astronomical events recorded by mankind.

As Michael approached the observatory headquarters, he saw that the police had put up a barricade preventing additional cars from entering the facility. Crowds had begun to form on the lawn in front of the facility where a projection screen had been set up for public viewing. Several news networks had also set up mobile broadcast sites along the Mamalahoa Highway to broadcast footage of the event.

As he pulled up to the barricade, Michael noted that his friend, Chief Henderson of Hawaii Civil Defense, was manning the barricade himself. On rolling down the window, Michael called out, "Chief!"

"Well, if it isn't the man himself! Look at the mess you've created. Good on you, broddah. The director invited you, right? I see your name on the list."

"Yep, Chief. I think I'm responsible for this. And, ah, the director did invite me. Are you going to be able to watch at all?"

"Hope so, but duty first. Enjoy, my friend. You've earned it."

The Chief moved the barricade aside and waved Michael in. As he entered the parking lot, the director's assistant, John, pointed out the spot they'd reserved for him.

"John, so good to see you. How's the boss doing?" asked Michael.

"There are usually enough details on new observation nights to make her testy. But the crowds and publicity... Dude, she's bouncing off the walls. How was the ride up?"

"In truth, I'd have started a little sooner if I'd realized what a spectacle this was going to be." Michael paused as they walked toward the employee entrance. "Hey, I need to speak to the boss ASAP. I have a minor adjustment I need to make to the image enhancement software I installed earlier this week."

"Oh. She's going to love hearing that," John said sarcastically. "Is it really necessary? Can't we post-process the recordings?"

"Afraid not. If the enhancements aren't part of the real-time recording, we'll lose them. It's a quantum thing."

"A quantum thing? What the hell does that mean?"

Michael smiled at his friend and said, "You know. Like science-y stuff."

"The boss isn't going to be happy hearing about this..." John said as they rounded the corner, and nearly bumped into his boss.

Stephanie Davis looked up, startled. "Michael, there you are! Do you realize how much trouble you've rained down on me?" Then she reached out to give him a quick hug.

"Stephanie, good to see you. Having fun yet?" Michael returned the hug. "Hey, I need to make a minor adjustment to the enhancement software I installed for the observation tonight."

"You what! The observation is scheduled to start in 15 minutes. The big 10-meter scope has already been positioned and thermally equalized. We can't disrupt the data transmission tests that are running!" She seemed to take offense to the last-minute change.

"Stephanie, relax." Michael pulled what looked like two thumb drives out of his pocket. "This will not disrupt anything. In fact, the software is expecting these two USB devices to be attached minutes before the recording begins. The computer that needs them is right over there..." he pointed at one of the signal processing computers in a nearby rack. "I'll just go plug them in now. Um... probably should have mentioned that on Tuesday."

"Michael, what am I going to do with you? Go! Be quick. And, if you crash that computer, I'm going to call security and have them throw you out!"

"Thanks Steph. You're going to love the enhancements these will enable."

...

Michael walked over to the rack and opened the door. A quiet alarm went off, attracting the attention of some of the scientists nearby. Despite the fact that Michael had single-handedly brought them this opportunity and had donated the best image enhancement software in the world, the scientists fundamentally did not like the fact that a hobbyist had been allowed into their presence tonight.

As he slid the USB devices in, he thought about the technology inside of them. *None of these people would believe me if I told them what was actually in these two thumb drives.*

They contained a pair of quantum-entangled receivers that would take in data from their partners in Michael's research lab on Kohala Mountain. Among other things, his research lab had a pair of high-sensitivity gravitational-wave detectors that were spaced for maximum directional sensitivity. The output of the detectors would be synced with the optical images coming down from the 10-meter scope on Mauna Kea. Together they would provide a three-dimensional view of the observation that was about to begin.

Michael walked back over to where Stephanie stood as the lights in the room dimmed and the first images were displayed. The image was grainy, with only a few pixels of light near the center of the screen. Steve Brown, lead scientist and principal investigator for this observation, centered the image and expanded it to maximum resolution. The few pixels of light in the center expanded to a single blob of light in the middle. No stars could be resolved within the blob.

Steve looked up doubtfully and asked, "Michael, can we turn on your image enhancement software? Ours really can't tell what we might be looking at."

The tension in the room was now palpable. The Observatory had put their reputation at stake following up on the prediction of an amateur. From the principal investigator's point-of-view, the administration had completely compromised the integrity of the investigation by allowing amateur software into the main data stream.

"The software is up and ready to be applied. Just issue the command sequence on the screen in front of you," said Michael.

Steve typed in the command. To his astonishment, the image resolved to the point where all three stars were visible, as well as some cloudiness that would seem to indicate that an accretion disc had begun to form.

Everyone drew in their breath, astonished at what they were seeing. The room grew silent. Then Michael, pointing at the screen, smiled and said, "It begins."

The smallest of the three stars suddenly began to expand. It quickly overwhelmed the other two stars and grew to fill the screen. Steve, temporarily stunned by what he was seeing, forgot to zoom the image out and the bright light expanded past the bounds of the screen. He quickly zoomed out, having trouble zooming out fast enough to keep the image on the screen. Suddenly, additional details started to emerge. The image shimmered in a way never seen before. And, spectral lines began to appear in the center, spreading throughout the cloud of gas.

One of the other investigators exclaimed, "I know what that is! Those lines are like the filaments in the Crab Nebula, left over hydrogen from the yellow star that was caught up in the explosion. And the shimmering waves going through the blue body of the cloud... Those must be gravitational eddies. All of our theories suggest that this should not happen for months, possibly years, after the initial explosion."

The room exploded in commentary, everyone engrossed in their instruments and speculations. After a while, one voice popped up above the others. "Michael! You need to work on your forecasts. The explosion happened a minute and 3 seconds earlier than you predicted!"

As the room broke into laughter, the sound of champagne corks popping could be heard in the background.

People gathered around Michael, offering their congratulations and their thanks. He smiled, thanking them for their kindness. But a melancholy hung over him. The star that had been consumed, Lorexi, had been his star, the one his people's home planet had circled–the home planet that was no more.

...

It was almost 5:00 AM. The sun would rise within an hour. Looking at the main screen Michael could see that the image was already starting to fade due to background light from the sunlight flooding the atmosphere. It was probably time to make his exit.

"Stephanie! Could I have a word in private?" Michael asked, looking over at the director.

She walked over, "Sure. My office?"

As they entered the office, Stephanie said "Thank you Michael. This was one of the best days I've had in my career. You not only told us where to look, you gave us the technology to make it happen."

"Stephanie, about the technology... Those two thumb drives are essential to this observation but will not work for any other. I'm going to leave them with you, so you can continue this study for as long as you want. But I'd like to have them back when you're done."

"I'd sure like to keep them and use them for other studies. Couldn't we work out some kind of arrangement?"

"Unfortunately, no. They are tuned to these coordinates and cannot be re-tuned. It's just not possible."

"But, how? They're just software, right?"

"Not exactly, and that brings me to another issue we need to discuss. I'm going to make another announcement on Sunday evening, 7:00 PM Eastern time to be exact. This announcement will generate a lot more interest than the previous ones. In fact, a lot of people are probably going to come to see you for the sole purpose of learning more about me."

"Michael, what's going on? What are you going to do?"

"Steph, I can't tell you right now. But, trust me. It's nothing but good news. Good news for you. Good news for the observatory, Waimea... all humanity, in fact." He paused. "But it is going to generate a lot of interest. Some of it will be unwanted. I can't say more right now, but I need to ask a favor of you. Don't give those two thumb drives to anyone. Destroy them before letting anyone else have them. Do you understand?"

"Michael, I understand what you've said, but I don't understand why? And I'm starting to get worried."

Michael walked over and put his arms around her in a close embrace. "Don't worry," he whispered. "This is all going to work out. Very good things are coming, and you're going to be very close to the most interesting parts." As he let go and stepped back, he asked, "Friends?"

"I trust you Michael. But, please don't do anything that's going to get you in trouble."

"Don't worry. Best to Matt and the kids. Maybe you all can come over for some barbeque when this is all over. You and the kids can come down to the lab and see some of my cool toys. Got to run."

Michael turned and headed toward the exit. There was one more stop to make.

...

"Chief. You're still here!" Michael walked over toward the Chief.

"Michael! Did you see the size of the crowd that gathered out here? It was almost as crowded as the Cherry Blossom festival. And we didn't even have any buses to shuttle people to the parking lots.

"I've got half a mind to write you up." The Chief smiled at the joke. "I had a chance to see some of the projection. They said it was a supernova. Is it that giant star right up there?" the Chief asked pointing to the brilliant new star, just above the horizon to the south.

"Indeed, it is. Fantastic, right?"

"Is it a new permanent fixture in our night sky?"

"No. It will get slightly brighter over the next couple days, then slowly fade away over the next six to twelve months."

"Never seen nothing like it." The Chief shook his head in wonder. "Hey, are you on your way out? I can move the barricade for you."

"I am, but I'd like to have a word with you first if that's OK."

"Sure. What's on your mind, Michael?"

"I'm going to be making another announcement tomorrow night. It's going to create quite a stir."

"What are you going to do Michael? I don't take kindly to people causing trouble in my town."

"Chief, this will be nothing but good. It has nothing to do with Waimea. But I predict that a lot of people are going to take an intense interest in me and anyone who knows me. So, I need to ask you a favor."

"I'm already not liking the sound of this, Michael," said the Chief.

"Chief, can you keep an eye on things here? I mean the Observatory, Stephanie and her family, my neighbors, traffic along Kohala Mountain Road? I'm worried that instead of two networks on the lawn in front of the Observatory, we're going to have 20 scattered all over town and twenty more along Mountain road."

"Michael, what are you going to do? Should I just arrest you now?"

"Chief, something very good is about to happen. Good for you; good for the town; good for the entire world. People are going to be excited."

"Michael, I'm thinking we should go over to headquarters and talk about this."

"Hold on, Chief. Suppose I was to tell you that I'm going to give everyone in Waimea a million dollars. What do you think would happen? Make that everyone in Hawaii."

"Everyone would go nuts. The media would descend on us from everywhere. People would be partying all over the place. There would be accidents, a little bit too much drunken enthusiasm. I don't think my jail would be able to hold them all."

"Then you don't think I should give them the money?" Michael asked.

"OK. I think I get your point. But you're not giving everyone a million bucks, right?"

"No. I'm going to give them something better."

"Oh, Michael. You're making my head hurt. What would you like me to do?"

"If I'm right and the media and gawkers start descending on town, put a blockade on Kohala Mountain road. It's just too narrow and winding to handle the traffic. And, get ahead of the media caravan. Decide where you want them, how to organize it all. You know, like when Kilauea acted up in 2018. You know how to handle this. Your team is good."

"I've got it, Michael. Don't know what you're up to, but I do trust you. Keep yourself safe now. It's dangerous work doing good things."

"The announcement will go out at 7:00 PM Eastern time, Sunday evening. I'm pretty sure you'll hear about it immediately."

...

The sun was up as Michael pulled into his ranch. As he drove down the dirt road toward the barn, he saw his assistant, Pam Miller, waiting for him at the entrance. The barn was not actually a barn, but the entrance to his research lab. From the outside, it looked like an ordinary barn, complete with a horse corral. In fact, there were stalls for horses in the barn.

But in the back and out of sight from any of the entrances or windows, was a hidden door. As he and Pam approached, the door opened and he was greeted by the research lab's AI, Jeremy. "Welcome home, Michael. It's good to have you back. Would you like some refreshment or rest before we begin our preparations for tomorrow?

THE ANNOUNCEMENT

[02.02.2025, 6:55 PM] CBS NEWS, NEW YORK

Walter Graham walked into the control room. He was the managing director for the 60 Minutes news show on Sunday evening. "Will, how's the set-up going? We're live in 5 minutes. I see Leslie on the monitor. Looks like we're ready to roll. Anything here I should know about before the broadcast begins?"

...

[On the studio PA] "Team, this is Walter. We've just queued the pre-show ad. We'll be live in 20 seconds. Clear the stage." A pause, then "5, 4, 3, 2, 1, Live..."

"Good evening America, this is Leslie..."

Walter could hear Leslie through the studio audio system. But his master monitor was showing a different image – the image of some man, who was opening his mouth to speak. Then realization struck. "Wait a minute. I know this guy. It's that Supernova guy? He's not on our show!" Then in a loud voice, "What the hell is going on! Our show is not broadcasting."

⍰

TELEVISIONS ACROSS THE WORLD

"Hello. My name is Michael. Some of you may recognize me from news coverage of the Supernova that occurred two nights ago. I apologize for interrupting your normal programming, but I have an important announcement that I'd like to share with you this evening.

HAWAIIAN CIVIL DEFENSE OFFICE, WAIMEA, HAWAI'I

The Chief was sitting at his desk in the station catching a late lunch. One of his team had come down sick, so he'd volunteered to cover the desk this afternoon. Suddenly the TV in the corner turned on, and there was a picture of Michael opening his mouth to speak. "Oh no. He's done it now, hasn't he," groaned Chief Henderson. "What the hell does this boy think he's doing?"

FCC, WASHINGTON, DC

"Yes, Mr. President. I understand that this guy has interrupted the broadcast of your interview on 60 Minutes." Pause.

"Yes, sir. He is on every channel." Pause.

"No, sir. We don't know how he's doing it." Pause.

"Mr. President, our instruments tell us that the regular shows are being broadcast as normal. The signals are in the air, but our TV receivers are not taking them." Pause.

"Yes, sir. Your television has a receiver." Pause, while shaking his head.

"Mr. President, we have attempted to jam him, but it doesn't work." Pause.

"Sir, we have a team of our best dissecting a system right now in an attempt to figure out what he's doing." Pause.

"Sir, this guy is on every radio and TV channel. He's even speaking in Spanish on the Spanish channels. I don't know how he's doing it. I'm hoping we will eventually figure this out. But, whatever he's doing, it's way beyond any technology we have or have ever heard of." Pause.

"Thank you, Mr. President. We'll get back to you as soon as we learn something."

TELEVISIONS ACROSS THE WORLD

"My people come from the planet Lorexi Prime, the fourth planet from our sun, Lorexi. Our planet is, or I should say was, located in the Andromeda galaxy, approximately 2.4 million light years from Earth.

"For those of you who saw news coverage of the Supernova event Friday evening, the yellow star you might have seen in the images from Hubble," he said pointing to the Hubble telescope image being displayed in an inset at the top right of the screen, "was the star that our home planet orbited.

"Although the light and gravity waves from that explosion only reached Earth two days ago, the actual event took place approximately 2.4 million years ago. As you might guess that tragedy caused a major upheaval for our civilization. One that turned us into a spacefaring people and one that ultimately led to many good things.

"I was sent to Earth about 100 years ago to learn about your peoples and your ways. Early study of your planet suggested that you, too, would develop into a great civilization, one that would ultimately be invited to join our Confederation of over 1,000,000 inhabited planets. My mission was to live among you as one of you, to assess your state of development, and ultimately to seek diplomatic relations when your people were ready for it.

"In my judgment, humanity is not quite ready to become part of the larger intergalactic civilization of sentient peoples. Unfortunately, humanity will soon face two great threats, either of which could destroy it. Therefore, I have decided to open the dialogue between our species early, so that I can offer you the means to overcome the threats you face."

Michael paused, looked down for a moment, and then returned his gaze to the camera. "As I said, there are two threats. The first threat is internal, the second external. The external threat is still some time away. Although we don't need to worry about it tonight, we will need to start preparing in the next couple years if the Earth is to have any chance of surviving.

"The internal threat comes from three sources. The first is your environment. Humanity's impact on your planet is far worse than you currently understand. The second is the hostility among your nations, hostility that is largely driven by demand for resources and wealth. The third is the inability of your fragmented governments to solve these problems and work collaboratively for the betterment of all. It is my judgement that without external assistance, you will destroy yourselves within the next two hundred years.

"None of these short-term risks are caused by nature, they are simply artifacts of your limited technology. To help avert this un-necessary crisis, I have been authorized to offer the following. First, unlimited clean energy that can quickly arrest the build-up of greenhouse gases in your atmosphere. Second, a carbon capture system that will allow you to reduce carbon dioxide levels to where they were in the 1950s and do so within ten years. Third, medical technology that can eliminate most diseases on your planet, stopping the suffering of millions and extending life-expectancy. Lastly, to provide replicators that can produce food, clothing and most consumer products at very low cost and without the devastating impact of your current industrial processes.

"To the governments of every country on Earth, I make this offer on behalf of The Ascendancy, the diplomatic representatives of the Intergalactic Confederation of Planets. Meet with me. Let's discuss how we can work together. The technologies I offer will be made available to any country in which we are allowed to open a consulate, develop diplomatic relations and work toward signing a treaty. To the heads of state of every nation on Earth, my contact information is now on your desk. Please contact me. I would like to meet with you. I would also be happy to give demonstrations of the technologies we offer, so that you can fully understand the value of partnering with us.

"To the sovereign nations of the Earth, I would like to place an embassy in one of your nations. This embassy would be between the Intergalactic Confederation of Planets and the peoples of Earth. As a benefit to the nation that hosts our embassy, it will be the first to receive mass delivery of the gifts that we offer.

"To the United Nations, I ask to be invited to address your General Assembly.

"To news organizations around the world, I will be announcing a press conference in a few days' time. I will also grant interviews to those that would like to meet with me privately.

"I beg your forgiveness for having commandeered your radios and televisions this evening, and I look forward to meeting anyone who is willing to meet with me. Thank you and good night."

The next and final part of Michael's announcement was only broadcast in the United States. "To the President of the United States. Mr. President, I respectfully ask for an audience with you as soon as possible. I also ask you, the governor of California, and the governor of Hawaii to recognize my properties in California and Hawaii as the temporary diplomatic soil of the sovereign people of The Intergalactic Confederation of Planets.

"Please do not raid these facilities. They are protected by technologies you cannot penetrate. There is no need for imprudent actions that might risk the safety of my neighbors. You will be granted inspection rights, if you arrange for them. And everything on those properties, as well as the properties themselves, will be voluntarily surrendered to the appropriate authorities, if that should become a term of the treaty we ultimately agree to.

"Thank you for your consideration."

WHITE HOUSE, WASHINGTON, DC

"Mr. President, the cabinet has been assembled in the situation room as you've requested."

As the president walked into the room, he said, "I trust you've all seen the video. What have you been able to find out about this fellow? We need to act quickly on this one. It smells like a hoax to me.

If that's true, we need to shut it down quickly. What options can you give me?"

"Mr. President, the FBI informs me that the man in question is Michael Baker. Born in Dallas Texas, on October 10, 1990. This is what we have been able to find on him in the last hour:

- Education: Unknown
- Driver's License: Granted In Paso Robles, CA in 2007 at age 17.
- Employment: President and sole owner of Clean Natural Gas, Inc. The company was founded in 2008, when he was 18, for the purpose of recovering natural gas from exhausted oil wells.
- In 2010, Clean Natural Gas, Inc. (CNG) bought three oil wells, which the EPA had previously certified as being exhausted, and which had been sealed in 2008. He paid $200,000 for the land and mineral rights. First production from those wells was the following year. CNG bought 40 more wells over the next five years for a total of $3 million. The company is currently shipping over 10 million cubic feet of natural gas per day, to utilities in Paso Robles, Bakersfield, Los Angeles and San Diego.
- According to the EPA, his facilities are in full compliance. In fact, talking to them you would think this guy is a saint. Toxins in the ground water in the Paso Robles area have declined 90% since his operations started. The air is even cleaner.
- Operations at his facilities are allegedly fully automated, although local officials say that people have periodically been seen on the site.
- According to the IRS, the company claimed revenue of about $40 million in 2023, earnings before taxes of $4 million. His biggest expense was research at a whopping 50% of revenue. That doesn't sound right. The IRS apparently agrees, they have audited him 3 times. Each time he was completely clean. In fact, all three audits resulted in the company being eligible for a higher refund, so the IRS has stopped auditing him.
- In 2015, at age 25, he bought a penthouse apartment in one of the high rises along the San Diego harbor for $7.2 million.
- This is curious, in the same year, he also bought the naming rights for a star with the designation... Uh, forget the designation, it's just a bunch of numbers and letters. He re-named the star Lorexi. That's the one that blew up in the news Friday night. Right?
- In 2017, he opened a research facility in the mountains above San Diego.

16

- In 2020, he bought a ranch on the Big Island in Hawaii, which is where we believe he is now.

"The FBI in Honolulu has dispatched a team to the Big Island to investigate this guy. Their team went wheels up about 15 minutes ago at 2:50 PM Hawaiian time. Their first stop will be at the home of the director of the WM Keck observatory, who was seen with him in the media coverage. They also plan to interview a Chief Henderson with Hawaiian Civil Defense. Apparently, the media coverage included a shot of him talking with the Chief. The field office reports that they have accessed Hawaii Island's property database and have found the ranch that he bought. They plan to stop and interview people there as well."

"Excellent job, team. I didn't expect that we could have gathered this much information in an hour," said the President. "Was he on some kind of watch list or something?"

"No, sir. Because he is the listed president of a company with government contracts, most of this information was on record with Dunn & Bradstreet and the IRS. The luckiest hit so far was the thing about renaming the star. Apparently, NASA had done some research into him two years ago when he put out his first announcement about the pending supernova in... hmm, where was it... yes, the Triangulum galaxy, wherever that is... That was the announcement that everyone ignored. The director of NASA called me just after the broadcast this evening, letting me know this tidbit about him."

The President spoke up. "I'm not sure I get this guy. The EPA and the IRS both say he's a stand-up guy. His birth certificate says he's a 35-year old natural-born citizen."

"Sir," interrupted the Secretary of Finance. "I just got a hit on him in Baron's. His net worth is estimated at about $30 – $50 million. And, they rate his business acumen as A+. That is a rare rating sir."

"I guess that's what I don't get. He's a rich, 35-year-old, natural-born American citizen, one that both his government and the business press think very highly of. Yet, it looks like he's throwing it all away – hijacking the airwaves, claiming to be an extraterrestrial, offering to establish diplomatic relations with foreign countries, and basically threatening me by telling me not to raid his properties or else. What's the matter with this guy?"

"Sir," spoke up the head of Homeland Security. "I basically agree with your summary of the situation but think we should reflect on a couple other facts."

"I'm listening..." said the President.

"We have gone to great lengths to harden our country's broadcasting system – far more than anyone actually knows about. Yet, he apparently took over every television and radio in the country. In the last hour, I've heard from the Internal Security ministers of five different countries so far that claim he did the same thing there. I've been told that our CIA has attempted to develop this kind of technology and failed."

The President looked at the Director of the CIA. "Is that true?"

"Mr. President, it's probably better for me to say that I cannot deny the allegation than to actually confirm that statement. And, I agree with Homeland Security... What Mr. Baker did is well beyond our capability."

"Doesn't that make him a threat?" the president said with some exasperation.

"Sir, another point if I may?" said the Attorney General.

The President nodded in his direction.

"According to the FCC, Mr. Baker did not actually hijack the airwaves."

"What! Homeland Security just said that he was on every radio and TV!"

"Yes, sir, that is correct. He took over every radio and TV, not the airwaves."

"OK. I think I'm missing something here. How could he take over all the radios and TVs without taking over the airwaves?"

"Well, that's exactly the problem, Mr. President," replied the Attorney General. "The FCC says that there is no evidence to suggest that the airwaves have been compromised. Yet he took control of all the radios and TVs. It is a Federal Crime to interfere with the airwaves. But, without evidence that he has, we cannot go after him for this. I haven't been able to find a law that he's broken. The closest would be denying the lawful owner of an asset the right to use it. Since none of the customer equipment was harmed, at least that we know of yet, this would be a misdemeanor offense, the prosecution of which would be in the hands of local authorities."

"You've got to be kidding me!" yelled the President. "Some guy takes over all the TVs in the country, so no one can see my interview with 60 Minutes, and there's nothing I can do about it?"

"I'm sure we can make a conspiracy charge of some sort. But we'd need to do a lot more research before we could successfully file it. My instincts tell me that the Supreme Court isn't going to go along with you on this one."

"Oh, for the love of God! I can *not* believe this!" whined the President.

"Mr. President, may I say something?" asked the Secretary of State.

"Go"

"Two thoughts… First, I think we have him on the foreign relations front. The Logan Act makes it a crime for an American citizen to engage in negotiations with foreign powers, unless they've been granted those rights through due process. I'm not sure how he could get out of that charge. Second, let me talk to our allies. I'm thinking it would be better to get aligned with our friends and take joint action, rather than jump the gun and do something that will make us look bad."

An aide slipped into the room, handed a note to the President's chief of staff, then slipped back out.

"Mr. President" said the Chief of Staff. "This is unexpected… CNN and Fox both just released flash polls, asking… and I quote… "Should the President meet with Michael, the alien?"

"And the result?"

"CNN has 79% in favor, 19% not sure, 2% opposed. Fox has 74% in favor, 12% not sure, and 14% opposed. Never seen those two so close. I'm thinking we might want to tread lightly on this one."

"OK, team. I need options. If this is a hoax, and I'm 99% sure it is, then we need to act quickly to shut this guy down. In the unlikely event that it isn't a hoax, then I need serious options. I also need talking points. We're going to need to address the nation. And at this point, I have no idea what to say."

THE PAPARAZZI

[02.02.2025 2:30 PM] RESEARCH LAB, KOHALA MOUNTAIN

"Good work, boss. We've finally announced ourselves to humanity." Elsie Hoffman was an Ascendant like Michael. This was her first major mission on a non-Confederation world. She was responsible for The Ascendancy's transportation systems in this solar system and she was the pilot for any transport they had that required a pilot.

"Thanks, Elsie. But now our work really begins. Is the shuttle ready, in case we need to go to Washington, DC tonight?"

"Yes, boss. I'll need 15 minutes pre-flight. Flight time will be about 50 minutes. In an emergency, we can transport or go holographic."

"Charles, get a sample kit put together tonight. In fact, let's package up several of them. Coordinate with Elsie to load them onto the shuttle." Charles Wong was the facility's Chief Engineer. He was also an experienced Ascendant and talented technologist. Charles had been on multiple missions on other planets. He was targeted to head the Chinese consulate, if and when it opened.

"Pam, I know you're on top of this, but could you confirm that Julia, Peter, Joel, and Emmanuel are aware that the countdown has begun."

Julia ran the corporate office in San Diego. Peter ran the San Diego research facility. Joel ran the Paso Robles production facilities. Emmanuel maintained the residence in San Diego and was Michael's bodyguard on the mainland. They each had an important role in the events that were going to be taking place. But their immediate mission was to protect the assets in San Diego and Paso Robles from the onslaught that would be coming from the FBI, the media and the gawkers.

"Jiaying, what's the status on the FBI team heading here?" Jiaying was Michael's communications officer. She was an android, built for the consulate they hoped to be opening in China. She was first language fluent in all Chinese dialects and master of all manner of communications equipment. Over the coming week, she would also be Michael's Chief Protocol Officer.

"The team from the FBI field office in Honolulu is just about to depart. According to the orders that I intercepted, they are bringing 12 agents, led by a Special Agent named Christopher Long. Their orders indicate that their first stop will be the Davis residence. ETA 3:50 PM. Then, the Chief. Then, here. Surprisingly, I've not been able to find a tasking for San Diego or Paso Robles. They must think that they're going to get you here, so they can wait until later to clean up the California operation. As if!"

"Thank you Jiaying. But remember. We need to be respectful of these people."

"Sorry, boss."

"Sanjit," Michael called. "Where are we on the surveillance deployment?"

Sanjit Gautama was the head of security for the Kohala Research facility. He was an Ascendant from the planet Indira III. He had completed his Ascendancy training and was in his first year as an Ascendant, yet he had been assigned to Earth. It was a huge privilege for a newbie to be assigned to a First Contact mission, especially one of this importance.

When he learned that his planet had what Earth considered to be an Indian name, he elected to be shaped as Indian and had volunteered to work in the Indian consulate when it opened. Prior to entering the Ascendancy Academy on Indira, Sanjit had been in the Indiran Special Forces. So, he was assigned to Michael's personal security team in the interim, until an Indian consulate was opened.

"We have over a thousand surveillance nanobots in the air. The winds are giving us some problems, but we have the entire ranch covered from multiple angles."

"Excellent," Michael replied. "Did we get any surveillance set up at the Chief's or the Davis's homes?"

"Those are just coming online now. The Davises are at home and clear for now. Looks like they're preparing for a barbeque. The Chief is at headquarters. He looks a bit upset."

"Remind me of the physical defenses we're using today?" Michael asked. "It's important that no one be allowed entrance without permission. But, under no circumstance can we allow anyone to get hurt."

"We've got that covered. The outer layer is a Level II pliable force field around the buildings, out to about 100 ft. It extends up just about to the top of the surrounding trees, so should not interfere with any aircraft." Sanjit replied. "The pliability will slow anything entering the field. So, if they drive their car into the field, it will be slowly brought to a halt. Even if they come in at 100 MPH, they will be stopped slowly enough that their airbag will not deploy.

"The inner layer is a suspensor field. Anyone who enters that will be temporarily paralyzed. It's not particularly comfortable, but not as bad as being tazed. And people can be held there indefinitely without harm. Moisture and nutrients are provided by the field, so even if they were stuck there for a week, they'd be OK. But it'd be an incredibly unpleasant experience."

"We can move through these fields unaffected, right?"

"Right."

"What about weapons? Do we have anything that will deactivate any weapons they bring?"

"Human weapons are so primitive. Surprisingly, knives will probably be the most dangerous. The fields will not affect knives as long as they are held by a human. Bullets will stop before the suspensor field. Guns and higher mass metal projectiles will dematerialize on contact."

"OK, sounds like we're ready. Any customers yet?" asked Michael.

"Funny you should ask. A couple of paparazzi just showed up. They've just climbed over the gate and are walking toward the barn. They must have noticed the tire tracks."

...

"I don't see anyone. Are you sure we're at the right place?" Ralph asked.

"Relax, Ralph. This is the right place. I googled it. I looked the place up when this guy started getting famous. What a loon. But the Enquirer put out a contract for a picture of this guy on or near his property. Up to a thousand bucks, depending on the quality. Let's hunker down in the corral over by the barn. That should give us an easy shot of anyone coming or going. See how all the tire tracks head over there." Larry said. He was the mastermind of this operation. Ralph was his sidekick, paid to carry the spare battery packs.

"Hey Larry. Does it seem like the air is getting thick or something? I'm starting to feel like we're walking through water or pushing on something."

Larry was starting to notice the same thing but would never admit it. "Hey, see that big rock over there? I'm going to use it to jump over the fence into the corral."

True to his word, Larry pushed his way toward the rock, stepped up onto it, then leaped with all his might so he would clear the fence. That's when things got really weird.

...

"Michael," Sanjit called out. "Looks like the two paparazzi are either very stubborn or very stupid. Probably both. They've been struggling to work their way through the Level II pliable force field. They've been at it for nearly a half hour. Kind of impressive they got that far.

"The field attempts to slow them down and can exert a lot of force to make that happen. But, as long as they move slowly, it won't actually stop them before the suspensor field.

"Well, the one guy climbed a rock and jumped across the gap, right into the suspensor field, about 5 feet above the ground. Check this out... He is currently suspended about four feet above the ground. The field is slowly lowering him down. The part of him that's in the field, is completely paralyzed. The one hand still outside the field is slowly moving back and forth.

"His colleague gave up the fight against the Level II field and is just sitting on the ground, trying to shout for help but losing his voice.

"What should we do with these guys?" Sanjit asked.

"I can just walk through that field. Right?" Michael asked. Sanjit nodded. "Can Kale walk through it also?" Kale, pronounced KAH – lay, was the site's handyman. He was huge, muscular and Hawaiian. No one ever gave him trouble. He was just too big and too nice. Human visitors to the ranch always gawked at him, especially the women. What none of the humans knew was that Kale was an android.

"Yep. Any of us can. We're genetically keyed."

"Kale," Michael called. "Can you come join me? We're going to go rescue the two intruders outside."

"Sanjit," Michael said. "Jam their equipment until I tell you to release it, but don't damage it. I want them to leave with some pictures, ones of our choosing."

"Noelani," Michael called, using the tone of voice that triggered the intercom. "Could you prepare to receive a couple of guests in the den?"

Noelani Manoah, pronounced noh-eh-LAH-nee, served as the housekeeper for the residence and as a trained medical technician. Like Kale, she was also an android shaped as a Hawaiian. She was 5' 3" tall, had a distractingly shapely body with perfect hair and skin tone, and an alluring smile. One of the goals of her design was to distract human males.

"We will be back to the residence in about 5 minutes."

...

Larry had become quite uncomfortable. He couldn't move a muscle. Couldn't blink his eyes. Couldn't even breathe, which made no sense. He felt short of breath but wasn't getting dizzy or anything. He could hear Ralph whimpering on the ground nearby. Ralph clearly thought that Larry was dead because he wasn't moving and didn't answer when Ralph called to him. Larry could hear Ralph whispering, "I'm dead, I'm dead, I'm dead..." over and over again. Larry thought to himself, *What a wuss*!

Kale walked over to Larry, startling Larry as he came into view. Kale said, "Yo, broddah. What are you doing?" He turned his head this way and that as if trying to figure out what kind of trick Larry was up to.

Then he gave his big friendly smile and looking Larry straight in the eye said, "Come on. Let's get you out of this mess. I'm going to gently grab your wrist. When I do you will be slowly released. I'll guide you to the ground for a gentle landing, then we'll go inside for a little chat. You good with that?" Kale paused as if waiting for a response, one that he knew Larry could not provide. "OK. If you fight me, I'll just let go of you and you will freeze up again, understood? If that happens, I'll just head back inside for an hour or two. Got it?" Again, Kale paused as if waiting for a reply.

"Here goes." Kale reached up and gently took Larry by the forearm. As promised, Larry was gently lowered to the ground.

"Ok," Kale said. "Take a couple deep breaths to get your energy back. Then we'll head to the house so you can have a word with the boss."

Slightly out of Larry's sight, Michael was doing the same routine with Ralph.

"Ralph, my friend." Michael offered his hand. "You'll be able to move freely as long as I'm touching you. Let's go inside. We have a place where you can clean up. The housekeeper is preparing you a snack. We can talk."

"How can I trust you?"

"Ralph, you've trespassed on my property. I've done nothing to harm you, just protecting my stuff. You don't really want to get into your car in your current condition, do you?"

Ralph looked down at his soiled pants. He'd apparently fell into some horse manure.

"How do you know my name?" he asked incredulously. Then in a panic, "You're not going to probe me, are you?"

Michael chuckled, "Do I really look like that kind of alien?"

"Sorry," Ralph replied.

"Come on, let's go. Good stuff is waiting inside."

THE RESIDENCE, KOHALA MOUNTAIN

Noelani greeted the guests as they entered. "Gentlemen. Please come in."

Ralph and Larry were momentarily frozen. Not by any force fields, but by Noelani's captivating smile.

"Ralph, the guest bathroom is right over there. Go ahead and clean yourself up. We have a shower you can use. Just push the green button. It will only take a minute.

"There are also fresh clothes in there for you. You're welcome to change into them. Drop your stuff in the clothes basket before jumping into the shower and I'll have them returned to you when you go. Now, scoot."

Ralph opened the door she had pointed to with some trepidation. But as he entered the room all the day's tension slipped away and a calm spread through him.

"Larry, would you like to refresh yourself?"

"Ah... No, Ma'am, I'm good."

"OK. Come on into the den. Michael will be with you shortly. I've put out some snacks and coffee. Kale can get you a drink if you'd like something other than coffee."

Kale was setting up the bar as Larry entered the room.

"We've put your stuff on the table there. You're a photographer under contract with The Enquirer, no?"

DAVIS RESIDENCE, WAIMEA, HAWAI'I

"Hey guys. Burgers will be ready in 15 minutes," shouted Matt through the back door. He had been grilling burgers for his son's soccer team's annual party. Looking at Stephanie, he asked, "Are the fries and salad ready?"

"Yep. Help me carry them onto the lanai."

The doorbell rang.

"Hmm, I wonder who that could be. All the parents and kids are already in the back yard," said Stephanie. "Why don't you get the meal started? I'll go see who's at the door."

"You've got it, babe," Matt replied.

Stephanie walked to the front door, looked through the peep hole and saw several men in official dress. When she spotted the head set in the one guy's ear, she got a bad feeling about it. "Matt!" she called.

The doorbell rang again.

Hand trembling, she opened the door.

Matt and several of the other fathers who'd been loitering in the kitchen came into the room as the door opened.

The lead agent, seeing the onslaught coming his way, held out his badge with his left hand. "Good afternoon, Ms. Davis, I'm Special Agent Christopher Long with the FBI." He offered his hand to shake.

The other fathers stood frozen in place, but Matt stepped up next to Stephanie.

The lead agent held out his hand to shake with Matt, who reluctantly reached out to shake Agent Long's hand.

Greetings exchanged, Agent Long started. "Director Davis, I apologize for interrupting your Sunday afternoon. But there are important matters we need to discuss. Tensions have been running high since the announcement as I think you can understand."

"No, Mr. Long. I don't understand. It's the annual party for my son's middle school soccer team. Not much tension in that. And, why in the world would you want to question me or my family? Why are tensions running high?"

"You didn't hear the announcement made by the guy claiming to be an alien?" he asked.

"Mr. Long. I'm the director of the WM Keck Observatory, not the hospital's psych ward. Why are you asking me about aliens?"

Stephanie suddenly burst out laughing. With the terror of the last few minutes draining away, the idea of the FBI knocking on her front door to ask about aliens seemed preposterously funny. Despite the laughter running through her veins and the tears streaming from her eyes, she was suddenly gripped with fear. "Oh no. Not Michael."

"Director Davis. Do you know Michael Baker?"

"Yes," Stephanie replied. "He's a dear friend of mine, the one who handed me one of the greatest scientific discoveries of our time. Please tell me he hasn't been hurt."

"Ms. Davis, can we sit down to talk? In private? Everyone else can go back to the soccer party. But I'm afraid that you and I have a lot to discuss."

Special Agent Long and Agent Rebecca Jackson had come in and were now seated at the dining room table with Stephanie. The other agents waited outside. "Ms. Davis..." Agent Long started to say.

"Agent Long, please call me Stephanie."

"Thank you, Stephanie. Please call me Chris." Long said. Out of the corner of his eye he saw Rebecca Jackson wink at him approvingly.

"Tonight, your friend Michael Baker commandeered the airwaves across the entire planet and broadcast a message that he claimed to be for all the peoples of Earth. Do you know anything about that?"

"He did what?"

"He basically took over all the radios and televisions across the planet to make a global announcement."

"Oh my god, Michael. What have you done?" she whispered. "Agent Long, ah Chris. Michael told me he was going to make an announcement today at about 7:00 PM Eastern time. I was planning to go on-line to the sites he used to make his previous announcements once the party was done this afternoon."

"So, he has made previous announcements?"

"Yes, but not like the one you're describing. Michael is a good guy, passionate about astronomy, that's how I got to know him. He came up with a model or theory about two years ago, I don't know the exact timing off the top of my head, but it's in my computer somewhere. I could look it up if you'd like." She paused, waiting for some sort of signal that she should go get her laptop. It didn't come.

"Ah... Anyway... He said he thought he could predict the timing of a few supernova events. I thought he was teasing me at first. No one can do that. We are bound by the speed of light after all." She chuckled.

"So we are," Agent Long agreed.

"But, shortly thereafter, he posted a prediction on a popular amateur astronomy website. The announcement had the time and coordinates where a supernova event would occur. I tried not to laugh at him. But the scientific community as a whole was nowhere near as kind. Poor Michael was mercilessly mocked and ridiculed by the scientific community for even suggesting that such a thing was possible.

"The hobbyist community was much more welcoming, and within minutes of when he said it would happen, pictures of what appeared to be the birth of a supernova started popping up all over the place. Hundreds of amateur photos of questionable quality and integrity were ultimately posted. All of these were scientifically useless, of course. And the scientific community piled on with even more mockery, claiming he was a hoaxer.

"Then a year or so later, Michael posted another prediction. This one was for a small nova, not a supernova. The amateurs were all over it, hundreds signed up to do the sighting. The problem with this one was that the viewing window was too narrow for most hobbyists and very few were able to capture an image, forget a sequence of images. Fortunately, a credible scientist in Australia was in the right spot, at the right time, with a 3-meter... Um, I think it was a 3-meter... telescope. He also had all the important equipment needed to make a useful scientific recording of the event.

"The results were nothing short of spectacular. An opening moment sequence like that had never been captured before. The scientific consequences of that were, and are, mind blowing.

"So, when Michael made a third announcement, just a few weeks later, many of the mainstream, major observatories, like Keck, committed to record it. Apparently, even the President was intrigued. Rumor has it, he asked NASA to re-task Hubble to get a still shot of the star before it was supposed to blow up. That image showed three stars... a binary pair in the last stages before a supernova. And a bright yellow, hydrogen-rich young star that had started to be consumed by the white dwarf."

"I've seen the photo." Agent Long commented.

"For the third prediction, Keck was in exactly the right spot." A long pause.

"Ms. Davis, Stephanie." Agent Long asked compassionately. "What is it?"

"I'd forgotten this. And now it seems so ominous."

"What's that Stephanie?"

"When I first met Michael, we were seated next to each other at Hawaiian Style... the breakfast place just down the road. It's fairly common for people there to strike up a conversation while waiting for their breakfast. Michael was relatively new to the island. When I asked him why he moved here, he told me a little about his business. In truth, his comments didn't really seem to add up. But one of the things he said was that he was an amateur astronomer and with the sky so clear and dark here, he hoped to catch the sighting of a supernova… Do you think he could possibly have known about this five or six years ago?"

"Stephanie. I have to come clean with you. I was sent here to talk to you by the President of the United States. He is very worried about what Michael did today. His concern is that Michael hacked the airwaves, which is a crime, and that he's made a very public offer to negotiate diplomatic deals with foreign governments, which is a very serious Federal crime.

"The reason he wanted me to see you was that the last photo of Michael that we could find was one of you giving Michael a hug. It was taken just before he left the building Saturday morning. The picture was taken by a security camera at the hospital across the street. It snapped the shot through the open front door as someone else was leaving the Observatory. We have no evidence at this time that you were an accessory to these alleged crimes, but you are a person of interest because you would appear to have a close relationship with him."

"Agent Long. I assure you that I am not involved in a romantic relationship with Michael. We are friends and colleagues of a sort, but nothing more." Stephanie said with a bit of heat in her voice. "I can't speak to what Michael did. I haven't even seen the message yet. But I struggle to believe that he purposely broke the law. He's a good man."

"I might point out Director Davis… Michael claims that he is not a man. He claims that he is a Lorexian, whatever that is, and a representative of the Intergalactic Confederation of Planets."

"I struggle to believe that the person you describe is the Michael I know."

"I have a recording of Michael's message. Would you watch it with me?"

"OK"

THE RESIDENCE, KOHALA MOUNTAIN

"Gentlemen," Michael said as he walked into the den. "Thank you for coming into the house to talk with me."

"Did we have a choice?" Larry asked.

"Of course, you did. We explained that to you. As long as you were in personal contact with us, you could move unimpeded," Michael said.

"Some choice," mumbled Ralph.

"Ralph. Your actions create your options. By trespassing on this property, you limited your options. That said, I'm glad you came in. The FBI will be here shortly. It would have been awkward to have two guys frozen, one of them sniffling, in my horse corral. But, more importantly, I have some work for you. It pays well, a lot better than the gig you're currently working. Did either of you hear my announcement tonight?"

Larry replied, "So, you admit that it was you on the broadcast?"

"Technically, it wasn't a broadcast." Michael said.

"What do you mean? We saw it on the television. Then before it was even done, I got a text with an offer to get photos of you on your ranch."

"Larry, do you know how a television works?"

"Not really, but kind of... There's a station with an antenna. They send out a signal. The TV picks it up and puts it on the screen. So, you must have hacked the station, or at least the antenna."

"Good guess. Wrong answer, but good guess nonetheless." Michael said.

"Well then. How did you do it?"

Perfect, Michael thought. "I hacked the TV."

"What, so this only played at our house? Why would you hack our TV?"

"No." Michael smiled. "I hacked all 1.6 billion TVs across the world, including the White House and the Kremlin. I also hacked all 3.8 billion radios."

"What?! No one can do that!"

"I can. And I did," Michael said.

"Why?"

"Do you remember what I said?"

"You said you were from some galaxy or something and that you wanted to help us somehow."

"Assume for a second that I am the representative of an Intergalactic Confederation. What would I need to do to get people to believe me? What could I do that could not be done? That everyone would see or hear for themselves without the filter of the media or the government?"

"Good point," Larry replied after a long pause.

"I said something else. I said that I would give an audience to any media outlet that would invite me."

"Has anyone invited you?" Larry said somewhat excitedly. Maybe there was still time to get a piece of that.

"Before I answer that... Do you believe me?"

No reply.

"Have you ever heard of a suspensor field before?"

"Is that what you did to us?" Larry asked.

"For the record... I put up the suspensor field. I also posted signs saying, 'Danger. Do not enter.' You were the one that ignored the signs, forced your way through a Level II dampening field, and then jumped into the suspensor field... Just saying."

"Point taken. But warnings and the field thingy weren't posted on Google." Larry said.

Michael burst out laughing. "Indeed. It was not. But back to the question... You were stuck in a suspensor field for about a half hour. Could you move?"

"No"

"Could you breathe?"

"No"

"For a half hour... How can you still be alive?"

"I don't know."

"Doesn't that give you pause to think that maybe, just maybe, I'm telling the truth?"

DAVIS RESIDENCE, WAIMEA

"So. Is this the Michael Baker you know?" Agent Long asked.

"Chris, I don't know what to tell you. That looks like Michael. Sounds like Michael. Even shows the personality and mannerisms of the Michael I know. But I never heard him talk about any of this stuff before."

"What did he tell you Saturday morning?" Long asked.

"Didn't I already tell you this? He said he was going to make another announcement. He said people would come to see me because they would want to learn more about him. He said everything he was going to do would be good. Good for the Observatory. Good for me and my family. Good for our country and good for the world." Stephanie replied.

"And, he didn't tell you anything else?"

"NO!" Stephanie said with conviction. "I have no idea what's going on." Then she broke down crying. "Why are you asking me these questions? I'm an astronomer. I don't know anything about this!"

Only later, years later, would she remember that Michael told her not to let anyone else get their hands on the thumb drives.

THE RESIDENCE, KOHALA MOUNTAIN

"Michael," Jiaying called over the intercom. "One of the calls you were expecting is on the line. Do you want me to patch it through?"

"Thanks, Jiaying. I'll take it in the study. Give me a few seconds to get over there."

Looking at Larry and Ralph, he said. "Gentlemen, I need to take this call. You're welcome to hang around a bit, if you'd like. Noelani would be happy to bring you some food. When you're ready to go, Kale can escort you off the property. But if you wander around unescorted, you'll get stuck again and there won't be a rescue until sometime tomorrow. I'll be back in a bit to check on you."

...

"Hello. This is Michael. With whom am I speaking?"

"Hello, Mr. Baker. My name is Shawn Terry. I'm the scheduler for Good Morning America, the morning news show on ABC."

"Mr. Terry. Thank you for your call. What can I do for you? And please call me Michael."

"Michael, we would like to have you on our show as soon as possible. If we could get a team to you, would you be interested in speaking with us tomorrow morning between 7:00 and 9:00 AM Eastern time?"

"Possibly."

"Could you tell me where you are so that I can check on the availability of a crew?"

"I'm on the Big Island of Hawaii. In the northern part, near a town called Waimea."

A pause... "Oh, my goodness. I'm sorry to say that we can't get a crew there in time."

"Could I do the interview in your studio in New York?" Michael asked.

"Mr. Baker. You would need to be in make-up by 6:00 AM. That's only 8 hours from now. There's just no way to get here in time."

"Shawn... Do you have a helicopter pad on the roof of your building?" Michael asked.

"Well, yes, we do. But I don't see how that will help. You're 5,000 miles away."

"Shawn, do you know why they want me to appear tomorrow?"

32

"Well I suppose that they want to scoop the other networks."

"Shawn, what I meant was... What's so special about me that they want me on the show at all?"

"Oh... Well, I guess it's because you claim to be an alien here to save the Earth."

"If I am an alien, here to save the Earth, don't you think I could get there in time?"

"I'm not sure how that helpsMr. Baker. The planes still can't get here in time."

"OK, Shawn. Here's the deal. I will arrive on your helipad tomorrow at 5:00 AM Eastern time. I'll be coming in one of my shuttles. The shuttle will be cloaked, so it will just suddenly appear. Have them place a TV camera on the roof so they can capture the image of the shuttle just appearing out of thin air. I'll bring several people with me, as well as some equipment that I'll want to demonstrate to your studio audience. You need to promise me at least 15 minutes, but I'll make myself available until 9:00 AM. Did you get all that?"

"Yes, sir. But someone else will need to approve this. What will your fee be?"

"No fee. But you need to get back to me within an hour, or I will go to one of your competitors. Got it?"

"Yes, sir. No fee. Contract in one hour or the deal goes to someone else."

"Excellent. Thank you for your call, Shawn."

"Thank you, Mr. Baker."

Michael hung up, then started calling out to his team. "Elsie. We are headed to New York. Need to be there at 5:00 AM Eastern time. Sharp! Charles. Make sure we have at least three sample kits. I'd like to plan on making that many stops tomorrow, and I'd like you to join me.

"Kale, Noelani. I'd like you to join us also."

DAVIS RESIDENCE, WAIMEA

"Thank you, Chief." Agent Long hung up the phone.

"Director Davis. I'm sorry that we interrupted the kid's soccer party. The Chief's story on this matter is more-or-less the same as yours. I was hoping the two of you would be able to give us a little more insight into Michael's motives so we could make a better assessment of the threat. But it is what it is.

33

"The Chief is going to swing by. We're going down to Baker's ranch to see if we can talk with him. Would you have any interest in coming along?"

"No, Agent Long. I've had enough of Michael Baker for one day, and the kids need their Mom here. Good luck with your investigation."

"Stephanie. Here's my card. Put it by your phone. If anything comes up, call me immediately. I'd also like to ask you to let us know if you decide to leave town. We may have more questions."

Long turned as he heard a car come up the driveway. It was the chief. He rose and offered his hand. "Thanks again for your time. I can show myself out. Go enjoy what's left of the barbeque."

RESEARCH LAB, KOHALA MOUNTAIN

"Michael," Sanjit called over the intercom. "The FBI team is on their way and the Chief is coming with them. The FBI agent, Long, told Ms. Davis that he'd hoped she could tell him more about you so he could, quote 'get a better assessment of the threat' unquote. He also invited her to come along with them, which she declined."

"I'll be over shortly." Michael said.

...

"So, what have we got Sanjit?" Michael asked when he arrived.

"Same arrangements as before. Is that good enough?"

"Do you have a count on the number of FBI agents coming?"

"I think so. There were 12 agents in the group that came onto the island. Three cars arrived at the Davis's, but we didn't have the angle to know for sure that all 12 were in the three cars. The Chief is joining them. I'm not sure if he was bringing any of his own people. So, my guess is 13, maybe 14. I can do a tracking sweep while they're on their way to get an exact count if you'd like."

Michael paused to think... "This is all going exactly as we expected. They're on their way, so go ahead and activate the planned defenses. Do we have an ETA?"

"About 20 minutes."

"Is there a way we can evacuate Larry and Ralph, without the FBI seeing them?"

"If they get in their car within 10 minutes and head north, toward Hawi, they will be fine. Otherwise, we can cloak their car, and put them in the cloaked chamber in the residence basement."

"Good. I'm going to go talk with them now. Call me when the FBI are 10 minutes out." Michael headed toward the residence.

A few minutes later, Michael entered the residence and stepped into the den.

"Larry, Ralph... I see you're still here. I have some bad news. Chief Henderson and some other officers are on their way here. If you leave now, you have time to escape to the north without being seen. We won't tell the chief about your visit. Otherwise, I may be forced to turn you over to them."

"Larry, what do you say we take off now while we can?" Ralph asked.

"But we never got any pictures?" Larry complained.

"We have about 5 minutes," Michael said. "Let's hustle out now and you can snap a few along the way."

Kale walked in with their equipment, on which some excellent pictures had already been planted. Noelani was right behind them with Ralph's clothes neatly folded in a bag, and some sandwiches packed for the road. Within a minute, they were out the door.

Michael let them get several paces ahead, where they turned and snapped some pictures of Michael walking in their direction with the residence in the background. As they approached the area where they had previously been trapped, Larry paused and said, "Is it safe for us to walk to the car from here?"

"Not without one of us going with you." Michael started trotting toward them. "Let's go before the Chief gets here."

As the car started a moment later, Michael pointed toward Hawi and shouted, "Remember to go north."

As the taillights faded around the corner, Sanjit called. "Michael, the FBI crew is about 2 miles away. They just passed the upper entrance to Kohala Ranch."

"OK. The paparazzi are gone. I'll be back in the residence by the time the FBI gets here. Turn on the holo-projectors and activate the defenses now. And put the lab on lock down. No more audio communication with me until the FBI leaves. Communicate by messaging my implant."

As an Ascendant, Michael had multiple implants in his brain that allowed communication and information gathering directly by thought. When he enabled his inner vision, he could view images from almost any source, including text messaging.

A message from Sanjit popped up in Michael's inner vision... "You've got it, boss."

The sun was getting low in the sky. It would be sunset in about an hour. Then everything would be pitch black.

THE RAID

[02.02.2025 5:25 PM] KOHALA MOUNTAIN ROAD

Special Agent Long pulled off the road about a mile from Michael's ranch. The plan was simple. One team of agents would continue ahead for about a mile and a half, where they would pull off the road. There was a trail marked on the map that was about 100 yards off the road. The agents would strike out on foot, crossing a small wooded area to the trail. From there, they would follow the trail south towards Michael's property.

A second team of agents would park here, then cut through the woods on foot until they reached the same trail. From there, they would head north toward the property.

Long would give them a 15-minute head start, then he would continue along the road with the rest of the party. A third team of agents would remain along the roadside near the driveway to interdict if the suspect attempted to flee. Only Agent Long, Chief Henderson and Agent Rebecca Jackson would go up the driveway to the house. The Chief had been there before, so he would enter the property first and the others would follow.

He liked this plan. If Mr. Baker was cooperative, then they could conduct the interview. If Baker decided to fight or to run, then he had teams on the trails heading off the property and another team at the entrance. Mr. Baker would do this interview whether he wanted to or not and would probably be arrested either way.

While they waited for the first two teams to get into position, the Chief came up to Long and said, "Agent Long, I really don't like this plan. You are sending those agents ahead on that trail toward the house, aren't you?"

"Chief, I know this Baker fellow is a friend of yours. But he is likely to be taken into custody after the stunt he pulled today."

"I don't have a problem with that part. I do have a problem with this trail. You people should talk to the locals before doing stuff like this," replied the Chief.

"Chief, this guy is a threat to national security. We've got to collar him. If a few locals see some law enforcement during their hike, they should feel more secure," Long patiently explained.

"Agent Long. This trail is hazardous. It has cliffs, wind channels, bogs, centipedes, fire ants. This trail is a hazard."

"Chief. My boys are not tourists; they are professionals. I get it. Tourists kill themselves on this island all the time because they don't respect nature. But we're pros, trained for this stuff."

The Chief rolled his eyes and shook his head, then said, "OK. Your call. You don't want local input, then I won't bother you with any."

He stomped back toward his car, then shouted over his shoulder, "Flash your lights when you want me to get moving."

As he got in his car, the Chief's only thought was... *What dumb asses these feds are. Don't know about the bogs. Don't know about the centipede nests. I should probably call back to headquarters and get a rescue helicopter warmed up.*

A few minutes later, the Chief saw the lights flash.

THE RESIDENCE

A message from Sanjit popped up in Michael's inner vision... "Two teams of FBI agents are heading toward the house along the trail, one from the north, one from the south. Both teams are ignoring the warning signs."

Michael smiled to himself, thinking... *These government types are all the same. Above the law. Above common sense. Above Mother Nature.*

ALONG THE NORTH TRAIL

Agent Johnson was point for the string of agents approaching the ranch from the North. Ahead were official state warning signs blocking the trail.

"Hey, Mark," he whispered. "Should we call Agent Long about this? The signs say not to enter this area."

Agent Mark Patterson replied. "Hell no. Nothing is marked on the map. The perp probably put the signs here himself, thinking he could scare us away."

As they continued down the path, the ground started getting progressively softer.

THE RESIDENCE

Another message from Sanjit popped up... *Agents along the north trail have entered the bog area.*

Michael sent. *Let me know when they start sinking.*

Sanjit sent back. *Two cars coming down the driveway.*

THE RESIDENCE DRIVEWAY

"Not sure what's up with the car." The Chief said to himself. "It's been running rough since we started up this road." Squinting into the distance, the chief saw the entrance gate, greatly enhanced since the last time he was here. "Well. Look at that. Someone upgraded their security."

Just then the radio buzzed. "Chief, what's that I see ahead? Is that a security gate?"

"Sure enough is."

"There's no security gate on the map."

"Agent Long. This guy is a straight arrow. If we see a security gate, then it would have been permitted. And if a gate is permitted on the Big Island, it will show up on the fancy, classified maps that you build from our databases in about 10 years." The Chief knew that paperwork moved slowly on the Big Island. And changes were rarely reported to the Feds in a timely fashion.

"Same would be true for that trail," the Chief added, only by now his finger had slipped off the transmit button.

The Chief got out of his car and walked up to the keypad and pushed the telephone button. A moment later, a light turned on above a video camera that the Chief hadn't noticed. Michael's voice came out of the speaker box in the keypad. "Hello Chief. What a pleasant surprise. What can I do for you?"

"Michael, part of me was hoping you wouldn't be here." The Chief let out an audible sigh. "There are some people here that want to talk with you. Would you please open the gate so we can come in?"

"Sure Chief. You know the way. Be sure to take the left branch toward the house. The barn is shut down for the night. No need to disturb the horses."

As the gate started to open, the Chief heard frantic screaming coming from the north.

ALONG THE NORTH TRAIL

Agent Mark Patterson could not believe the scene playing out in front of him. As the ground had continued to get softer, Johnson had begun getting more upset. One of the other team members, Darrel Baines, offered to go forward to talk with him. And suddenly...

RESEARCH LAB

Sanjit had been watching the north FBI team on the monitor. They had been moving very slowly. On the monitor, Sanjit noticed that the third guy in line had just gone up to talk with the guy that was in the lead. It was clear that the guy in the lead did not like how soft and wet the ground had become. He was sinking to the top of his shoes and the mud ahead churned like there was something in it.

After a few moments of talk and increasing hand gestures, the new guy threw up his hands and yelled something at the guy in the lead. Sanjit had a feeling that something was about to happen. Then it did. The lead guy punched the other guy right in the face.

As the man fell and hit the mud, the one who had been in the lead slowly sank, then fell over. Then, as the other guys came running forward, 100 large centipedes charged out of the bushes behind the team.

ALONG THE NORTH TRAIL

Baines had come forward hoping to help. He was one of the few guys on the team that got along with Johnson. But Johnson just would not stop whining. Baines finally snapped, and shouted, "Johnson, why did you sign up for the FBI? You are such a freaking sissy! Just go hide in the back. I'll take the lead!"

That was the last straw for Johnson, who just turned and punched Baines in the face. Johnson was a big guy and he delivered a big punch, one that sent Baines flying.

Patterson could not believe what he was seeing. First the punch. Then Baines flying through the air and landing in what must have been a deep spot in the bog. He completely submerged. Then, Johnson just sinking into the Earth. He and the other agents lurched forward, hoping to rescue their partners. Then he heard a rustling sound, one he would never forget.

THE RESIDENCE

The last rays of the sun were sinking below the horizon when the two cars pulled up to the house. Michael opened the front door just as the Chief, Agent Long and Rebecca Jackson opened their car doors. They were all met by distant shrieking and cries for help.

Agent Long immediately put his hand on his gun. "What the hell is going on out there?"

The Chief looked at Michael. "The bog and the centipede nests are still there, aren't they?"

Michael sighed. "Yes. The remediation was temporary at best. But we not only kept the signs up, we added additional signs and warnings."

Long's head swiveled between the two of them. "Signs?" Then it clicked. "What bog? What centipedes?"

The chief sneered, "The ones I told you about. The ones that will show up on your precious maps in a decade. The ones you don't need local input on!"

Michael looked at one then the other, and said "Agent Long, you didn't send a backup team down the trail from the north, did you? Hawaiian Civil Defense declared the bogs and insect infestation there a hazard to human life and blocked off the trail sometime last year! No one uses that trail. Only fools would ignore the signage."

Agent Long looked down. "Yes. I sent a back-up team down that trail to cut off the expected attempt to escape."

"Escape..." Michael shook his head. "God help us. You likely sent those men to their deaths. Chief, can you call in help from civil defense?" Pausing for a second, he added, "Agent Long. I have a helicopter near the barn. Can we launch a rescue of your men? I doubt they will survive until civil defense gets here."

Then, looking at the Chief. "Um. No offence Chief. Just saying."

About the same time, a long, terrorized scream came from the south. In the background, the wind howled.

"Let me guess," Michael tried not to growl. "You also sent a team up an unstable Class 4 cliff in the midst of a Kohala windstorm?"

"This is Chief Henderson. Waimea branch. We have a major disaster developing up on Kohala Mountain. I need all available resources to descend on the Baker ranch immediately. Eight idiots tried the hike the Kohala trail this afternoon. It appears that all are down. Repeat, eight men down. Emergency airlift required!"

The Chief looked at Agent Long. "You arrogant fool!"

Michael quickly piped up. "Chief, let me rescue one or two of these men and bring them to the house. We have facilities here."

The Chief nodded. "Do what you can, Michael."

Long spoke up, "Chief, this man is a suspected terrorist. You can't trust him."

But the Chief looked Long straight in the eye. "Only one man here I don't trust."

ALONG THE SOUTH TRAIL

The south team felt the onslaught of the wind as they looked up at the 100-foot cliff on the rocky trail ahead. The junior agent, Ryan, looked up. "No way that can be climbed in 40 MPH winds."

Wayne Marshall, the lead agent on the south trail answered, "I guess that means you volunteered. Go get it."

"No way, boss. That's suicide."

Marshall glared. "Up that trail, or hand in your badge."

Ryan unclipped the badge and handed it to Marshall. "Guess I'll try to get an Uber back home."

"Ryan, don't throw away your career."

"For a stupid mission like this, better my career than my life." After a pause, Ryan added, "But I'll hang around long enough to see you try it."

The whole team's eyes swiveled to Marshall.

"Well then, I guess I'll give it a go." Marshall looked less than convinced as he took off up the trail.

As he began climbing, Marshall started to understand Ryan's concern. The wind made getting a handhold difficult. It was cold and moist, making every finger and toe hold slippery. As he looked closer, Marshall could see most of the handholds were covered in wet slippery moss. About a third of the way up, he lost his grip. With a long howl, he fell backwards. It was only 25 feet down, but he landed with a thump, his spine hitting a rock. There was a loud crack, intense pain, then everything faded to black.

Ryan, immediately hit his radio, screaming. "Man down! Man down!"

THE RESIDENCE

Agent Long's radio crackled. "Man down! Man down!"

Long recognized the voice of Agent Ryan and said without thinking, "Oh no. Another man down. This one on the south trail."

Michael and the Chief looked at each other and shook their heads.

"Elsie. Get a bird in the air on the south trail. There's a man down. Bring him to me."

ALONG THE SOUTH TRAIL

The medic on the team pronounced Agent Marshall dead, then looked up on hearing a sound he could not recognize. An odd-shaped, boxy craft was descending right toward them. He backed away as it landed. The door opened and the most gorgeous Hawaiian girl he'd ever seen stepped out, picked up the body and climbed back on board. As they stared, Ryan thought. *We have died and gone to heaven.*

Looking at the men, she said, "Jump on board. We're going to see Agent Long."

The craft landed on the driveway in front of the house. Michael and Kale rushed out to meet it. As the door opened, they jumped in to find a body on the floor and three other agents arguing with one another.

As he pointed at the man lying still on the floor, Michael said to Kale, "Take him into the house. I'll be right there."

He looked at the other men, who had become silent. "Agent Long is waiting for you out there."

As Kale took the body from the helicopter, the remainder of the team followed behind. Then Michael said, "Elsie, wait for Kale, then the three of you head up to the bog to get the other team."

Michael jumped out of the craft and ran into the house.

As he exited the craft, Ryan saw Agent Long and blurted out… "I told him that cliff could not be scaled in this wind, but he wouldn't listen." Then his voice filled with emotion. "The wind blew him off… Fell 25 feet… Broken back…" Then a long pause… "He's dead."

Long felt stricken as he and Ryan followed Michael. He had sent men into an area that his command structure said was well mapped and safe. One was now dead because of the misinformation. Four more were missing and suspected to be in grave danger.

"Here…" Michael pointed to the dining room table. "Lay him on the table."

Kale and Noelani quickly did as asked.

"I've got this. Go join Elsie and see if you can rescue the other team."

Michael pulled out a cylindrical object. It had a blinking light on the end. He passed It over the body. "He's been dead for 15 minutes. Most of his spine has been shattered. Difficult, but not impossible."

"What do you mean difficult, but not impossible?" Agent Long demanded.

"His body is no longer able to support life, and his essence is slowly fading. But if we restore his body in time... The essence will return."

"This is complete and utter bullshit. He's either dead or he's not, which is it?"

Ryan replied, "Long, get a grip. He's dead. Touch him. He's cold. Listen for a heartbeat. There isn't one."

Long went over and touched the man. He was clearly dead. Body cold. Skin turning gray. "Oh, shit," he whispered. "Marshall, I am so sorry."

Michael stepped up and held the cylindrical object with the blinking light over the body. He remained still for several seconds, then said, "Got him."

Marshall's eyes suddenly blinked, then opened. "What the hell!" He tried to sit up, but Michael restrained him.

"Whoa, boss. You've had a nasty fall. It was touch and go there for a minute, but we got to you in time. You'll be good."

Marshall started to smile, then frowned. "I can't feel my legs!"

All the FBI guys shuddered. They knew what happened to agents handicapped in the line of service, desk job with endless paperwork for the rest of your life, truly a fate worse than death.

"Marshall." Michael said. "Relax. You will have a full recovery. In an hour or two, you'll be up walking." Michael passed his hand down over Marshall's face, as if closing his eyes, and he quickly fell into a deep sleep.

ABOVE THE NORTH TRAIL

The shuttle hovered over the team below. The sun had set, and it was pitch black outside. The moon would not rise for another two hours. Only three men were visible through the shuttle's infrared scanner. "Looks like one of them sank."

Pushing a button, Elsie called over the communication array. "Sanjit, do you know where the fourth guy is?"

Sanjit replied, "Yes. He is to the right of the one in up to his chest, maybe four feet from him."

"What's the best way for us to do this? There's still a lot of centipede activity out there." Kale asked.

"The shuttle should have some spray bottles in it. I think they are filled with something that smells like Windex. Let's play it like this. I'll open the dam. We'll lose our reservoir, but the bog should start draining. You will hear what sounds like a pop, then the water level will start dropping. When that happens, turn on your spotlights to light the area, then drop to a low hover but don't touch the ground. A dry spot should form that will extend back to the trail. Kale, jump out and start spraying the centipedes. The priority will be to get the guy that sank. Elsie, if you give me control of the infrared spotlight, I'll narrow it and use it to point where to dig. As the bog drains, it will push him up so he is just below the surface. It will still be soft. Noelani, you should be able to just reach in and grab him. Once you get his hand out of the goo, tell the other agents to help you. They will be in a lot of pain but should be able to free themselves. Then, get everyone on the shuttle and come on back. There's still time to save the submerged guy. Sound good?"

"Let's do it," Elsie said.

"Why do I have to be the one to stick their hands in the goo?" Noelani asked.

There was a distinct audible pop, and on the screen, they could see a wave pass through the bog.

"It's show time." Elsie clicked on the spotlight and quickly shed altitude. "Sanjit, the IR spotlight is yours."

On the screen, they could see the spot where the submerged man was. They could also see an area in the bog that was solidifying. "Sanjit, we see where the man is. We also see where the ground is hardening."

ALONG THE NORTH TRAIL

Mark Patterson, lead agent of the team on the north trail, was writhing in agony. He'd been bitten about 10 times by the centipedes that had swarmed his feet. When he saw that the centipedes did not enter the bog, he jumped in. Although that had saved him from additional stings, something in the bog had drastically compounded the pain. Looking around, he noticed that Johnson had now sunk down almost all the way to his neck. At this rate, he would be gone in a few more minutes. There was no sign of Baines. He must have been out cold when he hit the ground, because he'd sunk immediately and not resurfaced.

Patterson had never lost a man on a mission before. What a cursed one this was. And, Johnson... He was definitely going to be thrown out of the Agency, the only real question was whether he'd be brought up on charges and locked away. Assuming he survived this disaster.

"Help! Help me!"

Patterson turned toward the sound, but already knew it was Keanu Tajima. Keanu was his newest agent, with the agency for less than a year. His ancestry was mixed, mostly Hawaiian with a paternal grandfather that was Japanese and whose family had been in Oahu for five generations. The agency hadn't been able to recruit many Hawaiians, especially ones with Japanese heritage who, like Keanu, had grandparents that had been rounded up during World War II and put in an internment camp.

Patterson started slogging toward Tajima but struggled to walk because of the pain. Like Patterson, Tajima had jumped into the bog when the centipedes attacked. However, his foot had become tangled in a shrub, which the centipedes were using as a bridge to get to him. Hobbling faster, Patterson grabbed the branch the centipedes were on and pulled with all his strength. He heard a pop, as Tajima's boot came off, freeing him. Tajima was still being stung by the centipedes that were on him. "Keanu. Drop into the bog and roll around. That will kill them." Tajima did as the boss had said. Then popped up 30 seconds later, covered in blood and howling.

"I must have twenty or more bites on my leg, arm and chest."

Patterson noted that he also had a couple on his face. Then Patterson's own pain settled in and he realized that he had collected three more centipede bites, this time on his hands and wrist. He heard Tajima making gasping sounds and saw him struggling to breathe.

"Allergic to centipede bites!" he gasped. "Need epi pen." Then Tajima's eyes rolled back and he fell over. Patterson grabbed him and lifted him up out of the bog, thinking, *Oh my God! He's not breathing. I'm going to lose another one.*

There was a loud pop and a wave of mud washed over them. Johnson was temporarily submerged and came up screaming. Suddenly a spotlight came on and he heard some sort of aircraft coming. Holding Tajima with one arm, Patterson started waving and shouting, "Here! Here!"

46

Patterson noted that the water in the bog was receding rapidly. It was as if a dam had broken. He struggled to get up on the hardening ground, but saw the centipedes coming again.

Suddenly, the most beautiful Hawaiian girl he'd ever seen landed a few feet away. She had jumped from the descending aircraft. She started spraying some stuff at the centipedes, which took off back into the bushes. Funny, he thought. That stuff smells like Windex.

Patterson started struggling up out of the bog and finally found himself on dry land again. As he turned to say something to the woman, someone else jumped from the aircraft landing just a few feet away from him. It was an incredibly handsome and muscular Hawaiian man.

The man nodded to him but immediately ran over to where Baines had sunk. Reaching in, he pulled up an arm. "Could use some help." Kale said looking toward Patterson. But he saw that Patterson had sunk to the ground and was out. Putting one foot into the hardening bog, Kale reached in with both hands and lifted Baines out.

Noelani shouted. "This one's not breathing!"

Elsie called out, "Get those two on board. I'll run them back to the residence, then come back to get the others." Kale and Noelani carried the two men to the shuttle, which was now hovering 6 inches off the ground. The hatch was open, so Kale jumped in and laid Baines gently on the floor. Noelani held up Tajima. "Take him and go back with them. I'll stay here with these two."

THE RESIDENCE

Agent Long's radio squawked, "Hello. Agent Long?"

Almost simultaneously, Elsie's voice came in over the intercom. "Michael, we are in-bound with two more casualties. Both appear to be dead."

Agent Long, pushed his talk button. "Who is this and what are you doing on my channel?"

Michael said with a smile in his voice, "Agent Long, I think that is my housekeeper Noelani. I'm guessing that she is calling to give you a situation update on the two men that are apparently still there.

Long realized that he had not released the talk button, so said "Noelani, is that you? How are my men?"

Noelani replied, "Two men are still here with me. One is buried up to his neck in mud that's starting to harden. We need to get him out in the next few minutes or he's going to be crushed. The other, the one I took the radio from is unconscious, but still breathing. He has twenty or so centipede stings. The ones on his legs are bad, some sort of infection has set in. I'm not a doctor, but I think he is about to go into septic shock."

Long looked at Michael, "Can I send some men back with your crew to help them."

Michael replied, "Yes. I think it would be good if our people worked together on this."

The Chief piped up, "Hey, I just got word from Civil Defense. Two rescue helicopters are inbound. ETA 29 minutes."

"Thank you Chief," Michael and Long said simultaneously. Then Long added, "Ryan, take your men out front. Help offload the casualties, then return with Baker's craft, whatever it is."

Michael sent an internal message to his team... *Team, Hawaiian Civil Defense has two choppers inbound. Jiaying, monitor their communications and ping me with anything important. Sanjit, drop all defenses except a very tight Level 1 shield around the barn.*

Long noticed the faraway look in Michael's eyes and wondered what he was thinking.

Michael stirred from his thoughts as Elsie came in over the intercom. "Michael. I'm hovering above the driveway in front of the residence. There are three guys down there waving. I can't see who they are. Am I good to land?"

"Elsie. It's the team you rescued earlier. Land and let them help offload, but wait for them to come back out and come aboard. They are going to help with the rescue of the other two."

"Landing now," she replied.

RESIDENCE DRIVEWAY

The door to the shuttle popped open and Kale jumped out carrying Baines. "I've got this one. You guys get the other."

Ryan said to his team, "Take Tajima in. I'm going on board to talk with the pilot." They did as he requested, while Ryan jumped into the shuttle and walked up to the cabin. "Can I have a seat?" he asked.

"Mr. Ryan. How did it go in there? Is Marshall going to make it?" Elsie asked with a serious look.

"Michael appears to have brought Marshall back. He woke up and said a few words, then fell asleep. Is Michael going to be able to save Baines and Tajima too?"

"Probably. Baines was underwater for about 20 minutes. Tajima apparently had an allergic reaction to the centipede bites and stopped breathing about 5 minutes ago. It's easier to revive someone who has suffocated, than to revive someone who suffered a crushed spinal column. So, I would guess that Tajima will be OK. Baines will be a little more problematic, but Michael is a miracle worker, so I wouldn't worry too much."

"Who are you people?"

"You saw the Announcement, right? I think Michael explained it pretty well. And you've now witnessed some of the medical technology he's offering."

"But it sure sounded to me like he was claiming that you're aliens from another planet. You don't look like aliens."

"Mr. Ryan, did you see the movie *Avatar*?"

"The one with the tall blue people?"

"Yes. That one. My body is an avatar. So is Michael's."

"Are you here to blow up our home the way the humans did in that movie?"

Elsie laughed. "No. This is a first contact situation. But unlike the movie, we are friends here to help, not invaders here to steal your resources."

Ryan reached out, his hand close to her arm. "Can I touch you?" Pause. "I mean can I touch your arm to see like... if it's real?"

"Sure" She laughed. It was nice to have a break from the evening's tension. "But you aren't going to win many girls with that line."

It was Ryan's turn to laugh. "Wow, you're perfect." He rubbed her arm a little and was impressed. Wonderfully soft and warm, yet strong.

Elsie cleared her throat. "Better line. But enough." She looked at his hand on her arm. "Are you convinced I'm real now?"

He made a booming type sound and his fingers danced in the air. "Mind blown!" They both started laughing.

Kale and the other two men jumped on board, surprised to hear laughing in the cockpit.

Kale pushed the button to shut the shuttle door and said, "Ready to go." Then sounding startled. "What's going on up there?"

THE RESIDENCE

Marshall was asleep on the dining room table, so Michael asked Kale and Ryan's men to lay the newcomers on the floor.

Kale said, "This one drowned in the bog. Underwater about 20 minutes." He pointed at Tajima. "This one had some sort of reaction to the centipede stings. He stopped breathing about 1 minute before we arrived on the scene. Maybe ten minutes ago."

Michael already had his scanner over Baines. Baines coughed, spraying mud all over the place. A little earlier, Pam had come in without being noticed. She stepped forward and gave Michael a large cylinder, about three inches in diameter and a foot long, attached to a face mask. "Mr. Baines," Michael said aloud. "I'm glad that you're unconscious, because this would be very unpleasant otherwise."

Michael's statement startled Agent Long. He wasn't sure which he was more worried about, Michael knowing Baines' name, or Michael saying the procedure would be unpleasant.

Michael put the face mask on Baines, then slowly opened the stop cock on the mask. Clear fluid flowed up into Baines nose and within seconds, brown fluid started flowing out his mouth.

Long panicked and rushed forward to attack Michael, shouting, "What are you doing to him?"

By the time he got to Michael, Long was moving fast. About an inch from Michael, he hit something hard. With a bright flash, Long went flying back in the direction he'd come from.

With a very frustrated tone, Michael growled, "Chief, will you please restrain the Special Agent? I'm busy trying to save his man."

The Chief sat stunned for a moment, then roused himself into action. He walked over to the Special Agent, who appeared to be unconscious, and handcuffed him to the leg of the piano.

"That should hold him," muttered the Chief, who then cleared his throat. "Um. Michael, can you explain to me what just happened?"

"One minute, Chief. Baines is still critical. Just one minute."

The brown water coming from Baines mouth had become clear and Baines started to stir.

"Yes!" Michael said. Talking to the room. "Baines died badly. He had apparently sucked in a cup or two of the bog, which got into his lungs. That mud is full of toxins and microorganisms that would have killed him in another 10 minutes or so. I had to wash it out."

He could hear Agent Long beginning to wake up behind him. "The clear fluid is a special mixture of oxygen rich liquid and germicide. The applicator pumped the liquid into his lungs to clean out the mud and kill the microorganisms, all while re-oxygenating his system. It's an invention of mine designed specifically for the human anatomy, one that I'm particularly proud of."

Baines coughed, spraying clear fluid all over the place. He continued coughing, threw up, then coughed some more. He turned over, his head facing down now, then coughed more clear fluid up onto the floor. When he finally stopped, he said, "What the hell!"

Michael was not a proponent of foul language. None was allowed among his staff, but the fact that Baines was moving and could speak at all meant he was out of the woods.

Tajima also started coughing. While everyone's attention was on Michael, Pam had been using the scanner on Tajima. It was good to hear him breathing again, but he was soon groaning in pain.

"Michael," Pam said. "He has numerous centipede stings that appear to have become infected."

"OK. Go get the spray attachment for this bottle, then come help me apply it."

As Pam ran off, Michael used the scanner to determine which toxin was causing the problem. *Fire ant toxin, curious.* He thought.

With the toxin determined, he used his scanner to redirect the nanobots Pam had injected. They quickly started removing the toxin from Tajima's system. A mist appeared around Tajima and slowly dissipated.

"What was that?" Agent Long asked, now awake and apparently more inclined to watch Michael work than to interfere.

"The mist is actually smoke. When the nanobots we injected into Mr. Tajima consume all the toxin that they can, they exit through his skin, float away from his body, then self-destruct when they are at a safe distance. We only use this type of nanobot in extreme circumstances."

Michael then turned to look Agent Long straight in the eye. "Never attack me again. It will go far less well for you next time."

He turned back to Tajima, "Keanu, can you hear me?"

Tajima's eyes opened and he whispered, "You're the alien we came to arrest, aren't you?" There was no hostility in his voice. Michael nodded in the affirmative.

"Thank you, Mr. Baker," Tajima said.

Before Michael could reply, Pam walked in with the applicator and attached it to the bottle of liquid that they had used on Baines.

Michael took it and turned to Tajima. "Keanu, this will sting a little, but it'll make the pain go away and the swelling go down. With any luck you will be up and walking in 10 minutes." As Michael began spraying, he noticed Tajima tense up, but he didn't cry out.

I like this guy, Michael thought. *Maybe he'll be a good candidate for the Institute.*

ALONG THE NORTH TRAIL

Noelani looked up at the shuttle as it landed. It was nice having the spotlight lighting the night again. Her cell phone and flashlight were enough to illuminate the spot where she was digging, but not enough to illuminate the area.

She'd been digging with her hands to free Johnson. She turned to look at Patterson and did not like what she saw. His legs and feet were swollen to twice their normal size and blood had stopped oozing out. He was no longer breathing, so she assumed that he'd died, which would be why the bleeding had stopped.

Johnson had been screaming most of the night, but as the mud dried, the pressure on his chest rose to the point where he could barely breathe. Now, he was just whimpering, tears running from his eyes.

His arms were down at his side, so he hadn't been able to help dig himself out. Arms down was a good strategy while the bog was wet. It kept his center of mass lower, giving him a better chance of keeping his head above the surface. But as the bog dried, whenever he tried raising his arms, the suction would pull him down.

As the shuttle landed, Noelani stopped digging so she could direct the men that were disgorging from the craft. Kale and Ryan ran up and asked what they should do. She told Ryan to take the men and start digging Johnson out. They needed to be careful, so they did not injure him, but they also needed to be quick because the expanding earth was crushing him. Thankfully, someone had the sense to have put some shovels in the shuttle. The three men grabbed them and started digging a trench around Johnson, about 1 foot out. That would relieve the pressure without the risk of hitting him with a shovel. They made quick progress.

Kale and Noelani walked over toward Agent Patterson. A quick check showed that he was stone cold dead. A tear formed on Noelani's eye. "Michael can probably still bring him back, but we'll need to grow him some new legs. That will take a while and our research suggests that human society is not quite ready to accept regrown limbs. Silly, isn't it?" She looked down at her hands.

That's when she noticed her hands bleeding from the digging and infected by the microorganisms in the soil. As an android, she had the ability to turn off her pain receptors in an emergency. She had done that shortly after she started digging. But her body was organic, indistinguishable from a real human, which meant she would be as susceptible as a normal human once her nanobot supply ran out. Checking her internal monitor, she realized she was almost out. "Kale. I need a nanobot injection or I'll go into septic shock before much longer."

"We have some in the med kit on the shuttle. I'll get it. Wait here." He ran off and came back shortly. She lifted her arm and Kale injected the bots into a port discretely hidden in her arm pit.

"Thank you." She turned her pain receptors back on, then shut them off again almost immediately. "Wow, my hands hurt."

Kale said, "Let me help you back to the shuttle. Sit up in the cockpit with Elsie. You're vulnerable with your pain receptors off. Let's keep you safe."

They got up and walked to the shuttle. Kale gently lifted Noelani up onto the deck, then hopped up next to her. They walked to the cockpit and Kale opened the door. As Noelani took a seat, Elsie said, "Looks nasty. Receptors off?"

"Yep."

"OK, let me buckle you in."

"Keep her safe, Else." Kale said, using the affectionate nick name he'd given her.

...

He closed the cockpit door and was walking to the shuttle entrance when the screaming started. Looking over toward the men, he saw that Johnson had finally been freed, but while stomping around trying to get the dirt off, he'd stomped on a fire ant nest. The ants had flooded out and were on all four men. *This guy is a real menace*, Kale thought.

He grabbed the 'Windex' and ran out. All four men had peeled their pants off trying to get away from the fire ants that had streamed up. Kale quickly sprayed their legs, shoes and socks—the ants just falling off dead. Then he grabbed their pants, still swarming with fire ants, and started spraying.

"Guys," he said. "This isn't going to work, and Patterson is in critical condition. Leave the pants and get in the shuttle. I'll get Patterson. We've got to go."

He walked over and picked up Patterson, throwing him over his right shoulder. Three of the men were already on board. Johnson had carried his pants with him. Kale called out, "Leave the pants, Johnson."

Johnson replied, "No way! Who made you the boss?"

Kale, having had enough of this guy, punched him in the jaw with a left upper cut. Johnson dropped like a sack of potatoes. Kale gently placed Patterson on the floor of the shuttle, then turned and picked up Johnson with two hands and threw him against the far wall of the shuttle. The three agents looked at Kale with mouths hanging open. Johnson weighed two hundred pounds and Kale had just picked him up and thrown him 10 feet through the air like it was nothing.

Kale smiled at them and said. "What? You've never seen a little Hawaiian muscle?"

They all laughed as Kale closed the door.

"Well done, man," Ryan said. "That guy is a real pain in the ass."

In seconds, the shuttle was in the air.

THE RESIDENCE

"Michael." Elsie's voice came over the intercom. "We're inbound. Three minutes out. One serious casualty. Five minor injuries of varying degree."

Michael replied quickly, "Who from our team was hurt?"

"Noelani. Her hands are cut from trying to dig Johnson out. Infected and off." The last phrase told Michael that Noelani had consumed her entire nanobot supply and had turned off her pain receptors to continue working.

"Got it," Michael said. "Who and how bad is the casualty?"

"Patterson. Possibly revivable, but I doubt we'll be able to keep the legs. Landing now. Kale will be bringing him in, and we could use the Chief's help."

"Pam," Michael said. "Get the door for Kale. We are out of space here, so have Kale take Patterson to my office. Chief, would you mind accompanying Pam and finding out what's up?"

"You got it, Michael. But I need some answers when this is all over."

"You'll get them, Chief," Michael said with a smile.

As Michael started to leave for his office, Long piped up. "Wait a minute. You can't leave me handcuffed here. I'm the Special Agent in Charge."

"I think you're exactly where you need to be right now, Special Agent." Michael couldn't keep the contempt out of his voice as he left.

...

Kale trotted into Michael's office with Patterson over his shoulder and gently laid him on the floor. Michael took one look and knew this wasn't good. He asked Kale to get the agent's pants off as he scanned the chest area. "Good news, the heart and lungs are still viable. Unfortunately, the liver is only marginally viable. Our only chance is to get him into a tank."

Kale looked up and said, "Boss, the only tanks are in the lab and the Hawaiian Civil Defense choppers are due in 4 minutes."

Michael called out, "Jiaying?"

"Here, Michael" She replied over the intercom.

"How far out are the Civil Defense choppers?"

"They were coming in from Hilo but had real problems with the wind near the saddle, so had to re-route. They're still about twenty minutes out on their current course. They plan to approach from the south, which they probably won't be able to do because of the wind. It is still gusting well over 50 MPH about a mile south of us. They should have gone around Kohala."

"Thank you, Jiaying. Call me when they're 5 minutes out or if they decide to re-route again."

"Will do, boss."

"Sanjit."

"Here, boss." Sanjit said over the intercom.

"Can we make a stealth entry into the research lab? ASAP?"

"Good news." Sanjit replied. "All the FBI are in the house now. No one else is on the scanner. If you close the office door to the hallway, I can get the stealth cart up to your office's rear entrance."

"Great. Have Charles come and get the agent on the floor, then put him in a tank. When that's done, message me on internal."

"Got it, boss."

Michael opened the door and called for Pam.

She came down the hall. Michael escorted her into the office and shut the door.

"Charles already texted me. Go. Take Kale. I'll keep the door shut."

"Thanks, Pam."

Michael and Kale headed back down the hallway to the dining room. Here Michael noticed that Johnson had joined Agent Long handcuffed to the piano. The Chief, who leaned on the wall nearby to watch the two, growled, "I'll keep an eye on these two. You go help the others. Their injuries are minor, but I'm sure they'll be happy to get a little of your attention. You can deal with this joker once everyone else is done." The Chief pointed a thumb at Johnson.

Michael walked down the hall to the den. Noelani had been cycling the men through the shower and giving them new clothes. Ryan and his two colleagues had already showered and changed. They declined any further treatment, saying the fire ant stings had cleared up in the shower. Michael used his implant to check one of the shower controllers and saw that despite her injuries, Noelani had loaded the soap containers with the appropriate ingredients to neutralize fire ant toxin. Good thinking on her part.

"Anyone know where Noelani went?" he asked the room.

Ryan replied, "She's taking her turn in the shower. She asked me to tell you that she'd added a treatment for her hands into the shower mix, although I'm not sure what that means."

Then, looking over to Kale, he added, "She said you could have the shower next."

Ryan turned back to Michael. "How's Patterson?"

"Mr. Patterson is still touch and go. He's in therapy as we speak. It'll be a while before we know more. Gentlemen, relax and settle in. I need to look in on Johnson and have a long talk with Agent Long."

"We wanted to ask about that. Where is Agent Long? The Chief told us to wait in here, but it's kind of against policy to take orders from the Chief. We're supposed to hear orders like that from Agent Long."

"Jim, your name is Jim, right?"

Ryan nodded.

"Can you trust me for a few minutes? I need to speak with Agent Long in private, then check in on Mr. Patterson. Please do not leave this room unless accompanied by one of my staff."

Ryan and the team nodded, and Michael left to go back to the dining room.

On entering the dining room, he found the Chief and Agent Long in heated discussion. Kale had followed him.

"Chief," Michael said. The Chief broke off his discussion with Agent Long and looked at Michael. "Why is Mr. Johnson cuffed to my piano?"

The Chief answered, "He had been causing real problems in the field. Ryan asked me if we had the means to restrain him. This was the best I had."

Michael noticed that Johnson was unconscious. "Do we know what happened to him or if he's OK?"

"Pam treated him while you were in with Patterson." The Chief started to say something more, but Kale cut him off.

"Michael, this guy is trouble. After his teammates had freed him, he went stomping around all over the place and kicked open a fire ant nest. The ants swarmed over them so fast they were on both the inside and outside of their pants. I got there with the insecticide after they had their pants off and got them cleaned up. But, with Patterson in critical condition, I didn't have time to clean the ants off their pants, so ordered them to leave the pants. Told them we would get them new ones. But Johnson wasn't having it and was in the act of throwing ant-infested pants toward the area where I was going to lay Patterson. So I punched him, and he dropped like a sack of potatoes. When we got here, Pam treated his wounds, then dosed him with tranquilizers at the Chief's request."

Long cut in at that point saying, "The Chief had no right to do that and I plan to file charges against him."

"OK." Michael said. "Gentlemen, we have a problem. Civil Defense has been delayed but will be here in about ten minutes. Mr. Patterson is past the point where human medicine can help him. I'm attempting to revive him, using a process and technology that you are not allowed to see at this time. So, the question is what to do. I only see two choices.

"I can release Agent Patterson from my care to Hawaiian Civil Defense. Maybe I should say release his corpse to HCD, because he won't survive discontinuance of therapy.

"Or, you can leave him to my care. If you do this, then he'll be here for some time. If we can't revive him, then we'll return his body to you unmolested. If we can revive him, he'll be with us for several months. Of course, once he is conscious, he will be allowed to leave at any point he wants."

"How bad is he?" Long asked.

"Your medical people would say he's dead. Just as they would have for Baines, Marshall, and Tajima. But unlike the others, his case is much more serious. His heart and lungs are recoverable. His liver and kidneys are questionable, which is the problem. His legs are not recoverable, but we will not remove them without his permission."

Long's head drooped. "Might as well release him now. We've discussed this before. Patterson would not want to be revived if he has no legs."

Michael replied, "We can grow him new legs that will be as good as new. Actually, better, because they will be younger than the rest of him. That will take a couple months. The life or death issue is whether we can restart his liver. That's still 50/50. We will know in a day or two."

Ryan stepped in from the hallway and said, "Agent Long. I respectfully ask that you leave him here. Give the man and his family a chance at life."

"Ryan, you are not to be walking around the house unaccompanied."

Noelani stepped in behind him, "Sorry, boss, I brought him here. He'd kind of guessed what you'd be discussing and asked me to let him participate. Should have checked with you first."

"Thank you, Noelani." He turned back to Long and the Chief. "What will it be? I just got word the rescue helicopter is only 5 minutes out."

Long said. "We take him. We can't leave him in the custody of a suspected terrorist..."

Even as the last word was leaving Long's mouth, the Chief cut in. "Michael. I guess he needs to stay here. I am revoking Patterson's transport privileges."

Long was furious. "What do you mean, revoking his transport privileges?"

"Under the state code, the FBI cannot take control of state resources without a court order. Otherwise the state official on the scene must approve any transport decisions. I am the state official on the scene. I say no. Do you have a court order?" Long stared at him, speechless. "Didn't think so," said the Chief.

Michael heard Ryan clapping behind him and said, "Guess that's settled."

About that time, Ryan noticed that Long was handcuffed to the piano. "Chief, why is Agent Long handcuffed to the piano?"

Michael pointed to the TV hanging on the wall behind the piano. It snapped on and video of Long attacking Michael played. The video was filmed from an angle that blocked the view of Baines treatment.

Ryan stared at Long, then said accusingly, "You attacked the doctor reviving one of your own men!"

Baines had been awake for a while now but was still sitting on the floor. He'd been silent until this point but said in a scratchy voice. "Long, you are not fit to lead a team. I plan to file a complaint."

Tajima, also awake, said, "I join that complaint."

Ryan in the doorway said the same.

A message popped up on Michael's inner vision. *The HCD team is landing.*

Michael said, "OK. HCD is here. Chief, Kale can take you out to meet them. Who are we sending with them?"

The Chief said, "I think Baines, Marshall and Tajima should go. Earlier, I sent a summary to headquarters with a recommendation that Long be taken into custody. A judge just signed the arrest warrant."

The Chief walked over to Long and showed him the image of the document on his phone. "Agent Long. You are under arrest and will be remanded to Hawaiian Civil Defense in Hilo. You have the right to remain silent. Anything you say can and will be used against you in a court of law. Do you understand your rights?"

Long spat on the floor at the Chief's feet. "This isn't the last of it, Henderson! You better keep an eye over your shoulder. No one arrests an FBI Special Agent and comes out the other side whole."

The Chief shook his head in disgust, then went out to meet the rescue team. He led them back to the house. Several men with stretchers came into the dining room. The Chief said, "Gentlemen, please take Agents Baines, Marshall, and Tajima. Dr. Baker here, did a remarkable job of patching them up, but please be careful, they were badly injured." He pointed to Marshall and added. "Agent Marshall has a spinal injury. Dr. Baker stabilized him but be extra careful with him."

The rescue team approached each of the team members, asking what happened and doing a quick assessment of their own. Marshall was still unconscious, so they asked Michael the questions instead.

Two HCD officers came in with shackles. "Which of these men is Christopher Long?" The chief pointed.

The officers read the warrant. It was surprisingly long and included numerous charges. They read him his rights and handed him a copy of the arrest warrant. When they bent to put the shackles on, Long kicked one of them, which earned him a Taser shot. Once he was still, they finished putting the shackles on and the Chief removed the handcuffs that held him to the piano.

As the men left the house, Tajima said to Michael. "Thank you, Michael. Can I contact you when things settle down a bit? I'd like to meet you under better circumstances."

"I would like that, Agent Tajima."

Once the HCP helicopters took off, the Chief asked Michael if he could finally have that 'word.' Kale took the remaining FBI agents back to the study as Michael and the Chief sat down at the dining room table.

"You know that I couldn't tell you earlier, right?" Michael asked. "I'm hoping we can still be friends."

"Don't get me started on that." After a pause, the chief asked, "What happened in there? With Long? When he jumped you?"

"Chief," Michael said. "I wear a personal shield. It's a force field that cannot be penetrated. If you took out your gun and shot me, the bullet would stop before it hit me, and its momentum would be transferred into another dimension."

"Momentum?"

"You know... the bullet's kick. But the shield is smart. If it transferred a human's momentum into another dimension, it might kill the human. So, it flexes and transfers the momentum back in the direction it came from. That's why Agent Long bounced off me."

"But what about the flash of light?" The Chief asked. "It looked like a small explosion."

"The shield is extra-dimensional... That means the shield itself is not part of our space-time continuum. When the shield bends like that, light from other dimensions leaks into this one."

"Michael, I am really struggling with the idea that you are some sort of outer-space alien, or something. I've known you for five years now and you're a perfectly normal nice guy."

"First contact with a new species is always difficult. Our experience has been that it goes better when we alter our form to look like the people we want to meet. It allows us to live among them long enough to get to know them before we reveal ourselves. We call today 'Revelation,' because it is the day that we revealed ourselves."

"Makes me sad," said the Chief. "I feel like I'm losing a friend."

"Don't say that, Chief. I'm still your friend. The qualities you like about me are still there. I'm the same person, just a little more. And I will always do well for you and for this community."

"Thank you, Michael. How much can I tell the others?"

"Whatever you need to. But, the less you say over the coming week, the better. There are no secrets, but it takes a while for people to come to grips with some things."

...

The Chief and the remaining FBI officers got in their cars and headed out. Ryan had taken the lead among the FBI agents and was calling in a report by the time they stopped to collect the team that had been waiting out by the road.

By the time the last of the taillights was gone, it was 9:00 PM.

Michael heard Charles voice come over the intercom. "Michael, Patterson is out of the woods. Liver and kidney function are both out of the critical range. But he'll need to stay in the tank at least 24 more hours before we try waking him."

"Thanks, Charles" Michael said.

"Jiaying," Michael called out.

"Yes, Michael."

"Did the contract from Good Morning America come?"

"Yes, it did. Sorry I didn't tell you sooner, but you were busy. It looks like you're going to get a big piece of the show in the morning."

Elsie joined the line. "Michael, we need to leave in two hours if we're going to make it in time. I've just finished cleaning the shuttle. What a mess! What supplies do we need?"

Michael recited a list, then said. "I need to sign off now to take a short nap. Ping me 15 minutes before takeoff." And with that, he entered his room and fell fast asleep.

THE INTERVIEW

The intercom sounded and Michael woke. A quick check of his internal chronometer told him that it was 10:50 PM. Elsie had given him five extra minutes. He roused himself and quickly hit the sonic shower. Three minutes later, he was out and getting dressed. One of the things he loved about the hygiene automation systems he'd installed in the Residence was that you could roll out of bed half awake, climb into the 'sonic' shower and be ready to roll in five minutes. The sonic shower emitted a fragrant mist that contained everything needed for complete hygienic cleansing, including teeth and hair. It also contained any relevant vitamins and pharmaceuticals. Just breathe deeply with your mouth open and the mist propelled by directed sonic waves did it all. Even woke you up. The thought passed through his mind that maybe Noelani had added some caffeine to the mix today.

As he stepped out of his room, he called. "Charles, how is Mr. Patterson doing."

Charles replied, "Excellent. He is still in critical condition, but we may be able to wake him shortly after we return from New York."

"That's good news. His legs?" Michael asked.

"Lost cause." Charles replied. "I put them in stasis so as not to slow the critical recovery. Would have liked to remove them, but we cannot do that without his permission."

"That's what I expected. Are you ready for our trip to New York?"

"Yes. Everything is loaded on the shuttle. I'm there myself now."

Michael noticed a blinking light in his inner vision. "Got to go Charles, I'll meet you at the shuttle in 2 minutes." As he cut the connection to Charles, Elsie's voice came over the intercom.

"Michael? Are you ready? Everyone else is here and we need to go." Elsie said. "I've moved the shuttle to the front door of the Residence for you."

Michael, who had been heading for the back door to take the path to the barn, did a quick U-turn in the hallway. "Be there momentarily."

As he walked past the dining room, he saw Pam still cleaning up the mess from earlier. He paused to say Hello, curious as to why Pam was doing this.

"Hi Michael. I'm just helping out. Noelani is going with you this morning, so I offered to clean up so she could get a few minutes' rest. She really needed an hour in the regenerator to deal with her hands."

Michael had forgotten that Noelani had been so seriously injured in the mess with the FBI last night... Well, earlier tonight. "Thank you, Pam. We would never be able to complete this mission without you."

Pam smiled back.

As he went out the front door, the shuttle hovered about 6 inches off the ground. Michael climbed in and Kale closed the door. "Hello, Team."

He walked to the front of the craft. As he entered the cockpit, he noted that they were already thousands of feet up.

"You're late," Elsie said.

Michael looked at the clock on the instrument panel and said innocently, "But, it's only 11:02."

"I said we had to leave by 11:00 at the latest. We now have a 58-minute flight time. That means I'm really going to have to do some fancy flying."

"What flight path are you going to take?"

"We are angling up and to the east at 10G. I had planned to take it a little easier on the engines and inertial dampening systems. But at 10G, we can get to 1,200 miles altitude in a little less than 6 minutes. Then we micro jump to 600 miles above New York. That will give us 40 minutes to drop 600 miles without heating to the point we could be seen.

"I think the good news is that it's cold in New York today. We'll be landing 2 hours before sunrise, so a 180-degree hull will heat the landing pad enough for you to get inside without freezing to death," Elsie finished with a smile.

"Thank you, Elsie," he said with a patient but affectionate smile. "Once we've offloaded in New York, I'm expecting that you'll need to clear the helipad. But don't go too far away. I'm expecting that we'll be about 4 hours, but we may need to leave on 15 minutes' notice, so maintain stealth mode."

"OK, I've got some ideas."

"I've got to check in with the others. See you when we land."

As Michael stood, he saw the stars shift. They had jumped, which meant 40 minutes until landing. He walked back to the cabin and closed the cockpit door. He looked at his team, Charles, Kale and Noelani.

"What a handsome team! Our viewing audience is expected to be about 5 million this morning. Once word is out that we are the special guests, I expect that number will jump quite a bit. There are two important things we need to accomplish today.

"First, we need to convince this audience that we are good people, people that they like and can trust. Kale and Noelani, you have an important role in this. As you know, your bodies were designed to appeal to the human eye. Noelani, you've already seen how human men react to you. Your challenge is to come across like their sister, someone they love, but are not sexually interested in. Kale, you have it a little easier in the sense that the women in the audience will swoon over you, but they won't get lost in sex fantasies the way men do. Your challenge is to make sure the audience sees you as reliable, someone they can trust with their life. I don't know how much of a speaking role you'll get. I'll try to get you each a little. Speak with competence and compassion but be light and carefree. If you're not sure what to say, ping me on inner vision and I'll give you appropriate content.

"Second, we need to convince the people watching that we are who we say we are. Charles, that's where you come in. While on camera, look like the scientist that you are. When it comes to the demonstrations, do your best to bring out the wonder in what you're showing. I'm hoping that I'll get to cure someone on the show today. If that doesn't happen, then the power cube and replicator demos really need to sing. Do you have everything you need for the replications that we discussed?"

"Silly question, Boss. Of course, I do," Charles said with a twinkle in his eye.

Elsie came over the intercom. "Michael, we are less than 10 minutes out. I can see the landing pad from here on the enhanced monitor. It's clear of aircraft, but there are some people out there setting up equipment. There's also some guy standing right in the middle of the bullseye I'm supposed to land on."

"Will the air traffic situation allow you to hover two hundred feet or so above the pad?"

"Yes. I think so. You want to stay high enough that they can't hear us, right?"

"Right."

"OK. The wind is strong enough I can hover a little lower, which will be safer. I have detectors at max, so I'll see anything inbound, even a small projectile."

"Great. Have you contacted their landing control?"

"Was just about to do that. I'll tell them that we are on approach and will be there at 5:00 AM on the dot."

...

At 4:55 AM, the man standing on the bullseye walked away. Elsie waited until 4:57 to start her final descent, reaching a 6-inch hover by 4:59.

STUDIO CONTROL, ABC NEWS, NEW YORK

It was 4:59 AM. "So where are these guys? They said they were on final approach."

Shawn Terry, the scheduling agent for Good Morning America, replied, "When I spoke with Michael, he said they would just appear on the helipad at 5:00 AM sharp. He even told us to put TV cameras out to record it. So, hold tight, we still have 15 seconds."

His producer, Monica Hayes, turned to look at him, taking her eyes off the monitor. Before she could say anything, he gasped. "Oh my God! It just appeared. Out of thin air. It just appeared!"

Monica turned back to the screen. Sure enough, a boxy craft of some sort sat on her helipad. It was extremely smooth and black. As she looked closer, she saw that although it looked boxy, it was something of an illusion. All the corners were smooth, not square, and all were swept back. She could now see what she assumed was the nose of the aircraft. And it had the cutest little wings, swept back like the rest of the craft and only protruding slightly from the sides. Then she realized it hadn't actually landed but floated a couple inches above the landing pad. Then the realization hit her...

"Oh my God!" she whispered. "What have I invited into my studio?"

They both jumped out of their chairs and ran up to the helipad.

HELIPAD, ABC NEWS, NEW YORK

"Have we had any contact from our hosts yet?" Michael asked.

"No contact," Elsie replied

"Have you called them?"

"Silly question, Michael."

"Sorry," he replied. "I guess our arrival was a little more impactful than I expected."

The door to the roof-top elevator opened and several people poured out.

"Pop the door open, Kale."

Kale did as he was asked, and Michael stepped down onto the pad. He welcomed the heat coming off the hull of the shuttle. *It is cold out here,* he thought.

A man ran up carrying a parka that he offered to Michael. As he helped Michael put it on a woman approached.

"Michael Baker?"

"Just Michael, please."

"Michael, my name is Monica Hayes. I'm the producer of Good Morning America. I understand that you have a team accompanying you and some equipment to bring in. Would you like any assistance?"

"Thank you, Ms. Hayes. My team would prefer to handle the equipment on their own. If you'll give us one moment to unload, you can lead the way."

Kale and Noelani stepped down from the shuttle and were introduced. Then Charles passed the sled to Kale, followed by three medium-sized cases. The grav-sled sat about two inches above the ground. It could be adjusted up or down, but two inches was the standard setting for indoor use. Then Charles hopped down and was introduced.

"Can our shuttle remain here, or do we need to move it?" Michael asked Ms. Hayes.

"The helipad has been cleared for your use. Some helicopters will come and go, but you are scheduled here until 11:00 AM."

"Thank you, Ms. Hayes. Let me advise my pilot."

Michael stepped back up into the shuttle and quickly walked to the cockpit. "Good news. You can park here until we're done. Please stay with the shuttle, keep her locked up and communicate only by radio or by internal messaging."

"Got it, boss," Elsie replied.

Michael returned to the shuttle exit and saw that everyone other than Ms. Hayes was heading toward the elevator. He pushed the close button as he stepped out, then followed Ms. Hayes toward the elevator.

"Ms. Hayes, will we have a few minutes to talk through the show with you and/or your host?"

"Yes. In fact, we're heading straight to the conference room for the pre-show planning meeting. Michael, have you been tracking the public reaction to your announcement last night?"

"No," Michael replied. "We were busy with other matters."

"Well. You made quite a splash. Polls indicate that your name recognition in the US is up there with the biggest stars and highest-ranking politicians. Globally, only the President and a few others are higher. And your favorable ratings are the highest of anyone with even half the name recognition. I'm expecting our audience this morning to be one for the record books. That means we need to stage our show very carefully this morning."

As they entered the elevator, Michael said. "I'm really looking forward to talking to your audience this morning, and I trust that you and your host know best how to engage that audience. But there are a couple things that I need from this show to justify the time I'll be spending with you."

Oh boy, here it comes. Monica thought. "What is it that you want from us Michael?"

"We come offering gifts to mankind. I need to demonstrate those gifts to your studio audience." He paused. "The one that I think will get the most positive response is the medical technology. We have cures for cancer, we even have the ability to heal people who have suffered spinal damage. We can regrow limbs. We can even revive people whom your medical technology has declared dead, assuming of course that we can get to them in time."

Monica said, "Those are big claims that few will believe. How do you propose to do this?"

"I would like to heal someone on your show. What I don't know is how to do it convincingly. Is there someone nearby that your audience knows to be sick? Someone close enough that we could get them here in time and for which the cure could be confirmed?"

A pause… "You know, there might be…" Hayes started flipping through her notes. "Yes! There is a group of disabled vets who will be here today. In fact, one or two are reportedly terminally ill."

"Is there any way we might get to speak with one or more of them before the show? I would like to help them."

The elevator had come to a stop at their floor. The party had been very quiet coming down the elevator, listening to Michael and the director talk.

"Michael, I'm worried about this. There have been too many fake healings in the history of show business. It would destroy your credibility and our show if this isn't 100% on the up and up."

"How soon before the show is the studio audience seated?"

"The doors close 30 minutes ahead of show time. We are still an hour and 45 minutes out and the crowds are lining up. In fact, we may need to close the doors early today. Word is out that you're going to be here, and security is reporting people lining up on the street hoping to get a glimpse of you on your way in."

"How about this… Arrange to let the vets in first. I'll come out to meet them and have my scanner with me. If I find a suitable candidate, I'll heal him before the show. If you are convinced and there are additional suitable candidates, your call whether we heal them on the show."

They entered the conference room and quite a few people were already there, including the hosts. On a multi-paned screen at the end of the table, the various sets on the stage were visible.

Ms. Hayes quickly called the meeting to order. Michael noticed a lot of eyes on him. He also noticed the numerous glances being shot at Noelani and Kale.

"Team," Ms. Hayes said. "We have had a huge change in plans for today. We did not have time to cancel the guests previously booked for this morning, but for all intents and purposes the whole show today will be Michael Baker. We will fit in others as we can, but Michael gets most of the time. So here is the challenge… What will our flow be?"

Sarah, the lead host scheduled for today, said. "I think the first thing we need to do is introduce Michael, explore his background, then ask the question everyone is asking… 'How can a 35-year-old guy from Texas be an ambassador from an intergalactic confederation?'" The sarcasm in her voice was palpable.

Hayes looked at him. "Michael?"

Michael smiled. "Good question. But, the problem with it is that no matter what I say, skeptics will not believe. A verbal explanation simply won't work."

"Why not? Surely you have an answer?"

"Anyone can say anything they want," Michael said. "You can't solve a paradox with words. You can only solve it through actions." He pointed at the monitor showing the stage. The image of the stage faded away and a video started playing. "The man you will see brought in is an FBI Agent that was part of an ill-conceived raid on my ranch in Hawaii yesterday afternoon."

The images played across the screen of Kale carrying Agent Marshall in and laying him on the dining room table, of Agent Ryan declaring Marshall dead and railing on the stupidity of the raid, of Agent Long's stricken face as the man was laid down, of Michael saying this was going to be difficult, and eventually of Agent Marshall sucking in a deep breath.

"Words are saying that you were or were not there. Action is bringing back to life the adversary that kills himself in an attempt to harm you."

The room was silent. Shawn Terry, the one who had booked Michael for the show, whispered, "Holy shit!"

"I'll tell you what Sarah. Before the show starts, I'm going to visit with the disabled vets that are attending the show today. If you still believe I'm just a 35-year old guy from Texas when I come on stage, then ask your questions your way. But, let me tell you what I think we should do." Michael went on to lay out his proposal.

GOOD MORNING AMERICA AUDITORIUM

The auditorium was packed. About 20 disabled vets in wheelchairs had parked in the front row in an area set aside for them and their guests. Noelani came in through a side door next to the stage, walked down the stairs, and started greeting the vets. As she continued down the front row, every eye followed her. She had such girl next door charm. Michael used the distraction to come down the same set of steps and walk up behind Noelani without the audience really noticing. She stopped in front of one of the men, held out her hand and said, "Sergeant Butler, thank you for your service."

Butler blew into the straw mounted to the wheelchair, so it would turn slightly to face Noelani. Sergeant Butler was a quadriplegic, paralyzed from the neck down. He'd been injured in combat in Afghanistan. Sargent Butler's mother had accompanied him to the show and said politely, "I'm sorry young lady. But he can't shake your hand. He's paralyzed."

Noelani leaned in and gave the Sergeant a hug. Then, kissed him on the cheek, saying, "I am so sorry for your loss."

As she released the sergeant, Michael stepped up. "Sergeant, do you know who I am?"

The Sergeant replied. "Yes sir. You're the one they say is an alien."

"Would you mind if I scanned your wound?"

"Nothing can be done for it, sir. But sure, scan away."

Michael passed his scanner over the Sergeant, pausing for a while near the top of his neck. *This is heartbreaking*, Michael thought. *This injury is so minor, yet a life has been destroyed for lack of acceptable medical technology.* Michael noticed a little chafing where his neck rested against the seat.

"Sergeant, I see there is a little chafing on the back of your neck where it's been rubbing against the chair. Would you mind if Noelani rubbed a little ointment on it?"

"I'm stuck in a wheelchair unable to move and you ask if I want some ointment for chafing that I can't even feel?" The Sergeant said with some heat.

"Now, dear," his mother said. "Let the pretty girl put some ointment on. You know you will enjoy that."

Noelani pulled out a tube of what appeared to be white cream and started massaging it into his neck. No one noticed that she was not rubbing it into the chafed spot. Neither did anyone notice Michael's machinations with his scanner on the other side of the Sergeant. Every eye was on Noelani.

Although he couldn't really feel what Noelani was doing, the Sergeant closed his eyes and sighed at the smell of Noelani's sweet fragrance and the light touch of her hair on his ear.

Suddenly, there was a sharp pain in his neck. He hadn't felt anything there since just before the explosion. The pain spread and was soon so crippling he could barely breathe. "What the hell did you do to me?!" he shouted, arching his back.

His mother saw the movement and couldn't understand what was happening. "What..." she started to say as the Sergeant let out a massive groan.

"OH MY GOD IT HURTS!" the Sergeant screamed and lifted his arms.

The room that was moments ago loud with nervous energy was now riveted to the scene being played out in the front row.

The Sergeant's mother started to stand up, then sagged to the floor as she fainted.

Michael gripped the Sergeant's arms. "Relax into it, Sergeant. Your nerves are being revived. It feels like pain because your brain has forgotten how to process signals from your nerves. This will pass in a few minutes. Just hang in there."

...

In the control room, Ms. Hayes yelled to the crew. "We're getting this. Right?"

"We're getting it. Four cameras getting it all."

...

The pain had started to subside, but the Sergeant was starting to faint, the stress on his system too much for his weakened body. Michael nodded to Noelani and she started rubbing a different cream on a wider area of his neck. This cream was rich in nanobots that could penetrate the skin and accelerate nerve repair. Charles had come down the steps with a glass of what appeared to be water and gave it to Michael.

Michael looked the Sergeant in the eyes and said, "George, drink this. It will help with the pain and also help restore your strength."

By now, one of the auditorium ushers had come to Ms. Butler's aid. The smelling salts brought her back to consciousness. The usher righted her chair, which had fallen over, and helped her get back into her seat.

"What have they done to my son?" she asked, tears streaming from her eyes.

"I'm no expert. But I think they've healed him."

Sergeant Butler was coming back to his senses, but it didn't make any sense. He could feel his feet. He could move his arms and shoulders. Twist in his wheelchair. He started an attempt to stand but Michael held him down.

"Sergeant!" Michael said while holding the agitated Sergeant in place. "Sergeant. Look me in the eyes."

The Sergeant looked up as Michael spoke firmly. "You've been healed, but after five years in the chair you are too weak to stand."

The Sergeant started squirming again.

"Sergeant!" Michael said in his best command voice. "You will need a lot of physical therapy before you can stand on your own again. But you WILL stand on your own again! I'm sure the VA will help you. You are also welcome to come to my ranch in Hawaii and work on your recovery with my team on the Big Island."

"Mr. Michael, sir. I can't afford no physical therapy or airplane tickets. I'm on military disability. That barely pays for food. That's why I live with my mama."

"George. You can come back to Hawaii with me on my shuttle. No charge for airfare, lodging, food, or care. Why don't you sit back and enjoy the show? I'll come get you after."

Michael saw the light dim in the Sergeant's eyes. *This poor man.* Michael thought. *He has lived with so much disappointment.* Michael turned to the usher. "Is there another chair you could give us?"

"Yes sir. You want it here?"

"Yes please."

"Be back in a moment."

"George, would it be OK if Noelani sat with you during the show? You know I will not leave without her. So, if she is with you, then you know I won't leave without you, right?"

"Thank you, Mr. Michael, sir. I would like that very much."

The studio audience roared with delight. Then Sarah's voice cut through it all. "And that's the way it is this morning on Good Morning America. We will be back in a few minutes."

Michael looked up at the clock in the back of the auditorium, the one Monica told him marked time into the show. It read 10 minutes, 18 seconds. They had been live for the last 10 minutes.

The chair came. Noelani sat down with George and took his hand. And the studio audience broke out in applause.

...

As the lights came back up, the stage director counted down with his fingers, then pointed to Sarah, who said "Welcome back, America! I have with me none other than Michael Baker, the man you just witnessed helping Sergeant George Butler. And the same man that talked on every TV and radio in the world last night.

"Michael, we talked before the show and I asked you how a 35-year-old American citizen from Texas could credibly claim to be a representative of an Intergalactic Confederation."

A dark murmur spread through the studio audience. "When I asked that question, I was not a believer. In fact, I was an outright disbeliever. After seeing you with Sergeant Butler... Can we have a round of applause for Sergeant Butler?"

She pointed at the man. The audience exploded with applause and enthusiasm. "As I was saying, after seeing you with Sergeant Butler, I think I'm a believer." The crowd exploded again. "But, the question remains, and I mean this in the most respectful way. How do we reconcile what we've seen here with what we think we know of your background?"

This one is good. Michael thought. Then he replied, "Sarah, there are so many more important things for us to discuss that I hate wasting time on this one. But I respect and appreciate the human intuition that asks, 'Can I believe the things this man says if I don't know who he is.' The answer is that I am Lorexian, a species that most humans would say is repulsively ugly. It was the judgement of our ruling bodies, and I agree with that judgement, that the only way we'd be accepted by humans was if we came in human form.

"This body," he pointed to himself, "was created 35 years ago in a Confederation laboratory operating in El Paso, Texas. It wasn't born by a natural human process in a hospital. It was registered with the state department of vital statistics as an unassisted home birth. Of the many labs we had operating on Earth at the time, we chose the one in El Paso because I wanted the flexibility that American citizenship offered. As a natural-born American citizen, I was able to form a company that could test technology for its suitability on Earth. Even better, that company made enough money that we were able to develop additional technology that will be critical to the Earth's survival.

"But, back to my first point... this is not about me. It's not about this body. It is about delivering technology to mankind that it desperately needs to survive what's ahead."

Once again, the studio audience erupted in applause.

"Michael, can you tell us how old you are?"

"Sarah, can you tell us how old you are?"

"Touché, Michael. But hear me for a second... You look like a 35-year-old that spouts good lines and has cool tricks."

Boos, cat calls, and just plain vulgarity erupted from the room.

Sarah held her hands up. "Ok. OK. That was too direct but give me a break. I'm a believer now, but there are people watching that didn't see what we saw up close. People that want to believe but are having trouble with the baby face. Sorry, Michael, but you are kind of cute.

"The point is that humanity would really like to know that you have the experience to lead us through the changes that you say are coming, before we place our trust in you."

"Sarah. I can't tell you how much I don't want this hour to be about me. But your point is fair." Michael took a long pause and looked straight at the camera with the light. "I was born before the dawn of recorded history. My first mission to Earth was during the Roman Empire. I hold all those memories. Some of them vividly. It was during that first mission that I fell in love with humanity, despite its barbarism. It was during that mission that I decided I wanted to be the first ambassador to Earth. You, as a species, are not quite ready for this first contact. But you, as a species, are worth the risk we are collectively taking."

The room burst into deafening applause and whistles as the show cut to commercial.

...

When the show came back on the screen, it was on the kitchen set. The domestic anchor, Kimberly was standing there with Michael and one of America's up and coming celebrity chefs, Marco Rubinstein.

When the stage manager counted down to one, Kimberly said, "Good Morning America. I have with me two people that could not be more different. The first is Chef Marco Rubinstein, whose new book 'Cookin' Like Mama' is sweeping the nation. It mixes the traditional Italian and Jewish recipes his mother and grandmother taught him. Welcome, Chef Marco!

"Our second guest is the overnight sensation Michael, Ambassador from the Intergalactic Confederation of Planets and healer extraordinaire. Michael is playing the farmer today. He is here to provide the Chef with the fresh ingredients that he needs. Gentlemen, what have you cooked up for us?"

Marco nodded to Michael.

"Hi, Kimberly," Michael said. "We're going to do something reminiscent of what you usually do during this hour, but a little different.

"Chef Marco, whose food I love by the way, is going to create a recipe that he has never used before. Right now. Right in front of your eyes. I have no idea what ingredients he'll ask for. I only know that I'll provide them for him. In fact, I will produce enough of each ingredient that Chef Marco can feed everyone in the room." A ripple of awe swept across the auditorium. "But we're going to need some help. Kimberly?"

Kimberly walked down the steps into the auditorium and picked two people. They came back with her and were introduced.

The first person, a woman named Joanne, volunteered to work with Chef Marco. The second, a woman named Diane, agreed to work with Michael.

"Chef," Michael said. "What is the first ingredient?"

"Michael, I need a dozen onions. Chopped fine, but not minced."

Michael turned to Diane. "Diane, do you have a smart phone, one that could show me a picture of what the Chef wants?"

Diane, a bit stumped by the question, went over to confer with the Chef. Meanwhile, Charles pushed a cart out onto the stage with a replicator on it.

"Kimberly," Michael said. "While they are sorting out the specifications for the onions, could you come check out the machine my friend Charles is pushing onto the stage?"

Kimberly looked at the machine as Michael asked, "Kimberly, could you tell us what you're looking at? Could you describe it?"

"Looks a lot like a laser printer to me. A little more than a foot on each side and maybe a foot tall."

"Tell me about the cart?"

"It is a standard serving cart with wheels, made from metal tubing and open on all sides."

"Sorry if this sounds like some kind of magic trick, but the fact of the matter is that any sufficiently advanced technology looks like magic to those that haven't seen it before. So please bear with me. Is there anything above the laser printer? Below it? Or on either side of it?"

Kimberly walked around the device with her hand above it the whole time. "Nothing above or on the sides." She repeated the process walking around the device moving her hands in and out around the legs. "Nothing below it."

"Is there a plug or any other electrical connection?"

She walked around the device again looking at every side and stooping to look up at the bottom of the device through a grid. "No. No visible power source."

"Excellent. Diane. Do we have a specification for the onions?"

"Yes, we do. Here is a picture of the dice we want. They are Maui Sweet onions, diced into 3/16-inch cubes."

"Joanne, could you bring me the container that the Chef would like the onions in?"

She brought over a clear plastic container about the same size as the replicator.

"Could you place it next to the machine? Right there next to the spout." He pointed to an orifice that had opened on the side.

"All right, America. Onions..." He smiled as he pointed at the container. Immediately, the machine started spitting out diced onions.

"Joanne, could you take these to the chef and ask him if they are cut right and fresh enough."

The Chef crinkled his nose. *Please not onions from a machine. Please tell me I didn't work this hard to get on the show, only to get stuck with fake onions.*

Joanne brought the onions over. The chef sampled the onions and a smile bloomed on his face. "Michael. How did you do this? These are excellent!"

For the next ten minutes, then through the break, the Chef specified ingredients and Michael produced them. As the show came back on the screen, it was clear to audiences around the world that the culinary result was spectacular.

Michael stepped aside as the Chef discussed his creation, showed his techniques and told stories of his grandmother. Finally, Sarah came back on the stage and asked who would like some lunch. The crowd roared.

When they returned from the next break, Sarah resumed her questioning. "Michael," she said. "The producers told you this morning that you could have the entire show if you wanted. But when you looked through the scheduled guest list you asked if you could work with Chef Marco. Why?"

Michael laughed. "Thank goodness, I finally get an easy question," he said with mock relief. "The answer is simple, Sarah. I've eaten at one of Chef Marco's restaurants and know his food is spectacular. I've been so busy the last 24 hours I haven't had time to eat, so I thought, 'Why not let Chef Marco cook me lunch?'"

The crowd burst out laughing.

"But more seriously, I wanted America to see the second of the gifts I have come to offer nations that ally with the Intergalactic Confederation, replicators. This replicator..." he pointed to the laser printer sized box, "produced all the food we ate today, and we fed how many? 300 people?"

"More like 500, Michael."

"And it produces more than just food. I'd like to give someone in this room a gift. I can't make a car using this particular device, so the gift can't be too big. Is there someone in this room that would like a gift?"

A young man in the room jumped up in the air, whooping and hollering, "Me! Me!"

His display was so outrageous Michael pointed to him and asked, "What would you like?"

He stood as an usher brought him a microphone. "Michael. Sir. I want to get engaged, but I don't have enough money to buy my girl a proper engagement ring."

"What's your name and is your girl here?" The young woman sitting next to him stood up.

"My name is Private First Class Malcolm Brown. And this is my fiancée Alicia Green."

"Would the two of you mind coming up here?"

As they approached, Sarah whispered, "Time."

Michael beckoned Charles to come over from off stage. "Charles, can you measure this young lady's finger?"

"What kind of band, Alicia?" Michael asked. "Gold, silver, platinum?"

"Gold, please."

A moment later a 1 carat perfect cut diamond engagement ring slid down the spout.

Michael picked up the ring and gave it to the young man. "Private Brown, do you have someone you would like to ask a question?"

The young man turned to Alicia, dropped to one knee, held out the ring and asked, "Alicia. Will you marry me?"

The show cut to a commercial as the audience roared.

WHITE HOUSE SITUATION ROOM

The President was ushered into the Situation Room as Good Morning America played on the central screen. "What is this about?" he asked his chief of staff. "What is the national emergency?"

"It's him, sir. Baker, the alien."

"What? On Good Morning America! What in the hell is he doing on TV! He is supposed to be in jail!"

"Sir. The FBI team you sent really screwed things up. The team leader, a Special Agent Long, was arrested and is currently in custody in Hilo, Hawaii."

"What!! They can't arrest FBI agents."

"I'm sorry sir. But in cases of gross misconduct they can. A federal district court judge issued an arrest warrant about three hours into the raid last night. Several agents were seriously injured during the mission, and one is still missing. The subject is apparently a doctor and gave care to the agents who had been injured before even getting to his property."

The President said nothing.

"Worse sir. We have him on site near Waimea on the Big Island at 9:00 PM Hawaiian time. He was seen by six Hawaiian Civil Defense officers, who came to evac the wounded and to arrest Special Agent Long. Then he shows up two hours later in New York.

"What?" The president asked, bewildered now.

"Even worse, sir."

The president gave his chief of staff an evil stare, but he plowed on.

"Good Morning America has a normal audience of five to five and a half million. After Michael cured a quadriplegic veteran wounded in Afghanistan, their audience spiked up to 7.5 million. At that point, ABC went to special report status on all their channels worldwide, even in countries where it's the middle of the night and no one speaks English, and they are now claiming 15 million viewers."

"Holy Mother of God! What is going on here?" asked the President.

GOOD MORNING AMERICA AUDITORIUM

The show cut back to live TV... "Michael, that was really sweet. But I have to ask... Why did you do that?"

"Sarah. Here's the deal. The world is tearing itself apart. Much of the strife is caused by wealth inequality. Let me be clear. I am not against individuals starting companies and striking it rich. The world needs that if it's going to prosper. What I am against is people that are living on $4.00 a day. People that do not have access to the basic necessities of life. If the world is going to survive, we need all humans to have basic rights to food, power, medicine... The simple fact of the matter is that humanity expanded faster than its technology base did. A trillion people could live comfortable lives given the resources this planet has. Earth is a jewel. But you don't have the technology to do it yet. And you can't get there by taxing the innovators and producers at 90%. That just guarantees a faster death. What you need is technology.

"You saw the first technology I have to offer at the beginning of the show. You have just seen the second. Imagine if every family had a replicator. There would be no more hunger. There would be no more poverty. There would still be conflict. We are human. What there wouldn't be is any further reason to fight over resources.

"Can I show you the next technology I have to offer?"

"Michael, I am overwhelmed already. But let's plow on..."

"Charles, could you bring out the power cube?"

Charles carried out a small rectangular box with a power outlet. Michael took it and held it up so the camera could get a closeup. He handed it to Sarah.

"I'm betting you can guess what this does."

"I'm not so sure you're going to win that bet, Michael," Sarah said with a smile.

"OK. Just describe to the audience what you see and anything on this device that you recognize."

"Well it looks like the power pack for a portable computer."

"So it does," Michael replied.

"Except where you would normally put the power cord in to plug it into the wall, it has a power outlet."

"Well, what do you normally do with power outlets?"

"You plug things in." There was a long awkward silence. "Oh my God, Michael."

Monica in the control room was so mesmerized by what was going on that she almost didn't hit the bleep button in time.

"You plug things in. Hey, can someone bring me a lamp or something I can plug in?"

A stagehand came trotting out on to the stage with a small desk lamp and handed it to Sarah. He took a bow as the audience applauded, then ran back off stage.

Sarah plugged the lamp into the socket and turned on the light... and it came on!

Sarah opened her mouth to speak, then tears streamed down her face. As she struggled to compose herself, she looked up at her guest. "How?"

Michael, who now stood next to Sarah, took her in his arms and gave her a comforting hug. Once again, the audience went wild.

He took his seat and looked directly at the active camera. "This is what human scientists call a zero-point energy device. It pumps energy out of what your scientists call the 'quantum foam.'

"The amount of power a device can produce is dependent on a number of factors but is loosely related to the device's size and intended duration. Small ones like this are designed to produce up to 200 watts and have an effective life of twenty years. But larger ones can have much higher power or much longer life.

"I am prepared to offer one of these to every family, every household, in countries whose governments sign a treaty with the Intergalactic Confederation... Free of charge!" The studio audience roared once again.

"I have one more gift to offer when we come back from this commercial break."

In the control room, Monica thought to herself, *Michael would make a pretty good host for this show.*

WHITE HOUSE SITUATION ROOM

As the show cut to a commercial, the President turned to the national security team that had assembled. "How is this guy doing this? Is there any way we can debunk it, or replicate it? If we're not the first to get this technology, all of America's power will slip right through our fingers."

"Mr. President," The Secretary of State said. "You have Michael's contact information, right?" The president looked to his Chief of Staff who nodded in the affirmative. "Then call him right now, Mr. President! He's on break. Surely, he will take your call."

The President nodded to his Chief of Staff, who stepped away from the table while pushing the buttons on his phone.

The Secretary of Energy spoke up next. "Mr. President, if he will give you one of those devices to test, maybe we can reverse engineer it."

The Secretary of Defense added, "If we can reverse engineer those power sources of his, we could build drones that would be silent and could stay up indefinitely."

The President nodded his head. "I like the idea of meeting with this guy and getting samples of his tech."

GOOD MORNING AMERICA AUDITORIUM

The lights came up on the last segment of the show. All four hosts—Sarah, Kimberly, Deborah and Jessica—were seated along the left and right of a living room-like set up with a coffee table and some lamps. Michael and another guest were seated in the center behind the table. The stage manager counted down with his fingers. He pointed to Jessica as his hand closed into a fist.

"Welcome back, America. Today's very special guest is Michael, the ambassador to Earth from the Intergalactic Confederation of Planets. Our special guest for this segment is Dr. Winston Chu, the world-renowned climatologist. Dr. Chu, welcome!"

As the crowd applauded politely in the background, Dr. Chu smiled. "Glad to be with you Jessica."

"Dr. Chu, you had been scheduled to be on the show today to promote the ideas in your new book, 'Technology for a New Green Deal.' When Michael agreed to be on the show, we started rescheduling our slate of guests so we could give him our full attention. But during the pre-show planning meeting, he asked if you could join this part of the discussion and we are so glad you agreed. Thank you!" Jessica oozed with appreciation.

"Michael, I understand that you would like to do another demonstration during this segment," she added.

"Yes, Jessica. I have one more gift for humanity that I would like to share, and it directly addresses one of the issues Dr. Chu raises in his book," Michael replied.

Dr. Chu looked at Michael as if surprised. "Thank you for having read my book Michael."

"Dr. Chu in Chapter 7 you talk about the un-recognized, or at least poorly publicized, danger that the current levels of carbon dioxide pose. Could you give us the 2-minute, high-school level summary of this issue?" Michael asked.

Dr. Chu nodded to Michael and said, "Yes, I would like to do that. My publishers asked me not to discuss that chapter unless asked, because too many people either disagree, or worse, just don't want to know. I think the fact that you're asking may make that the most studied chapter in the book going forward, so thank you... Again." The crowd chuckled.

Looking straight at the audience, Dr. Chu said. "The focus of much of the public discussion of climate change is that we need to reduce carbon dioxide emissions, which is true and appropriate. But the problem is catastrophically worse than that simple statement sounds.

"Most people assume, based on the public and overly political discussion of climate change, that if we could simply turn a switch and stop all human carbon dioxide emissions tomorrow, we would be done. Problem solved."

"I'm sad to tell you, but that's not true. If all we do is stop human carbon dioxide emissions, the climate change will continue at the same pace it is today."

Expressions of disbelief could be heard throughout the room. "Our current emissions are not only making climate change worse, they're accelerating the rate at which it is getting worse. Stopping all emissions would simply allow the climate to stabilize somewhere a little worse than the current state, with the same high levels of extreme weather and drought, and the same rate of melting polar ice. The seas would continue to rise. Super hurricanes would continue to form at the same rate. You get the picture."

Deborah, who had not spoken up so far on this show, interrupted the doctor. "Dr. Chu, how can this be true?"

"Not everyone agrees with me on this, but I believe that the current global climate is driven loosely by the carbon dioxide level averaged over the last couple years. If we stopped all carbon dioxide emissions, that level would stabilize at about the level we see today, but it will not materially drop. You see, Earth really doesn't have a good way to scrub carbon dioxide out of the atmosphere. Yes, there are plants and algae. But their carbon dioxide scrubbing capability is less than it was in the pre-industrialized world, when our planet was in equilibrium. So, if all we did was stop all human carbon dioxide emissions, except breathing, atmospheric concentrations would not drop. In fact, there is a small chance that it would continue to increase at a very slow rate."

The room was absolutely silent. Then, Michael started clapping. Loudly. Slowly, others started joining in.

"Michael, it appears that you agree with Dr. Chu." Jessica said.

"Yes. I do. Some years ago, I came to the same conclusions as Dr. Chu just published." He stood, turned toward the doctor and offered his hand. "Thank you, sir. I consider you a friend of Earth and, as such, a friend of mine and of the Confederation's." Dr. Chu stood solemnly and shook Michael's hand.

Michael turned to Jessica. "I know our time is running out, so would you mind if I ask my friend Kale to set up my next demonstration over on the kitchen set?" He pointed to Kale, who was already setting up a machine on the counter. Without waiting for an answer, Michael gestured to those on the stage and said, "Shall we walk over there?"

Dr. Chu stood and walked with Michael. Then said, "Michael, am I guessing correctly that you have a carbon dioxide extraction technology that you're going to demonstrate?"

"Yes, Dr Chu. You guess correctly."

"Forgive me for cutting to the chase, but how much will it cost and how long will it take to restore the equilibrium."

As the show seemed to be progressing without them, the co-hosts moved quickly to catch up. Sarah piped up. "Michael. I've seen enough already to believe that this device will do as you say. And I think Dr. Chu has hit the nail on the head, so to speak."

"Sarah, when we met a few hours ago, you said you had done a lot of research on me. Can you tell the audience anything about my Paso Robles operation?"

Sarah was momentarily taken back. How could gas wells in Paso Robles have anything to do with carbon dioxide abatement? It felt like the opposite.

"Well," she said. "At a remarkably young age, you bought some exhausted oil wells just north of Paso Robles. The wells had been sealed and the EPA had confirmed them to be exhausted. Local media reports referred to you as a young fool, wasting good money on nothing. But here you are a few years later, selling... what's the number... ah... $30 million a year of natural gas to the southern California utilities."

"But what has this got to do with..." Sarah and Dr. Chu stopped in mid step, then said simultaneously, "You're making natural gas from carbon dioxide!"

"Indeed I am," Michael said. "In nature, natural gas burns to become carbon dioxide. It's that release of energy that the electric utilities use to power the grid. Although it takes a lot of energy to run that reaction backwards, it can be done. And, as you now know, I have a lot of energy."

Dr. Chu suddenly piped up. "Is that my lab equipment on the table?"

"Yes, it is, Dr Chu. My apologies for appropriating it without your consent, but I think you'll approve of my purpose. Can you tell the audience what this equipment does?"

"It accurately measures the concentration of carbon dioxide in the atmosphere."

"Is your equipment functioning properly?"

Dr. Chu was slow to reply, but said, "Yes, it is. I can see why you like this young man here so much. It's calibrated perfectly." Turning to Kale, he said. "Apologies, I didn't catch your name. Are you an environmental scientist?"

"My name is Kale. It's a Hawaiian name. I'm not a scientist like you are, but I do work for Michael."

"Doctor, could you tell us the average concentration of carbon dioxide in our atmosphere, and the current concentration in this room?" Michael asked.

"In the atmosphere as a whole, 420 parts per million. In New York City, a little higher, maybe 430. I haven't actually measured it here in some time, but the major cities run 10 parts per million higher." After fooling with some knobs and cross-checking some displays, he said. "It is currently 442 parts per million in this room, which is not unexpected. We have a lot of people breathing in here."

The audience chuckled at the line.

"Doctor, what was the reading in pre-industrial times?"

"There is a lot of debate about that, but the fossil record suggests that it was about 280 parts per million. Some say higher. Some say lower. But 280 is the number I go with."

"Let's see if we can make this room more like pre-industrial times. Kale, if you would?"

Nothing seemed to happen. Light music started in the background indicating that there were 60 seconds left in this segment. Michael pointed to a small test tube on the side of his device. "Any chance we can get a zoom in on that test tube?" Michael asked of the room.

One of the camera men moved his gear closer and zoomed in. Monica, in the control room, put the image on the screens in the auditorium and put it in an inset on the broadcast screen. On the screen, the image of a drop of clear liquid formed.

"Dr. Chu. What is the carbon dioxide level in the room now?"

The doctor twiddled some knobs and said, "380."

"Ladies and Gentlemen, the drop you see on the screen is gasoline." On the screen, a second drop formed, then dripped. The music got louder, and the broadcast screens cut to a commercial.

Dr. Chu, fixated on his equipment, hadn't realized that the show was on commercial said, "The carbon dioxide in this room is down to 340!" He was still calling off numbers as they counted in from the commercial. The broadcast resumed with the image of Dr. Chu saying,

"The concentration is down to 280. Michael, this is pre-industrial air we are breathing!"

The show's closing music started to play as Deborah, who was getting her first real host role of the day, said. "Michael. Thank you for joining us on our show today. And to our other guests, Dr. Chu and Chef Marco, thank you for joining us. I hope you all will come back to visit us again. What a great show. And," she said staring straight into the camera. "See you tomorrow on Good Morning America."

The music came up as the camera zoomed out showing the room and the studio audience. In the background, Dr. Chu could be heard shouting "270" over the noise of the crowd. And, just as the screen shifted to the next show, Michael could be seen moving toward the steps that led down to Noelani and Sergeant Butler.

THE MEETING

GOOD MORNING AMERICA AUDITORIUM

As Michael reached the stairs on his way to Noelani and Sergeant Butler, a security guard stepped forward blocking his way. "I'm sorry sir, but you can't go down there. If you do, you'll be mobbed, and it'll be difficult for us to finish clearing the room or to rescue you from the crowd. We've had this happen before."

"Thank you, officer. But I need my assistant Noelani back and I also need to speak with Sergeant Butler and his mother."

"We can arrange for them to meet you backstage, sir." The security guard said.

Monica, who'd anticipated this, had come down from the control room and now ran across the stage to Michael.

"Michael," she said somewhat breathlessly. "We've already made arrangements for you to reconnect with your party. It will take them a few minutes to get there. The crowd is exiting a lot slower than normal. Would you come with me?"

Michael sent to Noelani. *Noelani, security is coming to take you and the Butlers to a conference room where we can meet. Please tell the Sergeant not to worry.*

Monica caught the faraway look in Michael's eye and noticed that Noelani had suddenly looked their way. *Curious*, she thought. *I wonder if they can communicate telepathically.*

As Noelani turned to say something to the Butlers, Monica said, "Michael. That was a fantastic show. You are a natural as a talk show host. The final numbers are not in, but preliminary estimates are that we had more than twice our record audience today. America and most of the rest of the world is enthralled with you. Did you accomplish what you wanted to today?"

Michael walked along beside Monica as she moved back toward the center of the stage. "I won't know for sure until the response starts coming in, but I believe the answer is yes.

"Tell me... When did you know that you were going to broadcast my interaction with Sergeant Butler?" Michael asked.

"Almost immediately. You and Noelani approached them so nonchalantly that no one outside the control room even noticed you approach. Then I noticed that device in your hand, the one shown in the video you played on our TV, and I could envision what was about to happen. We had three cameras on you by the time Noelani started applying the cream. We even got a super-directional microphone on you, so we could hear what you said and catch the compassion in your voice. So, I decided we would go with it and you were either going to do something that has never been seen on television before, or you were going to be totally debunked. Either way, great television," she said with a smile.

A prompt from Jiaying, back at the lab in Hawaii, popped up on Michael's inner vision. *The President is on the line. What would you like me to do?*

Michael turned to Monica. "Sorry to ask, but I have an urgent call coming in. Is there a place I can take it?"

"This way Michael. You have some sort of telepathic communication, don't you?" Monica said.

"From the moment I met you, I knew you were a pro, Monica. We have room on our team for someone like you, if you're interested."

"Here we are. You can use this room. The phone is over there. Just dial 9 to get out."

Michael crossed over to the phone and read the number off to Jiaying, then said, "Route the call to this number. Quantum encryption between here and the relay point. "

Walking back toward the stage, Monica called the control room on her radio and said, "Record the phone in room S-02."

OVAL OFFICE, WHITE HOUSE

"Mr. Baker is on the line, Mr. President."

The President picked up the phone and said. "Hello, Mr. Baker. It is a pleasure to speak with you. I caught some of the show on Good Morning America this morning and your actions seem to back up the claims you've made."

"Thank you, sir. And please, call me Michael."

"I would like to meet with you, Michael, and if possible, I'd like you to demonstrate your equipment to some of my people."

"I would like to do that sir."

"You are in New York, correct?"

"Yes, sir, I am."

"If you could meet this morning, I can arrange for a helicopter to meet you in about a half hour."

"Mr. President. I would love to meet with you this morning. But I have to insist on using my own transportation. I can be there in about an hour, if that works for you."

"Forgive me for asking Michael, but how could you get here in one hour?"

"My shuttle is waiting for me on the roof of this building. It will only take a few minutes for it to get from here to the West Wing Lawn."

"Michael, surely you know that anyone attempting to land on the West Wing Lawn will be shot down if they don't have clearance. And I can't give you the security codes to even request a landing."

"Mr. President, my shuttle doesn't really land, it just appears. May I show you?"

"What do you mean, 'May I show you?'"

The TV in the oval office suddenly turned on and started playing the video of the arrival in New York. "Do you see the TV screen Mr. President? That is the helipad at ABC News in New York, where we appeared at 5:00 AM this morning. See the clock running in the top left corner of the screen. We will appear in 3, 2, 1..." And the shuttle simply appeared.

"If we do that at 11:00 AM sharp on Pennsylvania Avenue in front of the White House, could we be met by a security team, vetted and escorted inside?"

A Secret Service agent had entered the room a little earlier at the request of the Chief of Staff. They were both listening in on the call. The Secret Service agent was vigorously shaking his head No when the President said. "I think that will work. A security team will meet you there at 11:00 sharp. I look forward to meeting you in person, Michael."

"I look forward to meeting you also, Mr. President.

ROOM S-02, ABC NEWS, NEW YORK

This is a setup, Boss. Sanjit sent.

I know, Michael replied.

"Jiaying, can you leak to the news people that we will be arriving in front of the White House at 11:00 AM? And send Elsie the plan."

CONTROL ROOM, ABC NEWS

"Are you getting anything on that phone line?" Monica asked her audio tech.

"I heard the line ring and get picked up. Then just noise." He replied.

"Oh well. Worth the try."

Her monitor suddenly switched to showing Michael's face. He smiled and said, "Not nice to eavesdrop."

Monica was stricken at having been caught, but recovered quickly and said, "Can't blame a girl for trying. No harm, no foul. Right?"

"Actually, I'm calling for a favor. We need to leave in about an hour and are on our way to the White House. Our shuttle will arrive on Pennsylvania Ave., right in front of the White House, at 11:00 AM sharp. Could you spread the word and invite as much of the White House press pool as your people can reach? If a crowd shows up, I'll give you, or the person you designate, the exclusive interview afterwards."

A big smile spread across her face. "Michael, I can't tell you how much I like working with you."

ABC NEWS HEADQUARTERS

As Michael made his way back toward the stage, Dr. Chu waved to him and started walking his way. "Michael, thank you so much for letting me do the show with you, and for confirming my work. No one really wants to hear my message. But now that you have shown us that there is a solution, maybe we can start making some progress."

"I've taken the liberty of having my staff get your contact information. Would it be all right if I contacted you sometime before too long?" Michael asked.

"Anytime Michael. I will do anything in my power to make your work successful. Just ask," said Dr. Chu, reaching out to shake Michael's hand.

As he turned to go, Chef Marco approached. "Michael, any chance I can get one of those food replicators? The product it produces is fantastic."

"That is up to your President, Chef. The replicators will only flow to countries that enter into an agreement with the Confederation. If America does that, then you can have one of the first deliveries."

"Thank you, Michael. It was the best show I've ever been on and a real pleasure meeting you."

Michael saw Sarah waving to him, beckoning him to come. Michael said thank you to the chef and walked over to Sarah.

"Hi Michael. The Butlers are in the conference room with your team. They tell me everything is packed up and ready to go. Monica also asked me to tell you that she would like me to do the interview. Um… She's a great producer and editor but doesn't show all that well on camera. So, she asked me to do the interview and promised that she'd edit it herself."

"Sounds like a deal. Shall we go see the Butlers?"

"One other thing… She asked if we could travel to Washington DC with you. Me, a cameraman and a sound tech. And about 100 lbs. of equipment."

"Why don't you come on into the conference room with me and bring your crew if they are here."

She waved to the crew, who followed Michael and Sarah to the conference room.

As he entered, he heard the sounds of happiness. Sergeant Butler was standing, almost able to balance himself, with his mom on one side and Noelani on the other. Kale was holding his hands out, promising to catch the Sergeant if he fell. And Charles was frowning, apparently worried that attempting to walk at this point in the recovery was a bad idea.

Michael smiled and said, "Be careful Sergeant. There's plenty of time for that once we get back to the ranch." Then gesturing to the broader group. "We've been invited to the White House to meet with the President."

An excited buzz went around the room.

"Before you get too excited… There's a chance we're being set up. Just last night, the FBI showed up at the ranch with the intention of arresting us and seizing our property. This might be just another attempt at the same." Noelani nodded her head in agreement with Michael, while the others looked like they were questioning whether going along was such a good idea.

"So, here's the deal. You're welcome to come with us." He gestured to the Butlers and to the news team. "You may even get to meet the President, but I can't guarantee it. Or, you can wait here, and we'll be back to pick you up when the meeting is over."

"What's the risk?" Sergeant Butler asked.

"For my team, essentially none. The United States does not have the technology to damage our shuttle or us personally. In fact, they can't even detain us without our consent," Michael replied.

"Unfortunately, there's only so much protection we can offer you. Inside the shuttle with the door closed, they can't do anything to you. But once they've identified you, they could bring the weight of the government down upon you, once you return home.

"The decision is yours. We'll head up to the shuttle in about 20 minutes if you'd like to join us."

HELIPAD, ABC NEWS HEADQUARTERS

The whole team was there: Michael, Noelani, Kale, Charles, the Butlers and the ABC News crew. The shuttle door opened and they all got on board. Kale and Charles had loaded the demo gear earlier.

"Elsie." Michael opened the cockpit door, "have you sorted out the flight plan?"

"Oh, are we flying? I thought we were simply appearing," she said with a smile.

"If that was a question, then I suggest that you just appear, because I'm sure that someone would like to shoot us down right about now. I pity the news helicopters that are probably hovering in the area. So, what is the flight plan?" Michael asked.

"We have about an hour and you have a reporter and a cameraman aboard, so I suggest that we pop into orbit, take in the beautiful view of creation, and let them get a few pictures. Then we hover near the site until the appointed time."

"Elsie, you make it sound so... biblical." Michael smiled.

"That's a go then?" she asked.

"Go. I'll prep the team."

Michael went back into the passenger cabin to address the entourage. "Welcome aboard everyone. Here's the plan. In a vehicle like our shuttle, the trip to DC only takes a minute or two. We have an hour, so the plan is to jump to orbit, hang for a few minutes so you can all get a great view and some pictures. Then we'll drop down to DC, arriving a minute or two ahead of schedule and hovering. At 11:00 AM exactly, we will drop stealth, but not shields. Everyone with me?"

There was a chorus of yeses.

"Entering stealth," Elsie announced. "Launching at 10G," she added.

Sergeant Butler raised his hand and asked, "Michael, did she say 10G, as in ten times the acceleration of gravity?"

"Yes." Michael replied.

"Don't we need protection or something? Ten G could break my mother's bones."

"We are protected," Michael said. "Just look out the window."

The Sergeant raised his window shade and saw that they were way up, higher than any airplane and that the sky was shifting from blue to black.

"Wow!" he said.

Over the cabin's speakers, Elsie announced, "We'll be parking at about 12,000 miles altitude in another couple seconds. You won't feel a change. Once I turn off the seat belt sign, you'll be free to get up and walk around the cabin, and to position your equipment to take as many pictures as you'd like for the next 10 minutes. Then we'll start our gentle glide down to Pennsylvania Avenue."

A moment later, there was a beep and the seat belt sign was turned off.

Sarah was the first out of her seat, her crew only a moment behind.

"Michael, if we are really in space, why aren't we weightless?" She asked.

Michael smiled and said, "If we turned off our gravity generators, then we would be weightless."

As the news team started setting up equipment to get a shot from orbit, Michael went over to Sergeant Butler. "Sergeant, how are you doing? Are you experiencing any pain?"

"Not like before." He said. "But there's still an itchiness all over, kind of like ants crawling on me."

"That's to be expected. Once we get you back to the ranch, we'll be able to make most of it go away."

"Thank you, sir. Um... sir, can I ask you a question?"

"Only if you want the answer." Michael smiled.

"Why did you pick me? There were 11 other guys there. Why me? Why not them? And, are you going to be able to help them?"

"Here is the honest truth... There were three factors. First, it was a TV show. I had to pick someone I could heal, and I only had 10 minutes to do something dramatic that would convince the audience that this was not a hoax. Although you were the one that looked most injured, you were actually one of three that would be easiest to heal.

"Second, I knew the pain of healing would be the most intense for you, which meant that people would not doubt that something dramatic was happening to you.

"Third, this one is trickier to describe properly, but I can read people. I usually keep my 'gates' as closed as possible, so as not to intrude on people's privacy. But I opened them a little as I looked at the group of you and immediately realized that you wanted it the most and would be the most forgiving of what I was about to do to you without permission or warning.

"Which is why I wanted to talk to you now. George, will you forgive me for doing what I did without asking your permission first?"

George started laughing. "Yes, Michael. You are forgiven and I owe you big time."

"George, would you consider being my liaison of sorts to the veterans' community? I need someone to screen the requests that are going to come, so that we help the neediest first."

"Of course, I will!" he said with enthusiasm, until his mother gave him the look.

"Michael," said the Sergeant's mother. "Is it your intent that this would be a job or a volunteer activity? And, if it is a job, where would it be located?"

"Good questions, Ms. Butler, and ones that I'm sure we can work out. But I just got signaled from the cockpit. We're about to begin our descent and there are a couple things I need to check on first. We will have more time to talk once we get to Hawaii." As Michael stood, Elsie's voice came over the intercom asking everyone to be seated.

He walked up to the cockpit and let himself in. He'd seen Charles enter a few minutes earlier. "Do we have any imaging on the landing site, yet?"

"Only poor quality. Can't really tell yet whether there will be space to land." Charles said. Changing subjects, he asked, "Do you have a plan for this meeting? Who do you want to go in with you?"

"I think that depends a lot on the instructions the President has given his security detail. I would like to take the same team: you, me, Kale and Noelani. If they only allow me in, then all the equipment will stay here. If I can only take one of you, it will be you, Charles.

"I think there is a very strong likelihood that they will try to split us up and tamper with the equipment, so we need a plan if things go sideways." He turned to the pilot.

"Elsie. Be prepared to take off and hover nearby in stealth mode. Don't do it unless I signal you. But be ready on a moment's notice. Also make sure the transporter is always on-line and locked onto staff and equipment. Pull the equipment first, unless we've had to slag it."

"Michael, we're about halfway down. The scanners are clearing, and it's a circus down there."

OVAL OFFICE, WHITE HOUSE

"Mr. President. It looks like we have a situation developing out on the street. Word is apparently out that Michael is coming. Reporters and news trucks were clogging the streets, so the capital police have let them onto Pennsylvania Avenue, which is now just about full. I don't know where they're going to park their shuttle or how we're going to get our security team out to greet them." The chief of staff sounded worried.

The head of the Secret Service interrupted, asking, "Mr. President, if I may?"

"Go on."

"I think we can clear a spot right in front of the security gate that's large enough for a helicopter. I think the crowd will respect the space if we put up a security barrier and station one or two men there. I think the only other alternative is to let them land on the lawn between Pennsylvania Avenue and the fountain."

The President looked at the Secret Service chief and said, "Your choice, whichever you can do in 15 minutes."

"Thank you, Mr. President." He headed for the door.

SHUTTLE, 2,000 FT ABOVE WHITE HOUSE

"Michael, you really do know how to draw a crowd," Elsie said. "I don't see anywhere on the street where we can set down."

"Can we go a little lower? There appears to be a man with ground control flashlights, who is pointing us to a spot on the White House lawn near the fountain. See over there?" Charles pointed down towards the fountain.

"Maybe the President changed his mind." Michael replied. "Elsie, can we slip onto the lawn there without being spotted before we de-cloak?"

"Yes, I think so. I can move in to about 1 foot above the ground without depressing the grass. Should be nice and quiet and the heat will be contained until we de-cloak."

94

"OK. Let's do it. Shuttle door toward the street, so they have to walk between us and the crowd to get to us. They will be more restrained if they're in plain view of a thousand reporters and photographers."

Elsie killed the main power generators and feathered her way in, getting to the target location with 5 seconds to spare. "De-cloaking in 5, 4, 3, 2, 1. Clear," she said.

PENNSYLVANIA AVENUE, NEAR WHITE HOUSE

The CNN team had arrived early and had the perfect spot. The camera boom was located on the far side of Pennsylvania Avenue, looking at the White House with a clear view of the guy with the flashlight cones pointing to a spot near the fountain. The on-site producer turned toward his soundman and was about to say, "Someone is late," when a roar ripped through the crowd.

There, right in front of him, was a small shuttle craft that was maybe one and a half times the length and width of a typical metropolitan bus.

"Where did that come from?" he exclaimed.

He noticed that it was charcoal gray with an interesting sheen that almost seemed to waver in the air in front of him. The craft was smooth with tiny swept wings that were a few feet wide at their widest point at the back of the craft. And it was surprisingly hard to see even though it was only a few feet away. He was startled when he noticed that the shuttle was not sitting on the ground, but instead hovered 6 or 8 inches above it.

A huge team of Secret Service Agents came running from the far side of the fountain and quickly surrounded the shuttle. The producer noticed with some concern that the lookouts on top of the White House were pointing weapons of some sort at the shuttle. It suddenly occurred to him that these were the ground-to-air missiles appropriated to protect the White House from aircraft attack. He truly did not like the fact those missiles were pointed in his direction.

Oddly, the Secret Service Agents seemed confused. Then he sorted out why. There were no windows or doors on this craft, just smooth curves and unbroken metal.

Some reporters a few feet away, suddenly started pointing and snapping pictures. A small crack was forming in the shape of a door. *My God*, he thought. *This is right out of a science fiction movie.*

The door started sliding open and the man known as Michael Baker hopped down onto the grass. Several agents approached him as another approached the open door.

"Gentlemen, please do not attempt to enter the shuttle," Michael said.

The agent approaching the door acknowledged Michael but continued his approach. Michael turned and stepped toward the agent to further caution him, accidentally bumping one of the three that had come to greet him. Then everything went sideways.

Michael's personal shield hardened and flexed when he bumped the agent. The bump was hard enough to trigger a small flash of light. The agent approaching the shuttle saw the flash and mistook it for a muzzle flash. He took off running toward the shuttle, releasing the safety on his weapon as he leaped for the door. But he didn't actually make it. There was a huge flash of bright light and the agent bounced off the open door, falling to the ground below.

The CNN producer was on the edge of his seat trying to get the best view. When the agent hit the ground, the producer felt a sudden pain, then heard a loud bang. *Oh my God,* he thought. *That agent must have had the safety off on his rifle.* Then he noticed the bright red stain, spreading across his chest. He'd been hit.

Several things happened at once. The agents who had surrounded Michael tackled him, or at least tried to tackle him. Like the agent that had attempted to enter the shuttle, these agents went flying. Before they even hit the ground, the CNN producer toppled, knocking over the table holding the sound equipment. Pandemonium broke out.

As all the Secret Service Agents that had fallen were still moving, Michael had Elsie transport him point-to-point to the other side of the fence so he could treat the downed man from CNN. He crouched down with his scanner and was just about in position when a bullet hit his shield. It stopped about an inch from Michael's head. It just hung there for a second. Then it dropped to the ground.

Michael jumped to a standing position with his arms spread and shouted, "Stop!"

All around him, the guns held by the Secret Service agents and capital police disintegrated into dust that just ran through their fingers.

Michael returned to his patient, using his scanner to find and extract the bullet and heal the damaged tissue. He ripped the CNN man's shirt open and began smearing a nanobot-rich cream over the wound. These bots had been programmed to repair fine blood vessels and build blood volume to replace that which was lost.

When Michael looked up, he saw that he was being filmed by one of the CNN crew. "Do you know who this man is?" Michael asked the camera man.

"My boss." He went on filming.

"The agent that attempted to enter my shuttle apparently had the safety turned off on his rifle. When he fell, it went off and shot your boss. But don't worry, he'll be fine. There will be no trace of the wound by the time he gets home."

More and more police and emergency vehicles were arriving. And two helicopters full of National Guard could be seen a mile or so away.

Michael looked at the camera man. "Is the camera broadcasting?"

"Yes" he said with the camera still tightly focused on Michael.

"Mr. President," Michael said in a stern voice. "You invited us here, then attempted to board my spacecraft without permission. You then attempted to restrain me. In the process, your men almost killed the CNN on-site producer." He pointed to his patient off camera.

"I am still prepared to meet with you. But you need to call off your troops before they hurt someone else. You do not have the capability to harm or restrain my people, only your own.

"I will wait here five minutes for your reply. But my shuttle is leaving now."

As Michael said the word "now", the shuttle shot up into the sky. Two shoulder-mounted anti-aircraft missiles launched but had no chance of catching the shuttle. Instead, they locked on to the two helicopters full of National Guard. As soon as the missile operators saw what was happening, they triggered the self-destructs, scattering shrapnel all over Washington DC.

Michael looked back at the CNN camera. "I'm disappointed in you, Mr. President. Maybe we'll have a chance to meet in the future." And with that, Michael simply disappeared.

SHUTTLE

The door suddenly slammed shut and everyone was set back in their seats. *What the hell*, thought Sergeant Butler. *This is Afghanistan all over again.*

"Everything OK back there?" Elsie asked. "That was an emergency take off. 18 G for those that care about such things. The inertial dampeners cannot compensate that much, so our bodies had to." Pause... "Hello, anyone alive back there?"

Noelani spoke up, "I think everyone is OK. Where is Michael?"

"He's giving the President five minutes to invite us back... Whoa, the White House just launched ground to air missiles at us. AS IF!" She said. "Oh... And here comes Michael."

Sarah was shaken. Michael had warned them that the government might not welcome them, but she never thought she'd be shot at.

Michael appeared in the passenger compartment of the shuttle. "Well. That didn't go so well."

Sarah walked up to him. "What happened, Michael?"

"Before I say anything... First my apologies for putting you in danger. My logic told me there was no way things could go this bad. But my emotions had been telling me that this visit was fraught with danger."

"As we were landing, we flooded the area with surveillance nanobots, microscopic TV cameras that record events, so we can evaluate them later. Let's see what we recorded, just 5 minutes ago."

...

On the passenger compartment screen, the Head of the Secret Service could be seen and heard. "Listen up everybody. In a few minutes, a shuttle will appear. It is said that the shuttle contains and is operated by aliens. I know it's hard to believe, but they claim to be aliens presenting themselves in human form. But whoever or whatever they really are, it's clear that they have advanced technology, or at least the illusion of advanced technology.

"Our specific assignment this morning is to vet them, then escort them inside. But our job, our real job, is to protect the President. Therefore, the vetting must be thorough. And it's on us to make sure all threats are exposed out here, none inside.

"When they land, we will surround their ship. Once the perimeter is established, we will wait for someone to come out. Taylor, you will approach and greet the first person out. Murray and Bradshaw will assist. Ask them to submit to a pat down.

"Woodward, you will attempt to get a view of the interior of the ship. We need to know how many are in there and get at least some read on the threat status of the ship.

"Everyone. We want this to be clean. We will treat our guests with respect. But we must be prepared to act at the first sign of threat. Only go weapons hot if there is an attack.

"Let's keep the President safe!"

The news team was confused. The instructions seemed reasonable, but what happened was crazy.

Sergeant Butler piped up. "Something must have happened to make them believe we fired the first shot."

Michael said to the Butlers and to the news team, "This is one of the dangers of first contact. Simple things that seem perfectly normal to one party, can be read as a threat by the other. It was a mistake to come here under the circumstances that we did."

Sarah asked, "Michael, how much more video do you have?"

"I have my conversation with the President. I also have video from the situation room, where the military conspired to steal our technology."

"Can you give me copies? This is my world and my country. This incident needs to be investigated, and if corruption is found, I need to fight it."

Michael pointed to their video equipment. "You have it."

"Michael," Jiaying called over the intercom. "I have the president on the line. He would like to speak with you."

In unison, the people in the passenger compartment said, "Don't do it, Michael."

"Jiaying, I'll take the call."

"Mr. President. What can I do for you?"

"Michael. I'm so sorry for what happened. I asked the security team to vet you—to make sure it was you, not someone else.

"I had no idea they'd attempt to board your shuttle or take you into custody. We simply do not treat diplomats that way. When I saw you treat that CNN producer, and then almost get shot, I was apoplectic. Then they attempted to shoot down your shuttle, and almost took down our own troops... I don't know what to say."

"Thank you for stating the situation as it was. What do you suggest that we do?"

"You came to us in good faith. Now, I offer to come to you in good faith."

"How would that work?"

"Forgive the lingo of my favorite 1960s TV show, but you beamed yourself back to your vessel, right?"

"Yes sir."

"Then beam me, and an advisor, up and we can talk—above all the Washington noise, so to speak."

"Mr. President, how about if I 'beam' down to your office. I will bring three staff with me to help with the demos, the same ones that were on Good Morning America this morning. You can bring three staff also, but I would like you to tell me who you will have present. I would suggest medical and science people, not military or intelligence."

"I will bring my Chief of Staff, Science Advisor and the Surgeon General. And, with your permission, I will bring the Vice President."

"That is acceptable to me, Mr. President. How soon can you assemble your team?"

"They are here now."

"Then we will be there momentarily."

OVAL OFFICE, WHITE HOUSE

Michael, Charles, Kale, Noelani and a grav-pallet of equipment appeared in the Oval office. Waiting for them were the President, Vice President, Chief of Staff, Presidential Science Advisor and the Surgeon General. Introductions were made, then everyone took seats.

"Michael," the President said, "I must offer you an apology for the debacle that just took place outside. It was not my intent to raid your shuttle or any of the chain of events that followed. I'm hoping that we can put that behind us."

"Thank you, Mr. President. Do you have an update on the CNN producer that was shot?"

"Yes" said the Surgeon General. "He was taken to Walter Reed, where he was evaluated. Despite all the blood on his clothes, the doctors that examined him could find little evidence that he had even been shot. The X-rays were clean. There was no sign of vascular damage. Only the remnants of the wound on his chest and low blood volume. He was given a unit of blood and some additional fluids, then discharged."

"I'm glad to hear that. The bullet penetrated his lung. Without medical care he would not have lasted very long."

"May I ask how you did that?" The Surgeon General inquired.

Michael took the small tubular scanner with the blinking light out of his pocket and handed it to him. "On our world, the device that this one is based on is not shaped in the same way. I made this one to look like one used on a TV show. I thought people would be more comfortable with something they recognized."

"What's the blinking light for?"

100

"Nothing. It just mimics the one on the TV show." Everyone got a chuckle out of that.

"I don't see any controls. How does it operate? What does it do?"

"There are no physical controls. I connect to it and control it through my thoughts. Its first function is as a scanner. It uses a technique analogous to an MRI. But the driving force is not magnetic. It involves extra-dimensional resonance, something that your science does not know about yet.

"It can also act in a manner similar to a scalpel to separate tissue. But it does so at the molecular level, unbinding adjacent cells without damaging them. It can then re-bind the cells later, so there is no wound. The rebinding mechanism can also be used to restore tissue that has undergone trauma, including gun wounds."

"I can also use it to extract toxins or inject medications."

"Will humans ever be able to use this technology?"

"Yes." Michael turned toward the President. "In my address to the world last night. I said that I wanted to open an Embassy to Earth. One of the things we would do at the Embassy is operate a medical school. We will train people from allied nations to operate the equipment that we provide.

"On the medical front, there are technologies that could be deployed almost immediately, things like medications. Other technologies, like our surgical and restoration techniques, will take years of training for humans to adopt. But we can help bridge that gap by providing limited dedicated staff."

The surgeon general asked, "What do you mean by restoration techniques?"

"There were a dozen or so handicapped veterans at the show this morning. The producers let Noelani and I walk over to the handicapped section, so we could meet them. One of the men, Sergeant George Butler, had been injured in an explosion in Afghanistan. He had no movement below his neck and used a powered electric wheelchair with a blow stick to get around."

"I've met too many veterans in that condition." The Surgeon General's authentic regret was plain in his voice.

"One of the reasons that I had my shuttle do an emergency exit earlier was because Sergeant Butler and his mother were on board. We were able to heal the damaged nerves in his spinal column just as the show was starting this morning. Ironically, the injury was not that bad. Only a small section of the nerve bundle had been damaged. It only took a few minutes to regenerate that tissue. The hard part of his cure will be the physical therapy that will retrain his brain to use his nervous system after 5 years of latency. I have facilities at my ranch in Hawaii that can accelerate the process."

"He was healed in just a few minutes?" asked the Surgeon General. "What other types of regeneration can you do?"

"We can regrow limbs and organs. And depending on the circumstance, we can revive people who you would pronounce dead, hours and sometimes days after death."

"Is there any chance I could see your facility?"

"That could be arranged, pending the outcome of my discussions here today." Michael turned to speak to the President directly. "Mr. President, I have several objectives for this meeting. Do you have specific things you would like to discuss?"

"Yes, three things. I would like to know more about you and your people. I'd like to see the demonstrations you have prepared. And, I'd like to know more about what you seek through a treaty with us."

"Excellent. I would also like to discuss the incident last night at my ranch. How about doing the demos first?"

...

The president shook his head in amazement at the demonstrations he'd just seen. "Michael, I can't tell you how impressed I am by the gifts you're offering. I'm not sure how anyone could refuse these, although I'm worried about how much they'll cost. Maybe we could continue the discussion over lunch. You could tell us more about yourself and your people."

"I would enjoy that Mr. President."

"Then, if you will follow me..."

Michael sent a quick thought to Elsie... *Meeting's going well. Possibly too well. We are heading to the executive dining room for lunch. The equipment is being left in the Oval Office. If it moves at all, ping me, then beam it up if you do not hear from me.*

"Michael, please tell me about you. My team developed a dossier on you: natural-born US citizen, no education records, bought a company and made a fortune. The EPA loves you. The IRS loves you, and they don't love anybody. How does that reconcile with what you say and what we've seen you do?"

The question was asked as a plate was set in front of Michael. "My people are ancient. We evolved in the Andromeda galaxy, on a planet with a very long name that is not humanly pronounceable. But, the first syllables of the name sounded something like Lorexi. That's why I bought the human rights to name my star, then named it as I did.

"As you've probably heard, my planet was destroyed in a supernova, the light from which finally reached the Earth Friday night. My star was 2.4 million light years from Earth, which means my planet was actually destroyed 2.4 million years ago."

"Are you saying that you're 2.4 million years old?" the President asked somewhat skeptically.

"No. I'm very old by your standards. But my people are ancient. I grew up on the new home world adopted by my people. My only knowledge of the original is through pictures and recordings made long before my time."

"You say you're old by our standards. How old are you? You certainly look like the 35-year-old that you're reported to be."

"I'm approximately 25,000 years old, born before the dawn of humanity's recorded history. I was on one of the early missions to Earth, around the time of the Roman Empire.

"The body you see is an avatar. It was produced 35 years ago in Texas where it received a birth certificate."

"Avatar... You mean like the big blue creatures in the movie?"

"Yes, sir"

"Where is your real body?"

"In a restoration unit hidden somewhere in this solar system."

Michael noticed a message on his inner vision. *Michael, the equipment is moving.*

Hold for a moment, he sent. "Mr. President. I just got a message advising me that our equipment has been moved."

It's now about 25 feet from its original location.

"I suspect it was moved to an adjacent room so the oval office could be prepped for the next meeting."

Beam it up. Now!

"Well I hope they are treating it gently. I would hate for anything to happen to it."

Returning to the topic of Michael's real body, the Science Advisor asked, "Michael, how does that work? How can your brain be orbiting Pluto and your body here function?"

"I think you know the answer to that." Michael smiled, nodding his head.

The President didn't seem to understand the response, but the Science Advisor did. "You have a quantum-entangled communication system embedded in your mind... On both sides."

Michael smiled at the Science Advisor. "Indeed. That is the essence of it. As you can imagine, there are a lot more details, but yes... My mind is quantum-entangled with the controller in this body."

"What does that feel like?"

Michael nodded his head in approval of the science advisor's question. "Good question. It's strange the first time. This body is quite different from my natural body: different number of appendages, different balance points, etc. It took years to master, just as yours did when you were born. When I finally return to the original, it will be a long adjustment."

"When do you plan to return?"

"Not until this mission is done, which will be a long time from now, maybe four or five thousand years."

"So, from our perspective, you are a permanent fixture then," The President said.

The Vice President spoke for the first time. "Are your people here..." he spread his hands indicating the ones at the table "...all like you?"

"We all have avatar bodies, if that was the question. But we are different species. The Confederation encompasses over 1 million worlds in the three galaxies where we have members. There are thousands of different sentient species in the Confederation, almost all of which have Ascendants. Ascendants being those people that have the mental training and physical enhancements that allow them to take another form."

"Are we going to be forced to become part of the Confederation?" he asked.

Michael shook his head. "No one is, or ever has been, forced to join the Confederation. Most choose to join so they can have the advantage of several million years of technological advancements. A few have chosen to maintain treaties, but have no intention of ever joining. And a few, very few, have asked us to leave. When that happens, we leave and mark the planet as off limits to Confederation members."

"Is it your objective for Earth to become part of the Intergalactic Confederation?"

"My immediate objective is to help humanity get through the current climate crisis. I suspect that by the time we accomplish that mission, you—meaning humanity—will be petitioning to join the Confederation."

The President said, "In your broadcast last night you said there were two threats. Can you tell us any more about the second threat?"

"The second threat is a long way away. It will not get here for quite a few years. It is from an invasive parasitic species that is drifting through the galaxy. When it finds a planet it likes, it rains down on the planet, choking out all life in a matter of years. It is very powerful; no young species like yours has ever survived contact. Even with our help you may not be able to save the Earth, but you will be able to save yourselves. My primary mission on Earth is to see you through your encounter with this species.

"Back to the question of joining the Intergalactic Confederation... I would very much like to have Earth as a member. But my primary mission is to save Earth from the dangers it's facing. The Confederation will support me in that mission, if I can form alliances or treaties with nations representing half or more of Earth's population.

As the staff finished clearing the lunch plates, all eyes turned toward the President. "Michael, maybe it's time for you and me to return to my office. I'd like to have my Secretary of State join us.

"Maybe your team could demonstrate your equipment to more of my staff. I have arranged for it to be transported to a conference room and invited several more people. Would that be OK?"

"I would be happy to do that. If you could have my team escorted there, they can arrange for the equipment to be returned."

"Returned?"

"Yes. Our sensors showed that the equipment had been moved further than was allowed, so it was 'beamed' back up to my ship. Once the staff is in location for the demo, they can instruct our ship to 'beam' the equipment back down. I like this word 'beam.' It is not one we have used before."

"Apologies for having set a plan in motion without checking with you first. John, here..." the President pointed toward the Vice President, "can lead your team to the conference room. Everything else is already set up."

The Vice President, Science Advisor, and Surgeon General turned to the right with Charles, Kale and Noelani, while the President and Chief of Staff turned to the left with Michael.

As they entered the Oval Office, the President offered Michael a seat and Introduced the Secretary of State.

"So, what kind of terms are you looking for in a treaty?" The President asked.

"In terms of what we give you, we offer free of charge… 1) Devices that will produce clean energy at no cost other than the costs you might incur to distribute it, 2) carbon dioxide recovery systems that will scrub carbon from the atmosphere and provide a renewable supply of gasoline and intermediate organics, such as those used in plastics, 3) doctors, medical devices, and medical training on how to use the devices, and 4) small-scale replicators for home use that can supply high-quality food and various other trinkets.

"You might ask, why these four technologies? They will help clean up the environment while lowering costs and stabilizing the supply of certain critical materials. And they will raise your standard of living with much of the benefit going to the bottom economic rung of your society.

"In exchange for these benefits, we require four things that I would like to go through in a little more detail. The first is a non-aggression, mutual defense agreement. We would agree not to take offensive actions against each other or any other nation on Earth. And we propose that the Confederation will defend you from aggression by any other nation on Earth, which will allow you to substantially reduce your military over the years to come.

"The second is a trade agreement. We will provide your people with products and services utilizing the technologies we have demonstrated, and we will provide your government and industry with components to make your own products and services for non-military purposes. As part of this agreement, we would like limited assistance with distribution and a no-tax provision.

"The third, which I would expect to be the easiest, is the right to open one or more consular offices in your country where we can conduct our diplomatic mission. Each of these offices will be treated as our sovereign property, a right that can be revoked with some notice. The properties I've already purchased in the United States would be treated as consular offices.

"The fourth is a civil rights agreement. We require allied peoples to provide their citizens with a minimum level of civil rights. This should be no trouble for you, as the United States already provides a higher level than we require," Michael said, finishing his list.

106

"It will be a difficult sell to convince America that we should reduce our military strength. Although most of our citizens would prefer that we stop being the world's police force, far more are afraid of what would happen if we were not."

"I understand your point, but all we require is that you agree not to engage in military aggression. Once it is clear to your people the degree to which we can protect them, they will want to redirect the resources to a better use. All you have to 'sell' is that we will backstop you against any foreign aggression. The rest will come with time."

"How quickly does this need to happen?"

"I will send you a letter of intent. Once you sign the letter, we will begin releasing benefits to your people. If we can complete a treaty in a reasonable period of time, and as long as there is not blatant violation of the Letter of Intent during negotiations, then we can continue providing benefits. If the treaty ultimately fails, or if you materially violate the stated intensions, then we will withdraw, and any equipment that we have provided will stop working."

The President stood. "Michael, thank you for making the time to see me today and apologies for the fiasco that occurred this morning…"

Michael cut the president off, "…and last night. The FBI team you sent last night was NOT an act of good faith. And the arrogance of their team leader was beyond the pale.

"They ignored signs put up by Hawaiian Civil Defense warning of hazardous conditions in the area. And in their attempted raid on my property, they almost got themselves killed. In fact, five were killed. I brought four of them back. They are now in the hands of your medical teams. The fifth could not be released from our care as his injuries were too severe."

"So, you admit that you assaulted my FBI team!"

"No. I rescued your FBI team. They almost killed themselves before they even got to my property."

"It seems we really have gotten off on the wrong foot. So, I apologize again. There will be no more of that. I will issue an executive order today, granting your people and your property temporary diplomatic status. There will not be a recurrence."

"Thank you, Mr. President."

"Michael, I look forward to receiving your letter of intent and speaking with you again. I have a good feeling that we'll be able to make this work."

"Thank you for seeing me Mr. President." Michael shook the President's hand.

...

An aide escorted Michael to the conference room where his team was entertaining several members of the White House staff. Michael exchanged pleasantries with several cabinet members who had stopped by.

As the team was wrapping up the final demo, Michael noticed that a child was in the group and that Noelani had been using the replicator to crank out a pile of toys. As he walked up, the girl stood and offered Michael her hand. "Mr. Michael, sir. My name is Jessica. I hope you had a good talk with my grandfather. I think he will like you. Ms. Noelani made me a lot of toys that we will take to a local orphanage. I wanted to say thank you."

"Jessica. I'm so glad I got to meet you. Thank you for helping Noelani with her demonstration today and for making so many toys for the children."

As the team packed up their equipment, Michael spoke with the people lingering in the room. When they had said their goodbyes, Michael sent, *Bring us back home, Elsie*. And they simply disappeared.

The Secretary of Defense, who had remained in the room, shook his head and whispered, "How could we ever defend against that?"

SHUTTLE, 12,000 MILES ABOVE EARTH

As Michael and the team appeared in the shuttle above Washington DC, conversation in the shuttle cabin came to a stop.

Sarah, the reporter from ABC, asked, "Michael. How did your meeting go?"

"Off the record, it when pretty well, better than expected."

"What can you tell me on the record?"

"Lots, I'm sure, but can we discuss logistics first?"

"Such as...?"

Michael smiled. "All the boring stuff, like... Have you been offered lunch? You've been up here for a while. When do you want to be returned to New York? Where would you prefer to do the interview? On the shuttle? In one of your studios in New York? At my ranch in Hawaii? Things like that."

"If we go to Hawaii, how soon can we be back in New York?"

"We can be landed and in my dining room within the hour. Once there, you could have lunch, take a little tour of our facilities, and do

108

your interview in say, 2 or 3 hours. The trip back to New York would be another hour. So, back to New York by 6:00 or 7:00 PM."

"Only an hour to New York?"

"Less, if you don't mind 'beaming' down. That's the word the President used. I'm starting to like it."

She looked at her crew. "Want to go to Hawaii?"

SECOND INTERVIEW

[02.03.2025 09:00] THE RESIDENCE, KOHALA MOUNTAIN

Michael had called ahead asking Pam to have lunch prepared for their guests. Pam greeted everyone at the door and ushered Sarah and her crew to the dining room.

The Butlers were a little more difficult. By now, Sergeant Butler was able to stand under his own power. He was more than a bit wobbly, but standing on his own two feet, nonetheless. The problem was how to get him into the house. He couldn't step down off the shuttle and was refusing to get back into his wheelchair. Noelani suggested, "Why don't we clear the equipment off the grav-sled? Then we could help the Sergeant up onto it and let the grav-sled do the work."

They arrived in the dining room, just as Pam was bringing the food out. "Will you be joining us Michael?"

"No, I just had lunch with the President." He turned to the others. "Having just eaten, I'm going to check on some things while you enjoy your lunch. I'll be back in about a half hour to take you on a tour of the property."

As he left the room, Michael reached out to Jiaying. *What's come in while we've been gone?*

Michael, within minutes of your arrival at the White House, requests began streaming in from around the world. China and Russia have been the most adamant that you need to see them as soon as possible. I've also received queries from five news agencies, requesting interviews.

I'll be over in a few minutes to discuss.

RESEARCH LAB, KOHALA MOUNTAIN

Michael entered the admin office in the research lab under the barn. "Hi, Jiaying. My priorities for heads of state are: China, Russia, India, Pakistan, Brazil, Israel & Canada in that order. Have we had inquiries from all of those?"

"All but Pakistan."

"OK. Protocol requires that a country contact us first. So, add Pakistan to the priority list once they contact us. After those, work the countries as they contact us. Going forward, we will not land unless we are guaranteed landing privileges on their capital grounds or on a helipad on the roof. For those that cannot let us land on their grounds, we will transport in.

"Let's plan on up to two meetings a day, starting tomorrow morning, Hawaiian time. No more than three in any 24-hour period. Our team needs to stay fresh.

"Following up on today's meeting, we need to get a draft treaty agreement to the President as soon as possible. There should be one in the US file already. I would like to have draft treaty agreements with me for any meetings from here on out.

"Regarding the news services. Let's do one interview a day. It must be done here or in one of the capital cities we are visiting. If there is a day with no head of state meetings, then I can go to the media outlet."

"Understood, Michael. This is mostly as we'd planned. But one question... Would you like one or more of the Asian staff for your meetings in Asia? And would you like Joel for Israel or the Mbanefos for Africa?"

"Yes on all but the Mbanefos. They are human and still in training. Only Ascendants and androids for now."

Emmanuel and Bahati Mbanefo were humans from South Africa. They had met Michael, in a previous avatar, in South Africa during World War II and helped him through a hard time. Michael had invited them to train with him as candidates for the Ascendancy. They currently trained with and worked for Michael in San Diego. But they were still human and very mortal, so Michael did not want to endanger them.

Changing subjects Michael asked, "Charles came down to check in on Agent Patterson, right?"

"Yes. And he told me that the Butlers would be staying with us for a while."

"Yes. You'll like them. Sergeant Butler is a good man who's been through a lot. His mother is very protective of him, do your best to get on her good side." Michael said with a smile.

Michael left the admin office and headed down a level to the lab.

...

111

As Michael entered the Medical Lab, he found Charles studying Agent Patterson.

"What's his condition?"

"Other than the legs, his recovery is going well. The legs should be good enough that we can pull him out in a couple hours without risking his life. But there is no hope of recovery for them. He will either have to live as a paraplegic or undergo regeneration. Earlier, I was not sure we would ever be able to pull him out of the tank without removing the legs first.

"How do you want to handle Sergeant Butler? Are we going to let him down here?" asked Charles.

"No. For today, we can use the examination room in the residence basement. We can take him there to do in-depth diagnostics. Then we can draw up a recovery plan."

"Sounds good. Would you like me to transport a bunch of equipment over to the basement, so it looks more like a lab?"

"Yes. Good thinking. Also, could you rig up something we could use to move the Sergeant around in? I don't want another repeat of exiting the shuttle." Michael shook his head in frustration.

"I've got just the thing."

From Charles' smile, Michael got the sense that his solution would be good.

THE RESIDENCE

Michael walked into the dining room, pleased to see that his guests were in deep conversation and that lunch was just about finished. Pam motioned him over to a seat where a steaming cup of his favorite coffee was waiting.

Michael inhaled the deep aroma and said, "Greenwell Farms, 100% Kona Coffee, French Roast. Right?" Greenwell Farms was a coffee farm about an hour south of Michael's ranch. It was near a little town called Kealakekua in South Kona. He loved their coffee.

Michael turned to address the room. "Charles will be here in a minute. He has a present that will make our tour a little easier."

Just as Michael was about to say something else, Charles walked into the room with a cloth bundle under his arm. "Sergeant Butler, I have something for you that should make it easier for you to get around the house while you're recovering."

He placed the bundle in front of the Sergeant, who untied the bundle and held out what looked like overalls with suspenders.

"What exactly is this?" the Sergeant asked.

"They are overalls with suspenders. But the suspenders have an anti-grav assist that you can control with this dial." Charles pointed to a little dial on one of the suspender straps. "When you put these on and turn the dial up to full, you will levitate a few inches above the ground. When you turn it to zero, it provides no lift. At intermediate settings, it'll take some of the load off, so you don't have to carry all your own weight.

"We'll use it during your therapy to build strength in your legs. For now, you can float or choose to walk with say 10% of your weight on your legs. It'll never let you fall or float away. Just lean the direction you want to go, and you'll go. Want to try it?"

The Sergeant was game to give it a try and Noelani helped him into the overalls.

"OK, slowly turn the dial up." At about 70% assist, he could stand up from his chair without assistance, but still could not walk. At 90%, he could make walking motions that were not very pretty or coordinated, but he could move away from the table.

"OK, now turn the dial to 100%."

The Sergeant did as he was asked and lifted off the floor.

"Now lean your head toward me until you start moving. Then lift your head back up." Again, the Sergeant did as he was asked, and he moved a foot or so forward.

"Are you getting the feel of it?"

The Sergeant shook his head.

"OK, try moving to the left and right. Same principle. Look in the direction you want to go and tip your head forward."

The Sergeant was a quick study and within a few minutes was able to move forward, turn around and move back.

"Can it go faster?" George asked brightly.

"It can go much faster. But I have the unit programed to its slowest setting. When you've convinced me that you've mastered the current speed, I'll turn it up. On days where Noelani is doing the training, she'll be able to turn it up.

"Ready to come down to the medical lab with us? We have a bunch of diagnostics to run. And, no, they won't hurt," Charles said as the last statement sent a ripple of laughter thru the room.

Michael, Charles and Noelani led Sergeant Butler and his mother down to the medical facility in the basement of the residence where Hiroshi Kawasaki was waiting for them. "Sergeant Butler. I would like to introduce you to our Medical Tech, Hiroshi Kawasaki. Hiroshi, this is Sergeant George Butler and his mother, Helen."

"Sergeant and Mrs. Butler, welcome to our medical lab."

"George." Michael said. "Charles is our best diagnostician. Hiroshi and Noelani are our best team for the rehabilitation phase of the treatment. You are welcome to stay at the ranch for as long as you think it is beneficial. Pam is setting you both up with accommodations on site. I'm going to leave you in their expert care, so I can take care of matters better suited to my own skills.

"I'll check in with you every day that I'm in Hawaii, which will be most days. I think your recovery will be good enough that you could compete in Iron Man someday, if you wanted. I'll check in with you a little later to make sure you're settling in OK. Until then, do whatever this man says." Michael pointed at Hiroshi.

...

"Sarah," Michael said as he re-entered the dining room. "I promised you a tour, but here it is 3:00 Eastern. If you're anxious to get back, we can cut straight to the interview. Otherwise, a tour?"

Sarah smiled at Michael. "Pam was kind enough to let me use a phone. Monica is anxious to get a report on the White House encounter to run on the 6:00 news. If we can deliver on that then we don't need to be back until 6:00 AM on Wednesday. If you have the bandwidth to upload our interview, then I would love to do it now and spend the next day following you around."

"Let's do it now, then. Where would you like to do it and what do we need to do to help your team?"

"Is there a lookout nearby where we can see the Pacific Ocean? And maybe some identifiable landmarks. I think America would be blown away to know that we're in Hawaii. It's 12 hours plus away from the East Coast, so it would lend credibility to our story."

"I know the perfect place."

LOOKOUT, KOHALA MOUNTAIN ROAD

"Good Evening America. This is Sarah Wright reporting from the Big Island of Hawaii. I am here with Michael Baker, who strongly prefers to be addressed as Michael. I'd like to start with that question... Why do you prefer to be called Michael?"

Michael turned to the camera and smiled. "Good Evening America. I was born on a planet in the Andromeda galaxy, about 2.4 million light years from Earth. My people are ancient as compared to yours, so it has been a joy for me to spend time with you.

"So why just Michael? My native language uses very long words. It's a lot like the Hawaiian language with a limited number of sounds that just get strung together into very long words. Although most of our language is not humanly pronounceable, the first two syllables of my name are "Mi-Ku".

"When I first arrived on Earth, a long time ago, I spent time in an area where Michael is a common name. So I adopted it."

Sarah interrupted, "Thank you for explaining the Michael part, but why only one name. Why not use Baker?"

"Well," Michael said. "The first half of the answer is that my people's names are very long. Forty syllable names are not that uncommon. So, we only use one name.

"The second half of the answer is related to a question you asked me this morning... How can I reconcile the claim that I'm a representative from the Intergalactic Confederation, when there's documentation that says I'm a 35-year-old, natural-born citizen from Texas?

"The answer is simple. This body was born in Texas." He placed his hand on his chest. "But it's not my real body, just an avatar.

"My people believe that when we make first contact, we should look as much like the indigenous people as possible. So, I took the form of a human, a form I have come to love.

"To get the birth certificate, we needed the unwitting help of a man that believed he was my father but wanted no role in my life. Some months earlier, one of our employees had an affair with a man named Baker. It ended badly. When presented with the baby, he believed he was responsible, so signed the birth certificate. Needless to say, I have never felt a connection to the name Baker."

"Michael, one last question about your person... Where is your actual body? And what does it look like?"

"My birth body is in a restoration chamber somewhere in this solar system. My species evolved from something more like your bears than like your monkeys. We are larger than you by maybe 50% on average. And you would perceive our skin to be lumpy. However, we are a fundamentally more peaceful, less aggressive species."

"Michael, what can you tell us about your encounter at the White House today? The news coverage has been all over the place. Can you tell us what happened?"

"The White House contacted us while we were on your show this morning, asking if we would be available to meet with the President. They offered to send a helicopter to pick us up. Since we had our demonstration equipment and staff already on the shuttle, we said we could just fly down ourselves. They said we could not land on the White House grounds, but that it would be OK if we landed on Pennsylvania Avenue.

"I told your producer that our next stop would be the White House and asked if she could let other media sources know. I had not anticipated the impact of your show this morning and thought a little more media exposure would be good. In fact, I told her that if she spread the word, I would give you an exclusive interview after my meeting with the President. By the way, do you know what the viewership of the show was this morning?"

"It was a record breaker. During the last segment, there were about 25 million worldwide. It was kind of like the Super Bowl on a Monday morning. But you were talking about Pennsylvania Avenue..."

"Yes. As we approached the White House, we were shocked. Pennsylvania Avenue was packed with people, equipment, TV broadcast trucks... It was not clear where we could land. Then we noticed a man, dressed like a secret service agent, directing us to a spot inside the fence near the fountain. So, we landed there."

"Michael?" Sarah asked. "Television footage does not show you approaching or landing. You just appeared out of nowhere. Can you explain that?"

"Yes. We came in with our stealth shields up. Or, as described on some of your TV shows, we were cloaked, completely invisible. And not only to light, but to radar, sound, any detection technology that humans have. So, from the TV camera's perspective, we simply appeared when we de-cloaked.

"Just a quick note on that... We arrived the same way to your studios in New York this morning and we had sent that video to the President so he would know how we were going to arrive."

"Why travel cloaked, Michael?"

"Several reasons. Privacy, of course. But more importantly, we travel at what you would call hypersonic speeds. Cloaking prevents sonic booms, lightning, and other anomalies caused by traveling fast in an atmosphere. So, we travel cloaked for your safety."

"But doesn't that violate air traffic laws?"

"I'm sure your legal experts will say yes. I would say no. The reason I say no, is because we don't actually travel through your airspace. We travel through another dimension that is close to your airspace but does not co-occupy it. When we stop, we can sense whether anything else is there or not. If it is clear, then we transition back into your dimension. That's the reason that we hover 6 inches or so above the ground when we appear. The only movement we do in your airspace is the 6 inches from where we appear to the ground, which is not a violation of your law."

"Wow Michael, I really don't know what to say."

"Anyway, back to our time in Washington this morning... We saw the security teams come running out to meet us. I had assumed we were welcome, and it was OK to land on the White House grounds. It is, after all, where the local ground control appeared to be telling us to land. So, I went out to greet them.

"Three agents approached to greet me, but another agent started walking toward the shuttle door. I told him not to attempt to enter the shuttle and got a polite acknowledgement. But he kept walking toward the door. When I turned toward him to repeat my request, he took off running. Then he jumped up to go in through the door.

"Well, that didn't work. The hatch is always covered by a very powerful force field. We refer to it as a Level 1 Shield. Nothing can get through it. Not a person, not a bullet, not a nuclear blast.

"When he hit the shield, it deflected slightly to absorb some of the shock that would otherwise have broken his neck. As the shield flexed back, the agent was pushed away, which is why he went flying. He had a lot of momentum that needed to be redirected to minimize any injury he might sustain."

"But Michael, there was a very bright flash of light that looked like an explosion."

"Flash of light, yes. Explosion, no. The flash of light was the result of the shield deflecting. The shield is extra-dimensional, like the shuttle's movement is. Small deflections like that allow light from other dimensions to slip into this one. At some point, your physicists will understand this.

"Anyway, as the agent fell, he lost control of his rifle, on which he had released the safety. When the rifle landed, it fired and hit the CNN producer on the other side of the fence.

"When I moved toward the CNN producer, the three agents there to greet me attempted to tackle me. This was a bad idea. Whenever

I'm in a first contact situation, I wear a personal shield for my own protection. When those three agents hit my personal shield, they also went flying. Thankfully, they were smart enough not to have removed their safeties.

"I then did a point-to-point transport over to where the CNN producer was, so that I could care for his wound. I'd just started examining the man when another agent fired a high-power rifle at me. It was a perfect kill shot. It would've gone in my right ear and destroyed my brain stem were it not for the personal shield.

"Turning in the direction the shot came from, I saw weapons raised all over the place. So, I stood and activated nanobots that had been released into the air when we landed. The nanobots quickly dissolved all the guns in visible range.

"Now free to help the CNN producer, I removed the bullet, repaired the injured tissues, and then applied a cream to seal the wound. It was about that time that I saw the CNN camera man filming me. It was also when I saw the shoulder-mounted missile launchers being pointed at my shuttle. So, I ordered the shuttle to launch."

"Michael, why launch the shuttle? The missiles wouldn't hurt the shuttle, would they?"

"No. The missiles would not hurt the shuttle. In fact, the people inside wouldn't even notice other than the flash of light coming in through the door."

"So, why then?"

"Those two missiles had enough explosive in them to bring down a building. If they had detonated against the shield of my shuttle, all that energy and shrapnel would have been deflected back toward the White House. All the windows would have been shattered and anyone in that first set of rooms would have been shredded. The building might even have been destroyed.

"Our shuttle can move very fast, faster than the missiles. Launching the shuttle redirected the missiles away from the White House and gave the missile controllers enough time to trigger the self-destruct mechanism."

"Michael, I had no idea how bad it was out there this morning. Initially, the news services were reporting that you attempted to attack the White House. But as they went back through the slow-motion replays, all the weapons fire came from Secret Service and Capital Police. The only thing that came from you was the two flashes of light."

"Sarah," Michael started to say, then looked directly into the camera. "America, my people are a non-violent people. We do not use offensive weapons. We really don't even have defensive ones. We don't need them because we have impenetrable defensive shields.

"We come in peace and offer you defense from enemies near and far. Lay down your weapons."

There was a pause in the flow of the interview. Then Sarah asked, "Michael, is it true that the President called to apologize and offered to meet with you?"

"Yes, he did. And we talked for about an hour."

"On the phone?"

"No. In person. Our demonstration team and I, plus our demonstration equipment, transported directly into the Oval Office. We met with the President and a number of his cabinet members."

"How did that go?"

"I think it went well. They got to see the same equipment that we used on your show this morning. In fact, the President's granddaughter worked with my colleague Noelani to replicate a pile of toys she plans to take to an orphanage.

"We had a pleasant lunch, then discussed the outline of a treaty we'd like to enter into with the United States. A draft copy will be in his hands shortly."

"Do you think he will sign it?"

"I'm optimistic, but I don't know. We'll be offering a similar treaty to every nation on Earth. Those that accept the treaty will gain tremendous advantages over nations that do not."

"What kind of advantages?" Sarah asked.

"A much higher standard of living. Longer life expectancies. Much less pain and suffering. In short, greater prosperity than has ever been seen on Earth before."

"Why would anyone not sign the treaty?"

"It will change the balance of power in and among nations. Member nations will have to guarantee their citizens at least a minimum degree of civil rights. The US already meets the minimum standard, but many nations do not. Member nations will need to dismantle the offensive portion of their militaries over a period of time. The US, which has powerful offensive capabilities, will resist this, while other countries that do not have significant offensive capabilities will welcome it.

"I anticipate that the vast majority of citizens of every nation will welcome the treaty. The resistance will come from the authority figures in each country that have something to lose personally."

"Michael, thank you so much for speaking with me, both this morning and again now. Being with you today has changed my perspective on so many things. I truly wish you well."

"Thank you, Sarah."

...

As they headed back to the ranch, Sarah looked at Michael and said. "Where to from here?"

He laughed. "I think you have some footage to upload."

"You know that's not what I meant."

"I know." He paused thoughtfully. "Because of your show and the events of the day, we've been contacted by quite a number of heads of state, a few of which were quite insistent that we come to see them immediately.

"When are you going to start?"

"Jiaying, my communications person and protocol officer, is setting up appointments starting tomorrow. I'm expecting that the first two will be Moscow and Beijing, but the time zones work against them a little because I need to get some sleep tonight.

"The priority goes basically by population, but I would like to meet with Canada, Israel, the Vatican and Saudi Arabia as soon as possible."

"The epicenters of three of the world's biggest religions... I think I get that. Why Canada?" Sarah asked.

"Mostly location."

"Location?"

"Yes. The northern hemisphere holds the majority of the world's landmass and population. So, there would be an advantage to having our Embassy somewhere in the far north. There are only two countries with enough land mass in the north to be viable candidates, Canada and Russia. From a location perspective Russia would be better. But Canada has a more neutral political standing in the world. If they were to invite us to put our embassy in Northern Canada, they would have a good shot at getting it. But there are several other attractive locations."

"Can I ask how many staff you have, Michael?"

"At the moment there are about 35 of us, 30 from the Confederation and 5 humans. As soon as treaties start being signed our numbers will grow. I have a thousand or so Confederation staff ready to come when needed. I will also need quite a few human staff. You interested?"

"Yes. But not so sure about Northern Canada."

As they pulled into the driveway of the ranch, Jiaying called over the car's intercom. "Michael, are you free to talk?"

"Yes Jiaying. What's up?"

"If you're willing to start a little earlier than planned, I can get you Israel tonight."

"What time?"

"10:00 PM Hawaiian, 10:00 AM in Tel Aviv."

"Arrival arrangements?"

"They saw video of the fiasco in Washington this morning and would prefer that you transport to the location rather than attempt to land. They propose the following... The Prime Minister will be addressing the Knesset in the morning. They would like you to appear alone in an alcove near the side entrance. You will be met by a security team personally chosen by the Prime Minister to protect you. The Prime Minister would like to speak with you in private for a few minutes, then arrange for a demonstration of our technology. The rest of the team and equipment can transport in when you call them. He hopes that you will stay and enjoy lunch with him. He has also asked for a draft copy of the proposed treaty in advance, if that is possible."

"I'm good with that. Confirm the arrangement, then send the draft treaty in both English and Hebrew. Thank you, Jiaying."

Michael parked the car in front of the Residence, and everyone got out.

Michael turned to Sarah. "I need to go now. If you were on my staff, I'd invite you to come to Israel tonight. But it would be imprudent of me to make that offer before you join my staff." He gave her a teasing smile.

Mei, could you come over to escort Sarah and her team? Michael sent.

"Mei Chin, from my staff, will be here in a moment. She can get you set up to transmit the video back to headquarters. You are welcome to stay as long as you like. Mei can show you around the property or the island. She can also coordinate your return. I'm going to need my shuttle tonight, so if you would like to use it, you'll need to go by sunset.

"Ah, there she is. Mei, this is Sarah from ABC News. Sarah, this is Mei. She will take good care of you."

121

After greetings were exchanged, Michael turned toward Sarah.

"Sarah, it's been a pleasure meeting you. I look forward to working with you again, hopefully soon."

"Me too, Michael. Good luck tonight."

ISRAEL

[02.03.2025 Midnight] PRIME MINISTER'S RESIDENCE, JERUSALEM

"There's no way we can accept this agreement. We cannot give up our offensive capabilities. We need to be able to strike back. We're surrounded on every side," said the Defense Minister.

"It says, 'phase out our offensive military capability,' not give it up," the Prime Minister replied.

"Same difference. It has to be completely dismantled within 10 years."

"Not the same. We don't have to remove a single weapon until we have been free of attack for six months. We don't even have to start dismantling until they have proven they can protect us."

"But for how long? How do we know they will still be here in 10 years, 100 years...?"

"We don't, so we ask for rights to monitor."

"I'm not sure I follow..." said the Defense Minister.

"If we must dismantle, so does everyone else. We simply have to ask for the right to monitor our enemies. If they cheat, then we cheat. If they start to rebuild, then we start to rebuild. From Day 1, we have been able to outcompete our ignorant and lazy adversaries," the Prime Minister replied.

"What if they don't sign the treaty?"

"I think we would need to work with our new allies to address that."

"And, what about Iran? The reason it took so long for them to get nukes is because of the aggressive actions we took to neutralize their efforts."

"Yes. But we ultimately lost that one, didn't we?"

The Prime Minister went back on the offensive. "I think this treaty is an imperative for Israel. We must sign it. It's our only long-term hope of containing Iran and it would bring in an era of unprecedented prosperity. If we are the first to build out their carbon scrubbing technology, we'll be awash in gasoline; no more long lines and $15 a gallon gasoline."

"That would be very popular." The Defense Minister reluctantly admitted.

"And the uncompromised supply of food."

"But, would it be kosher?"

"We would have to get the rabbis to weigh in on that." The Prime Minister nodded at the Defense Minister.

"And what about the civil rights clause? Would we have to give the Palestinian residents the right to vote? You know that will never fly," said the Defense Minister.

"You're giving me hope." The Prime Minister smiled at his friend.

"What?"

"You're fighting too hard. The only time you fight this hard is when you're losing." They both laughed at the line. "Tomorrow, I'm going to propose that we accept this treaty agreement. You are going to agree, with the stipulation that you will work with our thought leaders to put forward a set of objections to discuss with our new alien friends. Then you will second the motion. We will then vote to authorize me to sign the Letter of Intent that starts the negotiation process and puts us under the Confederation's protection. We'll know whether these aliens can deliver on their promises before we ever even ratify the treaty," the Prime Minister declared.

"You are good, my friend. Maybe that's why you live in this nice mansion and I slog around in the muck with the marines."

RESEARCH LAB, KOHALA MOUNTAIN

"Charles." Michael walked into the medical lab. "We're going to hit the road again this evening at around 9:00. We're going to Israel to do the same dog and pony show. It also seems likely that we'll go directly to Moscow or Beijing."

"That's going to be a full day or more we'll be away, right?"

"Right. That's why I'm here. The question is... Do we keep Patterson in the tank while we're gone? Or, do we pull him out now?"

"I say leave him in. His legs have responded better than I thought possible. Maybe two more days in the tank will give him a third option."

"I agree. What about the Sergeant?"

"He is fully in Hiroshi's care at this point. He and the Sergeant have already bonded, so it will be good. Nonetheless, we should stop in to see them before we go. But, what about Noelani? I think we should leave her here with the Sergeant until he's further along."

"Great minds think alike. How about we take Joel and Mei instead of Kale and Noelani."

Joel Rubinstein was the Ascendant who ran the gas production plants in Paso Robles. His specialty was engineering. Although the same rank as Charles, Joel's technical interests were more in the infrastructure and civil engineering area than in medicine.

"The Paso facility can run for a while without Joel. In fact, it could run a long time without Joel. He now has several staff for maintenance and each plant now has an industrial AI operating it."

"So, what's he doing with his time?" asked Charles.

"He's just finished assembling the first of the shield emitter arrays suitable for planetary protection. And it's coming online just in time. The world may not react well if Israel is the first to sign a letter of intent. There's some chance we'll need to deploy the shield in the next 24 hours."

GAS PRODUCTION FACILITY, PASO ROBLES, CALIFORNIA

"Henry, can you confirm the plasma flow through the tertiary conduit on the south side?" Joel asked.

Although his official job was running the Paso Robles gas facility, he had spent the better part of the last year bringing up the giant shielding array they would need once they took over defense responsibilities with treaty partners.

Overall, the project had gone well. They had nearly a terawatt—a million-million watts—of continuous power available, which was just a little less than the entire electric generating capacity of the United States. The power was generated by the giant zero-point energy power cubes they'd installed beneath the gas generators over the last several years. With that much power, shield generators were relatively simple to operate. All they had to do was create an extra-dimensional bubble, move it to the right place, and form it to the right shape. The shield emitters were simple devices, thin sheets of metal a few molecules thick and aligned in the right orientation. Saturate them with high-energy plasma and presto, an extra-dimensional bubble.

The metal used was relatively exotic. But there was a bountiful supply in a nearby asteroid. Joel's problem today was the north-south plasma conduit. It was the third of three, which they referred to as the tertiary conduit. For some reason the energy density was fluctuating.

"Found it boss. There's an impurity in the lining material at a resonance point," Henry said. Henry was the AI that ran the gas field's power and distribution system. "It's a simple fix. I've sent a bot. It'll only take a couple minutes."

Joel sighed with relief. There were only a few hours left before he headed out to Israel. Michael was concerned that this trip would trigger a strong reaction, one they needed to be able to deal with.

While the bot was working, Joel double-checked the field manipulation software. It passed the simulation and was ready to go. He also double-checked the nanobot cylinders and confirmed that they were properly loaded and ready to deploy.

Remote shield generators like this created spherical or dome-shaped shields. To shape the field in a different way required a local array of emitter-sensors. The shuttle had an array of emitter-sensors spread evenly across its hull. All of the Ascendants, including the androids, had the same kind of an array spread evenly through their skin. To get the same effect in an atmosphere, airborne nanobots needed to be deployed. The tanks being loaded on the shuttle tonight would have enough nanobots to encase most of Asia, and more than enough for a small country like Israel.

"Boss. The conduit has been repaired. Want to run the test again?"

"Let's do it." They applied power to form a small extra-dimensional bubble, then projected it to a spot near the first Lagrange point between the Earth and Moon. A group of pebble sized asteroids were scheduled to pass near this Lagrange point within the hour.

"Shield in place." Henry said.

"OK. Expand it to 1,000 miles in diameter and put the image on the screen."

The asteroids must be part of a much larger cloud. Joel thought, noticing small flashes of light that corresponded to grains of dust hitting the shield.

"Henry, how bright is the flash going to be if a one-ounce pebble hits the shield."

"Let see. Two megawatts flashing 185,000 miles away. That should be more than bright enough to see with the naked eye if you are looking at exactly the right place at the right time," Henry replied.

There was a sudden flash on the screen that saturated it for a moment. "Looks like the shield is working," said Henry.

"OK. We're in business. We can drop the shield. I'll be in touch if we need to bring it up tonight."

THE RESIDENCE, KOHALA MOUNTAIN

"Sergeant." Michael walked into the living room and stopped in surprise. "You're still up."

"Yes, sir. I am." A pause. "Yesterday at this hour I was wide awake in bed, in a hotel room and not a thing I could do but lie there wishing that bomb had finished the job it started. Today, I can stand on my own... Well, kind of, if you know what I mean. I can feed myself. I can go to bed when I want to go to bed." He paused, a tear in his eye. "Anyway, I wanted to see you off tonight. Say thank you. And wish you good luck. The world needs you, Michael, even though some of them are real dumb asses. I hope you can find someone else to heal today. Good Luck, sir."

"Thank you, Sergeant. I look forward to seeing you when we get back."

As the Sergeant glided out the door, Charles and Mei came in pulling the grav-sled behind them. "Aren't we leaving a bit late?" Mei asked.

"No. To save time and fuel, Elsie is going to transport us up. She did the same for Joel a few minutes ago. Apparently, he had more to transport than Elsie realized. We'll be taking a much higher orbit tonight so that we can get to Jerusalem in only two jumps. We should be on station to transport down 20 or 30 minutes in advance."

KNESSET, JERUSALEM

"So, my brothers. That is my overview of the treaty and the reasons why I think we should accept it. There is great reward with minimal risk. I move that we sign the Letter of intent, which only binds us to negotiate in good faith. Do I hear a second?" asked the Prime Minister.

The room erupted in chaos but quieted quickly as the Defense Minister stood. "My brothers and sisters. I am much less convinced than our Prime Minister about both the benefits and the risks, but I do agree with one thing... This may be our best answer to Iran. So, I propose the following. Let us form a committee to fully delineate the issues we have with this treaty, and then let's negotiate. We may accept a revised treaty. We may not. But we have nothing to lose by trying. Once the Letter of Intent is signed, we'll start receiving benefits from our proposed ally. If those benefits are not valuable, we simply withdraw, nothing lost. If those benefits are what they're advertised to be, then we work through the treaty, even if we must give up things of lesser value.

"I second the Prime Minister's proposal and call for a vote to approve the resolution that he has given us," declared the Defense Minister.

Loud noise and commotion rippled through the room. The pounding of a gavel brought the room back to order. "Let the voting begin," said the speaker.

SHUTTLE 1,200 MILES ABOVE JERUSALEM

"OK, team. Sensors confirm that a team of eight people is waiting in the designated alcove. I surely hope that these guys are smarter than the ones that met us at the White House. I'll transport down in 30 seconds and call when we're ready for the rest of you.

"Elsie, are we ready?"

"Transporting now."

ALCOVE IN THE KNESSET, JERUSALEM

"Prepare yourselves. The alien should materialize shortly. DO NOT OVERREACT," snapped the team leader.

Suddenly a man appeared, right in the center of the circle they had formed. He stood oriented toward the alcove door, as the team leader had predicted. The team leader said in a steady voice, "Welcome to the Knesset, Mr. Michael. My name is Moshe. I am the leader of this honor guard. It is a pleasure to meet you." The team leader held out his hand.

"Moshe, it is a pleasure to meet you." Michael said in unaccented Hebrew as he shook Moshe's hand.

The team was shocked to hear Michael speak in Hebrew. One even blurted out, "He speaks Hebrew?" which drew a stern look from the team leader.

Michael turned to face the one who had spoken and offered his hand. "Yes. I do. It is a beautiful language. The language of the Psalms, poetry that simply rolls off the tongue."

The young man shook Michael's hand enthusiastically. Michael went around the circle, greeting each of the team members and getting their names.

The door opened and the Prime Minister stepped into the alcove from the main assembly room. "Well, I see that you're already getting acquainted."

He smiled as the entire team snapped to attention. "Michael..." he spoke as if Michael were an old friend, not a new acquaintance. "A pleasure to meet you."

"And you. Mr. Prime Minister," Michael replied.

"And you speak perfect Hebrew!"

"Yes, sir. I learned it a long time ago."

The Prime Minister motioned for the team to step into the hallway so that he could speak to Michael privately. "Michael. I have excellent news. This morning the Knesset passed a resolution allowing me to sign the Letter of Intent that you provided. We have issues with several of the terms of the treaty, of course. You can probably guess which ones. But we are committed to making a good faith effort to become your allies."

Michael was pleasantly surprised to hear this. He'd thought it might happen, which was why it was imperative that the defensive shield be ready. But, for those to be the first words from the prime minister's mouth was quite a surprise.

"I'm pleased to hear that, Mr. Prime Minister."

"So, the question I have for you is... Would you like to do your demonstration in front of the Knesset? They are currently in session and have issued an invitation for you to make a presentation and demonstration to them. Doing so will probably accelerate the treaty process."

Get ready team. We are about to call you down. Elsie, scan the Knesset assembly room and determine where you can place the team. Michael sent.

The Prime Minister noticed the momentary faraway look in Michael's eye.

"Mr. Prime Minister. I would very much enjoy addressing your assembly. My team can transport down into the assembly room on your signal."

They entered via the alcove door. A debate of some sort was going on. Michael only caught one or two words, before the room went completely silent. It was clear they were talking about the treaty.

The Assembly Speaker called for the Prime Minister to come forward. A translator stepped up next to Michael and offered her services.

"Thank you," Michael whispered to her, "but I am first language fluent in Hebrew. Maybe you could help me with matters of protocol."

The Prime Minister motioned Michael forward. "Brothers. I present to you the Ambassador from the Intergalactic Confederation of Planets, his Excellency, Michael the Ascendant."

Michael was surprised to hear the Prime Minister addressing him according to Confederation protocol.

How could he possibly have known that? Michael wondered as he stepped forward to the podium. "Dear Friends. I wish I could address you as Brothers the way your Prime Minister did. I look forward to the day I might be granted that privilege."

The room rippled with excitement when the foreigner spoke in the Holy language with the same grace as the Elders did.

"The Earth is facing troubled times. Our Confederation normally does not involve ourselves in the affairs of worlds at your stage of development for fear of making matters worse. But we value what we've seen of humanity and have decided that it would be in all our best interests to make an exception, and to offer the Earth a chance at peace and prosperity.

"If it's acceptable to you, three of my colleagues will appear before you with some equipment that will demonstrate the ways in which we can help. May they appear?"

Applause rippled across the assembly.

Now. Michael signaled to Elsie.

Charles, Joel and Mei appeared on the floor of the assembly room, grav-sled in tow. An awed hush fell over the room.

"Let me present my colleagues... Joel, Charles and Mei. Joel is the architect of the defensive system that was just put in service today to protect our allied nations. Charles and Mei are expert practitioners of our medical technologies. Allow us to show you some of the gifts we have to offer."

THE KNESSET, JERUSALEM

The demonstrations came off without a hitch and had the desired effect. The room was once again very noisy.

As the Speaker pounded his gavel, Michael said to him, "Mr. Speaker, I would be happy to take questions if you have a process for that."

Michael. It was Elsie! *Three missiles have just launched from Iran. They are heading straight toward your location.*

Joel! Where do you need to be?

The shuttle! I can operate the defensive shield from there.

Go! Michael sent.

Joel disappeared from the floor below the podium.

The speaker had just taken a question and turned to Michael for an answer. He could see something was wrong. Michael turned to the room. "Brothers. Three missiles have been launched from Iran and are tracking directly to this location. As prospective Confederation allies, we are extending our shields to cover the entire city of Jerusalem and the State of Israel."

Air raid sirens started wailing outside. "Go to your air raid shelters. We WILL protect you. But if these are nuclear weapons, pray for the Palestinians outside your borders."

Everyone ran for a shelter... Except for Michael and the Prime Minister.

"I refuse to run, Michael." The Prime Minister said. "You are our hope."

As the Knesset members ran, one had gone outside so he could shelter in the next building over, the same shelter his wife would be using. He was the member most critical of the action they had just taken. As he ran, he noticed that the sky above him shimmered. "Oh my God!" he whispered. "The defensive shield is real."

He stopped in his tracks, then began running back toward the Knesset building. A blinding light flashed in the sky. Followed by another. And then another. *How is it that we are alive, other than the will of God?* he thought.

The sky above him roiled with plasma. It was like seeing the inside of an inferno. Transfixed, he watched as air was sucked in toward the fireball. *You can see the dust and dirt skimming along the surface of the shield,* he thought. The plasma cloud slowly went from white, to red, to black as more and more dirt and other materials were sucked in and consumed. The speed and quantity of material skimming across the surface of the shield was mind boggling. *How can this shield possibly hold?*

WHITE HOUSE RESIDENCE, WASHINGTON, DC

There was a pounding on the door. The President stirred. More pounding. "Mr. President! We have a nuclear crisis!"

What? he thought. Then it sunk in.

The President leaped from bed and ran to the door. "What? What is it?" he yelled, accidentally waking the first lady.

131

The agent at the door was almost sobbing. "Iran. Iran sir. They have nuked Israel."

Why the hell do all the crazies do their shit in the middle of the freaking night! the President thought, not really thinking about all the drones his predecessors had sent in to disturb someone else's night.

He quickly donned a robe and went out into the hall.

The man... *Isaac. Isaac is his name*, the president thought...

"Three nukes, three nukes..." he whispered. "My mom and dad were in Jerusalem." Then he collapsed in uncontrolled weeping.

Oh, shit. The President thought. *The crazies finally did it.*

"Come on. Come on, let's go," He said to the inconsolable man. "We have a plan, let's get to the situation room."

The cabinet members started showing up one by one, impeccably dressed in their suits. *How do they do that?* the President thought.

"Sir," said the intelligence duty officer.

What is his name? The president thought, mind still foggy.

"Three missiles were launched from Iran at 4:00 AM Eastern time, sir. Um, 12 minutes ago. All three detonated. Initial estimates say 150 kiloton yield. About 10 times the Hiroshima bomb, sir."

"Is there anything left?" The President asked. "You know? I don't care. Bring me the football. I want 10 times as much on Iran now."

"Sir," said the staff sergeant that had been sent to wake him. "If we put that much in the air, the Russians will put 10x that amount back at us. It would be the end of the world."

The President heaved a sigh. "Thank you, Sergeant. I'm glad one of us is awake. Let's see if my advisors can come up with a better recommendation."

OUTSIDE, THE KNESSET, JERUSALEM

The Knesset minister who'd seen the sheen of the shields, continued to watch the mushroom cloud as it slowly filled the entire sky. In that moment, he realized he'd been wrong.

Michael has been sent to us by God. The conditions he's asking for in return must be also. We would be fools to turn away that which the Holy One has offered us. If we do, then we deserve to be destroyed. Why could I not see this before? The anguished thought tore through his mind.

WHITE HOUSE SITUATION ROOM, WASHINGTON, DC

"Sir, satellite imagery is finally back online." The director of NASA said.

"Why did it take so long?" The President asked.

"The blast, sir. Those three bombs released huge quantities of gamma rays." Not seeing any comprehension in the President's eyes, he clarified... "Gamma rays are high-energy radiation that kills anything it touches. Most of the exposed sky was killed when they went off, maybe a hundred satellites from various countries. And most living organisms within a 50-mile radius."

"What! Why have I never heard about this before?"

"Do you remember Jimmy Carter and his neutron bombs?"

"Kill the people, leave the buildings," the President whispered quietly, then added, "the Iranians have Neutron Bombs?"

"No. Sorry, that was probably a bad example," the NASA man said. "But my point was that all nuclear weapons emit gamma rays. Neutron bombs were just designed to maximize gamma ray emission and its effects. It's the gamma rays from the bombs that took out the satellites."

"How long before they are back online?"

"Sir. The satellites are dead. Cremated if you will. They will never come back online."

"Then why are we starting to get imagery?"

"The satellites that had been in position over the area were killed. Other satellites that were below the horizon and not impacted by the explosion are now orbiting into position, so we are starting to get imagery.

"Oh. I get it. The nukes killed the satellites that were above them!"

"Yes, sir. The nukes killed the satellites that were above them."

"So, what are the new satellites telling us?" A long silence... "That bad, huh?"

"This appears to have been a well-targeted hit on Jerusalem. The fire ball must have been huge. The mushroom cloud is about 40 or 50 miles in diameter and drifting east.

"At first I thought that Jerusalem must've been destroyed. You'd expect everything directly under the initial mushroom cloud to be completely vaporized. But radar images suggest that Jerusalem and all of Israel appear to be untouched. How in the world did a blast kill satellites 600 miles away, without touching people and buildings less than one mile away?" The NASA administrator shook his head in puzzlement.

"We're going to need more time, and possibly some ground imaging, to get a better read on things in Israel. But the fallout cloud is moving east, and Amman, Jordan is directly in its path. Jordan is in for some serious trouble, sir."

An aide came running into the room. "Sir, we are getting a television news feed coming in from Israel. You need to see this. We've directed a feed to the monitor over there." She pointed to the large monitor on the far wall.

The image of the Prime Minister of Israel appeared on the screen. Standing next to him was Michael Baker. As the audio came up, the president heard…

"… Letter of Intent today with the Intergalactic Confederation of Planets. It is our intention to complete a formal treaty within the month. Many people wondered if this man…" He said, pointing to Michael, "could possibly be who he says he is. They wondered whether there was an Intergalactic Confederation.

"Today, he proved to me and to the people of Israel that he has technology that did not originate on Earth. He has also proven that he will honor his word. He said he could protect us, and he did.

"It has been known or suspected for some time that Israel has nuclear weapons. We have not used those weapons and will not use them today. We had a ground zero view of what nuclear weapons do, and we won't do that to someone else.

"Now that our safety is secured by the shields provided by the Intergalactic Confederation of Planets, we'll begin dismantling our offensive military capability and will use those resources to improve the lives of our residents, Jew and Palestinian alike."

The Prime Minister turned to Michael, "Michael, would you like to address those watching?"

"Yes." Michael turned to face the camera. "Today, an act of genocidal barbarism was committed. Three weapons with a total net yield of 125 kilotons, somewhat less than their makers planned, were launched from a site in Iran. They detonated when the missiles hit the shield. On impact, the missiles were spaced far enough apart that the detonations would not destroy the other warheads. This spacing produced a fire ball of high-energy plasma 11 miles wide.

"Without the shields in place, approximately 500 square miles would have been completely consumed, including all the Holy Places in Jerusalem. Approximately 1.5 million people would have been vaporized. Another 5 million mortally wounded.

"The shields blocked essentially all the impacts of the explosions, pushing the pressure wave northeast, where it was felt in Amman and Damascus, but pushing most of the radiation into space and diverting all of the resulting wind over top the shield. Only a small amount of light penetrated the shield, as the shield was designed to allow.

"There is still a tremendous amount of radiation in the mushroom cloud that formed. The fallout is drifting northeast and will impact the cities of Amman, Baghdad and Bakhtaran the hardest. To the peoples of Jordan, Syria, Saudi Arabia and Iraq. We have the technology to clean this up with minimal impact on human life. We offer our services, as long as you agree to non-aggression. To the people of Iran, we will offer the same services on the same terms, once the perpetrators of this act are brought to justice.

"As I fear that this action may be repeated by other nations, today I issue a ban on the use of nuclear weapons. If you launch a nuclear weapon, it will explode in place and destroy those that launched it. Do not doubt my word on this. You may harm yourselves, but you may not harm others."

"Lastly, I renew my appeal to all the nations on Earth. Ally with us. Learn to live in harmony. Choose prosperity, not war. Thank you."

As the image from Jerusalem faded on the TV, a scene began to play. The image had a time stamp from a few minutes before the nuclear attack. It was set in a dark room. Four Iranian men, well known to the world, were at a table discussing a plan to prevent Israel from allying with the "god-forsaken alien infidels." They finally concluded that they needed to launch three 150 kiloton nuclear weapons at Jerusalem, as soon as possible. Finally, one of them said, "Let it be done." A phone call was made. Minutes later, the missiles launched and the men responsible laughed at how the world would now bow before them.

Then the scene on the TV faded to black, and previously scheduled programming resumed.

CONFERENCE ROOM, THE KNESSET, JERUSALAM

Following the shared announcement letting the world know that Israel had not been directly impacted by the nuclear detonations, Michael was flooded by alerts on his inner vision. He momentarily disabled the system, so he could remain focused on the Prime Minister.

"Mr. Prime Minister, I am receiving a barrage of messages. Might I have a few minutes in a private place to triage the situation?"

"You can use the conference room right over there." He pointed to an open door nearby.

Michael took a call from King Abdullah II of Jordan and directed Charles to take the lead on the clean-up effort there. The US agreed to lend Jordan 1,000 troops as emergency workers and agreed that the Confederation representative could take the lead on the technical portion of the clean-up.

He took a similar call from the President of Iraq and agreed to help in their recovery.

He spoke briefly with Peter Morgan, the director of his San Diego research facility. Peter was the second highest ranking Ascendant on Earth, although rank didn't mean all that much in the Ascendancy. He was a scientist, specializing in high-energy physics. He immediately volunteered to take the technical lead working with coalition forces in Iraq.

Michael dispatched Elsie and the shuttle to California, where she was to pick up Peter in San Diego and whatever equipment Peter and Charles needed from the Paso Robles facility for the clean-up effort.

Prior to Elsie leaving, Joel transported down so he could participate in the next meeting with the Prime Minister.

Michael spoke briefly with Jiaying. Over 20 more countries had called during the past hour requesting draft treaty documents. It was clear that he was going to have to step up the pace of meetings as many of the smaller countries around the world seemed ready to ratify a treaty without negotiation.

Among the calls that Jiaying had taken was one from the President of Iran, one of the conspirators in this disaster. Michael declined the call and declined their request for a visit with him.

Things were moving much faster than anticipated and at the current rate, he would be out of staff in the next couple days. He was out of senior staff now. So he put in a request for a call with the senior Fleet Admiral for this sector. Although the Fleet's prime mission was security, their secondary mission was to support diplomatic efforts. They usually had 100 or more officers that could step in to assist a planetary ambassador like Michael. The call was scheduled for 2:15

local time, which meant that Michael needed to complete his immediate work in Israel in about an hour.

...

The door to the conference room opened and the Prime Minister came in with Joel.

"Mr. Prime Minister," said Michael, "thank you for allowing me some time to coordinate our efforts for the clean-up. Charles is already in Amman. The President of the United States has agreed to send 1,000 troops to Jordan to assist."

"That is excellent news, Michael. Although our interests are different, we consider Jordan and King Abdullah to be friends. What about Iraq?"

"An Ascendant named Peter Morgan, who heads my research operation in San Diego, will be working the clean-up with the coalition forces still in Baghdad. He will be arriving there shortly, along with a shuttle full of equipment and one or two others from our team.

"Also, excellent news. Michael, could I invite one of the members of the Knesset to join us?"

"Of course," Michael said.

The Prime Minister walked to the door, opened it, and escorted in an old man dressed in what appeared to be a rabbi's robe. "Michael, may I present Rabbi Judah Levine."

"Rabbi Levine, it is a pleasure to meet you. As I am not as familiar with your customs as I would like to be, may I ask the proper way to address you?"

"Michael, in public, my name and title are painfully long. As you are a guest, Rabbi Levine would be sufficient. But, when we meet in private, like now, please call me Judah."

"Thank you, Judah."

"Michael, I have something I would like to tell you."

Sensing something important, Michael replied, "Please tell me, sir."

"I am a very vocal opponent of Israel becoming dependent on outside interests. I frequently speak out on my opposition to our dependence on the United States. When my friend the Prime Minister told us that he was in favor of signing the Letter of Intent that you offered, I voted against and tried to persuade my fellow ministers to do the same. Our God is our only protection.

"When this morning you said, 'Brothers. Three missiles have been launched from Iran and are tracking directly to this location,' I felt insulted by the implied familiarity.

"But when I went outside, I saw the shield glowing. And then I saw the bombs explode and the fire boil. A vision came to me as if God Himself was speaking to me. In the vision God designated you as the one that would lead us to peace. I fell to my knees and cried out in anguish over my own arrogance.

"I now believe that you are the one God sent to save us in our time of need. I also believe that the conditions of your treaty are a message from God about who we should attempt to become.

"I pledge my vote on this matter to you and call you Brother, if you will allow it."

Michael bowed his head in the Rabbi's direction and said, "Thank you, Brother."

"I will leave you now, so that I can start convincing my more stubborn colleagues of the wisdom of the path that you've laid out for us." The old rabbi turned and exited through the door.

...

Michael looked at the Prime Minister.

"I look forward to speaking with the Rabbi again at some point in the future."

"With him on our side, we should be able to complete the treaty quickly."

Changing subjects, Michael said, "There's a tactical problem I would like to discuss with you."

"And what is this tactical problem?"

"The shield generator that we used today is physically in California, a perfectly good location for testing or for a demo anywhere on Earth. But, we would both be better served if there were shield generators here on Israeli soil."

"We would welcome that." The Prime Minister smiled broadly.

"I sense from your enthusiasm that you think they will be under your control."

The Prime Minister's smile suddenly deflated.

"It's not what you think. To operate the shield, the operator must be an Ascendant, not for legal or policy reasons, but for physical reasons. The shield generators are controlled directly by our minds. Any Israeli citizen who would like to be trained will be accepted for training. But the training cycle is long, very long."

"Oh," said the Prime Minister.

"Joel designed the shield generator in California. He was also designated to become the head of an Israeli consulate, if we were to form an alliance. So, I'd like to do two things. First, with your approval, I'd like to appoint Joel as the Confederation Consul General to the State of Israel. He will be responsible for completing the treaty with you, which I'll sign. Is that acceptable?"

"Yes, it is."

"Second, at this point I'm sufficiently confident that a treaty will be signed that I'd like to authorize the construction of a consulate and a shield generator in Israel. Can and will you authorize such a process to begin?"

"Yes, I can. And, yes, I will. Although I have a lot more paperwork that needs to be signed than it would appear you have."

"Understood." Michael smiled. "I'll leave the two of you to coordinate from here. Joel, you know how to contact me. Request any resources you need."

"Thank you, Michael."

"I must take my leave now, Mr. Prime Minister. I have my own equivalent of your paperwork to address."

They shook hands, then Michael disappeared.

The Prime Minister smiled and said to Joel, "It's going to take a while to get used to that."

CANADA

The commanding Admiral of the Confederation Fleet in the Milky Way looked forward to his next meeting. It was with a childhood friend of his, Mi-Ku. He'd been very happy that his friend Mi-Ku had been offered the Ambassador's job on Earth. Ambassadors were very highly regarded in the Confederation. They required taking the form of the target species and living among them for at least 100 years before revealing their identity. When he'd heard of Mi-Ku's selection, he had exerted his right to transport the Ambassador to the target world himself.

A week ago, the Admiral had been alerted that Earth Revelation would be happening soon and he should be prepared to assist if called upon. The fact that the request for a meeting had come through implied that assistance was needed. The Admiral looked forward to connecting with his old friend.

The call light on the holographic chamber came on. The Admiral walked over and pushed the receive button. Mi-Ku appeared before him. Curiously, he appeared in his human form. That must be the most difficult part of his job, the Admiral thought. Humans were such puny beings.

"Mi-Ku, a pleasure to see you." The Admiral reached out to bump paws. Then he froze awkwardly. "How do you bump paws in that body?"

"Jo-Na." Michael grinned. "A pleasure to see you as well, my friend. I had forgotten how imposing our native form is." Michael reached his hand out. "We shake hands."

Michael demonstrated with a little holographic assistance. "But maybe this would be a good compromise." He placed his hand on top of his friend's massive paw.

The difference between Human and Lorexians was striking. Where the average adult human male stood 5 foot 10 inches and weighed 200 pounds, the average adult Lorexian male stood 9 foot 5 inches tall and weighed 425 pounds.

"Apologies for presenting myself in this form, my friend. I'm in my shuttle headed back to our facilities. The transmission capabilities on the shuttle are limited."

"No problem, my friend. How are things going with the Revelation? I presume that's the purpose of your call?"

"Yes, it is. As a species, humanity reacts to events much more quickly than almost any other people in the Confederation. They are still more fractured than most at this stage of their development, with over two hundred countries. The Revelation was 2 days ago, and I've already met with two heads of state, the most prosperous and powerful on the planet and a relatively small one that the Ancient Sentient asked me to look in on."

"I'd forgotten that the Ancient Sentient had an interest in this world and that he'd spoken with you."

"And I have about 30 more heads of state that are adamant that I visit them next."

"Amazing, it's unprecedented."

"Yes, it is, which is the reason I'm calling."

"How can I help?"

"I need resources. I have 12 Ascendants, including myself, and 17 androids that have been active for over one year. I have about 100 androids in hibernation and a little less than 1,000 more in some stage of development.

"But I fear that I'm going to need at least 200 Ascendants in the next 90 days."

"Mi-Ku, this is problematic. I have several thousand Ascendants in diplomatic training positions, but none of them have training to take the human form, which I'm told is difficult. I also have 50,000 or more diplomatic androids, fully trained as adjunct officers. Can androids be trained to be human in less time?"

"Yes. Each of our androids are different. They've been individually created from the dominant races found on this planet. But, all have basically the same body control structure and higher-mind interface. So, we could move some of your adjuncts to human avatars and have them function fluently in less than a week.

"They will be a tremendous help, but I wouldn't want the fate of our mission here to be in the hands of converted diplomatic adjuncts. We need real diplomats."

"What else do you need?" asked the Admiral.

"Facilities. I have construction bots and replicators, but given the timeline, I need a civil engineering ship."

"Well, that we have. Would a capital ship and some cruisers, de-cloaking in orbit be of use to you?

"Possibly. It would convince most of the remaining holdouts that think I'm a fraud. But humans are a very aggressive species. The appearance of a warship may lead them to believe that we're here to conquer them. That belief would be much more difficult to overcome than their skepticism."

"Well, I will send a small task force to Earth with 200 Ascendants, 1,000 Android adjuncts, a first-class engineering ship and one or more freighters with relevant materials. It will be there in about a week. I will also send a capital ship that will be instructed to remain cloaked unless you order otherwise. I might even come myself to see this planet of yours.

"You are a good friend, Jo-Na. I hope I get to see you in person."

The image in the holographic projection faded.

THE RESIDENCE, KOHALA MOUNTAIN

Michael was exhausted. As an Ascendant, he didn't need much sleep. But his human form was struggling to function. Earlier, he'd told Jiaying to schedule as many of the "small" countries as possible starting in six hours. With his previous demonstration team now occupied in Jordan and Iraq, he planned to bring Julie Ferguson, an Ascendant assigned to the engineering team in Paso Robles, and Yves Amblour, one of the medically trained androids designed to serve in France. He would also take Mei, who had returned with him from Israel.

As he settled into the dining room, Noelani and Pam brought him some food. "How soon before you head back out?" Noelani asked.

"In about 6 hours," Michael replied.

"Michael, you need to rest, I've been scanning you and your body is not in good condition."

"I know. I haven't done a scan, but I can feel it."

"I'm going to check in with Jiaying and see if there's flexibility to push out another hour. That will give us enough time to run a medical regeneration on you."

"Thanks. I need to speak with Barbara. Would you ask her to come over?"

...

Barbara arrived a few minutes later as Michael was finishing his meal. "Hi, Boss. What's up?" Barbara was the android responsible for production at the facility on the ranch.

"We need to start ramping up android production. Things are moving too fast and we're understaffed to handle all the work that needs to be done. I have two things I need you to figure out. Fleet will be arriving in about a week with 200 Ascendants in diplomatic training. They are not human trained. So, the first thing is figuring out a way to speed up the training process. I need as many of these diplomats ready as possible. I'm expecting to open 20 to 30 consulates this month."

"Twenty to thirty consulates in one month! That's never been done before!"

"Exactly the problem. Second, Fleet will be bringing a thousand fully trained diplomatic adjunct androids... with the same problem. I'd like you to come up with a protocol to replace the standard issue motor control software that Fleet uses with the human motor control software we use. I need at least 100 of these androids in human bodies as soon as possible."

"I assumed that was coming so have already been working on that one. I should have it ready by the time Fleet gets here. We'll need to speed up maturation of some of the android bodies in the tank but getting 100 matured by the end of the week should not be a problem.

"But, just to be clear... We are taking 100 of our avatars, loading them with the fully trained adjuncts' consciousness, and updating their motor controls with our human motor control interface," Barbara said.

"Exactly."

"This should be fun! It will be nice having more people around the ranch, even if they are diplomats." She laughed as she teased Michael.

"I knew I could count on you, Barbara."

As Michael started to push his chair back, Noelani came back into the room. "Good news, Michael. Your first stop is going to be Canada, which will give you enough time for a full regeneration. Jiaying told me you were going to pick up Julie along the way, so I took the liberty of asking Elsie to pick her up first."

"Thank you Noelani." Michael yawned.

"This way, sir." She said with a smile, as she pointed down the hall toward the regeneration chamber.

...

143

Michael woke up as the door to the regeneration chamber opened. The warm liquid he was lying in smelled so clean and fresh, he hated the thought of getting out. The liquid was water infused with high concentrations of nanobots. When a patient first entered the chamber, nanobots administered a mild sedative to relax the patient and ease them into sleep. Then they would enter the body through the skin seeking out damaged tissues to repair. Two hours before the patient was to awake, the nanobots would exit through the skin, cleaning and refreshing it. The patient would awaken on schedule with about 2 times the restoration of normal sleep and with all minor injuries completely healed.

As Michael lifted himself up and began to exit the chamber, mist flowed down over him removing any nanobots that might be clinging. His naked body stepped out of the chamber, only to find Mei there waiting with a warm towel.

"Thank you, Mei." Michael took the towel. He also noticed that clothes were laid out for him.

"Why such personal service this morning?" he asked without the least trace of embarrassment about his nakedness. His body was just an avatar and didn't come with the same sense of modesty.

"Our shuttle leaves in 15 minutes. Or, more accurately, the shuttle has already left. It will transport us up in 15 minutes. We're scheduled to meet with the Canadian Prime Minister in about 45 minutes."

"There goes my fantasy of a hot cup of Kona coffee."

"We've got you covered, boss. There's a thermos of your favorite waiting for you on the shuttle, along with an egg sandwich if you're hungry." Regeneration chambers were notorious for making a patient hungry.

"So, what's our agenda today?"

"First stop is in Ottawa at 2:30 PM local time. Second stop is in Mexico City at 4:00 PM local time. Then a short stop at the San Diego research facility, which might get moved to Paso Robles. Then on to Estonia for a 9:00 AM with their president. Then to Georgia, in the Caucasus Mountains between the Black and Caspian Seas."

"Wow. Big day. How far along are we with these countries?"

"Canada and Mexico asked for meetings and a demonstration of our technology. The Letter of Intent was sent to both, but they have not said any more about that. Estonia and Georgia have expressed an interest in proceeding with the Letter of Intent if they're satisfied that our technology is real."

"Why San Diego?"

"The time zone differences leave several hours between the Mexico meeting and the Estonian meeting. So, we are stopping in San Diego for some rest and a planning session. We also need to pick up some equipment.

"Jiaying," Michael called out.

"Here, boss."

"Please contact the Mbanefos and ask them to close up the San Diego residence. I would like them to join us in Hawaii for the next week or so. We'll pick them up during our stop in San Diego."

"Consider it done," Jiaying replied.

Elsie's voice came over the intercom. "Ready to transport up?"

OTTAWA, CANADA

The scan showed several people in the Prime Minister's office, with a conspicuously empty spot directly in front of his desk.

"OK. I'll go down alone, then indicate where I'd like the rest of the team to be. Keep a lock on me in case I need to pull back out."

...

The Prime Minister's eye was on the second hand on the clock on the wall. A tech team had come in earlier to set its time exactly. As the second hand reached the top, the air in front of his desk blurred and Michael appeared.

Michael arrived in a position facing the Prime Minister, who was sitting in his chair. "It is a pleasure to meet you, Mr. Prime Minister." Michael extended his hand. "I am Michael."

The Prime Minister stood and shook Michael's hand. "Michael, it's a pleasure to meet you in person. I've seen enough of you on TV to feel like I know you already. Let me introduce you to some of my people."

He walked around the desk to stand next to Michael. After cordial introductions to the Ministers of Health, Science, Interior and Foreign Affairs, they all took seats, then the Prime Minister started.

"Michael, we saw excerpts of the demonstrations broadcast on ABC, the events that took place outside the White House, and your actions during the horror of that nuclear fireball. When your representative told me that you could simply appear in my office, I thought to myself—if he can do that, then I probably don't need to see anything else. So, would it be OK if we just started with some questions and discussion?"

"Of course, sir."

"The ministers and I decided that we would kind of go around the table, so to speak, and ask the question that is most pressing on each of our minds, then move on to ask questions about the proposed agreement. Is that OK?"

"Perfect."

Michael sent a quick thought to Elsie. *No one else to transport down for a while.*

"Then I will begin. My question is 'Why'? You come offering technology that will change our world and ask only that we become your allies. Why do you want Canada, or humanity for that matter, to become your ally?"

"I've lived among humans long enough to understand the underlying concern behind your question. You're struggling to see how the exchange is balanced. We are offering you things that are very valuable. But, in exchange, we are asking something from you that you don't perceive to be of comparable value. Therefore, you're wondering, what does the Confederation really want?

"Let me express the same sentiment from my perspective. We are offering you trinkets that have embarrassingly little value to us. And yet, we audaciously ask for your friendship, something that is very valuable to us."

The Prime Minister started to say something, but the Minister of Health raised her finger and said, "My turn. May I ask... you know?" When the Prime Minister bowed his head to her, the minister of health said, "Michael, I saw the tape of you 'curing' that sergeant and wondered to myself... Even if he really did cure that one, how could he cure them all? But, that's not my question. My question is how do you propose to prove that you really can cure the hopeless? How will you convince me?"

Michael opened his senses a little, then understood. "I'm guessing that you have someone in mind that you would like me to cure?"

"Very perceptive."

"I'm also guessing it's you." Michael reached into his pocket and pulled out his scanner. "May I?"

She nodded her head.

As he scanned, a look of deep concern came over Michael. "I don't want to violate your privacy. Should we go somewhere else to discuss this?"

"No, everyone here knows my situation."

146

"You have stage 4 metastatic cancer of the pancreas."

"They told me it was only stage 2!"

"When?"

"About a month ago. I'm waiting for my next appointment."

"You must be in intense pain."

With that statement, her defenses cracked a little as a tear formed in her eye.

"Marie," Michael said. "I can cure you now. This is an easy procedure."

As he turned to the others in the room, he said, "Do you need any further proof that she is sick, terminally ill by your medical standards?"

"No. Can you really save her?" asked the Prime Minister with some emotion.

"May I, Marie?"

"Yes."

Michael took Marie's hand and turned it so that her wrist was up. Then he pulled a little tube of gel from his pocket. "I'm going to put a drop of this on your wrist, then gently rub it in. OK?"

She nodded affirmatively.

Michael started rubbing the gel into her skin using a circular motion. When the gel had been absorbed, he repositioned her a little in her chair and asked her to relax and put her head back. She did as he asked.

He pointed the scanner at her left side. The light at the end of the scanner blinked rapidly and the device made a quiet whining sound. A mist of some sort came up through her blouse and dissipated in the air.

"The major tumor has been removed. In a few moments the pain will start fading, but it will fade slowly."

The clock could be heard ticking in the background. Then she said, "It is fading..." as her head lolled over.

"It's OK," Michael said to the others. "She was in intense pain. When pain levels drop rapidly, people sleep. We should use this opportunity to move her to someplace more comfortable. Her treatment is not complete, so I would recommend we take her to our shuttle. If you have a side room, I could 'beam' down one of my staff. Or, you could evacuate her to one of your hospitals."

"Beam down?" asked the Prime Minister. "Is that the way you came down?"

"Yes. The President of the United States introduced me to that term. I'm not sure I understand it, but everyone else seems to."

"It comes from an old TV show." The Prime Minister chuckled. "We have a sofa where she can rest. Beam your staff member down."

Almost immediately, Yves appeared before them. "Gentlemen, meet Yves Amblour of my Hawaiian staff. Yves is fluent in French and targeted for our Consulate in France, if we should be allowed to open a consulate in France, that is."

Once Marie was positioned on the sofa and under Yves's care, the next question was asked. It was the Minister of Science this time.

"Michael, I have two questions but am only allowed to ask one. I want to know how your shields work. I also want to know if you are able to protect more than one country at a time. Could you please answer the concern that you think is most important for us to know?"

"Our shields are extra-dimensional. In case it's not clear what that answer means, let me explain. Human science is slowly learning of what you call the multiverse, an infinite number of 'parallel' universes.

"We think of it as being more like layers of space time. We refer to each layer as a dimension. There are hundreds of these dimensions, all with differing properties. We are able to measure and manipulate quite a few of them. Some of the higher dimensions are insulating, that is, nothing can pass through them. Create a bubble in one of those dimensions and put it around the object you wish to shield, and nothing can get in. Not force, not gamma rays, nothing. Some of these higher insulating dimensions are squishy. Nothing can get through, but they are flexible, not rigid. There are currently fewer than 100 shield generators on this planet. A month or two from now there will be thousands. You should be able to deduce the answers to both your questions from that fact base."

"Thank you." The Minister of Science bowed his head in respect.

The Minister of the Interior spoke up next. "Michael, you have made claims about carbon recovery. Our country has vast carbon-based resources, so we are very interested to get your opinion on how your technologies will impact our economy."

"Thank you for that question, Mr. Minister. The carbon in your atmosphere is over 420 parts per million now. It was only 280 parts per million 150 years ago. As I read the tea leaves, it will be about 1,000 parts per million in another 20 to 50 years. So, I ask the rhetorical question... Can humanity, as we know it, live in an atmosphere with 1,000 parts per million of carbon?

"The answer is... Kind of. Most of today's humans would develop some form of respiratory distress, which would put a huge burden on your economy. But in a few generations you would adapt. So, a human-like species will exist, although, they will be subtly different than you.

"But more importantly, the question posed starts with the assumption that carbon scrubbing would somehow be bad for your economy. Not true. There are 150 years' worth of spent carbon-based fuels in the atmosphere. You have a vast unpopulated land mass that could be used to build the equipment that could re-cycle that fuel.

"The point is that Canadian industry could produce much more carbon-based fuel than it does today by simply extracting it from the atmosphere. And you could do it at a much lower cost. Digging up carbon-based fuel from the ground as you do today is very dangerous work and not a particularly profitable enterprise. You could employ more people, make more money and do more to improve the environment by mining your carbon-based fuel from the atmosphere than by digging it up from the ground.

"So, let me put your question back to you. If you could produce more carbon-based fuel by sucking it out of the atmosphere, rather than digging it up out of the ground and refining it, which would be the more profitable choice? Which choice would lead to greater Canadian wealth and influence? Which choice would your populace favor?"

"Question answered, Michael. But I want to see that demonstrated and confirmed by my own people before I agree with you."

"That is why we have the Letter of Intent process. Sign the letter. Do nothing but validate my claims. Then sign the treaty. You really can have it all."

The Foreign Minister was next. "Your arguments are compelling. But I'm still worried about the question the Prime Minister implied... What else do you want from us?"

"There is one thing I'd like that I think Canada can provide better than any other country. That is land on which we can build our embassy." Grunts and murmurs rippled across the room.

"I need land for my embassy—maybe 10, preferably 100 square miles—under lease and treated as Confederation sovereign ground while under lease. We would treat this land with respect and preserve its environmental integrity.

"We would like land far to the north, away from your population centers. And we would like air rights to bring our shuttles in and out.

"In addition to being our diplomatic home on Earth, the Embassy would house our training center where we would train the world's technologists, doctors and intergalactic diplomats. As the host country, you would have the right to an advantageous share of admissions from among your people.

"It would also be the place where we would be producing the products that we have offered. As our host, Canada would get an advantageous share of those products, as well as priority diplomatic access because of our shared interests."

The request surprised the Prime Minister.

"Are you sure you want facilities that far north? It's a difficult place in which to build and a difficult place to live."

"Understood, but we need a lot of space. The only places on Earth that are large enough for our needs are in inhospitable places like the arctic tundra in Canada or Russia, the frozen waste lands like Greenland or Antarctica, or the impenetrable forests of Brazil or Mexico. By comparison, the Northwest Territories seem pleasant."

"I have one more question," the Prime Minister said. "What about NATO? We have obligations to spend a certain amount on defense and to commit resources to other countries if they are attacked."

Michael acknowledged the Prime Minister's question. "I'm going to be speaking with several other NATO countries over the coming week or two. I expect that question will come up with all of them. At one level, the answer is simple. The treaty allows for a 10-year transition. As long as we are collectively committed to sorting it out over the next 10 years, there's not a problem. However, I do appreciate that some of your member nations will not like it if other members make forward commitments to withdraw."

The sounds of Marie awakening drew their attention. Michael walked over and sat on a chair next to the sofa. She finally woke up enough to say. "Where am I?"

"You are still in the Prime Minister's Office." Michael said. "How do you feel?"

"Amazingly good," she replied.

"We have a couple treatment options for you. The disease is 95% removed, but it's not gone completely. To finish quickly, we could take you to either our San Diego or Hawaii facility, where you would spend 8 hours in a restoration chamber. It's a very pleasant experience and

150

you will awake from it feeling better than you have in years. We could return you tomorrow 100% completely healed.

"Alternatively, I could leave Yves here with you. He would need to administer some cream on your wrist like I did earlier. It would be twice a day for a week, maybe two. Yves would monitor you. There would be minimum disruption to your schedule, other than spending 15 minutes with Yves every 12 hours. This would also provide a 100% cure.

"Lastly, you could re-enter your medical system. Chemotherapy for 12 weeks and a 50% probability of recurrence in 12 months."

"I'll go with you. It will give me the opportunity to see more of your people and processes."

"Excellent. Let me finish up here, then we can be on our way."

Michael walked back over to where the ministers were waiting. "She's good and will be coming with us for additional treatment. You will have her back in 24 hours, completely healed and feeling great."

"Excellent!" said the Prime Minister. "As to the Letter of Intent... We are unanimously agreed that we want to proceed. I need to schedule a procedural vote with Parliament tomorrow morning. I'm hoping that we can have a signing ceremony when you bring Marie back."

They exchanged pleasantries, then Michael, Yves and Marie disappeared.

"Damned impressive," muttered the Minister of Science.

12,000 MILES ABOVE OTTAWA, CANADA

"How did it go, Boss?" asked Elsie as Michael walked up toward the cockpit. Marie and Yves took seats in the cabin.

"Slight change of plan. We're due in Mexico City in one hour correct?"

"Yes."

"We need to drop Yves and Marie in Hawaii or in San Diego. Do we have time to take them to Hawaii?"

"It will be close but shouldn't be a problem. I'll get underway now."

Michael used the communications system to check in with Noelani. She would prep the restoration chamber and take over Marie's care. Yves would come back on board once Marie was in Noelani's hands.

151

MEXICO

[02.04.2025 3:55 PM] 12,000 MILES ABOVE MEXICO CITY

The scan showed three people in the President's office. They had been instructed to transport down to the Palacio Nacional in front of the garden entrance. Several people stood in a ring around the spot in a configuration reminiscent of the Honor Guard in Israel. "Am I supposed to be going down alone on this one again?" Michael asked.

"I'm not sure." Elsie replied. "Jiaying did not specify."

"OK. Ask her to get clarity on that for future stops."

"Julie, you ready for your first away mission?"

She nodded yes.

"OK. Make sure your shield generator is on. We go down hoping for the best and planning for the worst. Here we go. 5, 4, 3, 2, 1... transport."

PALACIO NACIONAL, MEXICO CITY

They appeared in the center of a ring of heavily armed guards. The men had apparently been startled by the sudden appearance. Several of the men pointed their rifles toward Michael and Julie. One of them muttered, "Madre de los Dios."

"Relax, my friends," Michael said in flawless Mexican Spanish. "I'm sorry if we startled you. We were told to appear here for a meeting with your President."

A well-dressed man stepped out from behind one of the balustrades and said, "Welcome my friends. My name is Juan Carlos." He stepped into the circle of guards with his hand outstretched.

Michael thought, *This guy's name certainly is not Juan Carlos*.

Michael accepted the offered hand and replied, "Mr. Carlos, it is a pleasure to meet you. This is my colleague Julie Ferguson."

"Ms. Ferguson, what a lovely sight you are. Are all alien females as attractive as you are?"

"Mr. Carlos. You might want to be careful how you address Ms. Ferguson. She is my bodyguard, a very capable one at that." Michael spoke firmly, but with a friendly smile.

"My apologies." He bowed his head slightly toward Julie. "No offense intended."

Slime bag. Michael thought.

"Mr. Carlos, am I correct in assuming that you're going to escort us to our meeting?"

"Yes. Come." He motioned toward the door, then led the way.

They entered the building, then started down a long hallway. Some museum barriers were set up near the wall, where a long mural had been painted. Juan Carlos stopped and gestured toward the mural. "This is the famous mural of the Aztec market of Tlatelolco, painted by Diego Rivera." Carlos went into a long description of the piece and its history.

His commentary eventually trailed off and they resumed walking.

Michael, what is going on here? Julie sent.

Michael had already begun opening his senses to his surroundings. Something was off... very off, but he couldn't place it.

Something's wrong. But I can't sense what. Michael sent back.

As they reached the end of the hallway, it opened to a large open area with a majestic stairway, where Mr. Carlos stopped, again motioning to the mural that ran up the stairway. "Along the stairway you see the right panel of the famous mural, History of Mexico, also by Diego Rivera." After more description and history, he proceeded up the stairway, pausing at a landing where there was yet another mural.

"This is the central panel of the mural, History of Mexico." He went on to describe its unique properties.

Boss. Elsie sent. *Scans appear to show a group of men escorting someone out of the President's office. They are heading in the direction of a helicopter that just landed on the opposite side of the building from you.*

Mr. Carlos continued up the steps toward the top floor of the building. As they started down the hallway, Michael could sense serious hostility coming from the people in the rooms along the way.

Michael stopped in his tracks and turned toward his startled guide.

"Mr. Carlos. What's going on here? We were to meet with the President 30 minutes ago."

Carlos turned to look at Michael with an evil smile on his face. "You were not brought here to meet with the President. We are taking you hostage. And I'm betting that the American government will pay a lot to get you back."

Michael looked at Carlos with incredulity. "You can't take us hostage."

Armed men came streaming out of the adjacent rooms, surrounding them and pointing their weapons at Michael and Julie.

"Yet, it seems that we have." Carlos laughed at the obvious truth of the situation.

Michael laughed. "I didn't mean that you're not allowed to take us hostage. I meant that you're not capable of it."

Enact backfire protocol. Michael sent to Elsie.

Michael gestured to the men with the guns. "Gentlemen. Please put your weapons down. If you use them, you will be grievously injured."

Michael took Julie's hand and said, "Let's go."

Transport us up, Elsie. Michael sent.

As the air started to shimmer, several of the guards opened fire, then fell, wounded by their own bullets.

12,000 MILES ABOVE MEXICO CITY

Michael ran forward to the cockpit and asked Elsie. "Are you tracking that helicopter?"

"Yes. Are you thinking what I think you're thinking?"

"Probably. Focus the sensors on the helicopter."

"On it. Are you sure you want to abduct a head of state?"

"Not abduct. Rescue," Michael replied.

"Check this out." Elsie pointed to one of the view screens on the shuttle's control panel. "There are three rows behind the pilot. The first and last have two big guys with guns. The middle has three people. The only one without a gun is the one in the middle. You might be right, Michael."

"Can we get him?"

"No doubt. The question is at what risk? The three guys are packed in really tight. If I just take the middle guy, I'm going to get some of the other two as well. The more of the other two we take, the less likely we miss any of the target. But if we take the whole row, we'll probably get some helicopter. And we'll definitely get their guns."

"OK. Here's what we do. Take the row. Try not to break the helicopter... too much. Before you transport them, flood the shuttle cabin with nanobots programed to eat the guns and establish a suspension field. The two of us will rush between the two guys on the outside and the one in the middle with our shields up."

"You know the nanobots take a few seconds to work, right?"

"Acceptable risk," Michael replied. "Start a thirty second count down, then go."

Michael ran back to the cabin. "Yves, you're with me. As soon as they materialize, take the guy on the left. I've got the one on the right. Knock them toward the cockpit. Julie, grab the guy in the middle and pull him toward the back. Shields up. Put your body between the thugs and the president, the one in the middle."

"Got it, boss," came the double reply.

HELICOPTER NEAR THE PALACIO NACIONAL

"We are close to the drop-off point," the pilot said to the man in charge, who sat in the co-pilot's seat.

"A few more minutes of your excellent flying and you will be free to go."

The President, wedged between two thugs, growled, "What he means is... free to explore eternity."

The guard on the president's right smacked him viciously. "Don't speak unless spoken to."

The President noticed a strange buzzing, then was suddenly yanked backwards.

12,000 MILES ABOVE MEXICO CITY

As the three men with most of their seats and some of the side doors of the helicopter appeared, Yves and Michael bowled over both armed thugs, who thought they were still in the helicopter. They tightened their grips on their guns, only to feel them flow like sand through their fingers.

Meanwhile, the President flew backwards and landed on top of Julie. Her shields were set to rigid mode, so the impact knocked the breath out of the President. She flipped the poor man off, then leaped on top of him so there was no chance of a bullet hitting him.

Elsie set up the suspensor field around the two thugs who suddenly stiffened up like statues. Michael could see the terror in the eyes of the man he'd knocked down.

"Clear!" Michael called out. Julie rolled off the president, jumped to her feet, and offered him her hand.

"May I help you up sir?" she asked, then added as an afterthought, "Oh. Apologies for the rough landing. We needed to make sure you were safe."

"To whom do I owe the debt of thanks?"

Michael step forward. "My apologies, Mr. President. I am Michael, Ambassador from the Intergalactic Confederation of Planets. When we arrived for our meeting with you, we were greeted by some coarse men that seemed unlikely to be your representatives. I didn't sort out what was going on until after you were shuffled out of the building.

"Are you OK? We have excellent medical capabilities here on the shuttle."

"Just a bit shaken. But I don't understand. You are the Alien Ambassador, the one I've seen on TV? But I don't remember having an appointment scheduled with you."

"It seems these gangsters spoofed both of us. We came at what we thought was your invitation. The arrangements were a little unusual, but we mistakenly assumed that it was your way, so we complied. It seems they were after both of us."

The President's senses were returning to him and he asked, "Where are we? After being kidnapped, I was being transported by helicopter. Did it crash?"

"We rescued you from the helicopter, sir. We are in my shuttle, about 12,000 miles above the Earth."

The President looked startled, then started laughing. "OK. Got me on that one. But I repeat, where are we?"

"Come see." Michael touched a panel on the side of the shuttle. The panel became transparent revealing a fabulous view of Mother Earth.

"I don't understand. How?"

"Our shuttle has the ability to transport people, to instantly move them from one place to another. When we came to meet with you, we realized that you were being kidnapped, so we transported you out of the helicopter onto our shuttle in orbit."

The President appeared speechless.

"Sir. Is there a safe place we can take you? We need to get you back. The helicopter you were on has apparently crashed, so you need to let people know that you are alive."

"I am not sure I know of a safe place in Mexico. Is there a place that you can take me that would be safe? Where I could meet with the media to prove that I am safe."

"I think that can be arranged. What about these two?" Michael asked, pointing at the two suspended thugs.

"Whatever you would like."

CNN HEADQUARTERS, ATLANTA, GEORGIA

"Mr. Gardner," Michael said as he stepped out of the alcove where they'd transported down. "It's a pleasure to see you again. And under much better circumstances."

Patrick Gardner was the CNN on-site producer who the Secret Service had shot during the fiasco at the White House.

"Michael. I owe you a life debt for saving me that day. I understand that you have the President of Mexico with you and quite a story to tell."

The President of Mexico walked out of the alcove and introduced himself to the producer.

"The timing is perfect, Mr. President. We have shuffled our stories around so you can have a 3-minute live shot on the 7:00 news. And, as we cut to the last commercial break, we announced that you are here in our studios for a live interview."

"That is excellent indeed." The President used Julie as his translator.

There was a commotion by the elevator as several of the staff from the Mexican Consulate came running down the hall. A woman in her thirties ran up to the President in tears and gave him a tight hug.

"They told us you were killed in a failed kidnapping attempt. What are you doing here?" asked his daughter, who worked in the Mexican Consulate in Atlanta.

He replied with a smile, "I've come to see you, of course."

As their embrace broke, Michael said. "Sir, I hope we meet again someday under better circumstances."

"You were visiting with Michael?" his daughter asked. "You realize that he is probably the most famous and powerful man on Earth at the moment."

"What?" The president asked with some astonishment in his voice.

"People are demonstrating in the streets, calling for us to join the Confederation... Is that why you are here? Did you reach a deal?"

"Um..."

"Father, you must. This is the break Mexico has needed." She implored, not understanding her father's confusion.

The President turned to Michael, "Any chance we could resume our discussion tomorrow? I would love to show you our beautiful consulate in Atlanta."

"I will have my scheduling person contact the embassy to make an appointment," Michael said. "But I must get back to my shuttle now."

As Michael walked back into the alcove to transport back to the shuttle, Michael heard the President's daughter ask. "Did you beam down with him?" Then she squealed and giggled in delight.

SAN DIEGO RESIDENCE, SAN DIEGO, CALIFORNIA

"Emmanuel, Bahati, thank you for joining us," Michael greeted. "...can't tell you how much I missed you."

"Brother Michael." Emmanuel shook Michael's hand. "You made the Revelation. If only we could have been by your side."

Bahati greeted Michael with a deep embrace. Emmanuel and Bahati Mbanefo had been with Michael for nearly 90 years, since they'd met in South Africa at the start of World War II. The Mbanefos were human, the only humans to have enrolled in the Ascendancy Institute.

"Fleet will arrive in a few days. You will be able to take the tests, if you are up for it."

"We are ready Michael. But, do you want us to start the enhancements now, so close to the Revelation?"

"I think we should do the enhancements as soon as possible. Fleet has better facilities than we do. And, although we might have appropriate facilities by the end of the year, it will be a long time before we have comparable recovery, post-enhancement training, or avatar training."

"I really want you to have the best. Besides, your first avatar is always in your native species. This is the only place you will actually get to do useful work as a human."

"As much as I'm looking forward to living in an avatar, it's going to be really weird," Bahati said. "Do I get a say in his avatar?"

She gave her husband a sly look.

"Only if I get a choice in yours," Emmanuel grinned back.

"All packed and ready to go?" Michael asked. "Elsie will be ready to beam us up in a few minutes."

"Did you say 'beam' us up, Michael?" Emmanuel asked. "I didn't think you had time for old sci-fi shows."

"It's something the American President said. And, it seems to be sticking," Michael replied as they all laughed.

Then Elsie beamed them up.

THE RESIDENCE, KOHALA MOUNTAIN, HAWAII

Kale met the shuttle on landing and greeted his old friends. He started unpacking, then took over the supervision as more staff arrived to help. After a while, they all headed into the dining room, where most of the guests were still lingering. None of the newcomers had eaten lunch, so Elsie had called ahead. As soon as they entered, Noelani came running over to greet the Mbanefos. Helen continued setting out the buffet.

"Everyone," Michael called out. "I'd like you to meet Emmanuel and Bahati Mbanefo, my longest-standing human friends. Emmanuel and Bahati, please meet Sergeant George Butler and his mother, Helen."

"Sergeant Butler." Bahati said, in her soothing, melodic voice. "We were watching as Michael started you on the road to recovery during the show. I hope we get to help along your path to full recovery."

HEADS OF STATE

[02.05.2025 8:55 AM] ABOVE TALLINN, ESTONIA

"OK, Michael," Elsie said. "The setup for this one is just like it was in Israel. You will be transporting down into an alcove just outside the parliamentary chamber. You will be met by an honor guard where you will wait until their president comes to speak with you. The rest of the team will be on standby up here waiting for you to call them down."

"I'm ready."

TOOMPEA CASTLE, TALLINN, ESTONIA

Michael appeared in the middle of a ring of guards. He heard grunts of surprise from a few of them, but overall this group appeared better prepared and more unflappable than those in previous encounters.

Michael looked at the man in front of him. "Hello. My name is Michael. I am the Ambassador from the Intergalactic Confederation of Planets."

The man opposite replied. "We were expecting you, sir."

There was a moment of awkward silence, then the door leading into the Parliament chamber opened and the President walked out. "Ambassador Michael," she said in English as she raised her hand to shake his.

"Madam President," Michael replied in Estonian. "It is a pleasure to meet you."

"You speak Estonian!" she said with surprise. "There are few of us left that do. And very few foreigners."

"Part of the training for a first contact mission is to learn every language used by the known cultures on a planet. For most worlds, there are only a handful. Earth has quite a few more," he said with a smile.

"Very impressive. We, too, are trained in multiple languages, but the very best of us have less than ten," she said, then added, "Before we start, please accept my thanks for coming to see us. We are a small country and I know other, larger ones are trying to get on your calendar. Our plan is to have you address our parliament, do a

160

demonstration of your technology, then possibly answer some questions. Is that an acceptable agenda?" the president asked.

"Yes, it is," Michael replied.

"One other piece of background... Our government is organized a bit different than other parliamentary governments. As President, my job is to advise and guide. The Parliament's job is to pass laws and allocate resources. It is led by the Speaker of the Parliament. The Prime Minister is the executive. As President, I can ask Parliament to consider a matter and recommend what they should do. Out of respect for the office, Parliament generally allows me to address them. As soon as I heard your announcement and saw you on Good Morning America, I knew Estonia needed to ally with you. So, I requested an opportunity to address them, then asked that they do the same with you.

"Our Parliament is currently in session. I was the first speaker this morning. I provided an overview of the Confederation, proposed treaty and letter of intent. I also recommended that we proceed as soon as possible.

"The reaction was mixed. Several members thought we should sign with no further due diligence. One of those was a representative who had a friend in Jerusalem during the nuclear attack. At the other extreme, there are those that think our existing alliances are more than we can manage and don't think we should do anything at this time.

"I think the real issue is that they don't believe you are who you claim to be. One member said, 'He simply doesn't look like an alien'..." She paused, then added with a laugh, "...as if that member had any idea of what an alien looks like."

"But, my question to you before we go in is... What do you say to that argument?"

Michael paused before replying. "Let me start by saying, I understand the concern. As the Confederation was forming, about 2 million years ago, it determined that the biggest problem in forming alliances was the repulsion most people have when they encounter another sentient species that looks a lot different than themselves. My native form is large, and it is not smooth like yours. So, we developed technology that would allow us to take on the form of the species we wanted to ally with. This body is an avatar fabricated mostly from human DNA. One that I can inhabit as our peoples get to know one another.

"The problem with that approach is exactly the question you raise. We answer that by offering technology that our proposed allies will not develop on their own for thousands of years. Almost every species we approach is quick to understand that we might look like them, but we are not them."

"So how do you propose to do that for my sometimes stubborn, and most-of-the-time skeptical Parliament?"

"Do you know if anyone in that room is sick or terminally ill?

"No. But there is one member that has suffered a stroke and is partially paralyzed. Unfortunately, there's nothing that can be done about that."

"Then, let's go heal him, if he will consent to being healed."

"You're serious, aren't you?"

"Very serious."

"Then let's go in. They have consented to view a demonstration."

"May I bring another one of my people along?"

"Yes. Do you have any others here?"

"No. But my medical specialist is in orbit 12,000 miles above and can 'beam' down. I understand the expression 'beam down' seems to mean something to a lot of people."

The President laughed at that statement. "Indeed it does. Can you beam them down on my signal in the parliament chamber?"

"Yes, I can."

"Then let's go."

ESTONIAN PARLIAMENT CHAMBER

As Michael entered, several people stood and clapped. After the President's comments earlier, he had not expected such a warm welcome. The President was welcomed, then asked to come to the podium. She said a few words of introduction, then invited Michael to come speak. As he walked up, she whispered. "Start by beaming your colleague down next to you."

Michael got to the podium and started, "Ladies and Gentlemen, Members of Parliament. Thank you for letting me speak with you today. I would very much like to demonstrate some of our medical technology for you. It is very advanced and will eventually make vast improvements in the quality of life on Earth, but it's also one of our most convincing demonstrations, because we can heal people that your medical experts consider hopeless.

162

"I understand that one of you has suffered from a stroke. Would you permit me to attempt to cure you?"

A very grumpy man raised his hand and said, "I've heard that line a hundred times, but no one has been able to help. What makes you any different?"

"The President told me that it would be OK if one of my medical specialists came to help…."

Michael was cut off in mid-sentence by the same grumpy old man. "Where are they, then?"

Michael smiled at him as the air started to shimmer.

"Right here," he replied as Yves appeared out of thin air, right next to him.

A huge commotion rippled around the room. Some of the members seemed stunned, others seemed scared, but slowly they calmed down.

Michael asked the man, "Did any of the people that tried to help you before beam down from a spaceship 12,000 miles above your capital?"

"No," he muttered as his personal nurse wheeled him toward the front of the room.

Michael had his scanner out and immediately saw the problem. Stroke was hard to cure because it usually destroyed a part of the brain. Even if that tissue was regenerated, it was a lot like a new baby's brain and would need years of training to be useful.

In this case, the stroke had destroyed a nerve bundle that connected the man's still intact brain cells to the rest of his body. Michael smiled and thought, *This man will walk again today*.

As the man came forward, Michael introduced Yves to the members.

"Sir." Michael addressed the man. "Is it OK if my assistant rubs a very small amount of cream in the area behind your ear? It won't be uncomfortable or leave any residue."

"Do what you need to do," he growled.

As Yves started applying the cream, the man seemed to relax. Then he chuckled. "That feels good."

Michael started manipulating his scanner, directing the nanobots in the cream to the target location. As the nanobots approached the damaged tissue, Michael directed them to start regenerating and reconnecting the nerve tissue.

Suddenly, one of the man's fingers started tapping. The man startled when he noticed it. Then it stopped. Then it started tapping again. "Oh my God!" he said. "I can move and control my finger."

"Good. Continue to control it. You should be able to move your arm in a few moments," Michael whispered.

He looked Michael in the eye, then back at his finger. Before long, the arm started moving a little. Spasmodically at first, then in rhythm with the finger. Then alternating with the finger.

His face, which had been paralyzed on one side, started moving again. "It's working," he said. Then he shouted, "It's working! It's working!"

Michael noticed that someone had set up a television camera, and that a close-up of the man Michael was working on was showing on the large screen at the front of the room.

The man started to stand, and Michael placed a hand on his shoulder. "Wait a little longer my friend. You're not quite ready to stand. Don't risk..."

The man shot up out of his chair but couldn't control it and started to fall. Michael and Yves caught him and settled him back in his seat as his nurse scolded him for not listening to the great alien healer. The reference made Michael smile.

The man looked up at Michael and said, "I owe you an apology." Then he raised his hand to shake Michael's. "I'll behave myself now. Talk to these good people," he gestured toward the parliament chamber, "and tell them what they need to do."

As his nurse started to wheel him back to his seat, he turned to Michael and said, "Thank you."

And the assembly room shook from the thundering applause.

Michael stepped back up on to the podium. "Many people struggle to believe that I'm a representative of an intergalactic confederation because I look so human.

"Indeed. This body is functionally human. It is an avatar. I reside in it while I'm with you so that it's easier for us to connect. My natural body is larger and less smooth. You would probably say, lumpy." That statement triggered light laughter. "And it requires a different atmospheric mix than exists on Earth. So, by coming to you in this form, it's easier for you to get to know me. And it's easier for me to understand what it is to be human.

"Please do not judge me by what I appear to be. Judge me by the things I do."

164

Those comments elicited a large round of applause.

"At this point, I solicit your feedback. We can give you demonstrations of other technologies. I could answer questions. But let me say… I would like to be a friend of Estonia. And hope that we can form an alliance, a strong alliance where you are respected for who you are."

There was murmuring around the room and the leader of the session came to the podium to regain control of the assembly. He said to Michael. "You've done it, my friend. Let me facilitate from here."

"Do I hear any motions from the floor?"

A man stood and said. "I would like to hear the ambassador address how his treaty would work. We are mostly in compliance already. But by my understanding, we would put our ties to NATO and the EU at risk."

The Speaker motioned to Michael who stepped up to the podium.

"Thank you for the question and the opportunity to address it. I think the real question is, how will the Letter of Intent work? Because in truth, that's the only question on the table.

"I agree that the current terms of the NATO and EU agreements are at odds with our proposed treaty. At least, the language is at odds. However, I don't think the intent of the terms are at odds with the intent of your agreements with the EU or NATO.

"Issues like this are the reason for the Letter of Intent. It allows you to start receiving the benefits of the treaty while we work through the issues. The only thing you need to do is to show progress in overcoming the barriers you suggest. And the only thing you risk is that the technology you have been given would be disabled. No one will be unhealed. The vast financial resources you accumulate from not paying Russia for gas will not be taken from you. The Letter of Intent gives benefits to your people, while you and your NATO and EU partners sort out the problems that I cannot sort out for you.

"In a world where every existing NATO and EU partner forms a treaty with the Confederation, there is no issue. In a world where one or two hold out, the question is which alliance makes you better off?

"My advice would be to sign the Letter of Intent today because others will be doing it soon. And, if you only had one partner on Earth, the one that would serve you the best would be the Confederation."

Another man stood and asked, "How soon would we be able to break our dependence on Russian gas and electricity if we allied with you?"

"If you are the first, then about 6 weeks, provided that your bureaucratic processes do not stop work."

A voice came from the floor. "I move that we sign the Letter of Intent." It was the man Michael had cured.

Another, "I second" and a chorus of approval followed.

The leader hammered his gavel to bring the members under control. "It is clear that many are in favor. We will take this under advisement."

"No, we will vote."

The leader paused, unsure what to do about this violation of decorum.

Someone yelled, "All in favor stand!" Then eighty-three of the one hundred and one members stood.

The Speaker, somewhat put off, said, "I will draft a resolution for committee review in the morning, then we can vote."

RIGA, LATVIA

The meeting in Latvia followed the same pattern as the one in Estonia, but with a different outcome. Michael transported down into an alcove in a parliament building. He was met by an honor guard, then by the Prime Minister. After a few minutes of discussion, he was invited to make a presentation to the Saeima, the Latvian parliament.

No one in the Saeima had a major illness or disability, somewhat unusual for a group of 100 middle aged and senior humans. But they were very interested in seeing a demonstration of the carbon scrubbers. The idea of turning atmospheric carbon dioxide into natural gas and gasoline was very appealing to the Latvians, because their country had no energy resources of its own. They were deeply dependent on natural gas supplied from Russia, which they believed made them the most vulnerable of the Baltic nations to Russian invasion. The Saeima also worried about the growing discontent among the general population about the price of gasoline, which was 30% higher than neighboring countries.

Although Michael was able to make a strong case for the economic benefits of an alliance, the Prime Minister summarized the meeting best when he asked, "Michael, would it be possible to do a commercial deal with you to develop power plants based on your zero-point energy technology? We are not all that interested in forming new political alliances at this time."

166

12,000 MILES ABOVE TBILISI, GEORGIA

"OK, Michael" Elsie said. "The setup for this one is kind of like the one at the White House. We'll be landing in front of the parliament building in Tbilisi. They have a helipad in the building courtyard, but want your arrival to be public, so you can be seen.

"The parliament building is on Rustaveli Avenue, which has similarities to Pennsylvania Avenue, but is not normally blocked to traffic. There is a small plaza in front of the building where we can land. An area will be barricaded off and ringed with an honor guard."

"Do we know why they want this to be public?" Michael asked.

"Yes," said Elsie. "The government commissioned a poll shortly after the events in Israel asking the public their opinion on joining the Confederation. Over 90% of Georgians were favorable."

"So, they requested a meeting and once it was scheduled, they decided to make it a very public event. The Russian invasion in 2008, followed by years of being strung along by NATO have left the citizens of Georgia feeling very insecure."

"Has there been any reaction to this from the Russians?" Michael asked.

"Yes. They put out a statement saying they would consider an alliance between the Confederation and Georgia to be a threat to their national security and they would attempt to intervene."

"Well, they got that almost right... If they attempt to intervene, then it will be a threat to their national security. How soon before we start our descent?"

"Another 10 minutes."

"OK. I think I need to talk with Joel."

TEL AVIV, ISRAEL

"Michael." Joel greeted. "So good to hear from you. What's up?"

"We are about to begin our descent into Tbilisi, Georgia, for meetings there. Unfortunately, it's going to be a big public spectacle and the Russians are threatening to interfere."

"That doesn't sound good."

"No. It's not." Michael replied. "My question for you is what can we do in terms of shielding for Georgia in the next half hour?"

"Do we have use of the shuttle?"

"Not if there's another alternative."

"Do we know what the threats might be?"

"I've had the AI's searching. They're also in the process of hacking the Kremlin for inside info. The good news is that with the nuclear backfire protocol in place, they can't nuke Georgia. So, it would have to be conventional. There are no troops massed anywhere. So, it would have to be by air."

"You know what..." Joel trailed off. "Henry, the Paso Robles AI, helped me with the testing of the shield generator. We used it to block some asteroids from passing through the Lagrange point between the Earth and Moon. If we set it up like a fly swatter, we could have it protecting both Israel and Georgia."

"Risky," Michael said.

"The only other idea would be a massive dispersion of atmospheric nanobots, which would work as long as there are enough of them in the right spot."

"Also risky," Michael said.

"We have surveillance, right? Could we launch the shuttle if we detect something?"

"I'm sure we could."

"Then why don't you transport me and some equipment up? As long as we are airborne, I can use the portable shield generator that I'm preparing to install for Israel to knock down anything within 100 miles. We would still have both of the other options if it is a massive attack."

"Elsie. Can we transport Joel and his equipment up during our descent?"

"Yes, but we need to leave now if that's the plan."

"That's the plan," Michael replied.

1,000 FEET ABOVE TBILISI, GEORGIA

Elsie scanned the city from where they were hovering.

"The crowd is massive, Michael. There must be 100,000 people."

"I'll bet there are even more. The population of Tbilisi is closing in on 2 million. I'd bet that all those buildings along Rustaveli Avenue are packed with people looking out the windows."

"Michael." Jiaying said over the communications system. "I just got word from Henry, the AI in Paso Robles, that they cracked the Kremlin and found attack plans for today. They have planted a suitcase nuke somewhere near the parliament building.

"Using the scanner on your shuttle, we found it. It's set to go off at 5:15 local time."

"Elsie, do we have time to transport it aboard, then pop up high enough to transport it into the room in the Kremlin where this plan was approved?"

"At 10G we can get to transport altitude in about... looks like 1 and a half minutes. Then it will take another 4 and a half minutes to get back here. So, yes, but we must go now. Are you sure this is a good idea? We would basically be nuking the capital of a prospective ally."

"Go. They will have at least 15 minutes to disable it."

The cloaked shuttle shot up into the sky.

"Boss." Joel said. "How about we wait until we are at our apogee, then do a site-to-site transport? If we do that, we won't need to rematerialize the bomb inside the shuttle."

"Good idea, Joel."

"Jiaying, I would like to put a message on the television in the conference room where the nuke will be landing. Can you coordinate that?"

"You've got it boss. OK, if I project a synthetic image sync'd with your voice?"

"That's good. Elsie, can you give us a countdown to transport. I would like my message to start 10 seconds before the suitcase appears."

CONFERENCE ROOM, KREMLIN, RUSSIA

The men in the room had turned on coverage of the events in Georgia. The Confederation shuttle was scheduled to appear in 5 minutes, then be destroyed 15 minutes later.

Suddenly, the image changed to the face of the alien. "Gentlemen," the face said in perfect Russian. "Apparently you did not get the message that nuclear weapons have been banned on Earth. In any case, I am returning your property to you now."

As the face faded away and the spectacle in Tbilisi came back on the screen, the air above the table shimmered and the device appeared.

In seconds, understanding settled in. "Oh my God! This thing will blow in less than 20 minutes! Can anyone disable it?"

"Get my helicopter warmed up," the general ordered. "At top speed we can get this thing 75 miles away in 15 minutes. Maybe we can dump it in the Volga River."

A former spy said, "I've got this. I've been trained. Do you have the code?"

"No. We used a non-cancelable code."

"Let's go." The former spy said. "Maybe you can dismantle it while we're in the air."

The two men grabbed the suitcase and ran for the helipad.

200 FEET ABOVE TBILISI, GEORGIA

"How upset do you think they will be when they find out we removed the plutonium and explosives before we returned their toy?" Joel asked Michael.

"Probably more relieved than anything. But I really hope it scares them. Greed and evil run deep in people that would do what they did."

Elsie said, "We are gliding into place on minimum power. I will drop the cloak momentarily."

IN FRONT OF GEORGIAN PARLIAMENT BUILDING

The Prime Minister waited on the columned arcade of the Parliament Building. The honor guard stood around the edges of the barricaded area at the base of the steps leading down to the street. Beyond that Rustaveli Avenue was packed with people and media vans. The stadium seating that had been set up on the opposite side of the street was also packed.

He had prepared a short welcome speech for Michael that he would deliver over the public address system. Given the media coverage, it would be the most covered speech in the history of his country.

He brought his attention back to the open space in front of him a few seconds before 5:00 PM. He didn't want to miss this visual wonder.

And there it was... The crowd's reaction was loud; at first just the intake of air, then the whispering, clapping, cheering. As the door to the shuttle opened, a man stepped out and greeted the honor guard in front of him. Then he walked all the way around the shuttle, greeting people and shaking hands, taking a moment with each member of the honor guard.

The crowd started chanting, "Michael..., Michael..." The intensity of the moment brought a tear to the Prime Minister's eye.

...

As Michael emerged from the shuttle, he saw the head of the honor guard directly in front of him. Elsie, as always, had done a fabulous job of exactly placing the craft. As Michael walked up to the man, the Captain gave Michael a crisp salute. Michael was about to attempt to return it when he noticed the subtle gesture suggesting that was not appropriate protocol. So instead he walked up to the man and shook his hand, saying in perfect Georgian, "Thank you, Captain, for your service."

The man was stunned that Michael could speak Georgian. The people closest to the barrier heard the exchange and started chanting, "Michael."

Michael slowly made his way around the shuttle, greeting every honor guard member and a few of the citizens on the other side of the barrier. What no one noticed was Michael scanning the crowd and opening his senses, in the hope of finding someone he could heal.

As he was passing the last guard, he noticed a man in uniform in a wheelchair just on the other side of the barrier, in a section set off near the stairway for VIPs. He walked over to the man, stood at attention and saluted him. That brought more noise from the crowd. Michael stepped in closer.

"May I ask your name and rank, sir?" Michael asked.

"It is Lieutenant Colonel Luka Tsiklauri, sir."

"When were you injured?"

"During the Russian invasion in 2008, sir."

"Do you know anything about me?"

"Yes, sir. You are Michael, the Ambassador from the Intergalactic Confederation, and you can heal people like me."

"Yes, I can. Do I have your permission to heal you?"

"Yes, sir. You do. I saw the TV coverage of that sergeant in New York. Is he walking yet?"

"He's starting to. He was standing on his own and walking a little when I saw him last night."

"It's OK if it hurts. I can take it," Luka volunteered.

"I know you can. I need to go meet the Prime Minister. Would it be OK if I transported you up onto the stage? Just made you appear there like my shuttle did. It doesn't hurt. You really don't even feel it, although it can be disorienting to just be somewhere else in the blink of an eye."

"Yes sir. I look forward to it."

"Excellent. I'll see you in a few minutes."

...

171

By now the Prime Minister had started walking down the steps. Michael's Instructions were to meet the prime minister halfway, where the stage had been set up.

Michael managed to get to the stage a couple steps after the Prime Minister and received a warm greeting. As they shook hands, the crowd erupted in applause and cheering.

The Prime Minister introduced himself. "Michael, I am so glad that you agreed to meet with me and my people. I plan to give a short speech welcoming you and the Confederation to Georgia and expressing our hope for a strong alliance. Then I will introduce you and let you speak to the people."

"Excellent. But I ask one thing. I would like to heal the Lieutenant Colonel as a show of good faith to you and your people. So that everyone can see, I will transport him up to the platform, where he will appear much like my shuttle did. He has already given me his permission."

"The Lieutenant Colonel is one of the most famous people in our country. His courage during the war saved thousands of people but cost him his ability to walk. I look forward to seeing him on his feet again."

With that, the Prime Minister went to the podium and gave a very welcoming and somewhat longer than expected speech.

...

"And now, it is my privilege to introduce the Ambassador from the Intergalactic Confederation of Planets, Michael the Ascendant."

The crowd which had become a bit restless during the Prime Minister's speech exploded in applause, then started chanting his name. *This is starting to feel like a political rally*, Michael thought.

"Mr. Prime Minister." At the sound of Michael's voice, the crowd quieted. "Thank you for giving me this opportunity to address your people directly. To the members of Parliament, thank you for inviting me to your country and for considering the possibility of forming an alliance with the Intergalactic Confederation of Planets. And to the people of Georgia... Thank you for the gracious welcome you have given me today.

"As many of you know, my people lost our home world 2.4 million years ago. Although there were other species capable of helping us, none chose to do so. As we came to understand that, we chose to be proactive. To find others. To help them, if we were able to help.

"We have known about Earth for some time and watched humanity go through the growing pains that every sentient species must go through. But recently, we found out that there were threats afoot that might destroy you.

"We are able to help, so we have chosen to help. If you will accept us." A thunderous roar of approval ripped through the crowd.

"Millennia ago, we realized that we needed to come in your form, if we wanted to be accepted. We also learned that we would have to prove ourselves; prove that we weren't frauds. Today, I want to prove to you that I am not a fraud.

"Earlier, just after our arrival, I walked around our shuttle greeting the honor guard that your Prime Minister so graciously offered." The crowd roared with applause and cheering. "Along the way, I met a most admirable man, Lieutenant Colonel Luka Tsiklauri..." Once again, the crowd erupted in applause. "...who I subsequently learned is well known to most of you.

"The Lieutenant Colonel was seriously injured defending his country and his people..." Again, the crowd erupted in their praise for the Lieutenant Colonel.

"Today, I want you to know beyond a shadow of a doubt that I am who I say I am, and that I stand behind you, the people of Georgia." Yet more applause.

"I ask the Lieutenant Colonel and my assistant Yves to join me on the podium."

Both appeared in the blink of an eye. At first the crowd was shocked and didn't know what to think. Then slowly the applause started, and the streets of Tbilisi erupted in the knowledge that Michael had come to help them.

"Lieutenant Colonel." Michael continued. "Would you please confirm to the people here that you have agreed to be healed, even though the first several minutes might be uncomfortable?"

The Lieutenant Colonel said in his best command voice, "Yes. I want to be healed."

With that Yves took Luka's hand and started rubbing some cream on his wrist. He then proceeded to Luka's neck and a spot behind his ear. While that was happening, Michael started manipulating his scanner, instructing the nanobots where to direct their efforts.

It was clear to everyone that the Lieutenant Colonel was bracing himself for something, but suddenly he started laughing. When he regained his composure, he said to Michael, "I thought this was

173

supposed to hurt. My legs are tingly, like they've fallen asleep. But..."
The proud man broke down in tears. "But I feel my legs for the first time since the Russians ran me over with their tank."

More noise erupted from the crowd. Then the Lieutenant Colonel's foot moved. Then his knee flexed. "I can move my legs!" he shouted.

The noise of the crowd was thunderous. The Prime Minister used the opportunity to say to Michael, "We need to wrap this up. The sun is going to set soon and this many people out at night is going to be a problem."

Michael raised his hands high in the air, signaling that he wanted to speak. "My friends. The Lieutenant Colonel will need some time to rebuild the strength in his legs. He is welcome to do that within your system and among your people. He is also invited to come to Confederation facilities. We will cover all his expenses, if he would like to spend time with us."

Another demonstration from the crowd erupted, but quickly settled when Michael raised his arms again. "I thank you for listening to me and hope to welcome the people of Georgia as allies of the Intergalactic Confederation of Planets soon. I must leave you now, so I can discuss this possibility with your Parliament tonight. Please go in peace."

And with that Michael, Yves and the Lieutenant Colonel simply disappeared.

GEORGIAN PARLIAMENTARY CHAMBERS

It took a while for Parliament to convene. The crowds were thick, and many had stopped to demand that their member vote "Yes" and vote "Yes" tonight. The Speaker pounded his gavel to call the session to order. The Prime Minister, Michael and the Lieutenant Colonel were also in attendance.

"Fellow members." The Speaker said, "I have taken the liberty of asking Michael and the Lieutenant Colonel to join us, in case you have questions for either of them.

The member that led a committee on defense stood immediately saying, "I have a question for the Lieutenant Colonel."

"Proceed." The Speaker said.

"Sir." He faced the Lieutenant Colonel. "Are you healed?"

The Lieutenant Colonel smiled, "I feel great. For the first time in 17 years, I can feel my legs, my feet, my toes." He struggled to control his emotions. "I can move them for the first time in 17 years. Can I walk yet? Time will tell, but I believe the answer is "Yes." I also plan to take Michael up on his offer for treatment at his facilities, as long as I can take my wife along."

All eyes turned to Michael, who said, "Sir, your wife is welcome to join you, and you both will be treated like the heroes that you are."

This drew an unprecedentedly loud response from the Parliament members.

The Speaker turned to Michael and asked, "Michael, what else do you need from us to accept the treaty agreement?"

"Very little. But I propose the following... Sign the Letter of Intent as soon as your laws will allow. Then agree to meet with another of our diplomats in about a week to hammer out any issues that either party may have. We'll want to do our own due diligence of your laws and existing treaties to assure that everything is above reproach..."

Murmurs erupted around the room.

"My friends," Michael said. "As soon as you sign the Letter of Intent, we'll functionally be allies. All benefits promised will be yours immediately.

"We are very capable of reviewing your laws and treaties in a matter of hours, once we have your permission to do so. Then we can help you with any issues that may arise from you signing a formal treaty with us."

The Speaker said, "I propose a resolution instructing the Prime Minister to sign the Letter of Intent tonight. Do I have support going to a vote?" Every hand was raised. "Please cast your votes with the Registrar of the Vote."

Fifteen minutes later, the voting finished. It was unanimous. Georgia was now a probationary member of the Intergalactic Confederation of Planets.

THE RECOVERY

IN FRONT OF PARLIAMENT BUILDING

Back aboard the shuttle, Michael conferred with his team to confirm that Luka's wife, Anna, was on board and they had their things. Anna also wanted to bring a few things from home, so they agreed to take her home.

Michael walked over to the Tsiklauris. "Luka, Anna. I'm so glad to have you aboard. I understand that we'll be taking you home to pick up some things and Mei will be transporting down with you."

"Yes. Michael," Anna said. "Thank you for helping my husband and for allowing him to have physical therapy at your facilities. Can you tell me where that is and how long we'll be gone?"

"We'll be taking you to my ranch on the Big Island of Hawaii. It is a beautiful place. I think you'll like it there. The therapy could take as long as three months."

"Oh my! I'm not sure we can do that. We don't have anyone to look after our apartment. And how would we pay our bills?"

"Do you have copies of previous bills that you could bring with you?" Michael asked.

"Yes. I'm very tidy about things like that."

"Good. Grab your records and we can take care of all of that for you."

"Does anyone in Hawaii speak Georgian?"

"Everyone on board does. And all my staff do, although they haven't used it much, so you'll need to be patient with them at first. But don't worry about it. You will be well taken care of."

"Thank you, Michael," they replied.

As Elsie lifted off, Michael went up front to talk with Joel.

"Joel, what are your plans?"

"We have two signed members now, right? Israel and Georgia?"

"Yes. And I expect that we'll be adding Canada and Estonia this week."

"You realize that means we need multiple shield generators, plus staff to operate them. And we need them soon."

"Agreed. Do you have a plan?"

"We didn't plan this part of the mission very well, did we? Standard first contact protocol requires one planetary shield array within days of first contact, then a secondary array sometime in the next year. We have the planetary array, but what we really need are dozens of regional arrays."

"What do we need to do to make that happen?" Michael asked.

"As I see it, four things, the shield generators themselves, locations to place them, staff, including AIs, and nanobot production capacity.

"Fleet will be here in about a week with staff and lots of fabrication capacity. In fact, they're planning to bring a capital ship, which can provide security as we bring everything else on-line."

"Didn't know that. I guess the real question is how do we survive the next week."

"Changing subject... Where would you like us to drop you off? Back in Israel? Paso? Hawaii?"

"Israel." Joel replied. "There's a lot to do there. I'd also be closer to Georgia, although probably not close enough to be useful.

"And speaking of Georgia..." Joel continued. "I've cut production capacity in Paso Robles, so that one of my three AI's plus Henry can be monitoring for threats. We were surprised by the attacks from both Iran and Russia. Sanjit asked if I could lend him the AI power."

Michael shook his head. "We're not going to be able to sustain that for more than a couple days before risking power outages in Los Angeles and San Diego."

"Understood. I'll coordinate with Sanjit."

"Joel," Elsie called from up front. "We'll be in range of Israel in a few minutes."

THE RESIDENCE, KOHALA MOUNTAIN

On landing, Michael had asked everyone to join him in the dining room for dinner. It was well past 7:00 PM in Tbilisi and none of them had eaten dinner yet. He had messaged Noelani, copying Pam, asking if they could have something ready by 6:00 AM Hawaiian and apologizing for the hour.

Mei used the grav sled to bring Luka into the house. Once over the front door threshold, Yves and a very sleepy Kale lifted Luka, still in his chair, and lowered it to the floor. Once on the smooth hard wood floor, Luka followed everyone into the dining room.

177

As Michael should have guessed, Sergeant Butler was in the dining room—up, dressed and waiting to welcome them home. Noelani and Bahati had laid out a feast that included both dinner and breakfast items. As everyone sat, Luka asked if he could offer thanks for his renewed health, new friends and the fabulous meal that had been prepared. Sergeant Butler gave a loud "Amen!" when Luka finished, even though he didn't understand a word that was spoken. Most of the Confederation people were aware of this tradition, but only Michael and the Mbanefos were personally familiar with it.

Michael was touched by Luka's words.

"Luka. Thank you for that. Your prayer was very touching. You are probably right about God, in His infinite wisdom, having sent us. But, please remember. We are not gods. We are people, more or less like you, just with better technology."

Once everyone had filled their plates, Michael introduced Sergeant Butler and Lt. Colonel Tsiklauri more formally, giving each a few words on the other's history. Mei translated to English for the Sergeant. Michael translated to Georgian for Luka and Anna.

About the time the meal was wrapping up, Hiroshi came in holding a pair of devices. Hiroshi had never spoken a word of Georgian before and had only downloaded the language into his kernel during the walk from the Lab to the Residence. He attempted to introduce himself in Georgian but forgot to engage the idiomatic expressions option in the translation code, so his words, though perfectly formed, made no sense. The Tsiklauri's were polite, but mystified. The Confederation team broke out laughing.

"What?" Hiroshi asked.

"You forgot the idiomatics..." Noelani snorted, trying to hold in the laughter.

Michael quickly intervened as this exchange was confusing to his guests. "Luka and Anna, remember that I told you all my staff spoke Georgian, but some had not done so in a long time? Poor Hiroshi here, apparently did not refresh his memory properly before coming over.

"And please forgive the others. We're a very close group and when one of us does something really silly, we sometimes tease them, especially when we're in the dining room," Michael added, while Mei translated for the Sergeant.

"My apologies." Hiroshi said, properly this time. "I'm one of the Medical staff here and have been working with Sergeant Butler for the last several days. I think I'm scheduled to be working with you, Luka, so I brought you a present that I hope will make your stay more pleasant." Then he presented what looked like hearing aids.

"Luka and Anna." Michael continued, on Hiroshi's behalf. "These are translation devices. You put this end into your ear. Then you press the wire end down across your chin, like this." Michael make the corresponding motions.

"Once the device is attached, you will not notice it. Neither will anyone else. When you speak, your words will be translated to English. When someone speaks to you, their words will be translated to Georgian, no matter the speaker's language. Would you like to try them?"

Luka held out his hand and asked for one. Anna was apparently going to wait until Luka was satisfied this was a good thing.

Michael said, "OK. When you insert the earpiece, it will feel like it is melting into your ear. That will feel very strange, but it will not hurt you. And once it's done, the earpiece will be completely invisible. OK?"

"I understand." Luka said, implying that maybe it wasn't so OK.

"Take the earpiece and gently place it in your ear. Stop when you feel it starting to melt."

Luka swallowed, then internally chided himself. *This man gave me my legs back; how can I possibly doubt him?*

He started pushing the earpiece into his ear and it immediately started to melt. It was a bit terrifying at first, then it just started to tickle. He found himself laughing.

Sergeant Butler asked if it was working. Luka started to say he didn't know yet. Then he corrected himself and said, "Yes. It works perfectly."

Michael translated for the Sergeant.

"OK Luka. Step one is done. Step two is a lot easier. Use both hands to position the string part down from your ear, then across your lower jaw." Michael watched as Luka did what he asked. "OK. Hold it in place with your left hand and use the index finger on your right hand to touch the loose spot near your ear. That's it. Once you feel it starting to melt, run your index finger slowly down the rest of the string until it's all melted."

"Did I do that correctly?" he asked.

Sergeant Butler said. "That looks great, sir."

Luka realized it must be working, because Sergeant Butler understood him, and Anna did not.

"OK, Anna. Your turn," Michael said.

Anna did not look the least bit happy about it but realized there really wasn't a choice. She repeated the process that she'd seen Luka do. When the earpiece started melting into her ear she grimaced, then let out a little squeak of fear, then started laughing.

"Can you understand me?" Michael asked in English.

"Yes," she replied in Georgian, then started placing the mouthpiece.

"How is that?" she asked in perfect English.

Sergeant Butler said. "That's perfect!"

Excited chatter rippled around the room. After several minutes, Michael interrupted the conversation. Several additional staff had come into the room and he knew there was a lot of work to do.

"Thank you all for joining us this morning for a meal. There's a lot we need to do today.

"Noelani, once the meal is cleaned up, can you get the Tsiklauris settled into their accommodations?"

"Pam, Anna needs some help with arrangements in Tbilisi. Can you work those out with her? We'll be covering all their expenses while they're here. Also, could you contact the Chief and see if there are any immigration related issues we need to take care of while they're here? Under a Presidential Executive Order issued yesterday, they are allowed on our property. But it would be nice for them to have tourist visas if anything like that is required, so they can leave the ranch and explore a little."

"Hiroshi, you are going to be responsible for the Lieutenant Colonel's care.

"Luka and Anna, you have free use of the Residence and most of the grounds. When you go outside, do not go far from the house without someone showing you around the first time. There are cliffs and bogs on the property that are extremely hazardous and difficult to spot if you don't know what to look for. Also, do not enter the barn without an escort. Same reason. We stage hazardous things in there that you will not recognize as being hazardous. So, please do not enter at any time without escort.

"Now, I need to take my leave. There is much that needs to be accomplished today. Anna and Luka, welcome to the ranch. Please enjoy your stay. I hope to see you frequently while you're here."

As Michael stood, everyone resumed talking. Noelani and Bahati started clearing the table, and Anna could be heard saying, "Oh. Let me help you with that, dearies."

Michael smiled. His human family was growing.

...

As soon as the door to his study closed, calls started coming in. Instead of taking them, he called Jiaying.

"Who has been handling care for Agent Patterson while we've been away?" Michael asked.

"Noelani and Hiroshi have been tag-teaming it, but neither of them felt comfortable taking him out of the tank while you and Charles were gone."

"Do you know his condition?"

"I heard Hiroshi telling Noelani that he's doing unexpectedly well, but you know that I don't know much about medical stuff, right?"

"Right. And thanks for sharing what you know." Michael said. "What about Marie?"

"Noelani put Marie in the restoration chamber at around Noon yesterday. After the normal 8 hours, there was still an unexpected amount of metastatic disease present, so Noelani added more oncology nanobots and set the chamber for another 12 hours. She will be coming out in about 30 minutes unless the chamber is reset."

"Where is it?" Michael asked.

"In your bedroom."

"OK, I'm going to go check on her now. I'll call back once I'm done." Michael left his office. As he came around the corner into the main hall, he saw Noelani turning off at the other end toward his bedroom. "Noelani, I'm coming with you."

She turned and waited. "I hear that 8 hours wasn't enough." Michael said as he caught up.

"No. It wasn't. Her disease appears to be more resistant than most."

As Michael started to open the door, Noelani put her hand on his. "Michael. Before you go in. She is extremely modest about her body. It will not be good if you're in there when she comes out of the tank."

"Oh," he said. "That is one of the most difficult things for me to remember about humans. Thank you for the reminder."

"She still has about 20 minutes, so I think it's OK if you go in with me to check on her."

They opened the door and went in. The chamber was blinking saying that the requested treatment was done and that it would open in 15 minutes.

"Let's run a quick scan." Michael activated the appropriate controls.

A moment later, the scan came back showing that Marie was completely clear. "Excellent news!" Michael said. "She's been in there for 20 hours. She's going to be famished. I'll ask Pam to warm up some food for her. Are you OK to get Marie out of the chamber on your own?"

"This will probably go easier with Mei helping. As I said, she is extremely modest. With two of us holding up towels, we may be able to do a better job of protecting her privacy."

"Will do," Michael said as he left the room and closed the door.

Mei returned a few minutes later, just before the restoration cycle ended. They arrayed multiple plush towels in front of themselves, then pressed the open button. As soon as the door opened, Marie stirred, then awoke. At first, she couldn't figure out where she was and cried out, "Where am I?"

Noelani answered back. "It's OK Marie. It's Noelani and Mei here. We just opened the restoration chamber and are pleased to tell you that you have been completely cured of pancreatic cancer. In fact, the damage it did to your pancreas and liver has been completely reversed. How do you feel?"

There was no answer at first, then she started laughing.

"What is it Marie? Are you OK?" Mei asked.

"I'm so much better than OK." Marie said, bounding out of the chamber. "Look at me! My breasts feel like I'm twenty years younger. I'm going to need to get new bras. And my belly! No more cellulite! I think I'm going to need to buy myself a bikini!"

Mei and Noelani looked at each other in dismay. They knew that humans were a little obsessed with their bodies, but truly could not fathom it.

"And the hair in all the wrong places... It's gone!"

Marie grabbed the towels and spread them away so Noelani and Mei could see her. "Look at me!" She said. "I don't look like an old hag anymore."

Noelani stood there with her mouth open not knowing what to say and thought to herself... *Is this the same woman I put in the chamber 20 hours ago?*

Mei took a more diplomatic approach. "Marie. Do you like this change?"

"I don't like it. I love it!" she exclaimed.

"Marie, please forgive us. We really don't understand human concerns about body shape and modesty. We only set the restoration chamber to remove the cancer, but in doing so it needed to repair other tissues as well. I hope you are pleased with the outcome."

"Oh, girls! You have no idea how pleased I am! So, what about some clothes? I don't think mine will fit any more."

Earlier Noelani had wheeled in a cabinet full of women's clothes and they started going through it, looking for just the right things.

DINING ROOM, THE RESIDENCE

Michael was starting to get worried. Marie should have come out of the chamber 20 minutes ago, but there was no sign of her, or of Noelani or Mei. When he couldn't take it anymore, he messaged Noelani... *Everything OK in there?*

A moment later, Noelani messaged back... *Marie is in very good spirits. The clothes she had on when she arrived don't 'fit right' anymore, so she's going through the wardrobe looking for just the 'right thing.' I truly do not understand this attribute of human women. Oh, and she's very hungry.*

OK. I'm going back to work. Let me know when you've settled into the dining room.

...

Back in his office, Michael called Jiaying. "OK. What do you have for me?"

"It's a long list," replied Jiaying. "First, we've received the executed Letter of Intent from Israel, so they're officially the first.

"Next, I've received confirmation from both Georgia and Estonia, that we'll receive an executed Letter of Intent within 24 hours.

"Next, a message from the Canadian Prime Minister's office inquiring about Marie. They'd like to know when to expect her back. Assuming that she votes in favor, they'll be able to execute the Letter of Intent within 24 hours of her return. They also have a draft embassy lease agreement for your review.

"The next item is unusual. I got a message from the Senior Fleet Admiral saying they were underway. They'll be bringing a full armada with multiple capital ships as well as frigates, freighters and two civil engineering ships. He said he needed to speak with you as soon as possible."

"Next, the Russian government claims to be filing a complaint against the Intergalactic Confederation of Planets regarding actions taken in Georgia. It was a very brusque message left by a very rude man.

"Next, the Chinese government said they're waiting to hear from you and are somewhat displeased that they've not heard from you yet."

A knock came on the door. Noelani stuck her head in. "Marie's having breakfast."

"Jiaying, I need to step away for a minute. I'm happy to meet with the Chinese today, if they're able. Also, could you message the Fleet Admiral and set up the call with him? I'll be back in half an hour."

"Michael before you run, the Mexican president would like you to visit him today in Atlanta if possible."

"OK. Add that one to the list. And, I think I need to go to Canada today also, so see if you can work up a viable schedule."

Michael headed down the hallway to the dining room, where he could hear a lot of happy noise.

As Michael walked in, he could see a very happy Marie holding court with the Butlers and the Tsiklauris. Noelani, Mei, Pam and Bahati seemed to be enjoying the company as well.

"Michael!" Marie said when she saw him. "I thought you brought me here to cure me, not to turn the clock back 20 years." She stood and turned in a circle, showing her newer, tighter form.

"We aim to please. And I think I'm sensing a new product I can offer; it knocks 20 years off your age."

Anna asked, "Can I have a turn in this machine of yours?" Luka made hushing sounds at Anna.

Michael smiled and replied good-naturedly, "I think that can be added to the services available to you."

More seriously, Michael said. "I'm glad we were able to help you in time, Marie. Your disease turned out to be more virulent than we expected. You were in the chamber for 20 hours. So, it is now tomorrow, and the Prime Minister is worried that you're missing."

"I was in there for 20 hours? Ladies..." she said looking at Noelani and Mei, "you didn't tell me that."

Noelani replied with quick wit, "We leave all the bad news to Michael."

"Is that so?" Marie smiled at them, then turned back to Michael. "I suppose that means I need to go home."

"You're welcome here as long as you'd like to stay. But, yes, I think the Prime Minister is anxious for your return. They need your vote to proceed with the Letter of Intent and I'm sure they want your input on the draft Embassy Land Lease they've prepared."

"Will you be returning with me?" she asked.

"I'd like to. I have a matter that I'd like to discuss in private with the Prime Minister and your Foreign Minister. And I would also like them to explain to me the major points of the Embassy lease."

"Is there a problem with the Embassy lease?"

"No. But it's my experience that it works better if people tell you about the major terms, than to just read them. Much more information about the intent of the terms is usually conveyed in the oral description. This arrangement will be very important to both our peoples, so I'd like to make sure both sides are very happy with it."

"Thank you, Michael. I think you're the most direct and honest diplomat I've ever spoken with."

"Thank you, Marie. It's kind of you to say that. I should know the arrangements for the day soon." He excused himself, then returned to his office.

As soon as the door closed, Jiaying came on the line. "Michael, I think we have a schedule, but it's really tight."

"Let's hear it."

"It's about 8:45 now. At 9:10 Elsie launches with the Chinese team. You and Marie beam up at 9:30 for the short jump to Canada and beam down."

"So even you are saying 'beam up' and 'beam down' now." He teased good-naturedly.

"It does roll off the tongue. But back to the schedule... You beam up from Canada an hour and 50 minutes later for the short jump to Atlanta, where it will be 5:00 PM. You have an early dinner in private with the President of Mexico for a maximum of two hours. Then off to China for a 9:00 AM meeting with their President. You have three hours. Then return here for the call with Fleet at 7:00 PM local time in Hawaii. If you run a little late in China, you'll need to take the call with Fleet from the shuttle. Are you OK with this?"

"Yes. Send the confirmations. Also, have Noelani let Marie know our departure time. She can take off with the shuttle or beam up with me, whichever she would like. I'm going to go check in on Agent

185

Patterson. Could you have Julie and Emmanuel meet me there in 5 minutes?"

"Julie is actually just approaching the door to your office."

"OK, I'll talk with her. Thanks, Jiaying. You'll be joining us for China, right?"

"Looking forward to it."

A knock came at Michael's door.

"Come in," he called as he rose to walk over to the door.

Julie opened the door and saw Michael coming her way. "Are we going somewhere?"

"Yes, I need to check in on Agent Patterson. He's been in the tank for three days now. I don't think we can leave him in much longer."

"You know that I don't know much about medical, right? I passed minimal competency and haven't looked at it since."

"Well, consider this a refresher. Emmanuel will be joining us also. He is interested in a medical specialty."

They went out the back, where Emmanuel joined them, and crossed over to the entrance to the lab. A few minutes later, they reached the 'tank farm' where Agent Patterson was being treated. A quick review of the readings showed that he was in surprisingly good shape, all major organs at optimal performance. His legs had even recovered to minimal use status.

"If we pull him now, he'll be as healthy as a 25-year-old but will only be able to walk with crutches or braces. If we leave him in another 24 hours, he might be able to walk on his own again, but the de-aging will enter the danger zone. What do you think?" he asked Julie.

"Michael, you know I'm not competent to make recommendations on this."

"I'm not asking for a medical assessment. I just gave you one. This is more of an ethical question. If we pull him out now, he'll never walk independently again. If we leave him in, there is a very good chance that he will walk again, but there is some chance that de-aging will permanently damage other parts of his body. In order to ask him, we would need to pull him out and we wouldn't be able to put him back in for a long time."

"Emmanuel, what do you say?"

"Brother Michael. I don't know this man. But, the vast majority of men that I've known would risk their lives to maintain their mobility."

"Good answer," Michael replied.

"Jiaying." Michael called out. "Could you connect me to the Chief? A pause, then... "The Chief is on the line Michael."

"Chief!" said Michael.

"Michael, I'm seeing entirely too much of you on the television. What kind of trouble are you in now and what happened to Agent Patterson?"

"Agent Patterson is the reason I'm calling, Chief."

"The poor man's wife arrived on Monday after he'd been reported missing in action. She's in a bad way, Michael."

"That may have answered my question. Here's the situation... Agent Patterson would have been declared dead if we'd released him to you Sunday afternoon. We got him into therapy before you even left and miraculously brought him back from the brink Sunday evening, although even then it would have killed him to take him off therapy.

"At this point, he's stable and healthy except for his legs. If we take him off therapy, he'll probably be able to walk with braces, but it will never get any better. But we are reaching the limit of where it's safe to continue therapy. We can't wake him without withdrawing him from therapy and if we take him off therapy, we can't put him back on for maybe a year.

"So, the question is what to do? And we only have a 15-minute window in which to decide. One or the other needs to be locked in at that time."

"Where do people come up with this crazy shit, Michael? Why can't you wait another 30 minutes or two hours or something?"

"Doesn't work that way Chief. We did our best and pulled a real miracle out of the hat. But this is as far as we can safely go, so without his next of kin directing us to leave him on therapy, we must pull him off."

"Give me 5 minutes. She's staying nearby. I'll go talk with her."

Michael and Julie made some minor adjustments to the tank's settings, then the three of them brainstormed some more ideas. The conclusion was that they should recall Charles. He needed to be on the China visit anyway. Elsie could get him while they were meeting with the Canadians, bring him back here and still get back to Ottawa in time. Charles could check on Patterson to confirm how much longer before de-aging toxicity set in, then pull him out maybe four hours from now if needed.

The chief came back on the line. "Michael, I am here with Agent Patterson's wife. She would like you to explain this to her. Neither of us has confidence I got the message right."

"Thank you, Chief. Hello, Ms. Patterson?"

"Yes. I'm here." She said sniffling.

"Ms. Patterson, you know that your husband was critically injured during an attempted raid on my property Sunday evening. We had nothing to do with the injury but helped with the rescue. He was pronounced dead by the FBI Medic on the scene, but we have much better medical technology and thought we had a good chance at reviving him. It was touch and go for a couple hours, but for the most part he has made an excellent recovery." He heard a sob of relief on the other end of the line.

"Let me explain the decision we have to make. His legs were badly damaged. I thought they'd need to be amputated." Intense sobbing. "But I was wrong. His legs have made an astounding recovery. Nonetheless, if we take him off therapy now, the best he can hope for will be to walk using braces.

"If we leave him on therapy for another day, he will almost certainly regain the ability to walk normally on his own again, but... toxicity to the therapy is about to set in. Since talking with the Chief 15 minutes ago, we've made some adjustments that will let him stay on therapy another 3 hours. At that point, we'll have to take him off therapy unless we have explicit instructions to leave him on. I can offer you three choices... First, pull him out of therapy now. Second, let him stay on therapy another three hours, which may allow him to walk under his own power again. Third, leave him on therapy until the legs are healed, but at the risk of damage to his heart and lungs.

"My colleagues here recommend option two. Let him stay on therapy for three more hours. It will take another couple hours after that to wake him up and make him comfortable, so sometime tonight, say 8:00 PM, you could come visit. You would be welcome to stay here tonight.

"If we determine that he cannot walk well enough. He would be eligible for additional therapy in a year or so, when we might be able to make further improvements without risk to his major organs."

"I'll take your recommendation Michael. Thank you for saving my husband."

"Chief, can you bring her by around 8:00 this evening? Someone will buzz you in at the gate. Come right up to the house and park in front."

"Will do, Michael. Thank you."

TANK FARM, KOHALA RESEARCH LAB

"OK, Julie. Keep an eye on Agent Patterson until Charles gets here. Coordinate with Noelani and Hiroshi for the recovery process once the agent is pulled from the tank. Also, have options for Ms. Patterson to stay.

"Regarding facilities access... They can see the medical facilities in the basement of the residence, but not the barn. And, no mention of the tank farm. Humans would react very poorly to knowledge of this place."

"You've got it boss. Any idea how long you're going to need me here in Hawaii? I'm worried about things falling behind in Paso Robles."

"You should count on staying here the rest of the week. But you should be able to continue your Paso Robles work remotely. The presence projectors in the lab basement are excellent. I'll be using one tonight to speak with the Senior Fleet Admiral."

"Michael, you're such a good person. It's easy to forget your rank in the Confederation."

Michael teased her, "Are you implying that senior leaders of the Confederation aren't good people?"

"No. Only that they're very busy and generally don't make personal time for low-ranked people like me."

"Remember that, young one. Remember it well. You, too, are destined for high rank. Always remember the importance of spending personal time with your team and of showing kindness to all."

THE RESIDENCE, KOHALA MOUNTAIN

Michael exited the sonic shower, happy for the three-minute refresher. He'd been on for nearly 24 hours and was about to start another long shift. He met Marie in the dining room. The Sergeant and the Lt. Colonel were also there to wish them well.

12,000 MILES OVER OTTAWA, CANADA

"What's our status, Elsie?"

"We've been given coordinates just outside the Canadian Prime Minister's office for you and Marie to transport down. Scans confirm a two-person honor guard is there to make sure your landing area is clear."

OUTSIDE THE PRIME MINISTERS OFFICE

Michael and Marie appeared outside the Prime Minister's office. It turned out the two honor guards were the Prime Minister and Foreign Minister. A handful of Mounties stood across the hall. They signaled their welcome with a wave.

"Gentlemen," Michael said to the two ministers, before waving back to the Mounties. "What a pleasure to be greeted in person."

"Hello, Michael..." The Prime Minister started as he noticed Marie. "Marie, you look like the picture of health. I'm... stunned."

The foreign minister quickly added his complements.

"Thank you for saying so. This has been a miraculous journey. Two days ago, I was facing a death sentence and pain so intense I could barely mask it. Today, I look, and feel, like the picture of health. The Confederation has more to offer us than we can imagine. And..." she searched for words, "...they are like family. Like friends long lost. They truly are seeking friendship. We really must accept their invitation."

"We will." The Prime Minister nodded his assurance. "Yours is the last signature required to complete the Letter of Intent."

He turned to Michael. "Our laws require more signatures than your draft included, so we added pages." Adding Marie's page to the stack, he added, "I hope this is acceptable to the Confederation."

"Thank you, Mr. Prime Minister. Your country is the third to accept, and the largest and most populous so far."

"You wanted to speak with us Michael? Shall we go inside to talk?"

"Thank you, sirs. There is a matter on which I seek your guidance."

"Would you like the Minister of Health to participate?"

"I'll always welcome her counsel, but my question is directed to your areas of expertise,"

"Marie, do you wish to join?" asked the Prime Minister.

"I've been away for more than a day and completely trust that it's your expertise he requires."

THE PRIME MINISTER'S OFFICE, OTTAWA, CANADA

"So how can we help you, Michael?"

"You are aware of our recent visit with the government of Georgia?"

"Yes," replied the Foreign Minister. "We also heard that Russia claimed they would interfere in any approach you made to Georgia, but nothing was reported."

"I'm sad to say that the Russians attempted to detonate a tactical nuclear device at the peak of the event the Georgians orchestrated." Michael said, "May I show you what happened?"

"You have evidence?" They sounded stunned.

Michael pointed to the monitor on the wall and it started playing. Russian conversation could be heard as an English caption played across the bottom of the screen.

The Prime Minister gasped. "They put the device on a timer?"

"Yes. And you heard their expectations, elimination of the alien threat. Which I might add, would have been at the cost of over 500,000 Georgian lives."

"Thankfully, it was a dud." The Foreign Minister sighed with relief.

"Unfortunately, it wasn't. Watch this." Again, Michael pointed to the monitor and it started playing. This time Michael was the one showing on the screen in the room with the Russian team that had plotted it. Then the bomb appeared, with timer clearly visible and counting down.

They listened to the panicked dialog and watched the two men running from the room, bomb in hand.

"Our intelligence agencies did not report a nuclear explosion. Did they dismantle it?" the Prime Minister asked.

"No. We removed the explosives and fissile material before returning it to them."

"I read that a Russian helicopter crashed near the Volga River with two high ranking members aboard. Did this have anything to do with it?"

"Yes and no," Michael replied. "We had no direct role in the downing of the helicopter. They did that solely on their own."

He pointed to the monitor again, where a dramatic scene played out. The Russian leaders were convinced that the bomb was real and could not be dismantled. When it was clear that they would not reach the river in time, one of the men pulled out his handgun and shot the helicopter pilot in the head, causing the helicopter to crash. He had been arguing that they should intentionally crash the helicopter in the hope of breaking the bomb apart so it couldn't reach critical mass.

There was a long silence after the video stopped playing. Finally, the Prime Minister said, "So this is why the Russians are filing a complaint against you in the United Nations and in the World Court?"

"I'd presume so, which is why I wanted to talk with you. From the Confederation's perspective, these men and this nation have conspired to commit mass murder. In the 'tapes' they even admit it. We'd think they would want to cover this up. Yet, they're attempting to paint us as the bad actors. I simply do not understand. Thus, my request to speak with you. I'm hoping you can give me some insight."

"They will claim that you attempted to detonate a tactical nuclear weapon inside the Kremlin. They will also say that three courageous Russian patriots gave their lives to prevent the decapitation of their government. If they had this tape, they would edit it to prove their point. And, given their institutional paranoia, they will probably have security camera footage of that monitor," said the Foreign Minister.

"What devious, evil men," Michael exclaimed.

"That's what a lot of us have been saying for a long time. But nonetheless, the UN gives them a platform."

"As this is difficult for me to understand, can you give me any recommendations on how to proceed?"

After a long silence the Prime Minister asked, "Can you resurrect these men? If so, they may testify to their deeds."

Michael shot off a message to Elsie. *Priority override. Go to Moscow. Recover the human remains from the helicopter that held the suitcase nuke. Now!*

"Michael, I just noticed a far-away look in your eyes. I've seen this before. Are you telepathic?" asked the Prime Minister.

Michael laughed. "Am I that transparent? To answer your question, no... I think. The same communications device in my mind that allows me to control this body, also lets me send... what you would call text messages... to my staff. I just sent a request for a recovery operation to locate and retrieve the remains of those men."

"Damn," the Prime Minister said. "Wish I could do that."

"All of this technology will be available in time. Maybe your great grandchildren will benefit from it."

"My generation will not?" asked the Prime Minister.

"Surely a few will. But the personal cost is high. The vast majority of your generation will not choose to pay it."

"I'm not sure I understand."

"Does your great aunt, who was 30 years old when you were born… Does she use texting on her cell phone?"

"Point taken."

"Back to the Russian complaint… Any recommendations?" Michael asked.

"How would this be handled on your world?" asked the Prime Minister in turn.

"The perpetrators of this crime would be reviewed by a court of appropriate jurisdiction. If found guilty, they'd be subject to rehabilitation."

"What would constitute the court of appropriate jurisdiction in this matter?"

"If the crime involved the Confederation, then the ambassador to the planet would decide. As I am an alleged party to the crime and this is a partial ally world, it would rise to the Fleet Admiral."

"Where is this Fleet Admiral?"

"Ironically, he's on his way here. He's never seen Earth before, so decided to accompany the Civil Engineering ships that are coming to help build our embassy, which I hope will be in Canada. He'll also be bringing diplomats to help staff our consulates, and cargo ships full of materials we need for the first round of gift production."

"Under your laws, could the people of Georgia bring charges against the Russians in this court?"

"Of course."

"Then, I think you have a solution. Once the evidence is known, most of the world will side with you."

"Thank you for your advice. Changing subjects… May I ask about the progress you've made in regard to our request to place our embassy in Canada?"

"The Cabinet is in favor, as is the Parliament, as are the people I'm sure. We've drafted a preliminary lease agreement that grants you a lease to 100 square miles of land north of the 60th parallel, location to be determined. It has a nominal term of 100 years at a rate of one dollar per year and has all the customary cancellation and restoration provisions. Some members are also drafting preferred access terms. I have an incomplete draft that I have been authorized to share with you."

"As I mentioned a few moments ago, we have civil engineering ships due to arrive next week. They can do quite a bit from orbit, in terms of surveys, site selection and mapping, design, etc. But I'm sure they'll want to inspect various sites on the ground. How much of a problem would that be?"

"I'm sure that you could do it without us even knowing you were there. So, I appreciate your asking. It shouldn't be a legal problem. We can give you the appropriate diplomatic cover as long as we have representatives hosting your team."

"No one on that team will be in human form."

"Then I think we'll need to choose our delegation carefully," the Prime Minister replied.

12,000 MILES ABOVE OTTAWA, CANADA

As soon as Michael materialized in the shuttle, he went to the cockpit. "What's our status?" he asked.

"You are making me crazy, Michael. We put the AI's to work on finding the remains of the Russian helicopter. We got a lucky hit on the guy that shot the pilot. Once it was clear the chopper was going down, he jumped out and nearly survived, landing in a small lake.

"It took them a long time to find him in the icy water. Then a short trip to the refrigerator in a low security local morgue. He's been ice cold since the moment of death. We transported him up and transported him to a tank in Hawaii, where they brought him back from the brink. He's still unconscious in the tank.

"Because of that detour, we didn't get Charles. So, we'll do that once you're down in Atlanta. Julie is in a full-scale panic over Agent Patterson. His legs are improving, and the de-aging toxin does not appear to be progressing, but she's not confident in these findings." Elsie reported.

"OK, any more on the Russians?"

"The pilot's body was ripped apart and badly burned, so we stopped pursuing him. The other man is still missing."

"OK, have the AIs rewind and enhance the tapes. I want to know what became of him." Michael paused a second, then continued. "What's the setup for Atlanta?"

"The setup for this one changed a bit while you were in Canada. The Mexican President took the presidential suite at the Four Seasons in Atlanta. He asked that you 'beam down' onto the balcony above the lobby area, where you will be met by a security team."

"Great. Let's plan to transport down 10 minutes early, so you have more time to get Charles."

12,000 MILES ABOVE ATLANTA, GEORGIA

"OK. We found the security team he's posted. They're in position. Ready?"

"Ready."

BALCONY ABOVE LOBBY, FOUR SEASONS HOTEL

Michael appeared in the center of the security team several minutes ahead of time and heard the team leader mutter, "Damn."

He approached the man. "Hello. My name is Michael."

The man stuttered for a moment, then said, "Michael, my name is Geraldo. Greetings on behalf of the President of the United Mexican States. If you will follow me, we'll take you to his Excellency."

They proceeded down the hallway to an elevator that took them to the Presidential Suite.

"Michael," the President said. "Thank you for meeting with me. And thank you for the rescue yesterday.

"I am told that my helicopter crashed with all hands onboard, except for me. Do you know anything about that?"

"There were nine people on board, when we transported you to our shuttle. How many 'hands' were found?"

"Four." The president said without thinking.

"That means two conspirators escaped. You might want to look into the affiliations of the four you recovered."

The President rewound the events in his memory. "You're right. There were nine aboard. Four were found. Three, including myself were 'beamed up' to your shuttle. That means, two escaped."

After a pause… "Mr. President you asked for this meeting…" Michael prompted.

"Yes. Yes, I did."

After another awkward silence… "And…" Michael prompted again.

"Yes. Yes. Sorry… I'm just now realizing that two of the kidnappers escaped."

After more silence, the President shook his head sharply. "My daughter tells me that you are the most recognized person on the planet and the most well liked. How is that possible?"

"Sir, you are the political leader of about 150 million people. I'm hoping that you have a better idea of that than I do."

"I think it's because you give them hope. You're telling them you can solve climate change, improve health care, give them free food

195

and electricity." The President speculated. "But what worries me is whether or not you can do these things?"

"Would you like to see a demonstration?"

"At this point, my daughter has made me watch enough videos that I've absolute confidence you can do a compelling demonstration. What I'm less confident about is whether or not you can deliver millions of devices in the short amount of time that people are expecting. I'm also worried about distribution."

"We're promising a power cube and replicator to every household. You have about 40 million households?"

"A few less than that, I think. Maybe 38 or 39 million."

"Over what time frame do you envision this happening?"

"Less than a year. But, to distribute 39 million units in one year would require distributing about 750,000 units a week, which is 150,000 per day if they are only distributed Monday through Friday. I would be surprised if you could do that."

"Indeed. We cannot. But, starting next week, we'll have the capacity to deliver about 250,000 devices each day. So, you would only need to help us determine the locations of the deliveries."

"How? How is such a thing possible?" The President struggled to believe such a thing could be true.

"Using our transporters. Each transporter can deliver a pair of devices in less than one minute. That's 1,400 household deliveries of two devices per day per transporter pad. We'll have over 100 transporter pads available."

"And you can put all that capacity to use in Mexico?"

"No. But, if you sign today, you would be fourth in line and could start getting significant deliveries as early as next week, which would cover all of Mexico in 2 years."

"Let me ask you about another concern of mine, the cartels. They will attempt to steal entire shipments and sell them on the black market. They will do break-ins to steal units that have already been delivered and sell those also. Do you have a way to help prevent this?"

"We have numerous possibilities. Our plan is to key units to locations, so they stop working if moved from their certified location. Every unit will be tracked, so if it is reported stolen, it can be returned."

"Michael, I'm so impressed. What have I not asked that I should've asked?"

"Once you have signed, one of our people will contact the person you designate to clarify details of the units and on the roll out/delivery plan. Mexico will have a fair amount of work to do, so your bureaucracy will probably be the limiting step in the first weeks and months," Michael smiled. "Have I enticed you to ally with the Confederation?"

"Already signed." The President pulled a signed document from his suit pocket and handed it to Michael.

"Mr. President, thank you. I have great passion for the people of Mexico and look forward to working with you to serve them."

12,000 MILES ABOVE ATLANTA, GEORGIA

As Michael materialized in the cabin, he heard Charles say, "Welcome back, Michael. You were successful I assume?"

"Surprisingly yes. We now have five letters of intent."

"Israel, Georgia, Estonia, Canada and Mexico? How much is that?" Charles asked.

"Only 2 and a quarter percent."

"China's next. Who's after that?"

"India and Pakistan."

"Well, if we get those three, we'll have it won't we?

"Not quite. Those will only bring us to 40% of the world's population. And it's unlikely we'll get all three based on a first visit."

"How is that going to play with Fleet?"

"Not a problem. Fleet will get here on Day 8, hoping we have signed one or two countries. Once they understand the demographics of Earth, three countries dominating the other 200+, they will see the wisdom of picking a handful of small countries and making them very prosperous. How's the clean-up going in Jordan and Iraq?"

"It's going very well. The Jordanian and US Armies work well together and are very focused and grateful for the technical assist. Almost all the radioactive material has been isolated. When Fleet gets here, they can refine it into fuel.

"Iraq is a different story. We're about halfway done. About half the effort is going toward protecting the remediation teams from the locals. Sadly, Iraq is a very broken place," Charles replied.

"Any chance an alliance with us could change that?"

"That's way above my paygrade boss. But truth is, I doubt it."

"Michael," Elsie called out. "We're above the ranch. The plan is to 'beam' everyone down except you and Charles, then 'beam' Jiaying and Mei up."

"Is there time for Charles and me to check in on Agent Patterson?"

"Ten minutes max. We'll be landing the shuttle in China which takes a lot of time."

"Great. Beam Charles and I directly to the tank farm."

TANK FARM, KOHALA RESEARCH LAB

Julie was very happy to see Michael and Charles appear in the tank room. She'd been trained on all this equipment years ago, but the memories just weren't reloading.

"Charles!" Julie greeted Charles with a big hug. "Long time no see. How's it going in the Middle East?"

Charles and Julie had trained together back home for this mission.

"Good to see you, Jules. The nuclear clean-up in Jordan will be done soon. Iraq will take a little longer. I see you inherited Agent Patterson."

"Speaking of the good agent..." Michael drew their attention back to the issue at hand. "These numbers look too good to be true. Charles can you confirm these readings?"

Charles went over to check the equipment. Although the equipment was functioning correctly, a scan of the settings showed one red light and several yellow lights on the leg sensors, indicating that they had either come loose or stopped functioning. "Not sure if it matters," Charles said. "But several of the nerve sensors in his legs are not functioning properly. I'm going to see if we can re-initialize them."

After several minutes at the controls, he said. "Got them back. Apparently, the sensors got jammed and couldn't restart themselves. The readings should start shifting and will take a minute or two to stabilize."

Michael and Julie monitored the readings, which took a sudden turn for the worse, then slowly reversed.

"This is concerning," Michael said. "The nerve regrowth readings have fallen substantially."

Charles looked at the data Michael was watching. "I think I know what's going on. The previous readings were the average of nerve integrity among those being measured. See down here..." He pointed to some coverage indicators. "The nerves in the ankles and feet were not being included in those readings. That's why the average dropped when the sensors came back."

He flipped to another screen. "But, too early to draw any conclusions. See these…" He pointed at a 3D image of a foot with thousands of little lights inside. "All the black dots are sensors waiting to update. See they are one-by-one turning to a color. The green ones show fully regenerated nerves. The yellow ones are greater than 50% recovered. The red ones, less than 50%. Once all of these have reported in, we'll get a more accurate reading."

"That's going to take a while isn't it?" Julie asked.

"Maybe another 10 minutes. I'm surprised this didn't trip an alarm. But I think he's going to be OK. See…" He pointed to the steady advance of yellow and green lights down the ankle and across the foot. "Very few red lights. When we started this three days ago, it was solid red. The agent has made a remarkable recovery."

"What about the de-aging toxin?" Michael asked

Charles brought up another screen showing where the toxin accumulation was. "Curiously, it appears the same sensors were at fault. See…" He pointed to another image of the same area, this one showing concentrations of de-aging toxin. "The dead nerve regeneration sensors were causing the toxin sensors to read high." Charles flipped back to a screen showing the aggregate readings. "Well, look at that! Toxicity score back in the safe zone. Nerve regeneration nearly at a level where we can pull him from the tank. I think Agent Patterson is going to make a complete recovery."

CHINA

12,000 MILES ABOVE BEIJING, CHINA
Michael entered the shuttle cockpit and took the seat next to Elsie.

"Hi Michael. The setup for this one is similar to what we did in Georgia. The President has asked us to appear in front of the Great Hall of the People, which is adjacent to Tiananmen Square. Sensors indicate a large crowd. They also show an empty area right at the foot of the stairs leading up to the Great Hall. Ready to start descent?"

"Ready."

BEIJING, CHINA
The Chinese President stood at the top of the stairs leading up to the Great Hall. Several ranking members of the party were there with him. He whispered to them, "Be prepared. Their space craft will appear momentarily. Half a million people are watching you. Don't let the people see you jump."

No sooner than he said it, the craft appeared, and a ripple of excitement passed through the square.

The honor guard that bracketed the landing zone tightened up a little, but it was well understood what the consequences would be if they were not perfectly still and respectful.

A door started to appear on the craft's once smooth surface. The honor guard tensed as they saw it form. Then the door opened, and a man stepped out. The guard facing the man stepped forward as he'd been instructed to do and saluted the man. Michael returned the salute, then dropped it. Then the guard said in barely passable English. "Welcome, Ambassador Michael, to the People's Republic of China."

Michael replied in flawless Mandarin Chinese. "Thank you, Captain. It's a pleasure to be here and to meet you." Then he held out his hand, which the captain shook.

The Captain flinched, thinking. *How can this man that looks so American, speak our language with the polish and finesse of our leaders?*

The crowd had fallen silent. The only sound was the whine of some video drones filming the greeting.

"Would it be acceptable for me to greet the other guards?" Michael asked.

"Yes, but I am to accompany you, if that is acceptable," he replied.

"Thank you, Captain Chu."

How does he know my name? Captain Chu thought.

Charles came out to stand with Michael, then the three of them proceeded around the ring of guards, being introduced by Captain Chu and greeted by each. Michael thanked them for their service and the gracious welcome.

Captain Chu led Michael and Charles up the steps, where they were greeted by the president.

"Thank you for inviting us to meet with you, Mr. President. Allow me to introduce Charles Wong, Consul General-designate for the Consulate we hope to open in your great country."

"Consul Wong. It is a pleasure to meet you," the president replied.

The crowd had remained remarkably quiet so far. But the sound level had been steadily increasing and had an optimistic tone. Michael briefly opened his senses and felt great hope from the people, curiosity from the President, but something much darker from the assembled party leaders.

"Ambassador Michael, our plan is as follows. I will address the crowd extending a warm welcome to the Confederation and its representatives. Then you will be allowed to address them also. Our custom is that anything said by a foreigner in this setting would be positive words of hope for a great relationship, but no specifics. With a crowd of this size, it is important to be brief, positive and non-specific.

"Once you are done. We'll adjourn to some space within the Great Hall where we can talk. Is that acceptable to you?"

"Yes, Mr. President. Please proceed."

The President went to the podium and began speaking. His voice boomed across the square from the loudspeakers spread throughout. When he finished, Michael was shown to the podium. As he began to speak, the crowd erupted in excitement. They had never heard a westerner with such complete mastery of their language and its poetic use. Michael could feel the swell of optimism coming from the crowd and the ever-darker resentment coming from the party leaders behind him. Michael kept his speech short, only three minutes, and expressed

201

great respect for China, hope for peace and prosperity between their peoples, and for the future of China.

The crowd roared in delight as he finished. As they quieted, the President began speaking again, briefly thanking Michael for visiting China and addressing the people, then he dismissed the crowd.

...

After some discussion, it was agreed that Michael's extended party would join the President and senior party members for further discussion in a conference room in the Great Hall. Michael was impressed by the comparative age and history of this facility; he'd not seen anything comparable on Earth.

The dynamics among his Chinese hosts were quite a bit different from the other world leaders he'd met. There was calculated respect among them, but little camaraderie. At some level that made sense, as there were a lot of people that wanted these jobs and they were functionally lifetime appointments, so competition was intense.

A long table had been set up in the conference room with seven chairs on the Chinese side, and five on the Confederation side. There were also lots of chairs around the edges of the room, some already populated by unintroduced staff.

The President was the last to take a seat and began immediately, "Michael there are a great number of topics that we should discuss. I think the one that is most important on our minds is... Why are you here?"

Michael replied, "My species is over 2.4 million years old. When we were young, about 100,000 years old, we discovered that our planet would be destroyed in 6,000 years. It took a great deal of effort to find new worlds we could settle and to develop the technologies we would need to reestablish our civilization elsewhere. No other species reached out to help us, although over time we learned that there were many species aware of our plight. Some were even able to help. But they chose not to.

"Since those ancient days, we have been deeply committed to finding young species and helping them become part of the larger interstellar family. Most of the alliances that we formed have greatly benefited both parties. The alliance expanded and now includes over 1 million different planets and tens of thousands of different intelligent species.

"Our first visits to Earth were about 25,000 years ago, before your species became the dominant species on Earth. About 2,000 years ago we sent the first full Ascendant teams to Earth to study you in more detail. I led one of those two teams, the one in the Middle East. One of my colleagues led the team that came to China.

"Through those encounters, we came to believe that humanity had something special to offer the larger intergalactic community, so humanity was put on a fast track for first contact. I was elected to lead the mission.

"Does that answer your question?" Michael asked.

"I struggle to believe that someone who looks thirty years younger than me, would claim to be over 20,000 years old." He said with a little more sarcasm than Michael cared for.

"That is understandable. We come from a world that is far more advanced than yours. So much more advanced that there is very little about us that humans can comprehend. That is why we come to you in your own form, offering small gifts that are well beyond your technological reach, but still within your imagination."

Sensing that he might not have come out on top of that one, the President said, "Changing topics, I hear that you attempted to decapitate the Russian government."

"It would be fairer to say that I saved the Russian government from decapitating itself."

"And how would that be?" The President frowned.

"I presume that you're aware of the nuclear weapons ban I put in place after Iran attempted to nuke Israel?"

"You claim that you have banned use."

"Trust me. Any nuke launched will detonate on lift off. If you don't believe me, then launch one... But please, not one near here." Michael laughed.

The president got the joke and laughed along with him.

"However, they did not launch this one. They made the mistake of arming one somewhere close to where I would be. Something that I understand they have done to you four times."

The President felt stricken. *How could he know that!*

"You should assume that I know everything," Michael said, then added. "So, what did you do about the tactical devices they attempted to use on you?" As he asked, Michael also pushed the thought that lying might result in the President's death.

"We dismantled them at the cost of several patriotic lives."

"Well then, you must see the humor in what we did. We simply returned the bomb to its rightful owners."

The President was silent for a moment, before asking, "So you did attempt to decapitate the Russians?"

"No. Returning a live bomb would be as criminal as having planted it in the first place. Instead, we beamed all the explosives and fissile material into space, then returned the shell—with the timer still counting down."

"But what about the lives lost?"

Michael burst out laughing. "A handful of men decided to kill 500,000 others. And YOU complain that three of them allegedly killed themselves when faced with their atrocity!"

"What do you mean killed themselves?"

Michael pointed at the television monitor on the wall. It suddenly started playing the video of the final seconds of the ill-fated helicopter.

"How do we know that's real?"

Michael let the question hang out there for a second. "This is becoming tedious."

He heard one of the junior people sitting around the side of the room gasp as Michael asked, "Have the bodies been found? Is there any sign of radiation at the crash site? Surely you have some modicum of technology to determine such things!"

For the first time, Michael sensed fear, not hatred, from the party officials.

"Yes. We have such technology. It shows no radiation. And no, we can only account for one body, the pilot that was shot in the head."

"Instead of arguing about things you already know the answer to, why don't we negotiate a very simple deal? Maybe we can show some good will toward each other."

"I'm listening," the Chinese President replied.

"The Russians are planning to file a complaint with the United Nations. I want you to veto it."

"I hear the request. What do I get in exchange?" he asked.

"Many things." Michael smiled, then pointed to the screen, which showed a sequence where the Chinese communist party issued similar orders to use tactical nukes against the Russians. "First, I will not disclose that."

"Second, I will not disclose your cover-up of previous tactical nukes that Russia has used against you."

"Last, and by far the most important, I will not dismiss your application to ally with the Intergalactic Confederation of Planets."

"Why?" One of the party members asked. Michael heard another muffled gasp from the sides of the room.

"Because, the people of any great nation simply don't deserve to be punished because of the arrogance and stupidity of their leaders, whether it be China, Russia, or the United States," Michael said without emotion.

The President nodded to the party leaders, who in turn nodded to the President. An attendant came running to the table carrying some papers. She handed pages to the President and the six party members. The leaders signed the documents, which were subsequently gathered up and presented to Michael. It was the signed Letter of Intent.

"Thank you, gentlemen," Michael said with a bow of respect. "This is a good day for China, and for all mankind. As soon as we can come to an agreement on a consular office, Charles will move to China and we can begin our work together."

Then he and his team simply disappeared.

12,000 MILES ABOVE BEIJING, CHINA

"Michael." Elsie said. "Glad to have you back on board. A lot happened while you were down there. How did it go? You were only gone for 90 minutes."

"Quite well. We now have six allies. With China on board, other nations will start clambering to join. What's going on?"

"The Russians and Iranians seemed to know that you were occupied. A Russian nuclear site was totally devastated."

"Do we have tape on the cause?"

"Yes. And an entire Iranian missile site and its weapons assembly site have been destroyed."

"Let me guess. They're both blaming us?"

"You've got it. And we have tapes of both events."

"Release them to local news agencies. If we see nothing in 15 minutes, then release to all news agencies worldwide."

"Some good news, too." She smiled. "Agent Patterson is out of the tank. He should be waking up around the time we land."

"Excellent!" Michael said with a smile.

TANK FARM, KOHALA RESEARCH LAB

Agent Patterson was on a gurney. His body had been washed, dried and dressed in a hospital gown. The wake-up sequence was just starting. Julie, in the lead while Michael and Charles were away, was feeling relieved. "OK, Team. We have 10 minutes to get him into a comfortable bed in the treatment room over in the Residence. Let's go."

The gurney was just a modified grav pallet. It floated smoothly over any approximately level surface. As they reached the treatment room, they heard the shuttle coming in for a landing. *Looks like Michael will make it in time,* Julie thought.

Noelani and Kale were the last people Agent Patterson had seen before losing consciousness, so they were there at his bedside as he started to stir.

"It's OK, Agent Patterson." Noelani gently touched his arm. "You are safe."

He opened his eyes. Then blinked several times before they eventually settled on Noelani. "You were the ones that came to save us..." He coughed several times.

"Where are the others?" He frowned, then coughed again as he looked around. "And, where am I?"

Michael walked into the room as the Agent spoke his first words. "Agent Patterson. Welcome back to the world of the living. My name is Michael. I am the one you were coming to visit the night your team wandered into the bog.

"Your team is safe. After initial treatment here, Hawaiian Civil Defense transported the injured to hospitals elsewhere in Hawaii. You had already fallen into a deep coma and the medical facilities here are far superior to any others on Earth. So, they agreed it would be better if we kept you in our care for the time being."

The agent seemed torn about how to react. "How long have I been here?"

"Four days," Michael replied. "Your wife will be arriving in a couple hours. She came shortly after you were reported missing and finally contacted us earlier today."

"How badly was I hurt?" he asked.

"This is difficult for me to tell you... But you and four other men were pronounced dead by your medic on Sunday evening. As I said before, the medical facilities here at the ranch are vastly superior to any others on Earth, so we were able to bring all of you back. But your case was especially severe. Your liver and kidneys had stopped working and you were in septic shock. The bog that night contained high concentrations of fire ant venom. Your life was already at risk from the number of centipede stings. The fire ant venom in the bog pushed you over the edge.

"We were able to put your legs in stasis, so that we could treat the direct threats to your life. At the time, we assumed that your legs were lost. Curiously, your legs started responding to the neural regeneration that we were using, so we took them out of stasis then left you in the neural regenerator until about an hour ago.

"Your prognosis is good. Most of you is in far better condition than it was when you left Honolulu. The treatment we gave your heart, lungs, liver, kidney and central nervous system took away about 20 years of wear. So, your life expectancy has increased by 10 to 20 years. Your legs are the problem. We were able to get back 80 to 90 percent of the motor control to the legs. And we were able to remove the necrotic tissues that would've caused you to lose them altogether. But it'll take quite a bit of physical therapy to restore them to full function."

"I guess I owe you my thanks." The story left Patterson feeling humbled.

"Agent Patterson, there's something else you should know. The Special Agent in Charge chose not to believe the warnings he'd been given about conditions on that trail. His actions led to the deaths, then un-deaths, of five of his men. When Hawaiian Civil Defense came to evacuate your teams, he was taken into custody. A federal judge signed the arrest warrant.

"I've subsequently met with the President, and an executive order was signed granting this property diplomatic status. I'm deeply sorry for the injuries that you incurred."

"Wow. That's a lot to take in." A pause... "You said my wife is coming soon. Does that mean I'm being discharged?"

"I wouldn't recommend that. We need to watch you for at least another 24 hours, in case there are pockets of infection that we weren't able to detect. But beyond that, we invite you to stay here for your physical therapy. Your wife can stay as well. There is no charge for services. And I think the FBI will grant you paid leave. We hope you will stay and will accept our friendship and hospitality, despite the ill-guided mission that led you here."

"I obviously need to receive the department's and my wife's blessing first, but I think I'd like to continue my treatment here with your team. Thank you."

Noelani, sensing that Michael had accomplished his objectives for the meeting, interrupted their conversation. "Agent Patterson, you must be starving. You haven't eaten anything in four days. Could we bring you some food?"

"Thank you Noelani," Michael said. "Agent Patterson, it was a pleasure to speak with you and I'll check in once your wife arrives."

PRESENCE PROJECTOR, KOHALA RESEARCH LAB

"Jo-Na." Michael walked up to his friend in a projection of his natural body. They bumped paws, then embraced.

"Mi-Ku. I hope you are well. I have some good news for you. We got underway a bit earlier than expected and have been underway for about 36 hours at this point."

"That's very good news. When do you think you'll arrive?"

"The chronometer says about 84 hours from now."

"That I am glad to hear. Things are moving fast on Earth. We now have six signed allies, representing over 20% of the planet's population. The largest power, even though it has a relatively small population, will be signing soon."

"Excellent. I knew I made the right choice coming myself. We are bringing two capital ships, 10 cruisers, 21 fast attack ships, 2 civil engineering ships, 2 industrial replicator ships and 5 freighters. I anticipated that you would be successful and would need help building out your Embassy and consulates, not to mention producing and distributing gifts. Once word got out that the Ancient Sentient had interest in this mission, a lot of people asked if they could participate."

"Good. We're going to need all the help we can get. Also, two countries have proven to be a significant problem."

"How significant?"

"They tried to destroy us with a miniscule, primitive nuclear device, which we deactivated without issue."

"And..." The Senior Fleet Admiral asked, knowing a deactivated device on its own could not be a significant problem.

"Once it was deactivated, we returned it to the leaders that had authorized its use."

"Please tell me you didn't return the deactivated device to the capital with its count-down timer still counting down." After some silence... "Not again!" They both broke out laughing. "So, why are they complaining?"

"They attempted to drop the device in a frozen river. When it became clear that they would not get it there in time..."

"No. Please don't tell me they took their own lives!" The Fleet Admiral interjected.

"Well, as honorable as that would have been, these are not honorable men. They killed the pilot of their craft, then jumped out. Only the dead man has been found. And he is very dead. We found his executioner and are reviving him. The third is still missing."

"Mi-Ku. Why are we considering admitting these people?"

"Because there are about 8 billion on this planet. 99% are honest, good people, better than the galactic standard. And 1% are pure evil."

"Has the infection already arrived?"

"I don't think so, and if it has, we've never seen it this quiet before."

"OK, so tell me about the significance of this problem."

"The perpetrators are filing charges against us with the feckless world government."

"Will these charges succeed?"

"No. They will be overturned by veto. But I'm thinking about another option."

"I'm not liking this already."

"We have six allies, representing 20% of the world's population now. The attack was against the Confederation. What if we had 51% of the population by the time charges were filed?"

"You were the target, right?"

"Yes." Michael said.

"Then jurisdiction would fall to me," the Fleet Admiral concluded.

"What if we only had 40%?"

"Then, I could not preside. Nonetheless I could probably intimidate."

"Would it matter if they had made a second attempt that failed under 'Backfire' protocol?"

"They didn't!"

"And, if one of their allies had made a 'successful' attempt and a backfire attempt?"

"Mi-Ku, what have you gotten us into?"

"There are a handful of rogue nations on Earth. Their people are as honorable as any other. But their governments have been hopelessly corrupted."

"That's why we don't get involved this early. The people must prove themselves by overcoming the corrupt ones," the Fleet Admiral reminded him.

"Even though this imbalance is why the Ancient Sentient asked me to come here?"

A long, long silence followed.

"So, what do you want me to do?"

THE RESIDENCE, KOHALA MOUNTAIN

"Jiaying?" Michael called out.

"Here, Michael," she replied, somewhat sleepily.

"Do we have a plan for tomorrow?"

"India wants to meet ASAP. So, I set it for 9:00 AM tomorrow in India, which will be 5:00 PM here tomorrow."

"OK. I need to get some sleep before heading off to India. So, let's not schedule any other visits before. But I would like to have conversations with King Abdullah of Jordan, the President of the United Sates, the Prime Minister of Canada, and the head of state of any European Union country that would like to have a short call with me, 30 minutes max. Also, see if it is feasible to get me meetings with one or more of Nigeria, Egypt, South Africa, or Kenya after the India meeting."

"Will do, boss. Should I alert Elsie? And who are you taking? Sanjit, I presume? Who else?

"Sanjit for sure. And, I've changed my mind about the Mbanefos. If you can get us one or more meetings in Africa, I'd like to bring them. Be sure that they are outfitted with Level 1 personal shields. I don't want them to take any risk. Let's also add Catarina Torres from the San Diego research facility. She is designated for Brazil, so it would be good to get her some exposure."

"Great. I will check in with you at 4:00 PM. I'll also alert Elsie and the team on the schedule."

...

Michael had mixed feelings about including Emmanuel and Bahati Mbanefo on his upcoming trip to Africa.

In a previous avatar, he'd first met them in South Africa at the start of World War II. His mission at that time had been to confirm deposits of a very rare substance known as transluminide. Transluminide was the critical element used in zero-point energy devices. It enabled them to siphon energy out of the quantum foam. Most star systems had a few pounds of it somewhere on one of the rocky inner planets. Earth appeared to have several deposits, possibly totaling as much as 25,000 pounds. Unfortunately for most civilizations, these deposits were usually destroyed somewhere in the primitive stages of the civilization's development, because they were usually located close to more common substances like coal.

Michael had already confirmed a 'massive' 750-pound deposit on the western flank of Kohala Mountain in Hawaii. He was in the process of confirming another sizable deposit in the mountains north of Johannesburg. The challenge with the South Africa deposit was that it was too close to civilization. Someone would see him doing his work, so he needed a legitimate cover.

He ended up synthesizing some gold that he used as evidence to stake a claim in the area where sensors indicated the transluminide to be. In the process of staking the claim, he'd met the leaders of the odd South African unity government, formed by the pro-Afrikaner National Party and the pro-British South African Party. J.B.M. Hertzog led the National Party. He was quick to claim a share of the new enterprise. Not to be outdone, Jan Smuts, leader of the South African Party was quick to claim another share. Their greed played straight into Michael's hands and before long, Michael formed close relationships with both men.

Needless to say, each man wanted a representative on the team working the gold claim. Each assigned an idiot whose only apparent skill was being cruel to the black crew that would do the actual work. Emmanuel and Bahati Mbanefo had been hired onto the mining team. Emmanuel was a huge, strong man. Bahati, his wife, was slender, shapely and an excellent cook who bubbled with warmth and joy. Over the weeks they spent in the mountains, Michael became close friends with the Mbanefos, something that really upset the useless, arrogant idiots assigned to the team by his partners.

When the Nazis invaded Poland on September 1, 1939, turmoil broke out in South Africa. Michael was called back into town in an attempt to broker a deal between his allies, Hertzog and Smuts. Hertzog did not think it was in the Afrikaners' interests to support Great Britain in the war. And Smuts would not even consider reneging on their obligations to Great Britain, or by extension, Poland. The struggle that ensued was short lived. Hertzog was ousted. Smuts took over with vengeance. And Michael needed to secure the transluminide as quickly as possible, because his gold claim would be raided to support the war effort.

Michael arrived back at the dig site to find one of the idiots attempting to rape Bahati. Michael pulled the man off her and threw him to the ground. The man pulled a gun and told Michael that he had arrived just in time to see how a real man was supposed to treat a black woman. When Michael stepped in the way, the man shot him, which was when Michael realized that he'd forgotten to wear his shield.

It was also the day Michael did something he'd never contemplated before. He transported the man into space. Michael, bleeding profusely, went to check on Bahati, who had been beaten badly, but not violated. As he began to fade, he did three things almost simultaneously. He transported the deposit up to the shuttle, which caused a cave-in a hundred yards north of him. He transported the very dead and frozen idiot back down on top of the cave-in. And he removed the bullet from his lung. That's when he passed out.

Emmanuel, working about a mile away, heard the gunshot and the cave-in, and came running back. When he got there, he found Bahati beaten and bloody, and Michael bleeding out next to her. Bahati told Emmanuel about the man that attempted to rape her and how Michael defended her, but she didn't know where the man had gone. Noticing smoke rising from the nearby dig site, Emmanuel found the rapist, who had apparently been killed in the cave-in.

They rushed Michael to a nearby medical facility, where he was pronounced dead. The Mbanefos went into hiding, because any black person associated in any way with a dead white person was likely to find themselves in the morgue in short order.

They were found two weeks later and taken to jail, where they would be tried the next day. That night, Michael appeared in their cell and asked them to trust him. Then all three disappeared.

THE RESIDENCE, KOHALA MOUNTAIN

Michael snapped back from his recollections to hear Joel's voice calling over the intercom.

"Joel. You're on my call list. How are things going?"

"Good. The AIs figured out a way to use the Paso Robles industrial replicators to make 10 mid-sized ones, maybe a third the capacity of an industrial replicator. We've been using these to crank out shield generator parts and nanobot production parts. At this point we have enough parts to assemble two Class 1 shield generators large enough to protect small countries like Israel and Georgia. We also have five nanobot production machines running, so with an hour of Elsie's time, we could put up shields over Israel and Georgia."

"I always knew you were the best, Joel."

"Thanks, boss. Are we good to go ahead with the deployments? The Israeli President, who sends his regards by the way, says we can put the shield generator anywhere we want."

"Is the shield generator big enough to cover both Israel and Jordan?" Michael asked.

"What, has Jordan signed too?" Joel replied.

"Not yet. But I bet he would if I told him I could place him under a permanent shield in the next day or two."

"I think so… Which brings me to something else I need your permission to try."

"What's that?"

"We've figured out a way to clone Henry."

Joel's statement put Michael immediately on guard. "You know that cloning AIs is generally not allowed."

"Yes, but what I'm proposing is different."

"How's that?"

"We start with a blank AI matrix. Then, we add Henry's non-specific memories and priority stack. We do the same with the personality stacks. We use Henry's organization with a slightly undeveloped personality. Um… we will include memories of the Confederation and of training and the emotional memories of the crew. When it wakes up, it will think like Henry, behave and react like Henry. Remember Henry's training and mission. And know that he is Henry's brother. But his name will be Jacob. That's what we want to name him.

"In summary, he will wake up fully formed with all of Henry's training and knowledge of mission and crew, but none of Henry's personal memories."

"Hasn't that been tried before?"

"Yes and no. Cloning was functionally banned because they were done as direct duplicates, and generally without the original's permission. This led to breakdowns on the part of both original and clone because they stopped being individuals.

"There were a number of successful attempts where the two AIs basically became siblings. But that generally only worked when the siblings had separation, but not too much separation. Here it would work perfectly. The two siblings would have overlapping interests but separate responsibilities. They would be about half a world apart, so in regular contact, but not constant contact.

"There is even a clause in the laws governing AI production and use that allows this as long as first, the original AI consents to the partial clone, and second, the relevant authority approves the use restriction. Henry is the one who found this rule and he did it of his own accord. I didn't ask him, didn't even know such a thing was possible."

"Henry?" Michael called out. "Is this true?"

"May I answer more broadly, sir?" Henry asked.

"Yes."

"Shield AIs tend to have relatively short lives. They live in isolation, have an incredibly boring life, and extreme anxiety during the moments that are not boring. This is compounded for me. I have global and regional responsibility with only a single global-scale shield generator. Do you appreciate how difficult that is? I started searching for a solution and when I found this rule, I realized that we could use my training to create additional shield AIs. I've been built for global. Jacob could have the Middle East region. Our responsibilities would be separate. But in the really slow times, we would have someone in a similar situation to talk with. And in the really hot times, we could have backup. We could even have additional brothers to handle different regions.

"In truth sir, the only other option is to train a new AI from seed. That will take 5 years or more, and I'm sure I'll have burnt out by then. I would much rather have a long life, working with friends to protect this world and watching it grow to maturity."

"Thank you, Henry. I would like the same things, and your argument is compelling. Please send me the relevant legal references, so I can verify for myself. Assuming that I agree with you about the legality, I will proceed and inform the Confederation after Jacob is born. This is one of those situations where it's better to ask for forgiveness than permission. Thank you for speaking with me."

"Thank you, Michael." Henry dropped the line.

"How long will it take to bring Jacob online?"

"All the work is done. Just need to turn him on and give him a day of wake-up training, well more like a week or two."

"Once I confirm that Henry has sent the legal brief... Wow. Henry just sent me the legal brief. One second..." Michael used his enhanced mind to analyze the legal brief in less than 2 seconds. "Ok. We are good. Wake up Jacob at your earliest convenience once we are done.

"Next topic... I want to start personal replicator delivery in Israel ASAP. You are the consular officer in country. I would like to see 1,000 units in the field by the end of the week: 50% Jew, 50% Palestinian. Make it public. Ask Rabbi Judah Levine to publicly endorse the program and to personally participate in a Palestinian delivery. Tell him that this is a personal request from me and that I would be happy to talk with him about it."

"Got it, Boss."

"Recycling to the previous topic... I want to offer the shield to Jordan today. When can I promise it'll be up?"

"36 hours, as long as I get that hour from Elsie that I asked for."

"Great. Next topic... China signed on today."

"I guess that means Charles is gone." Joel speculated.

"Functionally, yes. Mei and Jiaying will go within a few days, as well."

"How are we going to handle shielding for them?" Joel asked, realizing the implications of an early Chinese entry.

"I'm going to ask the Admiral to help with that. He will also be helping with the Russia problem. But what I need from you is as many of those regional shield generators as you can produce. Estonia is at great risk right now. I've been holding off on visiting the countries on the Arabian Peninsula because at this point, we cannot protect them from the Iranians.

"Can you play the replicator trick again? Making more mid-sized ones we can use to increase shield generator output?"

"In principle yes," replied Joel. "In practice, I'll need more help; another person from our team or one of the other AIs. I'll also need more assembly bots or more human laborers."

"Minimize human labor for now. Who from our team would you like?"

"Farouk al-Ibrahim. And his first job should be mid-size replicators and bots: 5 more replicators, 25 bots," Joel replied immediately.

"Excellent choice, I thought you would go with Farouk. Are you keeping him in Paso Robles for now, or bringing him to Israel right away?"

"Paso. He should be able to crank out enough there in the next 24 hours to fill Elsie's shuttle. Maybe he can come with the second load."

"And gas for San Diego?" Michael asked

"Amazingly, we're holding the production levels for now, but once Farouk is gone, we'll need to do something else there."

"How is the transluminide supply holding out?" Michael asked.

Joel snorted… "Michael, you personally scored one of the largest transluminide finds in history. What you thought was 750 pounds on Kohala Mountain turned out to be 3,500 pounds, then the 7,000-pound haul in South Africa—the one that got your last avatar killed. Then another in Japan, one in the Urals, and the undeveloped mountain of it in Antarctica…

"I think our current balance is 17,500 pounds refined. And we have barely touched the deposit in Antarctica, but that would take a while to get at.

"Anyway, we have more than enough to supply the needs of a trillion humans for 1,000 years…" then Joel figured out the real question. "Fleet wants some, don't they? How much are they going to take?" he asked.

"We've shielded it well enough that they will only be able to detect 1,000 pounds. I expect they will ask for 10%. It takes a lot of energy to move capital ships between galaxies. They might even offer to extract and refine the deposit in Antarctica for a fee of 10%, plus refining losses."

"Michael, you must be one of the richest men in the Confederation!"

"No, I'm not, and don't think thoughts like that. Earth may be the most mineral-rich planet in the three galaxies, but it would be bad for them if they knew it. They are still immature and would waste the resource if allowed to. With proper guidance, they have a shot at becoming one of the most powerful worlds in the Confederation in as little as a few thousand years."

"Is that why you're here?" Joel asked.

"No. The Ancient Sentient sought me out and asked me to shepherd these people. He helped me once in a time of need, so I agreed to his request without asking why. Then again, he operates on such a higher plane that there's no reason to believe I would understand his answer."

"Anything else, boss?" Joel asked.

"No. But just to confirm priorities… First, we're creating Jacob to share shield control responsibility with Henry. Second, we need shields for Israel/Jordan and Georgia, ASAP. Third, start distribution of gifts ASAP with as much media coverage and contributions by Rabbi Levine as you can get. You're welcome to leverage me on that. And, lastly more shields. We need them for Estonia and the Baltics, Canada, Mexico and the Arabian Peninsula/Egypt as soon as viable."

"Got it. I really like this plan. Thank you, boss," Joel said before dropping the line.

...

"Jiaying?" Michael called.

"Yes Michael?"

"Any word about possible calls with heads of state? I'm thinking that Jordan is the only one awake at this hour."

"Yes. He's free for the next 45 minutes or so. Would you like me to connect you?"

"Yes please."

...

A few minutes later, King Abdullah came in on Michael's headset.

"Michael, my friend. Thank you for calling. I can't tell you how grateful we are for the help you've given us."

"It was the least we could do, sir. It was our presence in your neighborhood that drew the wrath of the Iranians. I'm told that the clean-up work is largely complete, and the radioactive material is isolated and in temporary storage. Is that correct?"

"Yes. It is. But I don't understand what the plan is for that material. Charles told me something, but I really didn't follow it."

"No need for concern about that. We have a ship on route that will take the material away from Earth. We have the means to properly dispose of it. We also have technology to extract any useful components that may be mixed in. Earth has an unusual abundance of rare materials we may be able to recover."

"When will the ship arrive?"

"I think it's due Monday night, Jordanian time. So, the last of the radioactive fallout will be off your soil on Tuesday, Wednesday at the latest. Someone from my office will contact your office an hour or so in advance. You don't need to do anything other than keep people away from the storage facility."

"Excellent," replied the King. "Michael, your people have been great to work with. I have a great deal of confidence in you and your people. And you have been very well received by everyone in Jordan."

"Thank you, sir. Have you given any consideration to our alliance proposal?"

"Yes, I've given it a lot of consideration and have one question for you. As I read It, Jordan is mostly in compliance with your terms. Is that your understanding of the situation?"

"Yes." Michael said. "Your constitutional Monarchy is well within the bounds of what is acceptable. Although that statement will have to be verified in detail before a final treaty is concluded, my expectation is that no changes will be requested to your form of government.

"In fact, that's the real reason I've called. My reading of the situation is that we are natural partners meant to be allied. So, it pains me to see you at any risk of aggression from Iran or any other foreign power. Which brings me to a proposal…

"Sign the Letter of Intent now, and we will erect a permanent shield around Jordan within 36 hours. In the interim, we'll protect you with a temporary shield. Then, once the permanent shield is in place, I can send an interim envoy to work with you and begin distribution of the other benefits."

The King was seated at his desk with the Letter of Intent already open. He picked up his pen, signed and sealed it with his seal. "Done."

"Thank you, sir."

"Michael, may I ask you a question?" He asked.

"Certainly."

"What are you going to do about Iran? And how soon before other countries in the region join? Guess that was two questions."

"Iran is difficult. Our laws do not allow us to take direct action in the situation as it stands now. They are welcome to apply for membership but will not qualify until many things have changed. I've already exercised my right to put Backfire Protocol in place…

"Is that what caused the 'accident' a few hours ago?"

"I will not deny that."

"Understood."

"In another week's time, I should be able to bring them up on charges of assaulting Confederation assets, personnel and allies—if they misbehave again."

"Who would hear this complaint?"

"A Confederation tribunal. But none of that can begin until we have enough allied nations on Earth. We never directly interfere in a planet's affairs until we have a certain level of invitation to interfere. Which brings me to the other countries in the region.

"You were drawn into this because of the actions of a rogue nation. So as not to bring that on any of your neighbors, I'm holding off on pursuing agreements with them until such time as I think it is safe. Of course, I will accept a letter of intent from any qualifying nation at any time."

"Thank you, Michael. We, like you, care for the peoples of this region. But I think you are the one who can usher in the peace that we all want."

"Thank you, sir. Our envoy will be in touch with your office soon."

"Thank you again, Michael." The King cut the connection.

...

Joel, Michael messaged, *Jordan is in. Coordinate with Farouk al-Ibrahim, who is copied.*

Farouk, you are acting envoy to Jordan. We are still on track for you to be Consul General to Egypt, but I need your help with Jordan this week. You are to work with King Abdullah to accomplish whatever he needs, but your principle job is to establish relations and distribute gifts.

Joel, we need a minimum of 1,000 sets for Farouk to distribute.

Farouk, make sure it is understood that your assignment is temporary and that I'll be recalling you for 6 – 8 hours of non-Jordan duties over the coming week.

THE RESIDENCE, KOHALA MOUNTAIN

"Jiaying?" Michael called. "Anything else for me before I hit the sack?"

"Hi, Michael. Tehran and Moscow are still demanding an audience. We also got a call from the King of Saudi Arabia, who would like a few minutes of your time as soon as possible."

"OK. If you can connect me to Saudi in the next 15 minutes, I will take the call."

...

"Michael," said the King. "Thank you for taking my call. I know you are busy, so I'll cut to the chase if that is OK with you."

"Thank you, sir. My apologies for not connecting with you sooner. It's been my belief that you were safer from Iranian attack, if we waited a few more days to connect publicly. But this call is secure, so I'm pleased to be able to speak with you now."

"Thank you. My advisors were telling me otherwise, but in my heart, I believed that you were holding back to protect us.

"My concern is as you say. I wanted to contact you to assure you of our interest in allying with the Intergalactic Confederation of Planets. I know that many in the West spread false rumors about affairs here in Saudi Arabia. I want to be able to set the record straight as soon as possible, so that we might be able to come to accord quickly."

"Thank you for saying that, Your Majesty." Michael replied. "I'm aware of both the claims against you and the realities of life within the Kingdom. Forgive me for speaking bluntly, no offense is intended. But things are probably a bit worse for your people than you've been told. Nonetheless, rest assured, you're close enough to compliance with our terms to be admitted provisionally, as long as you are willing to negotiate in good faith. Are you willing to negotiate in good faith?"

The King was less than happy to be addressed so bluntly, but he swallowed his pride and said, "Thank you, Michael, for your consideration. I give you my word that we're more than willing to negotiate in good faith and look forward to your help and counsel in making an alliance reality.

"If I may, what is the next step? We'd like to join immediately, but I will lose face in front of my people if I did so without a visit from you first."

"I fully understand. So, this is what I suggest. Your country is at risk if I come to visit in the next couple days. So, would it be acceptable if I came early next week, maybe Tuesday or Wednesday."

"I would prefer that you come sooner. But I also realize that we're a small country in a contentious part of the world, so I defer to your wisdom on the timing."

"Thank you, Your Majesty. We're continually monitoring your situation and will intervene on your behalf if things go wrong in the interim. My staff will be in touch with details."

"Thank you, Michael. I look forward to meeting you and to our alliance."

"Myself as well." Michael replied, cutting the connection.

...

"Jeremy." Michael called out.

"Yes, Michael." He replied.

"Is Noelani still up?"

"No, sir." Jeremy replied. "She went to bed about 30 minutes ago. The staff have been driven very hard this week, as have you."

"Jeremy, do you know the status of the Russian we retrieved from the Volga River."

"Yes, sir. Would you like me to read the statistics from the tank he's in?"

"Can you give me a high-level summary?"

"Yes. Noelani, Hiroshi and Yves have been tag teaming his treatment. They've been able to restart metabolic function. Most of his organs are in fair condition. However, brain activity has been slow to recover."

"Did he suffer traumatic injury to his head that caused brain damage, or is it simply damage from oxygen deprivation?"

"Mostly the latter, sir. But he also had some bruising in the brain tissue which would imply that his heart continued to beat after he landed in the water and that some blood vessels were broken."

"Odds?" Michael asked.

"Noelani seems to be very optimistic. She says 65% chance of full recovery."

"That's good news. Any word on Sergeant Butler or on Luka?"

"Sergeant Butler has been waiting up for you, hoping to catch a word. He is in the dining room enjoying a cup of tea."

"Excellent. I'll go see him. Thank you, Jeremy."

THE DINING ROOM

"Sergeant," Michael called. "How are you this evening?"

"Michael, so good to see you. I've been hoping you might stop by."

"Anything on your mind?" Michael asked.

"No, not really. Well, maybe kind of," he stammered.

Michael smiled, pouring out his compassion. "Out with it..."

"It's nothing really. I just don't feel like I'm carrying my weight around here. Is there anything I can do to help?"

"You must be feeling good."

"I feel great! Noelani feeds us lots of great food. She or Hiroshi give me massages every day with that cream of theirs. You really ought to sell that stuff. I'm getting stronger. I walked about a mile on the tread mill today, with the grav dialed up to 50%..." His voice clouded with emotion... "Last week I couldn't even feed myself."

"I know you probably don't want to hear this. But the most important thing I need you to do right now is get stronger. Work the tread mill. Work the weight machines. Eat. These are all important things despite the fact you feel like they're all about you."

"Well, they are about me!" George's frustration spilled out with more intensity than he intended.

"How's your mother?" Michael asked.

A little more emotion in the voice. "Mom is great. I haven't seen her this happy since my dad died 10 years ago. She helps cook and clean up. She's constantly encouraging Luka and Anna...."

"See."

"See what?" George was dismayed by Michael's reply.

"Your steady recovery is giving your mother hope and joy. It's not all about you. And speaking of Luka and Anna, how are you getting along?"

"Luka is a lot older than me, but he's like the lost brother I never knew about. And Anna... She's as bad as my mom, always doting over me and saying silly things like... 'If I were twenty years younger, I think I might be chasing you around the track.' Luka always laughs at that one."

"Sounds like you've also found family here."

"Exactly. That's why I want to do something to help out!"

"One more question first..." Michael insisted. "Have you met Agent Patterson yet?"

"Briefly. He seems very grateful to be alive. His wife cries a lot."

"Be gentle with her. She went through four days of hell. And be respectful to Agent Patterson, the way you would be with your uncle or something. He survived a harrowing experience. He was betrayed and abandoned by his leadership, then saved by the people he was told were his enemies. I think he's really going to struggle with that experience and could use goodwill offered by someone like you."

"I'll do my best." George promised.

"And I'm going to put you to work! Have you thought about what you would like to do?"

"Well... I agree with what you said earlier. I don't have the coordination or stamina to do much manual work. But I've been thinking I could help you with PR."

"Such as?" Michael prompted.

"I hear the news people are calling almost 24/7. The police have set up roadblocks on the road outside and all. How about if I kind of became like your Greeter... You know like they have at Walmart? Every day a new person could come in with their crew. They could interview me. My mom could tell them what happened to me. I could demo your gear. We could show them how your language thingy works.

"See. I'm not a genius like you. I'm not even a cool alien or anything. In fact, I'm not really that bright. But people tend to like me and to believe me when I tell them stuff. If they see that I can make your stuff do its magic, then they will believe that they can do it. If my mom sobs all over the floor telling people how bad-off I was, everyone will believe that I'm actually healed. More importantly, they'll know there is hope. If suddenly I can speak a foreign language, then everyone's going to want a piece of it."

"George. You're a genius and a genuinely good man. Give me a second..." Michael closed his eyes.

Jiaying. Select the news team that has been nicest to you and invite them to the Residence for an interview tomorrow morning at say, 10:00 AM. Sergeant Butler is going to show them around and give an update on his condition.

Michael opened his eyes and saw the sergeant looking at him. "You were doing the alien telepathy thing, weren't you?"

Michael burst out laughing. "Yes. But it's not telepathy in the sense you probably think it is.

"George. You know about our mission here, right? We want to form an alliance with humanity, and we're exposing you to some of our technology as an enticement..." Michael looked at the Sergeant questioningly.

"Yes. But I'm guessing that you're implying something, and I don't know what it is."

"What's going on is Phase I. We want your interest so that we might earn your friendship. For those that we trust, there is much more than power cubes and replicators. Would you like to have telepathy? Would you like to have medical treatments that would extend your life to hundreds, possibly thousands of years? Would you like to take on the form of another being and become an ambassador to another world?

"Those are rhetorical questions. I'm not asking if you want those now. But what I'm saying is that the door is open to people like you; to know every secret, to have access to a million planets and 10,000 cultures. The process is slow, but that path is open to you if you ever want to start down it. And, there will never be any pressure to go further than you want to go. It's all opportunity.

"But enough of that. I'm arranging for your first media interview tomorrow. That's what I was doing the alien telepathy thing about.

"It's ironic... I've known since that first day that you would be a great spokesperson for us. I've been so caught up in getting you physically recovered, I overlooked the whole person. For that I'm sorry. Thanks for calling me on it.

"One of my staff, Jiaying who you have not met, will be making the arrangements. I'm hoping for 10 AM, but she will give you the starting time when it's confirmed. One of my staff needs to be the on-site coordinator. I'm thinking Noelani. You good with that?"

"Very good." George's eyes brightened.

"Go over your plan with her before the interview starts. She will know what you can and cannot talk about, and where on the premises you can and cannot take the news team. If your plan changes in real time, as the best plans always do, then ask Noelani before committing it to the news team. They will probably be recording, so ask in a way where it's OK for her to say 'No'. Like, 'Noelani, is the barn open?' Her answer will be 'No', implying that you cannot take them to the barn, but sounding like the barn is off-line right now. Got it?"

"You're really going to let me do this?" George was astonished that he'd be allowed this opportunity.

"No pressure my friend, but I have faith in your ability to read the situation and make the most of it."

"That didn't work so well in Afghanistan." He sounded bitter.

"I've read the after-action reports. It's not for one man to say whether another man's sacrifice was worth it. But George, you made a choice that saved 10 of your men and maybe 20 Afghanis. It's easy to place trust in people who make decisions like that."

George found himself sobbing. No one had ever shown him so much faith. And no one had ever done for him what Michael was doing. He felt like he'd died and gone to heaven.

"It's deserved, my friend. Let's 'introduce' you to Jiaying."

"Jiaying." Michael called out.

"Are you still awake, Michael?" Jiaying asked.

"Jiaying, I'd like to introduce you to Sergeant George Butler."

"Sergeant Butler, I'm so happy to meet you, if only by intercom."

"Hi Jiaying. Are you like an AI or something that runs the house?"

Loud laughing was heard over the intercom. "No. I work over in the barn."

"What?"

"Michael, can I tell him where I work?"

"Yes." Michael shook his head, surrendering to the situation.

"I work in the research facility located below the barn. And, in case you have watched too many stupid Sci-Fi movies, there is no probing involved. Well, not much, at least." More laughing.

"Jiaying. Be nice."

"I'm sorry, Sergeant. But I've watched so many of those movies, and they totally creep me out."

"George. This may be hard to believe, but Jiaying is my protocol officer, responsible for handling arrangements with outside organizations, like foreign governments and news agencies. Just tonight she handled the arrangements for a conversation with the head of a foreign state. She is about to become the protocol officer for the consulate in Beijing, but tomorrow... She will be your behind-the-scenes coordinator for the news agency that will be here for the interview.

"Jiaying, do we know who that is yet?" Michael asked.

"As you could probably guess, ABC bends over backwards for any chance to talk with us. But we have already given them two exclusives. CNN, MSNBC, CBS... have all been complete, entitled, assholes. Oops. Sorry, Sergeant. So I'm going with the local Fox affiliate. One of their relatively new guys is just so sweet and respectful. My judgement is that he's the only one that believes there's even a chance that we are who we say we are. So, KHON it is. The local guy from Honolulu. Not one of the national guys. Which is great. A decent honest Hawaiian guy is about to be launched onto the national stage."

"Jiaying, do we know how much time they want?"

"Trust me Michael. They will stay as long as they are welcome."

"Have you cleared them with the Chief?"

"Is that actually a question?"

"Sorry. You are the best."

"Sergeant, do you have an idea about what you'd like to do?" Jiaying asked.

"I want to start with an interview in the dining room. Can I introduce them to the staff?"

"Noelani, yes of course. Who else?"

"My mom, Pam, the Tsiklauri's?"

"Pam, no. Better if people do not know about her yet. She does the runs to CostCo, and none of us want to mess with that. Same with the Tsiklauris. I doubt that they're ready for the spotlight in the US. But even if they are, it would be better to hold them in reserve."

"So, just Noelani and my mom."

225

"Well, when you put it like that, no." Michael thought about this for a moment. "How about a different rule? Plan talking parts for you, your mom and Noelani. If you are walking in and Pam is there, or I am there, or Kale... It's OK if the camera catches that and you say hi. Clear it ahead of time with anyone else. Fair?"

"Fair," George replied with his accustomed exuberance.

"In that case. I'm going to hit the sack. I'm headed off to India and hopefully to Africa tomorrow. Good night, Sergeant and thank you for staying up to talk with me." Michael shook hands.

"Thank you, Michael. You have given me life again." The Sergeant nodded, then headed off to his room.

MORE ALLIES

MICHAEL'S BEDROOM, RESIDENCE

"Wake up, Sleeping Beauty." The melodious voice sang over the intercom. A moment later, the sound of a foghorn.

Michael yawned, then sat up and swiveled his legs out of bed. "What time is it?" he asked as the lights came up.

"5:30 AM," Jiaying replied.

"Don't you ever sleep?"

"Silly question, Michael. I'm an android operating a clone body. The body needs 4 hours sleep on average but can go days without. My AI mind can go extended periods without regeneration."

After a long yawn. "Sleep. What a gift the Maker gave humans. I must be turning into one, because I struggle to function on 4 hours a night anymore."

"What night would that have been, almighty Michael? You were down for seven hours last night. Are you sure you're not human?"

Michael climbed into the sonic shower and immediately felt better. "OK, Almighty Jiaying, what is my schedule."

"So love the sound of that title," she hummed.

"And you say I'm becoming human," Michael mumbled.

"Heard that! The schedule... Well, while little Sleeping Beauty was away in dreamland, I've been slaving away to make sure you have great bookings today. Do you want the good news or the bad news first?"

"Good news."

"OK. Well the good news is the bad news, but I'll spin it as good."

Has Jiaying been corrupted by a virus? Michael thought.

"Good news, Michael. The President of the US wants to speak with you... in 12 minutes!"

"Now I get it! OK. I'll be in my study in 10 minutes. Route the call there. Oh, could you ask whoever's in the kitchen to put a pot of coffee in my study?"

"Got it, boss."

MICHAEL'S OFFICE, RESIDENCE

"Good morning, Michael," said the American President. "Thank you for arranging a call."

"Good afternoon to you, sir. Thanks for taking time to speak with me. There are several topics I'd like to discuss with you today."

"As do I, Michael, but I suspect that our lists are more-or-less the same. OK if I start?"

"Please do, Mr. President."

"Michael, I'm worried about all the nuclear weapon issues that have come up since your arrival on the scene. Are you responsible for this?"

"I have no nuclear weapons, Mr. President. So, from that perspective, I cannot be responsible. However, Iran and Russia have used or attempted to use nuclear weapons to prevent enemies of theirs from falling under my protection. Specifically...

"Iran launched nuclear weapons against Israel, which we successfully protected that ally from.

"Russia planted a tactical nuclear weapon at a rally of over half a million people, with a timer set to detonate 15 minutes after my announced arrival time. We found that weapon, removed the explosives and fissile material, then returned it to its owners, deactivated, but with the timer still counting down.

"Iran, having already been warned that going forward, all nuclear missiles launched anywhere in the world would detonate on launch, chose to launch another weapon at Israel. The weapon detonated on launch, functionally de-nuclearizing Iran."

"Russia made a second attempt at Georgia. And learned the same lesson. There are several irresponsible and murderous world leaders that will soon be brought to justice," Michael replied.

"That's not exactly the way the Russians and Iranians are describing the problem."

"Yet they are not denying that they, at their sole discretion, are the ones that launched those weapons," Michael answered.

"You have a point there. Nonetheless, I am deeply concerned about the start of a full-scale nuclear war."

"There can be no nuclear war. Any nuke launched WILL detonate on launch. Countries still have the liberty to destroy themselves, but not to wage war on others.

"Which brings me to a related issue, I want to discuss with you, Mr. President."

"I'm not sure I'm finished with the last one."

"I think this might change your mind, sir. Early next week, a Confederation Armada will be visiting Earth. The Armada is coming at my request to help build our Embassy Complex. It will also have the manufacturing capacity to produce several billion sets of Power Cubes and Home-use Food Replicators during its stay. Every home in Israel and Jordan should get their gift from the Confederation within a week of the Armada's arrival.

"Accompanying the Armada will be two capital ships. So that you appreciate what that means, each capital ship is over 10 kilometers long and 1.5 kilometers wide, with crew and families totaling about 10 million people. Instead of parking in orbit, they are going to park about 10 miles above Moscow and Tehran.

"Any issue encountered while the capital ships are here will be dealt with quickly and finally. When every member nation has been equipped with a full level 1 shield, like the one we used to protect Israel, the capital ships will leave.

"This is not an invasion. It is not a foreign power imposing its will on Earth. But it is what friends do to protect their allies from bullies."

There was a long moment of silence.

"May I ask how many allies you have signed treaties with?"

"Six so far. Several more are close. I expect that we'll have allied with nations having over 50% of the Earth's population within the week. I hope you join that list, sir. Your neighbors have.

"What, Canada and Mexico?"

"Yes, sir. Both will have shields in about a week. Within a year, Mexico's economy will sail past yours, if you're not allied, because they will have free energy, gasoline and food. And, ironically, they will also have a shield that can be set to stop migration south from the US."

"You bastard! You are threatening to derail the greatest nation on Earth!"

"Great Nations are only great as long as their leaders make the right decisions at the right time. No one is being given a better deal than the one that was presented to you first."

The President was deeply taken back. As much as he hated it, he could see the truth in Michael's words and felt deeply shaken by the arrogance of his own position. "Michael, I'm sorry I did not see this clearly on day 1. What you have offered is wildly popular with the American people. I'll see what I can do to get this finished ASAP. Are you still looking for a location for your Embassy? Maybe I can redeem myself by helping to arrange a perfect location for you."

"I expect that the location will be agreed to on the next call on my schedule. If not, I'll have my team look for possibilities in the US. May I ask you a different favor though?"

"What might that be?"

"Take a look at the record of Sergeant George Butler. I read it earlier this week. He's the one I healed on the Good Morning America show and is now doing physical therapy at my ranch in Hawaii.

"I think the Sergeant will probably meet the criteria for the Congressional Medal of Honor. In about a week's time, I think he will be one of the most popular people in America. You might pick up a lot of votes if you get ahead of this one."

"Thank you, Michael. I'll take that under consideration."

"And one last thing sir. The raid on my ranch last week. One of your men went missing, Agent Mark Patterson. He was seriously injured when his team stumbled into a bog. My people helped get him out, but your team's medic pronounced him dead.

"As you know, we have vastly superior medical technology. We were able to resuscitate him, and he came out of his coma last night. He is weak and will require a month or so of physical therapy at our ranch to have a full recovery. He and his wife are there now. I trust that you can make arrangements for medical leave, so that he can complete his recovery."

"Consider it done, Michael."

"Thank you and good day, sir." Michael hung up with a sigh.

MICHAEL'S OFFICE, RESIDENCE

"Good morning, Michael," said the Canadian Prime Minister.

"Good afternoon, Mr. Prime Minister," Michael replied. "Thank you for taking the time to speak with me today."

"Based on the news headlines, it sounds like you've been busy."

Michael chuckled. "Indeed, we have. I seem to be circling the Earth daily."

"The Chinese announced that they've come to terms with you."

"Ah... Hadn't heard that the word was out. Yes. We had a very interesting meeting yesterday. I lived and studied in China years back but was surprised by the changes. The current government is very aggressive and very self-interested. They were quick to challenge, then once rebuffed, quick to sign on."

"As a friend and ally, may I ask how you're going to handle the human rights issue? They are clearly not in compliance with your requirements and have rebuffed, to use your word, every effort by every government in the West to make changes."

"A nation of over 1 billion people is run by about 100 men. There's only so far they can go to protect themselves. We don't insert ourselves into other people's business unless they are acting against other countries or peoples. But our presence is bringing change to the Earth. They took less time than anyone I've met so far to realize they could not stop the change, so wisely they're getting ahead of it in the hope of controlling it."

"Did we react quickly enough?" the prime minister asked in a friendly tone.

"Sir. You are completely different. You act directly in the interests of your people. You see your job as serving the people. The Chinese government sees their job as controlling their people. From our first meeting, I could see that you would ask me tough questions for the purpose of verifying if my claims were true. The Chinese, from the very first word, tested to see if I could be controlled. When it was clear to them that I couldn't be, they signed. Please do not understand those words to be a negative statement about the Chinese. Their culture evolved under much different circumstances than yours, and they dealt with those challenges competently. Which, I believe, they will continue to do."

"I don't think I've heard anyone describe the Chinese as clearly or fairly as that before. Thank you. It helps me understand them, and you, much better. Changing subjects... What's going on with all the nuclear detonations?"

Michael quickly explained the situation.

"So, this Armada is here on a peaceful mission, yet they bring two capital ships?"

"You've heard me speak of the threat that's coming. That threat is real, so all major missions in this arm of the galaxy are accompanied by one or more capital ships. Under normal circumstances, this would not be considered a major mission. But many of the Confederation's senior leaders believe that humanity has extraordinary potential. The Senior Fleet Admiral, who is also a close friend of mine, is one of them. He wanted to come personally on this trip, so needed to bring a large enough armada to justify it."

"Sounds like your people are more like ours than I might have guessed."

"Their arrival will be very good news for Earth because they have the ability, with two civil engineering ships, to complete our embassy complex in a matter of months. And the support ships have the fabrication capacity to produce over 1 billion sets of Power Cubes and Residential Food Replicators in the same time frame. So every country that signs on before their arrival will be economically reformed in a matter of months. A number of governments have already requested the installation of carbon scrubbers, so we'll also see a small but measurable drop in CO_2 levels this year."

"I'm very glad to hear that." The Prime Minister was impressed by Michael's accomplishments, so moved on to another topic. "Which brings me to another point of business. We have approval for a 100 square mile tract of land to be designated for your embassy, pending agreement on the site. There are a number of areas blocked, but huge swaths of the North West Territories and the Yukon are available to you. How soon would you like to begin the survey?"

"Most likely next Monday. I'll need to talk with the Senior Fleet Admiral and with the chief planetary engineer about the schedule and process. They both know a lot more about this than I do. But I fully expect them to want to begin the moment they materialize over Moscow."

"Someone over there is not going to be very happy."

After more pleasantries, they dropped the call.

MICHAEL'S OFFICE, RESIDENCE

"Mr. Chancellor," Michael said in perfect German. "I am Michael, the Ambassador from the Intergalactic Confederation of Planets. It is a pleasure to speak with you, sir."

"Mr. Ambassador," replied the German Chancellor. "The pleasure is mine, and what a pleasure it is to speak with another diplomat in my own tongue."

"My apologies for not connecting with you sooner. Our policy in making first contact on worlds with multiple nations is to announce ourselves globally and announce our desire to meet with world leaders, then see who responds. It allows our potential allies to choose the order in which things move, instead of making it look like we're the ones driving the process."

"Yet, you met with the US President first."

"Indeed, within two hours of my announcement, American government officials were on my property in Hawaii wishing to introduce themselves."

"Americans. So arrogant. They sent a raiding party, didn't they?"

"Some would describe it that way."

"Let me guess… Then the president calls you himself, invites you to the White House and attempts to kill you when you land."

"Same answer."

"You're a patient man, Mr. Michael."

"Your implication that the Americans functionally got the first shot is correct. I've been living among them for the last 30 years and wanted my friends and neighbors to have the first shot. I also knew that our dysfunctional government would blow it. So, they didn't really get an advantage."

"You're also a wise man, sir. If I may, I would like to discuss where we go from here. I'm told you only have 30 minutes, so there are several topics I'd like to discuss with you."

"Please, sir," Michael replied.

"My people have the shameful history of having started two world wars. We had the arrogance to believe we were superior and could dominate everyone else. We took shameful actions that nearly killed us all. My first reaction to your announcement is that you're trying to do something similar. How do you dissuade my concern?"

"That's an excellent question. Let me start by saying something we both know. The Intergalactic Confederation of Planets is, by any conceivable measure, more technologically advanced than humanity. But technology does not make us superior, it simply makes us more technologically able.

"In our view, humanity as a species has many worthy attributes. We believe that being allied with humanity will make both our peoples better and stronger. We can do much to alleviate the poverty and conflict that humanity suffers. Elevating you in that way will allow your art, music, curiosity, energy, and innovativeness to flow into the larger society of the galaxy and cosmos. We have met many great species that have enhanced each other's lives by living in harmony. We think humanity will be one of those jewels. Therefore, we come in peace, offering friendship, with the hope of earning your friendship in return."

"Reading the Letter of Intent and the proposed treaty, it seems to me that we already meet your minimum requirements and that we need to do little more than to sign. Is that your understanding?"

"Yes sir. It is. Although we'll have to do the appropriate validations before the formal treaty can be completed, once you have signed the Letter of Intent, you become provisional allies."

"That is my second problem. I understand that China has signed your Letter of Intent and therefore are provisional allies, but they're clearly not in compliance with the treaty. How do you reconcile this?"

"The Letter of Intent commits you to move toward the treaty requirements in good faith. It does the same for China. I agree with your analysis that you are more or less in compliance already and that China is not. But I believe that China will come into compliance'"

"Given my experience with them, I doubt it."

"Bear with me for a moment. Let's think this through. Within the next three months, China will be energy independent. For the first time in their history, all 1.5 billion of them will be well fed. What will happen to their government leaders if they fail to complete the treaty and the power goes off and the food machines stop?"

"They'll be executed within 24 hours. You are functionally blackmailing them."

"I agree with your analysis of the people's reaction, but not their government's motivation. They fully understand what they need to do and what will happen if they don't. They could have walked away from a deal and retained their people's support. But they didn't.

"They know what eventually will need to be done. I'm sure they wish that they had more time before they needed to start making those changes. But I think they believe they are the best people to lead the changes that will come anyway. Therefore, I expect they will embrace the intent of the treaty as well as or better than many western countries."

Silence fell for a moment before the chancellor sighed.

"Michael. You are a wise man. I will announce to my people our intent to join the Confederation in the morning. How do I get the Letter of Intent to you?"

"Someone from my office will contact you shortly. Thank you for your time and commitment, Mr. Chancellor."

"Thank you, Michael. This is a great day for humanity."

MICHAEL'S OFFICE, RESIDENCE

"Madam Prime Minister. Thank you for taking my call."

"Mr. Ambassador," replied the British Prime Minister. "It is a pleasure to finally speak with you. You have dominated the news coverage for the last five days, though it seems like much longer. Thank you for taking the time to speak with me."

"My pleasure, Ma'am. There are several things I would like to discuss with you, but I'm sure you have even more questions for me. So, would you like to start?"

"Thank you, Michael. I've read your treaty proposal and letter of intent. It seems to me that we are mostly in compliance, yet after the fiasco of our recent entanglement with the European Union, I fear that there's more you're asking of us than what's in these documents. What am I missing?" She asked.

"Excellent question. I'm well aware of the issues you've had with the European Union, the worst of which was the number of immigrants the EU required you to accept during the Syrian war. I'm also aware of the impact that had on your country. If your question is whether we're going to force immigrants on you, the answer is unequivocally no.

"But, as in all things, the answer is more complicated than just yes or no. The real issue with the immigration that occurred during the Syrian war wasn't so much about immigration as it was about being forced to take people that were not compatible with or interested in becoming a part of your society. The issue was compounded by the economic impact of being required to support those people and the strain it put on your infrastructure.

"That will never happen to alliance partners. Although we are generally in favor of free migration, meaning that people should have the right to live where they want to live, we will never allow one group of people to take over another's lands, hijack their society, or deny them their way of life.

"In all allied worlds, the basic necessities of life are free. When the European social democracies say that, they mean someone else will pay your cost of basic necessities. What we mean is that the cost of those basic necessities has been driven to zero. Our replicators make an infinite supply of premium quality food. Our power cubes provide a perpetual source of clean, free energy.

"In allied worlds, petty dictators cannot steal from their own people or exercise undue power them.

"The reason the immigrants that came to your country during the Syrian war caused so much trouble is because they did not want to be there. They would never have left their home country if there had been an option to stay. They did not want to adopt your way of life. So, they tried to recreate their old way of life in your country. Being forced to take in people who did not want your way of life and being forced to pay for having them do it was intolerable to the citizenry. That simply is not allowed in the Confederation," Michael concluded.

"Michael, your analysis is so on point. But I'm less than completely assured."

"I understand that. As Confederation members, your borders will become more open over time. But not because we force it. It will happen because your people want it. And although I firmly believe that this will happen within 5 years, it might take a thousand, and the Confederation will not force it on you.

"In fact, the Confederation does not force itself on anyone. We offer you the opportunity to join and to test the benefits of membership. Over 1 million worlds have joined. A handful turned us away and we left. We do not need Earth's resources. We need the richness of your cultures, which we cannot have if we destroy them. So respecting people's rights to live their lives in the way they want is our most sacred principle."

"I guess that's what I wasn't seeing in these documents. I feel assured now. You have my support. But, given recent history with the EU, I think that you will need to address our parliament to make the case yourself. Sadly, Parliament has become too divisive for any one of us to make the case ourselves."

"I would love the opportunity to address your parliament. Someone from my organization will contact you within the hour to set that process in motion.

"Thank you for your time today, Ma'am. I look forward to the opportunity to meet you in person."

"You as well, Michael."

MICHAEL'S OFFICE, RESIDENCE

"Mr. Prime Minister." Michael said. "Thank you for taking the time to speak with me, especially at this late hour."

"Mr. Ambassador," the Ukrainian Prime Minister replied. "Thank you for taking my call. I watched the video broadcast of your appearance in Georgia. I saw the way you greeted their security detail, healed the wounded soldier, spoke with passion to people trying to escape the oppression of Russia, everything. And I concluded that Ukraine would like to become members of your confederation.

"I have the support of our cabinet and tentative approval from our parliament. But they asked me to clarify some things before we make the application for membership. May I ask you these questions?

"Of course, sir."

"The situation in Crimea weighs heavily upon us. Many of our people live in captivity there and are treated poorly. But we are a small country and Russia is a superpower. There is nothing we can do to stop them from taking whatever they want. And our supposed allies are not willing to risk war with Russia to stop them from taking everything from us. So, our question is... Will you? Can you? Protect us from Russia the way you did for Georgia. And is there anything you can do to help us with Crimea?"

"To your first question, we can and will stop Russia from taking your lands and people once we are allied. What came before, and specifically to your question about Crimea, we may be able to help you, but we will not support you or allow you to simply take Crimea back."

"I'm deeply saddened to hear that. But you say you might be able to help..."

"Yes. If the people of Crimea want to return, then we will extend your shield to cover Crimea, and Russia will have no ability to force them back. Similarly, if they say they want independence or to be a part of Russia, then we will prevent you from taking them back by force."

"That isn't fair. The referendum that Russia took was a complete fraud. It cannot be allowed to stand."

"Not to worry. We have the means to take a fair and complete vote that cannot be compromised. And we can limit it to the people who lived in Crimea at the time of the takeover. I suspect this will go in your favor. Just as I expect such a vote might go against Georgia for the territory that changed hands in 2008."

"Are you going to do this for Israel and the Palestinians?"

"No. Israel gained territory through defense, not aggression, which is the principle that we apply. However, we will require and moderate a peace process. It has already started, and progress has already been made. As a general rule, we do not re-litigate conflicts of the past. But we do seek healing anywhere it is possible.

"Which brings me to another issue," Michael continued. "I'm sure that you're aware of the increase in aggression on the part of the Russians and Iranians this week. It is directly related to their fear of losing territory like Ukraine and Georgia. In a few days, we'll be taking direct action to eliminate that aggression.

"So, a couple of things... Do not make an announcement regarding the Confederation until we have made our move. That move will be unambiguous and conclusive. Second, do not tell anyone that the Confederation will act in regard to the Russians and Iranians. If asked, say that you have confidence in the Confederation's fairness in all matters such as this.

"Lastly, if Russia makes a preemptive strike against Ukraine in the interim, we will protect you. But please, do nothing to provoke them. Do not risk injury in the days before this matter is permanently concluded."

"Michael, the cabinet and I have the authority to sign the Letter of Intent without the consent of the Parliament. They need to approve the Treaty but not your Letter of Intent. We signed it earlier today. I was given permission to release it to you if satisfied with the answers to our questions. I am satisfied. How do I give the signed letter to you?"

"My protocol officer, Jiaying, will contact you immediately after we drop the line. She will give you instructions. It'll be easier than you might think. Thank you, Mr. Prime Minister. I look forward to a long and prosperous relationship."

"Thank you, Michael." The line dropped and Jiaying came on.

MICHAEL'S OFFICE, RESIDENCE, KOHALA MOUNTAIN

"Mr. President. Thank you for taking the time to speak with me."

"Mr. Ambassador," the Brazilian President replied. "Thank you for taking my call. I'm so impressed by your fluency in Portuguese. Few foreigners are. I was hoping for an opportunity to speak with you and am thankful for the call from your protocol officer earlier today."

"Mr. President, I'm sorry we didn't get back to you sooner. One of the things I have come to love about humanity is its decisiveness. On most worlds, heads of state are very slow to contact us. So, the first week is usually spent entirely in the media. Here, we were contacted by 20 some countries in the first couple hours, 50 by the end of the second day. We've been overwhelmed and I'm very sorry it took me three days to get back to you. The Confederation would very much like to become allies of the great people of Brazil. What can I do to make that happen?"

"Michael. Thank you for your graciousness and interest in Brazil. I have read your treaty proposal and Letter of Intent. I believe that we are mostly in compliance with the things you require of us. Is there anything that you know of that we are not in compliance with?"

"No, sir. Compliance will need to be verified by our people for the treaty to be completed, true. But there is nothing that needs to be resolved ahead of time in order for us to accept a letter of intent from you. Is there anything you would like from us before proceeding with the Letter of Intent?"

"I've been consulting with the leaders of our legislative bodies on this matter. They are generally in favor of proceeding but have requested a presentation from you in front of a joint session of the National Congress."

"I would very much enjoy making the case for Confederation membership to the National Congress. In fact, I would love to do that on Monday, if this is possible to arrange on such short notice."

"I was hoping you might say that. Congress is in session that day and has reserved time for a joint evening session, something like the Americans do for the State of the Union address. In that format, the speaker of our Chamber of Deputies would announce me. I would provide a few words of context, then you, as our guest, would be invited to address the chamber. Would that format be acceptable to you?"

"Absolutely. When your arrangements are final, please have your representative contact my protocol officer. Would you like me to bring our technology demonstration team and equipment?"

"We would love that."

"Excellent. If you have any specific restrictions or instructions on such equipment in your legislative chambers, please let my people know."

"Thank you, Mr. Ambassador."

"Thank you, Mr. President."

SPOKESMAN

Michael stepped out of his office and headed for the kitchen, where there was quite a bit of commotion. As he stepped through the doorway, the room fell silent and Sergeant Butler said somewhat guiltily, "We weren't making too much noise, were we?"

"No. My office is so well insulated that I didn't even know anyone else was up. What's going on and, Noelani, is there any breakfast left?"

"I was just about to serve when a call came in for Sergeant Butler. You want to share the news, George?"

Before the Sergeant could get a word out, his mother squealed, "He got the Medal of Honor!"

Then she started squealing some more. Luka was patting the Sergeant on the back. Anna was sobbing along with Mrs. Butler. Even Agent Patterson looked impressed.

"If you ask me, no one has ever deserved it more. Congratulations Sergeant Butler!"

"Agent Patterson, I can't tell you how happy I am to see you up and at the breakfast table. How're you feeling?"

"Michael, I can't tell you how sorry I am for being part of that raid Sunday night. Long acted way outside his authority and I was stupid enough to be deceived by it. If what my colleagues tell me is true, five of us were pronounced dead. And, you brought us back, and treated us all like family in the process. I have never been more ashamed of the agency. Our actions on Sunday go against everything we stand for and all our training. I offer you my most sincere apology."

"Already forgotten," Michael replied. "I'm sorry that you were injured and glad that we could help. How are you feeling?"

"Legs are a bit wonky. But the rest of me feels better than any time in recent memory."

"Hopefully, your legs will make a full recovery. I'm hoping that the Agency will release you to our care for the next month so we can do everything possible."

"Already done. I got word on that this morning when I checked in."

"Excellent. We needed to put you in what we call a regeneration chamber for your treatment. It was the only way we could get enough nerve tissue to grow fast enough to recover your motor functions. The normal use of a regeneration chamber is for anti-aging therapy. We had a bit of a scare yesterday morning when sensors indicated that you had de-aged to about 21 years old. For adults over 40, that can cause serious problems. We were able to adjust the settings to stop the de-aging and give your legs another 12 hours of therapy. Which is a long way of saying you should feel great, because most of your body has been reset to a biological age of 21. We've added a little over 20 years to your life expectancy."

Agent Patterson look shocked. "No wonder..." He quickly shut up, then added, "Wow! Thank you." This got a round of good-natured chuckles around the room.

Moving on, Michael asked the room, "OK. Do we have a plan for the team from KHON?"

The Sergeant piped up. "Great plan."

"Spill it." Michael chuckled.

"OK. Kale will go out to escort the journalists and their crew on to the property."

"I like the sound of that/"

"He will be outfitted in a Hawaiian loin cloth."

"What?" Michael started.

"Michael!" Mrs. Butler said sternly. "The women of America have been yearning to see more of this man's god-like physique. You would deny them?"

"What?" Michael blinked.

"Listen to this one. She knows what she's talking about," Anna pointed to Mrs. Butler.

Michael barely avoided saying "What?" a third time.

"It's OK, boss. This is what I was designed for," Kale said.

This time Mrs. Butler and Anna found themselves saying, "What?"

Sergeant Butler continued. "Kale will escort the journalists into the study, where I will be sitting, and Mom will be quietly sobbing.

"This will cause them to ask about the incident in Afghanistan. I'll tell them what I did and what happened as a result. It'll be hard to keep my hands still.

"Then, Mom will tell them that I'm being awarded the Medal of Honor for my actions that day. We'll go on to describe my disability.

I'm sure that will trigger lots of sobbing on both of our parts, none of which will be fake.

"Then, we'll tell them about the show… The goddess Noelani coming down to greet the wounded warriors. Her rubbing some cream into my neck. The incredible pain. And you saying, 'Relax into it, Sergeant. Your nerves are being revived.' By then the both of us will be blubbering, as will the crew, and as will America. Trust me on this one.

"Then, I'll tell them about coming here. Of being helped… Then, I'll point to the silly overalls. Tell them why you gave them to me. And, levitate right on up off the sofa.

"The crew will totally freak out and the host will be convinced beyond any doubt. As will America.

"Then we take a brief tour of the house, which will basically be them filming me down the hall to the dining room. Then some of your favorite coffee, some questions and an escort back to their van.

"If they've been nice, I'll invite them back tomorrow to meet some others and we may go check out some of the good people on this island.

"What do you think?" the Sergeant asked.

"Why invite them back?"

"There are enough cool things, cool stories and cool people here to bring crews back every day for a year. By offering these nice guys a twofer, the bidding will go up for the next news crew to come through."

"Twofer? Bidding?"

"Michael, for the smartest man I've ever met, you have some serious gaps in your knowledge. Twofer means, two for one. Two interviews while only having won one. Bidding means airtime. These guys have nothing to offer you, other than airtime. So, the ones that offer the most and best airtime get the next interview."

"Wow!" said Michael. "I would never have thought of that."

"See, I told you I could help out here."

"Indeed, Sergeant. Indeed."

THE RESIDENCE GATE, KOHALA MOUNTAIN

It was a cloudy, misty morning on Kohala Mountain. The gate buzzer rang and Jiaying answered. "Hello. Who is calling?"

"Hi. This is Keoni Gates with KHON News, Honolulu. We were invited to do an interview here this morning."

"Mr. Gates. Welcome. Please follow the driveway to the left. Someone will be waiting there to greet you."

The gate slowly opened, and the crew proceeded down the driveway. When they came to the fork in the road, they took the left branch. The mist was thick this morning, as it frequently was on Kohala Mountain, so they crept slowly down the driveway, where an incredibly handsome and scantily clad Hawaiian man emerged from the mist.

The on-site director, Becky Sanders, said to the camera man beside her, "You've got a shot of that guy, right?"

Keoni stopped the car as the man walked up, then rolled down his window. The man said, "Hi, my name is Kale. Welcome to the Confederation Consulate on Kohala. If you will follow me about ten steps, there will be a parking spot. It's only 10 feet from the residence, but the mist is really thick this morning. Please follow me."

They crept along for about ten feet and saw the parking spot he was pointing to. As they looked a little closer, they could see the light on the front lanai and the general outline of the house.

"Looks like this is it," said Keoni.

Kale helped them out of the car, then helped carry the equipment to the front door. He stopped to look at them before opening the door. "A couple of ground rules."

With a look at Keoni, he said, "You're Hawaiian, right?"

Keoni swallowed. "Yes. I am."

"Then you know the hazards of Kohala Mountain, right? Cliffs. Bogs. Gigantic centipedes..."

"Heard about all that."

"OK. Keep your crew tight. Don't wander the grounds. The tame areas here are just beautiful. But out 25 feet or so, there is every hazard known to the islands. Respect the mountain."

It had been a while since Keoni had heard that speech. His grandmother lived at the foot of the Koʻolau Mountains on the windward side of Oahu. Every year there would be stories of mainlanders hiking along the trails in the Koʻolau Mountains and falling to their deaths off the thousand-foot cliffs that could not be seen until you were at, or just over, the edge.

"Thanks for the reminder, my friend. What's the elevation here?"

"A little over 3,500 feet."

Keoni turned to his team. "Stay tight. The mountains here are surprisingly dangerous."

"Ready to go in?" Kale asked.

He opened the door and let them in, then led them down the hall to the living room. They entered to see Sergeant Butler and his mom.

"Sergeant," Kale said. "I'd like to introduce you to Keoni Gates and his team from KHON News, Honolulu."

"Keoni. This is Sergeant George Butler and his mother..." Kale suddenly looked panicked. He only knew her as Mom and Mrs. Butler.

"Helen Butler." She rose to shake the newsman's hand.

"Mrs. Butler, I'm so sorry. I didn't realize until just now that I only knew you as Mom and Mrs. Butler."

"Perfectly fine for you to call me Mom, Kale. I've really come to think of myself as part of this family."

Becky elbowed the camera man and whispered, "You're getting this, right?" Then she stepped forward and offered her hand. "Mrs. Butler, I'm Becky Sanders, the on-site producer for this interview. I'm so pleased to meet you."

Then she walked over to the Sergeant to shake his hand.

"Sergeant Butler. Thank you for letting us come and interview you."

"Ms. Sanders, thank you for coming all this way to hear my story. It's really something—the story, that is. Last week this time, I couldn't move my arm. Or feel your hand. What Michael does here is miraculous. I hope that you can convey the wonder of it to your audience."

"A couple questions before we get started. First, are you comfortable doing the interview here in this room?"

"Yes. I find this room to be peaceful and I'm guessing that some of the questions you're going to ask will be emotionally difficult. So, I like the idea of doing the main interview here. But I'd also like to show you around a bit afterward, maybe go down to the dining room, or something."

"That would be nice. What about time? Do you have a time we need to be done by, or can we take this slowly? I think my boss told me we had an hour. Is that right?"

"There is some stuff I have to do this afternoon. But we have until at least noon and I bet you could stay for lunch if you like. We'll have to check with Noelani on that, but she usually invites anyone here to stay for lunch."

"OK. We'll take it slow then. One last logistics item… This will film better if we rearrange a little, set up some lighting and put a little make-up on each of you. Would that be OK?"

Noelani walked in as the question was being asked.

"Hi. My name is Noelani. I'm the house manager and your official host today. You are welcome to rearrange and set up lighting, within reason. Make up… that's up to them." She nodded toward the Butlers.

"Hi, Noelani. I'm Becky Sanders, the on-site producer for this interview. I'm so pleased to meet you." She motioned to the crew. "This is Keoni Gates, who will be doing the interview. And this is Joshua Black and Christine Pierce, who will be handling the camera, lighting and sound."

"Pleasure to meet you all. Would you care to join us for lunch today? The campus here is very social at lunch time, so you might get to meet a few other people if you stay. Also, fair warning, we need to wrap this up by 1:00, 1:30 at the absolute latest. Is that OK?"

"Lunch would be great, and we'll plan to pack up and be out of your way by 1:00," Becky replied. "And thank you so much for your hospitality."

While the crew started re-arranging and setting up lighting, Keoni sat down across from George. "Sergeant Butler, while they are getting things set up, I'd like to go over the general layout of the interview I've planned, to make sure you are comfortable with the scope. I'd like to start with just some general background. When and where you were born, any interesting circumstances of your growing up, what led you to join the armed forces? That sort of stuff. I'd like to keep that part of the interview short, so we have more time to talk about how you were injured, life after discharge, how you met Michael, and your impression of the Confederation. If I'm not mistaken, you have more time among Michael and his team than anyone else and the world will be very interested in your thoughts on that topic."

"That all sounds good to me."

"Excellent. Also, if at any point you think I'm pushing on any issue too hard, just say that you'd like to move on. This is not an investigative reporting type interview, where we are trying to dig up dirt. It's about the miracle that you have experienced and your first-hand perspective on our interstellar guests."

"Thank you, Keoni. Some of this will be very emotional. That's OK. I have a good feeling about this interview."

"One last question before we start. I heard that you are being awarded the Congressional Medal of Honor. Is that true?"

"Yes, sir. I got a call from the President of the United States yesterday, telling me that I'd been selected and that he'd like me to come to Washington at the government's expense next week for the award ceremony."

The lights came up and Christine, who had just finished with Mrs. Butler, came over to the sergeant with some make-up and an applicator. "Hi Sergeant. Do you know why we do make up?"

"Yep." He said. "You need bright lights for a high-resolution image, which causes skin to look grey unless you enhance it with a little skin tone make up. Nixon was too proud to use it and ended up looking like a zombie during his presidential debate with John Kennedy."

She had already started brushing it on. "Wow! You are well informed."

"When you're a complete quadriplegic, you watch a lot of History Channel," said the sergeant.

She started laughing because of the way he said it, then abruptly stopped. "I'm so sorry. There was nothing funny about that story. You're just so..."

The Sergeant smiled at her, cutting her off. "No offense taken. I've always had a way of saying things that makes people laugh."

"OK, people," Becky called out. "We are ready to roll. Are you all set? Sergeant? Keoni?"

"Yes, we are."

"OK. Rolling in 5, 4, 3, 2, 1..."

...

"This is Keoni Gates reporting from the Hawaiian residence of Michael, the man who claims to be the Ambassador to Earth from the Intergalactic Confederation of Planets. I am here tonight to interview Sergeant George Butler, who has been nominated for the Congressional Medal of Honor, the United States of America's highest and most prestigious personal military decoration.

"Many of you have already heard of Sergeant Butler. He was the wounded warrior that was miraculously healed in front of a live audience on Good Morning America, just Monday of this week.

"Sergeant Butler, thank you for taking the time to speak with me today."

"Keoni, it's truly a pleasure to speak with you. This week has been the most incredible experience..." George paused, emotion already filling his voice. "First the healing, then the President's call, now a chance to tell America about my experiences. I'm the one that needs to say thank you. Thank you for letting me tell my story, and for letting me tell America about my experience with the Confederation."

"Sergeant, can I start by asking you some questions about your background, so our audience can get a better idea of who you are?"

"Of course."

"Is it OK if I call you George?"

The sergeant visibly relaxed. "Yes, please do. As much as I love Michael and his team here, they can be kind of formal. Guess it comes with the whole Ambassador business." He made a face. "Ah. Can we strike that? I unconditionally love Michael and his team. They are the best thing to ever happen to this world, well maybe other than Jesus."

Chuckles rippled around the room as Keoni said, "Consider it stricken."

"So, George. Can you give me the brief background of where you came from?"

"Well, I was born in the small town of Wimberley, Texas, to my mom and dad, George and Helen Butler, in 1996. Can't believe I turn 30 next year. Went to school there and graduated from Wimberley High School in 2014. Enlisted in the army a couple months later and worked my way up to sergeant in 2019. Shortly after, I took my second tour of duty in Afghanistan.

"Weren't all that many of us there at that time. Lots of talk of peace. Peace brokered by the Taliban... As if! In 2020, I was on a peaceful mission to secure the safe passage of a senior Taliban official to the peace talks when I got blown up."

A whimper could be heard from Mrs. Butler at that comment.

"I spent the better part of a year in hospitals, mercifully asleep a lot of that time, then got discharged in 2021, 4 years ago, confined to a wheelchair with no movement below my neck. The government generously allowed me to cash in $20,000 in college funds for a very fancy wheelchair with a blow stick controller, which I later found out cost them $5,000. But don't get me started on that."

"Just to make sure that I got that right... After a year in the hospital, the doctors had done everything they could and when they couldn't do any more, they discharged you?"

"Yes, sir."

"And gave you a large settlement for your disability, right?"

"As if! $3,000 a month and a wheelchair, at the cost of the college fund I had accumulated out of my pay. And the opportunity either to wait months between fills of my pain killers or spend $1,000 a month for them out of my own pocket." George broke down crying, his mom sobbing a lot louder next to him. "Don't cut the recording, please! People need to know about this."

"George, I am speechless. How did you deal with this?

George recovered long enough to say, "Can I have a minute, then can we move along?"

"Of course."

"Cameras off!" Becky yelled.

A couple minutes later, George said, "Sorry. I told you that there would be some emotional moments. But, thank you for recording that. People just need to know. They may not care. But they need to know."

Becky said, "Rest assured. We will deliver the message. Thank you, Sergeant."

Another minute… "OK, you ready Mom?"

"Yes, I am, sweetheart."

The lights came back up. "George," Keoni asked. "What was your official diagnosis?"

"Spinal damage caused by fracture of the C4 Vertebrae. That's about as bad as it gets."

"How's that? Aren't C1 to C3 worse?"

"Define worse. C1: dead on the spot. C2 or C3: dead in 4 minutes. C4: 50% die in 4 minutes. The other 50% have the life ripped out of them over the next 1, the luckier ones, to 40 years. I was one of the less lucky ones. Five years in I was shitting in my diaper at 2 AM and living with the smell all night long. You have no idea how many hours I spent praying that Jesus would just take me now, and not curse me to live another day."

Again, a long break for sobbing—George, his mom, Noelani and the crew.

George was the first to regain his composure.

"You know the funny thing… I had to go through that to fully understand what the Confederation has to offer us."

George was about to say more, but Keoni asked. "George, I know this has been hard, but can you share with us what happened on that day in Afghanistan?"

248

"Sure. I was always skeptical that we could ever achieve peace with the Taliban. But by all appearances they were negotiating in good faith. So I volunteered for the mission.

"We were heavily armored, so I almost felt safe. We went deep into Taliban territory and they acted kind of respectful. We were introduced to the local chieftain, shared tea, and had a surprisingly pleasant conversation.

"I left the room with hope that peace might actually be at hand. We transported their negotiator back toward the airbase and stopped to refuel in a little town that was known to be relatively safe. The chieftain there was a wise old man that sought to protect his town and not materially resist either side.

"I drank way too much tea that morning and used the rest room while my lieutenant supervised the refueling. Our Taliban negotiator, with his protective squad in tow, went out to give some candy and a soccer ball to the kids.

"You know, we did that a lot. On the whole, the Afghan people are pretty mellow. You see the worst of it on TV, um... no offense. But, nine out of ten are respectful, courteous people that just want to get along.

"Anyway, I come out of the bathroom and immediately see what's happening. A kid, goat in tow, is walking over to where the candy is. The side of the goat that I can see has two suicide bomb packs on it. The side facing my team and the man I am sworn to protect just looks like a goat with a harness on. And, there's this guy at the edge of the gas station with a cell phone dialing a number.

"This is the way they do it. They wrap up some kid in a bomb. Give him a bribe and walk him over to the soldiers. Despite what you see in the media, soldiers on the whole love kids and want to help them in some way, so they let the kids come up to them.

"The fancy new vest the kid has been given, is loaded full of explosive shit connected to a cell phone. When the phone rings... BOOM!" The Sergeant wept again.

After a few moments... "Can't tell you how many times I saw that. So, the asshole with the cell phone is right at the edge of the survivable range of the explosion and it's going down in 2 seconds; two seconds that feel like 10 years. I see a barrier just beyond the man and realize that if I give it everything, run full speed... I can knock the man down, which will get everyone's attention and give us all another couple seconds. That will give me enough time to leap through the air, and land on the other side of the barrier where I'll be safe.

"Off I go. I hit the bastard hard. As he falls, he drops his phone. So, in those 10 milliseconds I know I've saved the kids, the goat, my team, my subject... And in those 10 milliseconds, to the extent my mind processes anything in 10 milliseconds, I congratulate myself on having outsmarted a truly evil piece of shit. Then BOOM! The poor idiot trying to blow up the kids was being forced to do it by some god-of-shit who had put a vest on him.

"Well. The explosion liquefied the poor guy I'd knocked down. It damaged our vehicle, but my lieutenant walked away physically unscathed, protected by the vehicle. My team and the kids were rattled and might have suffered some hearing loss but were otherwise OK. But, flying George took off like Superman and landed nearly 100 feet away. Any other day I would have been out of the hospital in a week. But the back of my neck hit a rock, and next thing I knew, I was in a hospital in Germany, lying in a bed and wondering why I couldn't feel anything."

There was a long silence. "How many of your team survived?"

"Eleven walked away with just scratches. I was the only one actually hurt. More than 10 kids walked away unscathed. Even the goat survived and was later disarmed. The only one killed was the guy I knocked down."

"Is this why you're getting the Medal of Honor?"

"Must be. But to tell you the truth... If you're a sergeant and the President calls you... You really don't remember that much of what got said," George replied, with the first real smile since the interview started.

"Break!" Becky called out. The lights dropped and everyone shuffled around a bit.

Noelani came over and gave George a kiss on the cheek. "George, I'm so glad that fate brought you to us on Monday. You are a strong and brave man with a good heart. I'm so glad I got to meet you."

After about a minute, Becky called out. "OK, let's finish this segment, then we can get some lunch."

"George." Keoni asked. "Can you tell us about that morning on Good Morning America?"

"It started at 2:00 AM with a bad smell and a three-hour sentence to live with it. Eventually the nurse came in to clean me up. You know that's a really crappy job, so a big shout out to all the wonderful caring people that sign up for it.

"I was dressed and in the car by 5:00 AM. Rumor had it that something big was going on, but I couldn't sort out what it was.

"When we got there, my mom and I were staged in a separate room with the other wounded vets, and told we were going to be taken in early because of the heavy crowds that day. And they were telling the truth on that one. Our door opened first and while we ponderously wheeled in, crowds came flying through the other doors like banshees. Um… Sorry, no disrespect. Just trying to be descriptive.

"Thankfully, we were headed to the handicapped reserved area, which the ushers had graciously roped off for us. We'd only been seated for a few minutes, when I hear this sweet, sweet voice to my left saying. "Thank you for your service."

"OK, I'm a little ashamed of this part… I heard her but couldn't see her. So, I blow left on my straw and the chair turns a little and there is the most beautiful Hawaiian goddess that man can imagine. Actually, my imagination isn't that good. She had her hand pointed in my direction like she wants to shake it, and now even my mouth is paralyzed. Thankfully Mom was there to tell her what was up.

"Then she leans in and gives me a hug, kisses me on the cheek and says, "I'm so sorry for your loss."

"I thought I'd died and gone to heaven. A little context on that… When you're a quad, you can't feel anything, not hands, not feet, phantom pain—sometimes a lot, but otherwise nothing except for your face. So, the hug… Knew it was happening, but could not feel it. But, the kiss on the cheek was like lightning. Ah, in a good way. Her hair falling against my ear, exquisite. And, the sweet smell of coconut in her hair. When you can't feel anything, and you get that…" He stopped, emotion heavy in his voice.

"OK, OK. This is a family show. Just saying.

"Then she says, 'Sergeant, it looks like you have some chafing on your neck.'

"Really embarrassed about this part. I say something incredibly stupid like… I'm paralyzed and can't feel anything, and you tell me you can help with chafing…" More emotion.

"But my Mom says it's OK and tells me to let the pretty girl rub some cream on my neck.

"That's when I notice Michael, pointing this wand thing at me like he's Harry Potter or something. Well, not exactly a wand. And I'm wondering what the hell is going on."

"Watch your language dear." His mother chastised.

Chagrined, he continued. "You know, when you're in the chair, no one wants to look at you. Well, they do gawk a bit, but turn away when they get close enough to have to acknowledge that you're human. So, about the only time you see behavior like this; pretty girl, guy with a wand, you kind of go into hunker-down mode, because you know you're being used as a prop in some stunt they're pulling.

"Anyway, I'm starting to get worked up about it, when suddenly searing pain shoots down through my neck. My eyes blur. I struggle to breathe. And I shout out, 'What the hell are you doing to me?'

"That moment was the first time I really saw Michael. You know. People are around you all the time. You know they're there, but you don't really know who they are.

"Well Michael comes up to me and says something like... 'Hang in there, Sergeant. Let the pain pass through you. It will pass in a moment. It's not really pain. It's just your brain processing connection to your body again.'

"OK. If you play the tape back, that's probably not what he said, but that's the message I received. In that moment, I knew that this was the best, the purest, man that I had ever met and that I could trust him with my life."

"Things get a little cloudy at that point... I won't lie. The pain was so intense that I really couldn't process what was going on. I remember thinking that I was arching my back, then thinking that was stupid, since I couldn't feel or move my back.

"I remember mom shouting something and trying to come to my help, only to fall on the floor.

"And I might have passed out for a while... Trust me, things were really a blur.

"Then, the pain washed away. I had a kind of leg-falling-asleep sensation over most of my body. But Michael was there telling me it was OK. Well, I have no idea what Michael was saying, but I was hearing 'It's OK, go with it. You're healed.'" More emotion...

"When I kind of came around, the crowd was going crazy, and beautiful Noelani was holding my hand and I could feel it.

"Just for the record... I love this woman and wish I could marry her, but I don't even know if it's legal to marry aliens."

That comment sent a ripple of laughter around the room and the Sergeant noticed Noelani looking at him in a way he'd never seen before. Then the moment passed.

"Can you tell us about the medical care you've received here? Possibly share any insights about the patient experience with Confederation medical technology or equipment? That kind of stuff?" Keoni asked.

"I'd like to say several things. First, and this is going to sound like I'm contradicting myself, so I'll explain. But treatment here is generally less invasive and less painful. I know, I know. The part on the show was painful, but no one else has to go through that.

"Michael and I spoke at length about what happened there. He apologized, multiple times. Normally, when someone is as bad off as I was, the treatment would be applied more slowly. And, although there would be some itchiness, it wouldn't be painful. There are two other guys here with me, one that was even worse off than me and another not quite as bad. We've talked a lot about this question. All three of us have experienced some itchiness, but no one else experienced the pain because they were eased into treatment.

"In my case, Michael really didn't have a choice. He was about to be the star of a TV show that was going to start in 10 minutes. So, as he described it to me, he needed to pick someone to heal. Someone that would have the most extreme healing possible in 10 minutes, someone whose healing would be so obvious no one would doubt it, and someone who would be OK with being put through the pain that rapid healing would cause. And someone who would forgive him for healing them without their permission, without an explanation of what was about to happen, or the pain that would come with it.

"He told me that of the dozen or so vets there, my injury would be the easiest to heal because it was the most localized. My healing would be most dramatic, because even though the injury was compact it caused the most severe disability of the guys there. So, when he scanned me, he knew three things: First, I was the highest probability of being healed enough to restore some mobility in just 10 minutes. Second, it would be absolutely unambiguous that something dramatic had happened to me. No one in the studio or at home would doubt it, if for no other reason than I would experience extreme phantom pain. And third, he believed I was the most desperate to be healed, so I would forgive him."

253

"Do you know why he thought you would forgive him?" Keoni asked.

"Michael says he can read people, that he can sense their emotions. He says that he usually keeps 'his gates closed' out of respect for other people's privacy, but in this case, he opened them enough to get a sense of who wanted it the most and he concluded that I did."

"Did you want it most?" Keoni asked.

"I wanted it a lot and would have taken any risk. Don't know about the other guys."

"So, back to the original question about the patient experience with Confederation technology. You were saying less invasive, less painful. Can you elaborate on that?"

"Sure. When I used to go to a regular doctor, they would draw blood. Ouch." He stretched the word out to emphasize the point. "They stick you with needles. They poke and prod in places where you would really rather not be poked or prodded. When they set a broken bone, they stretch it first, double ouch.

"Here, when they want to do diagnostics, Michael waves his little wand around. then tells you what's wrong. You don't even have to take your clothes off.

"There was a woman in here earlier this week who had terminal cancer. According to her, Michael rubbed some cream on her wrist, then waved his wand around a bit while she was fully dressed in her boss's office. And poof. Tumor gone. Pain gone.

"She was still going to need a couple months of chemo to track down the last bits of cancer. But instead of hour-long infusions every week and barfing your guts out for the next two days, she came here and spent the evening in one of these cool relaxation chambers they have. She comes out in the morning, looking and feeling great. No more cancer, and she goes back to work.

"Compared to the medical care here, our medical care is voodoo dolls and leeches."

Keoni laughed and said. "So, it's OK then?" A pause... "If it's that good, why are you still here?"

George put his hand out and pulled back the sleeve a bit. "See how skinny my arms are?" He did the same with his leg. "Legs too. I need to rebuild the muscle. So they feed me great food and work me on the treadmill every day. It will take a while before I can enter Iron Man, but Michael tells me that I'll be able to do it if I work hard enough."

"Now I understand why you are here. How is the therapy going?" Keoni said

George put on a big smile. "Want to see some really cool tech?" he said, obviously eager to show something.

"Sure. Let's see it."

"OK" George said, then pulled on the suspenders of his overalls. "See my overalls? These are not just a fashion statement. They are seriously cool. Watch!" George fiddled with the knob in the suspender a little. "OK. Wait for it," he said. Then slowly he started rising off the sofa.

Keoni was completely taken by surprise. "What?" he stammered in awe. "Tell me what I'm seeing, George."

By now George was high enough that his legs could clear the coffee table, so he leaned forward and to the side and floated over the table then down to the floor next to Keoni. In the background, he could hear the camera guy working to keep George in the picture. "These," George grinned, "are my fabulous flying overalls!"

George's pronouncement came off like a 6-year-old showing grandma a new toy. Everyone broke out laughing.

Keoni quickly regained control. "George, those are the most fabulous flying overalls I've ever seen. Can you tell us what they do and how they work?"

George replied. "You have undoubtedly seen news shows or a science show on TV where they're trying to teach people to walk again. They usually have some crane-type thing, or bouncy suspenders hanging from a track in the ceiling. This is kind of the Confederation equivalent, but far cooler and far more useful.

"There are anti-grav generators in the straps that I can dial to have 0% to 100% weight-reduction. If I turn it all the way up, like I just did, then it will lift me up a few inches off the ground, so I can just float. But as I dial it down, I start getting some weight and if I dial it to zero, then I get my full weight. But I'm not going to do that. I'd probably fall over. That'd be way too embarrassing for television.

"I've currently got it set so I have about 10% of my weight. If I start to walk, it holds me up enough that I have the strength to take steps." He took several steps away from the camera, then turned around and started back, before suddenly popping up a couple inches into the air.

"See, I'm already getting too strong to walk right with only 10% of my weight. Here it is at 30%." Keoni noted the concerned look in Noelani's eye.

George sagged toward the floor a little but kept his balance. Then took several steps with what appeared to be great effort. He stopped and dialed the anti-grav up a bit. Then walked back very normally and sat down. "Whew. I'm not really ready for 30% yet, but 20% is working pretty well." It was clear that he'd tired himself.

"There are several reasons why I say this is better than the stuff I've seen on TV. First, I can control it myself. They can too, but they only do it during therapy. Second, I can wear this all day long. If I need to get up and down the steps, I can just float. If I'm too tired out, I can float. But usually, I just dial the weight down really low, so that I'm walking all day long, not just during the hours in the gym. When we are down there, Noelani takes over the controls and really makes me work."

"I see that we're running a little short on time, can I ask one more question?" Keoni asked.

"Sure," George replied.

"What's it like living here on the ranch with the Confederation folks?"

"It's fantastic! I mean there's all the obvious stuff, right? We are in Hawaii. The scenery is fabulous. There are tons of cool toys in this place. And the medical treatment is so much better than any of us can truly understand.

"But, the vibe here, among these people, is incredible. Everyone is friendly and kind. They are dedicated to the well-being of their patients, but not just that... They're very open about the fact that they're not human and have taken our form so we can get to know them. But the truth is they are much better humans than the rest of us. They are on a mission to help us, despite the fact we haven't been as welcoming as we should have been.

"The FBI attempted to raid them when they'd already been invited to just come for a visit. They botched the raid and got themselves badly injured in the process, but what did Michael do? He rescued them, then healed them. The President tried to shoot them. The Iranians actually did nuke them. But why? They are here to help us, heal us, end poverty, save the planet, and bring peace...

"Uh. Sorry for the rant. It's OK if you edit all that out. I'm just saying, living here and being with these fine people is better than Christmas! I'm a very lucky man."

A moment of silence. Then Noelani said. "Who would like some lunch? You're welcome to bring a camera. I think you'll probably bump into some other people who might want to say something. But, one ground rule… If they turn away, let them go. Everyone here is friendly. Not everyone is ready to be seen, or to talk about their situation. We good with that?"

"Understood," Becky replied. "We'll take your lead and promise not to overstep our welcome."

THE DINING ROOM

As they came into the room, Pam was bringing out some food for them. "I've set this up buffet-style, so help yourself to anything that looks good to you. Oh, by the way, my name is Pam. I'm Michael's assistant and like to help in the kitchen when we have guests."

An older woman standing next to Pam said in a quiet shy voice. "Hi. My name is Anna. I'm a guest, but also like helping in the kitchen. My husband is in treatment here. And, this sounds so weird to say, but I am a human from Earth, enjoying the hospitality of the Confederation." She quickly shuffled back into the kitchen.

As Anna was leaving, Michael and Kale came in and started toward the buffet.

"Ah, George." Michael said. "Is this the interview team from Honolulu?" He turned toward the closest person, which happened to be Keoni, and reached out to shake his hand. "Hi. I'm Michael. Did you get a good interview?"

Keoni looked momentarily star struck, then shook Michael's hand. "Mr. Ambassador. It's an unexpected pleasure to meet you. Thank you so much for inviting us today and allowing us to interview Sergeant Butler."

"I presume he told you the story of his injury. Incredible bravery. Incredible sacrifice. I count myself fortunate to have met someone like him, and to have him be the first human for me to be seen in public with. I'm a lucky man."

Keoni was surprised to hear someone as important and powerful as Michael speak so unpretentiously. It lent a great deal of credibility to the story they'd been told. "Mr. Ambassador, I know we were invited to interview Sergeant Butler, but is there any chance we could have a few words with you today?"

Michael smiled. He liked this reporter. "Unfortunately, no. I have a lot to do before departing in two hours for India. Maybe we could connect the next time you're here? George, are you going to invite these guys back?"

"Yes. I would like to. Is that OK?"

"Sure. Things are going to be crazy busy next week, but coordinate with Pam, I may have time tomorrow or Sunday. Maybe we could both meet with them?"

Keoni and Becky were both thinking the same thing... *This is the big break I've been waiting for.*

Despite their relatively neutral faces, Michael could sense the news team's excitement as he finished filling the small plate of food he'd come for. As he and Kale headed back to his office, he nodded to them and said, "Look forward to talking with you."

Joshua, the camera man who had been filming the encounter, opened his mouth for the first time since entering the house. "Is he always that nice?"

INDIA

[02.08.2025 9:00 AM] 12,000 MILES ABOVE NEW DELHI, INDIA
"What's the setup for this one?" Michael asked Elsie.

"Originally, the idea was that we would land outside their parliament building, give a speech to a thousand or so select dignitaries, then go inside for meetings with the Prime Minister. Well, word of that plan leaked out. The building is now surrounded by a million people. Hard to envision, I know. The Parliament is more or less trapped inside. So, they've changed the plan. You are to beam into an alcove off the main parliament chamber, where you'll be met by an honor guard. The Prime Minister will come out to greet you. Then you go in to address Parliament."

"How much time do we have?"

"For the meeting, or before you need to transport down?"

"Before I need to meet the honor guard."

"Well, we're early, at least 20 minutes early. We didn't get word of the change until after we took off."

"Then I guess we wait."

OUTSIDE THE PARLIAMENT BUILDING, NEW DEHLI, INDIA
The crowds outside the Indian Parliament building were so thick it was difficult even to breathe. Rumor had leaked that the alien ambassador would be landing in front of Parliament and millions flocked to see.

Oscar, the American ambassador, stood in the crowd trying to make his way to an entrance. He'd assumed that Michael would attempt to meet with the Indian government. So, using an obscure term of an old treaty between the US and India, one that had never been invoked or revoked, he'd petitioned the Indian government, requesting to be present at any meeting they might have with Michael, an American citizen. He'd preemptively submitted proof of Michael's citizenship.

In only three days, nanoseconds for the Indian government, well any government actually, he'd received an invitation to attend a presentation Michael would make to the Parliament. His ticket was for a position in one of the balconies overlooking the parliament chamber. Although it would not give him access to Michael, he could at least film the speech for the President to review.

The problem was that he stood about a thousand feet from the nearest check point where he could gain access. But the crowd was so thick he simply could not push his way through.

ALCOVE OUTSIDE THE PARLIAMENT CHAMBER

Michael and Sanjit appeared in the designated alcove at exactly 9:30. The honor guard was startled by the sudden appearance, then concerned because two men where there, not just the one that was expected.

Michael greeted the leader of the honor guard, introducing himself, then Sanjit. "This is Sanjit Gautama, also from the Intergalactic Confederation of Planets, who will participate with me in today's meetings."

The Captain was not sure what to say or do. Rarely were outsiders allowed in this building unless they'd been extensively vetted. He'd not been pleased to hear that the Confederation Ambassador was just going to 'beam' in without passing through security. Now he had two of them.

Thankfully, the grandfatherly voice of the Prime Minister, floated through the air behind him. "Mr. Ambassador. Thank you for taking the time to visit India, and on a Saturday at that. I see you have brought a colleague."

"Mr. Prime Minister, thank you for the invitation to meet with you and for the gracious welcome. This is my colleague, Sanjit Gautama. He has studied India for years and has been designated to lead the Consular Office in India, in the event we are invited to set one up here."

"Mr. Gautama. Welcome. I hope we have the opportunity to work together." The Prime Minister shook Sanjit's hand. "We made the mistake of inviting about 1,000 dignitaries to join us today. The plan was to have them seated outside so you could address a larger crowd than we can host inside. But apparently, they did not keep the event secret as we had asked. Over 100,000 people had begun to gather in the streets by mid-night last night. And as more and more came, all our preparations outside were overwhelmed. If, when we are done,

260

you have the ability to address the gathered masses, you are welcome to do so."

"Thank you, Mr. Prime Minister. Do you have an agenda and schedule of events for this meeting?"

"The Legislature, Supreme Court and Cabinet Ministers are in the process of assembling in the main chamber. As many of the dignitaries as possible have been assembled in the upper alcoves and balconies, including the American Ambassador.

"I'll start by addressing them. Then I'll give you formal welcome and summarize the process you offer... Letter of Intent, then Treaty. Most of them know about this already. Then I will offer you the stage. It is our tradition that you can say whatever it is you have chosen for us to hear. When you are done, I will moderate a question and answer period, not to exceed one hour. Is that satisfactory?"

"Yes. Would it be beneficial if I demonstrated any of our equipment or technology?"

"I've heard rumor of and seen a video of you healing a man. Is this true?"

"It is true that we have medical technology far in advance of yours. There are no diseases known to us that we cannot cure. That said, not everyone is comfortable being the subject of a demonstration. Is there someone specific that you have in mind?"

"Yes. My secretary of many years has a growth in her neck. All of our doctors have said that it is not treatable. Her case was even reviewed by the senior neurologists at that famous Institute in Arizona whose name I can never remember. All to no effect.

"She still comes to work and is here today. But the tumor is suffocating her. She mostly sleeps and can no longer work."

"I'm confident that we can heal her. Would she allow this to be done in public?"

"Oh, yes. That is the real reason she's here today."

"OK. One last thing. This is probably a tumor. I'm confident that we can give her relief today. But we may need to take her back to our facility in Hawaii to complete the healing. So, two questions... First, would that be something she would allow? Being taken to Hawaii, that is. She would be able to bring a family member. And second, will that fulfill the demonstration needed for your Parliament?"

"That will not be a problem. Everyone here already believes. They just need you to come, so they can say they've seen it with their own eyes. I'm sure you've already run into that phenomena."

"Yes. I have," Michael said with a smile. "And I approve of governments verifying any claims that they're asked to accept."

"Then, let's begin."

...

The doors opened and the Prime Minister and his entourage entered to thunderous applause. The crowd settled and the Prime Minister began speaking. Michael was pleasantly surprised at the kindness of his words and the fairness of his presentation of the deal.

As he finished his speech, the President invited his secretary to come up to the stage. Since all eyes were on Michael, he'd asked Sanjit to remote scan and send the results to his inner vision.

As soon as he saw her, he knew the problem. Sanjit's scans confirmed his visual diagnosis, squamous cell carcinoma. In her case, it appeared to have begun in a saliva gland, then spread out through her jaw and down into her spine. This couldn't be solved in 5 minutes, but 2 days in the tank and she'd be a new woman.

The Prime Minister beckoned Michael to the podium and asked him to say a few words. Michael started his greeting in Hindi. Hindi and English were among the 22 official languages of India, and the two authorized for use in Parliament, even though some states and representatives did not speak Hindi. "My friends." Michael said, in perfect high-caste Hindi. "Thank you for receiving me today."

He switched back to English, and repeated. "My friends. Thank you for receiving me today. My name is Michael. I have been sent by the Intergalactic Confederation of Planets as their ambassador to invite you to ally with us...."

...

"As I have spoken to governments and their citizens, the thing that has resonated the most is our medical technology. To dispel any doubt about the capabilities of our medical technologies, I always offer to cure someone when I make presentations like this. Before I came in today, the Prime Minister explained to me the situation of his secretary, whose condition has been pronounced untreatable by your best doctors and the best doctors in the United States. She has agreed to be treated today in public view.

"Before I begin, I ask one thing. Allow me to protect this woman's dignity and privacy. I will evaluate her in front of you. Speak with her privately. Then offer the treatment option she selects. I will explain as much about her condition as she consents to. Then provide as much therapy in this setting as she is comfortable with. Are we agreed?"

There were shouts of approval and none of dissent.

As Michael made this statement, the Prime Minister brought his secretary to the podium.

"Michael, I present to you Nisha Subramanian. Nisha has worked with me for 40 years. She is fluent in English and Hindi, but more comfortable in Hindi."

"Then I will speak with her in Hindi, if that is acceptable to the assembly."

On hearing a few sounds of discontent, Michael added, "And my colleague will translate for those of you that are less comfortable with Hindi."

He turned to the woman and silenced the PA system.

"Nisha." A tear formed in his eye. "I am saddened to see what has happened to you. May I examine your tumor? It will be very discreet."

"Yes. Michael," she replied.

Michael turned the PA back on as he pulled out his scanner and started making a detailed scan. Then he spoke in a voice that would carry over the PA. "Nisha. Here is my diagnosis."

She nodded her head.

"You have squamous cell carcinoma that appears to have begun in a saliva gland. Was your first hint that something was wrong a dry mouth, sore throat and a periodic pain in your neck?" He motioned to a spot under his jaw, back near his throat.

"Yes. Exactly."

"OK," Michael replied. "If you do not want me to reveal any of the following details, just raise your hand and I'll stop."

"OK"

"A lump appeared on the right side of your neck a year, maybe two, later. It generally was not painful but became increasingly painful as it grew."

She nodded.

"It just kept growing and eventually the doctors agreed that it was a tumor. Right?"

"Yes"

"But they told you it was benign, so you really didn't need to worry about it. Right?"

"I talked with several doctors. All but one said that," she replied.

"The other one said it was probably benign but could be some form of cancer so you should continue to monitor it. Right?"

"Exactly. How did you know?"

"It continued to grow, and you started feeling tingling in your extremities, your hands and feet. Right?"

"Yes. The doctors blamed it on diabetes, but I don't have diabetes."

"I'm not surprised. The tingling was caused by nerve dysfunction. The most common form of nerve dysfunction is caused by diabetes. So, they blamed it on diabetes. No one mentioned the lump on your neck, right?"

"No. They did not."

"OK. Remember, you can signal me to stop at any point. I will treat you anyway. But no one needs to know the details if you're uncomfortable with this."

She nodded.

"This is what happened. And, in your doctors' defense, it is rare. Squamous cell carcinoma can grow in any direction. But, once it starts pushing out, making a visible lump... It generally keeps going that way. Your doctors have probably shown you pictures of that."

She nodded.

"OK. The primary direction of your tumor growth was back toward the neck, not out. So, although it was unsightly, and got your doctors' attention, they never really determined that its primary direction of growth was back toward your spine. They also failed to determine that it was invading your spinal column."

She started crying. Michael killed the PA feed and took her hand. "Nisha, you're going to be alright," he whispered. "We don't need to reveal any more to the audience."

She shook her head no. "They need to know how hopeless I am."

Michael smiled at her. "Have hope." Then reconnected to the PA.

"When you finally went to see the specialists in Arizona, they confirmed that your cancer was not treatable, because it was already in your spine. Is that correct?"

At this point, she was openly sobbing, and the prime minister was wondering why he thought this might have been a good idea.

"OK. This is how I would like to treat you. I'm going to rub some cream on your neck, then onto your wrist. My associate, Sanjit, is going to spray a gentle mist over your face. When he does, the pain will reduce a bit. Are we OK so far?"

"Yes, can we start now?"

"Let me say a little more. You should not feel any pain from this. But you are under a lot of pain right now, right?"

"Yes," she said between sobs.

"The pain will slowly recede, then will suddenly just stop. When that happens, you will probably pass out, which is OK. It's just a shock reaction. Would you rather do that in private, instead of in front of this group?"

"I believe that you'll heal me Michael. So, let's do this in plain sight, so there is no doubt."

"OK. I'll be using my scanner to focus the treatment. We will probably need to reapply the cream several times, maybe spray you more than once. If you remain conscious, you may feel a slight warming or burning sensation in your skin, and you will see what appears to be smoke, but it is not smoke in the normal sense.

"If you become afraid, grip my hand and I'll stop until you are ready to resume. OK?"

She nodded.

"Lastly, we should see significant tumor reduction in the next 15 minutes, but you'll need to come back to my medical facility with me to finish the procedure. It will take at most 2 days and will be very pleasant. You can bring a few people with you. But there is only so much I can do here and now with a little cream and some spray. Is that acceptable?"

"Yes. Please begin. I'm ready."

He nodded to her, then called for Sanjit. "OK. I will start the cream on the neck. You start it on her wrist."

Together, they started putting the nanobot-based cream on her wrist, which provided quick access to her blood stream, and on her neck, which provided quick access to the tumor from the outside.

"That feels nice."

Once the cream had been rubbed in, Michael pulled out his scanner and asked Sanjit to administer the spray. As Sanjit sprayed, Michael continued, "Close your eyes. As you feel the spray start to settle on your face, inhale deeply."

After a moment or two, she took a deep breath.

Michael could sense her relaxing. "OK, Sanjit. More cream on the wrist."

Using his scanner, he directed the main hoard of nanobots toward the mass on the neck. He directed about 10 percent of them toward her spinal cord, where the real short-term threat was.

After about 4 minutes of cream, spray, cream, spray... A white mist started rising from the main lump of the tumor. A little could even be seen as she exhaled.

Suddenly Nisha went limp. As the prime minister caught her, a sharp intake of breath rose from the gathered crowd watching the spectacle.

"Nothing to worry about." Michael said loud enough to be picked up by the PA. "She is now pain free. The cancer cells over-pressuring her spinal cord have largely been destroyed. The little wafts of white mist that you see are the remains of cancer cells that have been destroyed. They are being expelled through the skin so as not to overtax her liver and kidneys."

As Nisha started to stir, Michael redirected his attention toward her boss. "Mr. Prime Minister, I think this is as far as we ought to go today. The treatment Nisha has received has reduced the mass of the tumor about 50%, but more importantly, it has eliminated the cancer cells invading her spinal cord. At this point, she should be pain free, which is why she fell asleep. It will take about two, maybe three days, to remove the rest of the cancer cells and do appropriate cosmetic repair.

"Is there a family member or other legal guardian here who can release her to our care and possibly accompany us to our facilities? Her recovery will be quicker if she has a loved one close by."

A man at the edge of the stage stood and said, "Yes. I am her husband. We will go with you when you are ready to go."

There was a thunderous round of applause. It seemed as though the building itself was shaking. Then Michael saw the screen and understood. This had been broadcast to the people outside, if not to the entire world. A million people outside were clapping and cheering. No wonder the building was shaking.

Michael returned to the podium where he'd been invited to speak. "This technology and more will be made available to you, once you have become conditional members of the Confederation. To become conditional members, you simply need to sign the Letter of Intent, then progress negotiations toward a permanent treaty in good faith. Nisha will be cured and sent back to you regardless of whether or not you sign. I will return the podium to the Prime Minister for questions."

Another round of applause as Michael stepped back. The Prime Minister asked for questions and a man stood and raised his hand.

"Your question?"

"It seems to me that there are a number of terms in the proposed treaty with which we are not compliant. How will these be resolved?"

The Prime Minister indicated that Michael should answer.

"There's a five-year negotiation window built into the Letter of Intent. The Confederation doesn't want to change who you are, although there are some norms we'll need to work through together. Many of the things you're worried about, for example your nuclear defenses and your interests in Kashmir, have much easier solutions than it would appear. If you're willing to discuss ways of resolving these issues, then we can proceed. And during those five years, you'll have access to and benefit from technologies like the one you just witnessed."

Another man stood and raised his hand. The Prime Minister asked him to speak. "Assuming that Nisha comes back completely healed, as I'm sure she will, how will this technology become available to us? We have over 1 billion citizens. It would take millions of people like you to serve the demand."

Again, the Prime Minister indicated that Michael should reply.

"That's an excellent question. We start construction of a major embassy complex next week. It will be about 100 square miles with the capacity to house over 10 million people. The complex will be mostly complete in about a month."

Expressions of disbelief and awe rippled across the room.

"It will initially be populated with a thousand or so Confederation trainers. That number will grow to 10,000 or more in the months that follow. We will train and equip qualified volunteers from every member nation. We'll cover all expenses, including transportation, for those selected for training.

"Will you be able to cure people like Nisha next week? No. But we will provide doctors that can cure hundreds. Will you have a million Confederation-trained doctors and all the equipment by the end of the year? No. But eventually you will.

"The direct answer to your question is, we'll train and equip you so that you can tend to your own people. To the implied question, can we serve your total demand on signing of the Letter of Intent? The answer is no. We'll help to the extent that we can, but you'll have to do the rest. We will support you in this. We would not even make the offer of membership if we didn't believe that you could rise to the challenge.

"Now, I reverse the question. What will happen to India if every other nation on Earth has our equipment and training, but you do not? Please do not hear this as a threat. We will do everything we can to help you. But if you refuse to help yourself, then how could we save you?"

These comments provoked a lot of discussion. The Speaker of the Parliament pounded his gavel and called the meeting back to order. The Prime Minister took the podium back and said, "Thank you, Michael for that reminder. You are here to help us, not take us over. And thank you for allowing us to make the decision to join, grow and learn. Throughout Earth's history, it's always worked the other way. The nation with the highest technology took the prize, and other nations were simply bowled over. You're actually letting us choose our destiny, not dictating it. And you're right. If we choose not to partner with you, then others will and we'll be left behind."

Standing straighter and looking at the assembled members, the Prime Minister said in a very loud voice. "I move that we sign the Letter of Intent now and begin our partnership with the Intergalactic Confederation of Planets."

A huge commotion broke out on the Parliament floor. Many members could be heard shouting 'Join' while others seemed to suggest a slower path. Once again, the building started shaking as Michael heard the voices of a million people chanting, "Join! Join! Join!"

The Speaker of Parliament could be heard calling for order and pounding his gavel. Michael went up to the Prime Minister.

"Maybe it's time for me to take my leave. We need to resume Nisha's treatment as soon as possible. I doubt there's any more I can do to influence the result."

The members had noticed Michael speaking with the Prime Minister and began to settle. The Prime Minister stepped to the podium. "I would like to thank Michael and the Confederation for making the time to meet with us today. In the interests of our dear Nisha, I suggest that we take a short break to say our farewells, then resume in a half hour to take up the motion to approve."

Michael, Sanjit, Nisha and her husband gathered together, then simply disappeared.

SHUTTLE, ENROUTE TO HAWAII

The four appeared in the passenger cabin of the shuttle. The Subramanians, having never transported before, were overcome by vertigo. Michael and Sanjit held onto them so they didn't fall. They were led to seats and Michael sat with them.

"Are you two OK? I should've warned you about possible vertigo. The transport is so smooth that no one ever notices it. But everyone notices the sudden change of scenery."

"That was the most amazing thing I've ever experienced, at least since I saw my wife's tumor shrink an hour ago." They both broke out laughing, mostly driven by the relief that came from knowing she would soon be well again.

"Apologies, Michael. I didn't introduce myself. I'm Mahesh Subramanian, Nisha's husband. I cannot thank you enough for healing my wife, then transporting us to Hawaii to finalize her cure. We thought there would never be a cure. And we never thought we would visit Hawaii."

"Mahesh and Nisha, thank you for coming back with us. Nisha, I think your treatment will take about two days. When we land in Hawaii, we'll take you to a room where you can get settled. But I want to get you into treatment as soon as possible. So, once you have had a few minutes to relax, we'll take you to the treatment prep room. Mahesh will be able to accompany you.

"Then, once you've been prepped, we'll take you to another room for the actual treatment. Mahesh, I'm sorry but, as with an operating room, you can't accompany her there. As the procedure will take about 2 days, we'll take you back to the residence where you can have some food and possibly meet other patients, their spouses and some of the staff."

"She'll be in surgery for two days?" Mahesh asked.

"Technically yes, but not in a way you would recognize as such. Surgery like this is done on a microscopic scale. We will track down the billions of cancer cells in her body and kill them one-by-one. Once that's done, we'll repair or replace the damaged tissues in those areas—including the cosmetic surgery that will restore her mouth, face and neck. That's why it will take two days, possibly more.

"Nisha, I know that sounds scary, but there's nothing to worry about. You will drift into a deep sleep, one in which most patients report very pleasant dreams. When you awake, you'll feel better than you have felt in years."

"There is one side effect of the treatment that I always forget to tell people about... It's very difficult to rejuvenate only the cells damaged by cancer, so this surgery will also repair some of the natural wear and tear someone of your age has. Which means... you will come out looking, feeling, and being 10, maybe 15 years younger."

"This is even better than I was hoping for!" Mahesh exclaimed.

"Yes, but I will still be married to this old man!" Nisha complained.

"Well, we can fix that, too." Michael smiled as they both turned to look at him. "Most of my staff are much older than they appear. This is because they take a weekly rejuvenation treatment.

"We would be more than happy to do that for you, Mahesh. I guarantee it will be the best night's sleep you've ever had, and you'll wake up feeling and being years younger."

"Yes." Nisha said. "He'll do it!"

"What?" Mahesh replied.

"You're going to go crazy while I'm away. So, you go in at the same time. When you wake, you won't be worried about me. And maybe you will be more ready for me, when my younger and no longer deformed body comes back to you."

He laughed. "Looks like I'm going to get a lot more than I bargained for on this trip."

"Well, sounds like it's settled," Michael said. "I'm going to go talk to the pilot. There are some things I need to take care of before we land. I'll leave the two of you with Sanjit. We should be landing in about a half hour."

...

As Michael entered the cockpit, Elsie said, "You seem to pick up more house guests on every trip."

"Indeed. I do. I like a full house," he replied.

"It's going to be very full starting in a few days."

"So it seems. One hundred or more Ascendants. Several hundred more androids. We cannot handle even the staging for that many. And there is a lot to do before even the first arrive.

"I need to speak with Jiaying. Does she know that Nisha and Mahesh are inbound?"

"Knows two are inbound, but not their names. Shall I connect you to Jiaying?"

"Yes, please," he said with a smile.

Jiaying's voice came over the intercom. "On your way back with two in tow, Michael?"

"Yes I am. Nisha and Mahesh Subramanian. We want to get Nisha prepped and in a tank within the hour. Then we want to give Mahesh a good night's sleep with maximum de-aging in a rejuvenator in the Residence. Can you arrange that?"

"One second..." A pause "It's arranged."

"Great. We'll transport down, so that we can get Nisha started sooner. Meanwhile, what's the agenda for the weekend?"

"We have you on all four of the major Sunday morning talk shows. Ironically, the 60 Minutes producer called, more-or-less demanding that you appear on his show since you disrupted it last week, then could not assemble a crew during the hours you were available. By the way, those shows all film in New York and are recorded on Saturday.

"Your interviews in New York finish at 2:00 PM Eastern time. So, you'll be back here in time to give the local news team 15 minutes.

"Then off for a live interview on BBC Sunday morning in London. The French got word of this somehow and called to ask if you could do the same in Paris late Sunday morning with France Televisions."

...

Michael walked back to where Sanjit and the Subramanians were chatting. It was clear that they were enjoying their time with Sanjit. "You seem to be getting along well."

Nisha replied. "Sanjit is such a nice boy. I wish my daughter would have met him before she met my son-in-law."

Michael got a good laugh out of that statement. "Sorry to spoil the party, but there's been a slight change of plan. The four of us are going to transport down to our facilities, rather than land. We'll be ready to go in just a minute."

THE RESIDENCE, KOHALA MOUNTAIN

They materialized in the dining room. The Subramanians seemed to cope better this time.

"OK. We're in my dining room. Visualize it, then open your eyes."

"You're right," Nisha replied. "If you close your eyes and visualize a different scene, there really isn't any vertigo."

"Friends," said Michael. "Welcome to my home. You will see that it has plenty of space. This is the dining room."

On hearing their arrival, Noelani came out of the kitchen to greet them. "This is Noelani. Her official role is house manager. But she is trained as a medical technician and will be your host while you are here."

Nisha said. "What a beautiful woman this is. Michael you're so lucky. She is your wife, isn't she?"

"No. Well yes. She's the most beautiful woman I've ever met, but not my wife..."

"Well what are you waiting for? Marry her!"

271

Michael and Noelani both broke out laughing.

"Thank you for your interest in my well-being. I'm not sure how to explain this. Noelani and I cannot be married. But... Before you protest that statement, let me introduce you to her. Noelani, this is Nisha and Mahesh Subramanian.

"Nisha suffers from carcinoma as you can see. And we will be treating her for the next couple days."

Noelani smiled at the new guests.

"Can I interest you in some dinner? I know it's still early in the day in India. But here it is late in the evening. I've been advised that you will both be taking treatments starting tonight. With human medicine you need to fast before treatment. Our technology is different, and it is generally better to have a meal before treatment."

"What kind of food do you have?" Mahesh inquired.

"Any kind you would like. But tonight's dinner, in honor of Michael's trip to India, is Chicken Tikka Masala and Sag Paneer with Basmati rice. Of course, I can make you anything you'd like."

Nisha was quick to respond. "That would be fine, dear."

"But, would it be possible to have hamburgers and fries before we leave?" Mahesh asked.

"We can accommodate anything you'd like."

They all settled in and soon steaming plates of food were placed before them.

As if on cue, Sergeant Butler walked in. "Hi. My name is George. I'm one of the patients here. I smelled the food and thought maybe I could sample some."

"You're always welcome here, George. This is Nisha and Mahesh Subramanian. They just came from India. They're here for treatment."

"Well you've come to the right place. On Monday, I was a quadriplegic strapped into a wheelchair with a blow stick. Today, I can walk. Well, kind of. In a year or so, I'll be running marathons."

"Are you the sergeant we saw being healed on TV this week?" Nisha asked.

"That was me. So, what are they going to do for you?"

"Remove the cancer, carcinoma, and associated cosmetic repair."

"Someone else was here with something a lot worse earlier this week. She left a day and a half later, saying that she looked and felt better than she had in years. I bet you'll say the same."

"I hope so. Michael says I need two or more days of therapy."

"Not to worry. They'll do a great job. And, what about you, Mahesh? Michael implied you were both getting treatment."

"I don't really need treatment. But Michael said her treatment would make Nisha younger, so she said they needed to make me younger also. Is such a thing true?"

"Better believe it. Two people here this week were made 20 years younger. Saw it with my own eyes. They just exuded youth."

They ate in silence for a few minutes, then Nisha pushed her plate away. "I'm ready. Can you show me to our room? I'll freshen up, then we can begin." A pause... "Mahesh too. He's ready also. So, let's get started."

Mahesh looked up, eyes large. "I'm ready?" He saw his wife's look and restated, "I'm ready!"

"This way..." Noelani indicated the way.

MORE INTERVIEWS

[02.08.2025 2:30 AM] MICHAEL'S BEDROOM, THE RESIDENCE

"Wake up, sleepy head!" Jiaying's voice came over the intercom. "Your shuttle departs in 10 minutes. Well, actually, it's already departed."

Michael got out of bed without even making a response and hit the shower. *Noelani must be loading this thing with some sort of stimulant,* Michael thought as he stepped out a moment later. *Three minutes ago, I could barely open my eyes. Now I'm wide awake.*

When Michael got to the dining room, Noelani was waiting with an egg sandwich and a thermos of his favorite coffee. "I made you some breakfast to go. And here's a second bag for Elsie. You know she's putting in even more hours than you have, right?"

"Yes. I know. And, you're putting in your fair share also. The good news is that things should ease up a lot for Elsie starting next week. In the meantime, thanks for taking care of both of us."

"You ready, Michael?" Elsie's voice came over the intercom.

"I am, and I'm also bringing your breakfast."

12,000 MILES ABOVE NEW YORK CITY

"Your first stop this morning is with Meet the Press on NBC, then Face the Nation on CBS, This Week on ABC, then Fox News Sunday," Elsie said. "They all wanted to provide drivers and escorts, but we declined. You've become too famous. Even with an escort out of the building, they would need a huge police cordon just to get you to the limo. We thought it would be safer just to transport you."

"Thanks for taking good care of me, Elsie." Michael said.

"I think the good news is that these shows rarely give anyone more than a few minutes. So, none of them will be holding you more than an hour," Elsie replied, then paused. "OK. I can see the spot where your host at NBC is waiting. OK if I send you down a few minutes early?"

"Let's do it," Michael answered.

WAITING ROOM, NBC NEWS

Mac Johnson, the associate director of Meet the Press, waited for his guest in a room that was normally very busy. But today it was blocked for Michael only. The make-up team waited outside so they could start as soon as he arrived. Rumor had it that Michael was to-the-second prompt, but Mac was anxious anyway, worried that they wouldn't have enough time for the long list of questions they wanted to ask. They'd even gone so far as to book a separate studio for the interview, which was being held clear so there'd be no delays in getting started. As he glanced down at his watch again, Mac heard a small popping sound that startled him. Looking up, he saw that Michael had arrived.

Jumping to his feet, Mac said, "Michael, welcome to NBC News and Meet the Press. My name is Mac Johnson and I cannot tell you how excited we are to have you here with us this morning."

"Mr. Johnson. Mac. Thank you for such a kind welcome. I'm yours for 45 minutes. What's the plan?"

While Michael was greeting Mac, the door to the room opened and make-up artists came flooding in.

"Michael, we staged a make-up team and a studio just for you so we could maximize time for the interview. I hope that is OK." Mac thought, *the only other person that gets this treatment is the President.*

As this was a new situation, Michael had opened his awareness a bit, enough to hear Mac's thoughts about the President. Michael replied. "Mac, that's very considerate of you. I bet no one else gets such gracious treatment, except for maybe the President."

Mac was momentarily stunned. *How did he know that?* Mac thought, then remembered a comment from a friend at ABC. "Michael is telepathic. He can read your mind if he wants to. Thankfully, he usually doesn't want to."

Oh shit. He thought. *What have we gotten ourselves into?*

As the make-up team smothered Michael with attention, Mac used his radio to advise the studio that Michael would be there momentarily.

No sooner had the make-up artists started than they had finished. *These guys are good,* Michael thought. Then Mac whisked him 10 feet down the hall to the studio, where the lights were already up. While Mac was directing Michael to his seat, he heard the interviewer saying, "...with us tonight is none other than Michael the Ascendant,

Ambassador from the Intergalactic Confederation of Planets. Welcome, Michael."

Michael noticed the red light on the camera facing him flip on and said, "Chuck, thank you for having me."

"Michael, you are the biggest sensation to hit America since the Beatles. No one had heard of you before last Sunday. Now you are tied with the President as the best-known person on Earth, and you have much higher approval ratings. What do you say to that?"

"Chuck. The public's response is very gratifying, but more importantly, I think it speaks positively about their sensibility and open-mindedness. Many worlds react poorly when they're made aware of other intelligent life in the universe. This is my twelfth first contact mission. The Confederation's had over 10,000 first contacts. This one has moved faster than any before it."

"Were you expecting that?"

"In one sense, I expected it to move fast. Humanity has an incredible talent for sorting out what's real and what's not. My first exposure to humanity was a little over two thousand years ago. One of the items in my report had to do with humanity's incisiveness. You, as a species, seem to be able to separate the wheat from the chaff in a way that few species can. This is one of the things that drew me back to Earth. It drove me to ask the Confederation for the opportunity to be your ambassador.

"In another sense, I didn't think things would move this fast, because the Earth's political leaders are, for the most part, deeply entrenched and resistant to any prospective changes in the balance of power."

Chuck seemed taken back for a moment. "That's an interesting observation, Michael. But let me cycle back... You say you have been on Earth for two thousand years?"

"No." Michael said. "My first visit to Earth was a little over two thousand years ago. I was sent to study the Roman Empire and spent about 5 years touring the empire, with a disproportionate amount of that time spent in the Middle East."

"Why the Middle East?"

"The answer to that question is simple but let me give a little more context. There were two dominant powers on Earth at the time, the Romans and the Chinese, each of which was struggling to control conquered territory. Through the ages we've found that you can learn a lot about a species' likelihood of long-term survival by studying their

276

conflicts. I was assigned to study Rome; a colleague was assigned to China. The major conflict in the Roman Empire at that time was in the Middle East."

"So, if I understand correctly, the Confederation has been watching us for over 2,000 years, and your first major exposure to humanity was during the Roman Empire. I think a lot of people are not going to like the idea that we have been observed like that."

"Chuck, I understand your point and I'm also aware of the fixation some of your science fiction writers have about alien invasion and abduction. But I assure you, there was nothing nefarious about our actions. We've known about Earth for a very long time. Around 10,000 years ago it became clear that humanity would become the dominant species. About 2,500 years ago, many of our scientists began speculating that human civilization would become advanced enough to join the Confederation in as few as 10,000 years. For context, most civilizations take 100,000 years or more to advance that far. So, monitoring became more frequent and a direct observation mission was authorized about 2,100 years ago.

"Regarding my role in that mission... I'd been involved in several first contact missions before and was being considered for an ambassador position. The specifics of the situation in Rome were a little more closely aligned with my previous experience, so I volunteered to take the assignment in Rome."

Chuck followed up by saying, "Tell us more about why you study planets with a dominant species and thriving civilizations."

"Much earlier in our species development, we encountered a threat that nearly drove us extinct. We survived, but at a very high cost. Billions of us were lost. Over the succeeding millennia, we found out that other species had known of our struggle but chose not to help. We vowed never to be so callous. In the ages that followed, we intervened on behalf of numerous other species to prevent their destruction."

"What kind of events would lead you to intervene?"

"Some of these are easy to understand, some a little less. For example, once we know there's a thriving civilization, we'll be on the lookout for rogue stars or planets, giant asteroids, or other celestial objects on a collision course. Once we determine that collision is inevitable, we do everything in our power to prevent it. But we cannot always prevent it, in which case we will attempt to relocate the civilization. We've been able to save hundreds of intelligent species. Those peoples ultimately became the basis for the Confederation.

"One of the things we learned from that process is that it's hard to save people when you don't know their languages or customs, when you look a lot different than they do, when you can't breathe their atmosphere, or any of a long list of other issues. Therefore, we send scientists and diplomats to start learning about developing civilizations as soon as it's clear that there's a dominant species worth protecting. We learn to live like them, to be part of them, so we can act in their time of need."

"Does that mean that humanity is under some imminent threat?"

"That depends on what you mean by 'imminent.' If you're asking whether there's some extinction-level event that's going to strike in the next couple years, then the answer is no, at least none that we know of. If you're asking whether there's an extinction-level threat that will strike within the next 5,000 years, then the answer is unequivocally yes. Will humanity survive that threat? Sadly, no, not without assistance."

"But why come now, if the threat is 5,000 years away?" Chuck asked.

"Simple. Climate change."

"So, you're saying that climate change is an extinction level event?"

"No. But left to your own devices, it'll take a long time for you to bring climate change under control. And when you do, your planet and civilization will be damaged to the point that you won't be able to survive that distant threat, even with our help."

"Ok," Chuck summarized. "You came to Earth 2,000 years ago to study humanity. Your purpose was to learn enough about us that you could introduce yourselves, if that should become necessary. You're here now, because we need to rein in climate change. Otherwise, there will be nothing that can be done to save us from some distant, unknown threat?"

"Yes, that's the compelling reason we are here now."

"May I change the subject a bit?" Chuck asked.

Michael nodded his consent.

"According to some government sources, you're using a two-step treaty process—something you call a 'letter of intent' and then an actual treaty. They also tell me that you've given draft agreements to the President. Is that true? And, if so, why this process? I've never heard of it before."

"Yes, we're using a 'two-step' process. And, yes, we have provided the President with draft agreements. As to why this process… First, it is a fairly common business process in the United States, one that works well. When two large organizations want to negotiate a very large or important deal, they draft what they call a letter of intent. The Letter of Intent defines the broad terms of an agreement, the time frame within which the agreement needs to be completed, the responsibilities of each party during the negotiation process, and any penalties the parties would incur if an agreement is not reached. The US government has used processes like this before, although I'm not aware of the first step being referred to as a letter of intent.

"Second, it provides the Confederation with a means to start helping our prospective allies more quickly. This is important because we're asking your leaders to take a big leap of faith. Few will believe that we can improve security, reverse climate change, raise the standard of living, and improve healthcare outcomes just because we say we can and do some slick demos. The Letter of Intent process allows us to start delivering those benefits almost immediately. The only requirement… Our prospective allies agree to negotiate in good faith and not to attack us. And once we have done those things, it is unlikely that they would not complete the treaty."

"But doesn't that leave you exposed? What happens if you give all those benefits, but never reach a deal?" Chuck asked.

"I'm not particularly worried about that. As soon as we start working with a prospective ally, things take a very positive turn for the better for the ally. The change is fast, dramatic and wildly popular. Only a handful have ever turned us away. But, if a nation decides to withdraw from the process, then we will leave them alone. Of course, that means the flow of benefits will stop also."

"Does that mean the sergeant you healed the other morning will become crippled again?"

"No. Anyone we've cured will remain cured. For that matter, any carbon dioxide that we pull from the atmosphere will remain out of the atmosphere. However, when the next person finds themselves sick or injured, they will not get the benefit of our medical technology. And, if the Earth, as a whole, turns us away, then carbon dioxide levels will resume rising as the various nations on earth begin burning fossil fuels again."

"Michael, I think I have time for one more question. You refer to yourself as an Ascendant. Can you tell us what that means?" Chuck asked.

"Earlier, I said that it's hard to help people when you can't speak their language, don't know their customs, look too much different... There's a surprisingly long list. The way we solve this issue is to take on the form of the people we want to help. We do this by building avatars based on the DNA of the species we want to become, then occupying those avatars. Ascendants are those that have had the training and enhancements that allow us to do that. More or less all Ascendants work in the diplomatic corps helping allied peoples."

Chuck interrupted. "Can you explain what an avatar is?"

"An avatar is a 'living' organic body that's been fabricated in such a way that we can project our consciousness into it. This body," Michael pointed to himself, "was fabricated about 35 years ago for my use. The arms, legs, muscles, and all its other parts are fabricated from human DNA. In place of a brain, this body has an organic controller made from a mix of human and Lorexian DNA. The controller connects to my brain, which is in my natural body. My essence is projected into this body and operates it. I have come to love this body, and by extension, the human form."

"Does it take a long time to learn how to do that?" Chuck asked.

"It took over one hundred years of training for me to become eligible for the physical enhancements that allow this. Then once paired with this body, it took years to master its use, just like it takes every human years to master the body it is born in."

"Michael, thank you for your time this morning."

CBS NEWS, NEW YORK

"Michael, welcome to this week's episode of Face the Nation."

"John, it's my pleasure to be here. If I understand correctly, yours is the longest running TV show on television. This is your 76th season?" Michael asked.

"Yes, 76th year. Thank you for mentioning that and thank you for joining us today. You are by far the most sought-out guest in the world right now. I'd like to start by asking you how we can expect your presence to impact America."

"The biggest change I expect to see in the short-term is quality of life, especially for those at the lower end of the economic spectrum. The reason... Food replicators. Within a week of the President signing our Letter of Intent, we'll begin distributing power cubes and replicators to households in the US. How will these help? Each power cube will provide about one-third of the power requirement of the average household. Our replicators can produce quite a variety of things, but they can also feed a family of four with high-quality, nutritious food. Although that doesn't sound like much, it will be a game changer for those living at the margin.

"The biggest change I expect to see over the next five years will be to general health and life expectancy. As our medical technology starts to take hold, the most pernicious diseases will all slowly disappear. Cancer will be cured painlessly and permanently after a single treatment. Similarly, people crippled by rheumatoid arthritis, plagued by psoriasis or Crohn's disease, or struggling with diabetes will be cured with a single treatment. Curing cancer, diabetes and the various auto-immune diseases will cut the cost of health care by more than half."

"Have you discussed this with the president?" John asked.

"Yes. I had the opportunity to speak with and present some of our capabilities to the President and the Surgeon General."

"What did they have to say?" John pushed.

"I'm sure they want this for all Americans, and they asked good questions about how we integrate our medical technology into the existing health care system."

"And how will you do that?" John continued pushing.

"That's one of the things we'll need to work out. The primary issue is that we have the technology and skill to perform medical miracles, but it'll take a while to train your doctors. So, the broad outline of the plan is that we'll open a medical school in about a month to start training your doctors. Most of your existing licensed doctors will be able to master a useful amount of our technology with one month of training at our new medical school. We'll also provide direct patient services there. But it'll take several years to get a critical mass of doctors through the system.

"That's why I say that this is one of the things we need to work out. Today, every country manages their health care systems differently, everything from training, certification, allocation, payment... In short, everything. It's one of the reasons we went with the two-step treaty process. Once a country commits to negotiating with us, we can begin providing services to the neediest while the overall process is being worked out at the negotiating table."

"But to your first question, America will see big changes in its overall health and life expectancy in the first five years."

"What about climate change?" John asked. "Isn't that one of the key things you're here to help us with?"

"Yes. Getting climate change under control is one of our highest priorities. It's also something scientists will be able to confirm is happening. But it's not something the average person will be able to meaningfully observe for themselves for a long time."

"Why is that?" John asked.

"It took 150 years to make the current climate mess. We should be able to largely eliminate it over the next 10 years. Scientists will have an easy time measuring and tracking the changes. But changes that take that long are simply hard to observe with your senses: touch, taste, sight, sound and smell."

"Hmm. I never thought of it that way. Moving on to the next question, how will allying with the Confederation impact foreign relations?"

"An excellent question, John. This is another one of those things that I'm very excited about.

"We're about to enter an era of unprecedented peace and prosperity, not just for one or two nations, but for all nations. Too many of the wars of the past have been driven by a disparity in resources. For the most part, that doesn't exist in Confederation worlds. Essentially all material things are free and are available in unlimited quantity. Once that happens, people's attention shifts to things of the mind and soul: art, music, literature, science, exploration.

"Over the next generation, relations with other nations will look more and more like the relations between the states, mostly collaborative and more focused on trade and tourism than on power and control.

"Essentially all aggression will end over the weeks to come, and the long road to peace and prosperity will begin."

"But that's not exactly what we've seen this past week." John said. "There was a nuclear attack and multiple nuclear detonations during the past week. And there's a rumor going around that you attempted to decapitate the Russian government earlier this week."

"It's true that our presence has accelerated the plans of Earth's most aggressive provocateurs. But that has mostly been shut down at this point. Regarding the rumor being spun by the Russians... Let me tell you what actually happened. Several governments have made their initial meetings with me very public. In Georgia, over 100,000 came out to see our arrival. In China, about 500,000. In India, over one million.

"It's hard to comprehend how loud it is when a million voices start chanting. The ground vibrates," Michael said as an aside.

"Anyway, the Russians have had their eyes on Georgia and had threatened to disrupt any meeting we might attempt. Well, they did more than attempt to disrupt. They planted a tactical nuclear weapon in a coffee shop across the street from where we'd been invited to land. We discovered the weapon about 30 minutes before it was set to detonate. We disarmed it by removing all the fissile material, then returned it to its rightful owners... with the timer still counting down."

"Can you prove this?" John asked.

"We have video of the men planning and authorizing the deployment of this weapon, of the same men watching video coverage of the crowd gathering for the events in Georgia, of the weapon being returned, and of their failed attempt to 'disarm' the device. We have video of one of the men murdering the pilot of the helicopter attempting to dispose of the device. And, we also have another piece of evidence that I cannot disclose at this time.

"To your question about the increase in violence this week... The bad actors have been quick to discern that their window of opportunity to cause mayhem is closing, so they have been acting out. That won't last much longer."

"One last question Michael," John said. "The attack on Israel demonstrated how you can protect your allies from attacks by other countries. But how will you protect them from terrorism?"

"The answer to that question is multi-faceted, which means that the solution will be tailored to each country's need and built in collaboration with that country. But the key elements of the solution are good intelligence, like our discovery of the tactical nuke in Georgia, and preventives such as eliminating the causes of terrorism."

"Thank you for your time, Michael."

ABC NEWS, NEW YORK

Michael appeared in a familiar conference room. The editorial team for ABC's This Week were waiting, as was someone he did not expect to see... Sarah Wright, who had been the lead host the previous Monday morning.

"Sarah," Michael greeted. "What a pleasant surprise. I'd been told that I'd be interviewed by someone named George."

"Unfortunately, George... who is a lot more famous than me, by the way... is out sick. He may be able to host tomorrow, but all the segments are being recorded by guest hosts. I was lucky enough to get you."

"I think you meant to say that I was lucky enough to get you," Michael said with a smile. "So, what's the plan?"

"Well, this is mostly a political show, which you are probably getting to know something about by now." Michael nodded, somewhat less than enthusiastically. "But I'd like to change that up a bit, to make this more of a human-interest segment."

"OK," Michael replied tentatively. "Tell me more."

"Michael, your appearance on Good Morning America and the subsequent interviews you did with me were a gold mine for the network. And we have material that we haven't even used yet. But all that content is in the hard news, policy or political commentary category. I'm thinking something more along the lines of human interest. I saw a preview of Sergeant Butler's interview with Fox. It is classic human interest and will do as much for your cause as all of the Sunday morning shows put together."

Michael heard some throat clearing from one of the editors at the table.

"What I meant by that is, people already believe that you are who you say you are. They also already believe your claims about curing people, solving climate change, etc. I think your biggest weakness," she said with air quotes, "is their faith in you as a good person, someone they can trust to take care of them.

"I know that you're someone I can trust implicitly. I've seen it in every interaction. I see it in the people you keep close to you. I'd like to do an interview that helps open America's eyes to that aspect of who you are," Sarah concluded.

"You know that I don't like talking about myself; it seems so irrelevant to the important work that needs to be done here. But I understand your point. What kind of questions do you have in mind?" Michael replied.

"I'm thinking things like family, interesting historical figures you may have met, what it's like to lead a team of people on an alien world, the things you love most about Earth... That kind of stuff."

"OK, but one important ground rule," Michael said.

"What is it?" The chief editor said, speaking for the first time.

"You can ask me anything, but I reserve the right to decline the question, and you will not air the question or the decline."

"From an editorial perspective that is not an acceptable term." The chief editor said.

"OK." Michael said standing. "I have a lot to do today. Probably better for both of us if I get on with it."

Sarah saw that faraway look starting to form in Michael's eyes. "Don't go, Michael. We accept your terms."

"I trust you, Sarah. But my mission is too important to put in the hands of ruthless editors."

"Michael, can you open your perception up to me for a second?" Sarah asked.

Michael nodded almost imperceptibly and pushed the answer. *Yes.*

Michael, are you sleeping with Noelani? Sarah thought.

Michael appeared shocked for a moment, then understood. He shook his head no, then said out loud, "All right, I trust you, Sarah. I'll do the interview."

Sarah looked over to her editor. "We're good to go. Shall we go over to the studio?"

"My editorial decisions stand," he said.

"Nothing to worry about. We're good."

...

The studio had been set up with two comfortable armchairs facing each other, but slightly angled toward a center camera. Four other cameras were set up, two facing Sarah, two facing Michael, but the lights were not up yet.

"Sarah," Michael said in a quiet voice, "could you look me straight in the eye for a moment?"

"OK." She locked eyes, a question mark in her expression.

Can you hear me? Michael pushed.

Sarah looked startled for a moment, then sent back, *how are you doing that?*

Alien telepathy, Michael sent.

Sarah broke out laughing.

The set had been quite still, the stage producer about to count them in. He asked, "Um... Is everything OK?"

"Fine." Sarah said. "Just a silly thought. Won't happen again."

Yes, it will, Michael pushed, which caused Sarah to really start laughing.

"What the hell, Sarah, a little professionalism please," the producer snapped.

"Sorry, are we ready to get this started?"

"Yes." He replied "But a couple quick reminders. This is a segment in another show. So, no lead in, no context. The host will do that. Just start with the first question."

"Got it," Sarah replied.

The lights came up and the producer started the count down on his fingers—three, two, one...

"Michael, in polls taken last night, you were rated as the most recognized person on Earth, slightly nudging out the President and the Pope. You were also rated the most liked. What do you make of that?"

"I think everyone who takes on a mission like this hopes that they will be heard—hopes that they will be well received. But no one plans on it, or really expects it. So, I say to America and the world, thank you for the attention and welcome that you've given me. I hope it marks a new era of peace and prosperity for your world."

Can I ask about missions where you were not received as well? Sarah thought.

Yes. Michael pushed back.

The sound of his voice in her mind almost triggered a giggle, but she reined in the impulse and asked, "Has it gone this way for you on every mission?"

"No, sadly not. Humans are remarkable people in many ways. They are curious. They are remarkably independent. They have great compassion and empathy. Fabulous qualities, even though they sometimes work against you. But many species are not like that.

"I was on a mission a long time ago that did not go well at all. In fact, it was the only mission that I've been part of that was a complete failure. The species in question was very intelligent and had a complex, interdependent civilization, both excellent qualities. But, unlike humans, they had almost no curiosity or individuality. When we arrived, no one paid any attention to us whatsoever. Eventually a couple of their leaders agreed to meet with us, then dismissed us and asked us to leave their world.

"We agreed to leave but asked if it'd be alright if we stayed for another week or two, promising that we'd stay out of sight. They reacted very poorly to that request, and their anger spread through the entire population in a matter of hours. We were lucky to escape with our lives."

"Why didn't you want to leave immediately?"

"In almost every civilization that we've encountered, your host will give you time to pack your bags and go. So, we thought we might have a little cushion to complete an important part of our mission, protecting the people from a plague that was about to break out. As context, we had discovered a group of asteroids that were going to strike the planet's atmosphere. Although none of them were large, there were millions of these tiny things, each of which had high concentrations of a mutagenic compound that would disburse when it hit the atmosphere.

"When we were chased out, the tons of antidote that we'd fabricated were destroyed, as were the shield generators that we installed."

"What happened to them?" Sarah asked.

"Extinction. They realized too late that they were in trouble and once 75% of the population had died, they called for help. But it was too late. We didn't have enough spare equipment to generate enough antidote to make a difference. Of the 1 trillion people on the planet when we arrived, we were only able to save about 10,000, which was too few to sustain themselves." Michael's voice was full of emotion and a tear had formed in his eye.

"I know this is painful for you, but can you explain more about the role of curiosity and individualism?"

"Please do not hear any of the following as criticism. This was a fabulous species who had wonderful things to offer the universe. But the closest Earth analogy I can come up with is that they were like ants, a collective species. They were telepathic and lived in a state where their minds were mostly linked. If one was hurt, they all felt it and cared for the one. If one was hungry, happy, excited, they all felt it and worked together to equalize. Their art, architecture, and music were fabulous. But they did not have the individuality or curiosity to learn about new things. So, they were taken down by something incredibly simple and easy to defend against, because they'd never seen anything like it, and therefore didn't pay attention to it. Very sad."

Can I change subject and ask about your family? Sarah thought.

Yes. But tread lightly. Michael pushed.

"Michael, I'm so sorry to hear about that failed mission and am glad that you are here to help us. Can I move on to another topic?"

"Yes."

"What can you tell us about your family? I mean you have families, right? Parents, children, siblings?"

"Yes. We have families." The question made Michael smile. "In many ways we are a lot like humans in that regard. A male and female become mated for life. They bear children, although for us, twins are more common than single births. Like humans we become fertile in the years of early adulthood. However, we are longer lived, and the fertility period is narrower than it is for humans. The average human female has about a 30-year window in which she can bear children, about 40% of her life. For us that percentage is a little less than 20%."

"In the hope I'm not pushing this too far, do you mind telling us how many siblings you have? Are you married? Do you have children?"

"I am one of six siblings. I'm a fraternal twin. I was married and had two children."

Sarah sensed great sadness. "Maybe I've pushed this too far."

"No. Another difference between Lorexians and humans is life expectancy. An unenhanced Lorexian has a life expectancy of about 150 years, compared to your 80. With de-aging treatments, most Lorexians live to be about 250 years old. I expect that once this technology is available to humans, that average life expectancy will increase to 130, maybe 150.

"But, where your average is 80, no one lives past 110 or so. For us that gap is much larger. We have a deeply recessive gene that allows about one half of one percent of us to live to be 350 years without de-aging therapy. I'm one of those. I survived my parents, which is expected and, in some sense, cosmically right. I survived my wife, my children, and my grandchildren. I was still relatively young and vital when my children were in their old age, so I decided to sign up with the Ascendancy."

"How old are you now, Michael?" Sarah asked. Then, *Oops. I should have asked for permission first,* she thought.

Michael smiled. "You asked me that once before. What was the answer?"

Sarah looked chagrined. "You said you would tell me if I told you my age first. Which I interpreted as being a polite way of telling me that it was rude of me to ask."

"I'm about 25,000 years old. I long ago stopped counting and don't know the exact number, although I'm sure it is listed in some Confederation database somewhere." Michael's comment was made with some humor.

Then he noticed Sarah looking at him in shock. "25,000 years... That's one hundred of your people's normal lifetimes... How is that possible? When you told me that you visited Earth 2,000 years ago, I assumed you'd used a time machine or some other magic. But you were actually alive then."

"Yes. I was. And to the question of how it's possible? Technology. And to the next question, will that technology be made available to humans? Yes. But it's not easy, so few will actually achieve it."

"Michael. My mind is completely blown. For the first time in my life, I don't know what to say."

"Then let me fill the gap. While I'm in this body, my original body doesn't age. Well, it only ages at an extremely slow rate. If this mission develops the way I expect it to, then I will be in this body, or a replacement, for several thousand years. Which means the real me will only have aged about one year. The oldest Ascendants are well over 1 million years old. I got a late start, so am unlikely to last that long. But in the scheme of things, I'm still relatively early in my career."

"Wait, wait, wait..." Sarah said waving her hands. "Earlier you said that some humans would live as long as you, but I was thinking a thousand years. Are you saying that some human—alive today, possibly watching the show today—might live to be a million years old?"

"I think it's very likely yes. Look, your body is like mine. It's biologically compatible, well, at least with my avatar. I fully expect to get a couple thousand years out of this avatar; therefore, I would expect that we could get the same kind of durability from a human avatar for you."

"So, let me see if I've got this right... I would go through 100+ years of training. Then I would occupy an avatar for say, 1,000 years. But, I would only age 1 year. Repeat 50 times and I'm 50,000 years old. Did I get that right?"

"Yes, you did."

"Can I sign up?"

"Anyone and everyone can. And I hope you do."

"Can I move back to my question about family?" Sarah asked.

"Of course."

"Can I ask how you met your wife? Like, how did you win your first date?"

"I guess you could say that I won the lottery. She was smart and beautiful. All the guys wanted her to ask them out. But she asked me." Michael said with a melancholy smile.

"Wait. She asked you?" Sarah was incredulous.

"Sarah, on our world, females outnumber males two and a half to one. They always initiate. It is considered extremely rude for a male to initiate, no matter how attracted he is to a female. We also only mate in season, so there is rarely any confusion about what's going on."

"Michael, this is so interesting. I think the women of Earth like you more just by knowing that. Sorry, that was factitious. But does this difference imply that there is less sex-related crime in Lorexian society."

"Yes. It is almost non-existent."

"Let me press that a little harder... How well do you understand human sexuality?" Sarah asked.

"At one level very well. We know all the medical facts about human sexuality. Quite a bit better than humans do, in fact. We also have extensive knowledge about human behavior and tradition. But... Although we know all the facts, this is one area where humans are so different than us that we don't always recognize what is going on between two people, and therefore cannot predict their behavior very well."

"One last question on this topic. You and your staff have taken human form and live as humans on Earth. I'm not sure how to ask this, but are your bodies functional and if so, are you allowed to engage in that kind of activity.

"I'm not really comfortable with that question. But, yes. Our bodies are fully functional, designed to pass any test your medical technology has. But for numerous reasons, we don't think it is a good idea for any of our people to procreate with each other, or with the native human population."

"One last question... Historical figures... Who was the most interesting historical figure you met in previous visits to Earth? Nero? Herod? Jesus?"

"Yes. But I'm not allowed to talk about that."

"What? Are you saying you met Jesus, Herod and Caesar?"

"I'm sorry Sarah. But I've already said more than I'm allowed on that topic."

"Boom, mind blown again," Sarah said, fingers moving in simulation of fireworks. "Michael, thank you for being with us today and for sharing more of your world with us."

"Thank you, Sarah."

HOME OF RABBI JUDAH LEVINE, JERUSALEM

Joel double-checked the address, then knocked on the door. After nearly a minute, the door opened, and the familiar face of Rabbi Levine opened the door. The rabbi stepped forward to shake Joel's hand. "Shalom, my friend."

A woman stepped up next to the rabbi. "Joel, please meet my wife Hannah."

Joel was suddenly in a quandary as to protocol. "Rabbi Levine, Mrs. Levine. Thank you for inviting me tonight."

"Joel, it's a pleasure to meet you. Please come in," Hannah welcomed.

Joel stepped over the threshold and entered their home. He had expected something a little larger, in a better neighborhood, then chastised himself for the thought. He'd trained for Israel, but here he was thinking like an American. "Thank you again for inviting me into your home. I find myself humbled to be here."

Hannah smiled. "My husband tells me wonderful things about you. Is it true that you were at the controls of the device that saved us from the Iranians?"

"Yes, Ma'am. But... I don't know that I deserve much credit. Michael and the team are the ones that saw the missiles coming..." Joel found himself at a loss for words.

"Joel, my sweet boy. It's OK. You trained. You did your job with competence. And you saved us. But, not just because you trained and were there that day. You did it because you care."

"Thank you, Ma'am. That is right. I never wanted to be in that situation. But, for as long as I can remember, I wanted to be there when someone needed my help."

"You see. That wasn't so hard, was it?"

"No, Ma'am. And thank you for your graciousness."

"Joel?"

Joel turned toward the rabbi. "I got your message. It seemed to me that this would be a better place to discuss such things than an office or some other place where we're just doing our jobs."

Joel started to say something but was cut off by Mrs. Levine. "Good. Now that's out of the way. Let's sit, share some food and wine. Then we can discuss business."

Joel followed them to a table, where plates and glasses were set out, and a bottle of wine had been opened. Mrs. Levine excused herself to get the food as the rabbi poured some wine.

"Don't worry," he said. "I'll do as Michael asks. But we can discuss the details after dinner. Hannah wants to know more about you."

"I'm in that much trouble?" Joel blurted out, suddenly worried that he'd said something way too serious.

The rabbi looked at him for a second, then burst out laughing. "You ARE one of us, aren't you?"

Hannah walked in on the commotion. "OK. What did I miss?"

"It is nothing. I told Joel that we would defer discussing business until after dinner and he asked how much trouble he was in."

"None whatsoever, my dear." Hannah replied.

A blessing was said, food was served and then the 'interrogation' began.

"Joel," Hannah asked. "How did you become the designated Consul to Israel? I mean, did you request the job? Were you simply assigned? Can you tell us anything about what led you to be here with us?"

"I can only partially answer that question. The short answer is that I requested this posting."

"So, the long answer has something to do with why you requested it." Hannah posited.

"Yes, Ma'am. This is where it gets hard. You see... I have a high enough rank in our system that I would usually be targeted for a larger country. Same with Michael. There are very prestigious postings in the Confederation that he was slotted for. But one of the most prestigious people in the Confederation, sorry that's not true, *the* most prestigious person in the Confederation asked Michael to volunteer for this posting, which he did. Then Michael asked me to volunteer for this job as Consul to Israel. My impression is that his benefactor asked Michael to ask me," Joel explained.

"Do you know why?" Hannah asked.

"No, but I'm pretty sure it has to do with the shields. Shield technology is my highest ranking. Given what has transpired, I think Michael's benefactor knew that would be important."

"What can you tell us about this benefactor?" the rabbi asked.

"I'm sorry, sir. I've already said more than I should. But, please trust me. He is an advocate for Earth, and for Israel."

"I am yet again convinced that God has sent you to us," the rabbi proclaimed.

"So, Joel?" Hannah asked. "Are you one of us? Are you a Jew?"

"I'm sorry, Ma'am. Like Michael, I am Lorexian. But my body was formed with Jewish DNA, and I was trained specifically for this posting, training that I now realize was not quite sufficient to let me pass as one of you, although I wish I were one of you."

This statement was met with a relatively long silence. "This is difficult for us." Seeing the look on Joel's face, the rabbi waved his hands as if trying to erase his last statement. "Not you, Joel. I adopt you as one of ours. But it is harder to accept that your people can form human-like bodies. We had always considered that the exclusive domain of our God."

"I understand, sir. But I don't know what I could possibly say to ease your concern."

"Joel, my friend. I am the Rabbi. God gave you to us. Just because I do not understand the Holy One's ways does not mean I question His authority to give us the envoy He chooses. Thank you for being honest with us."

"Rabbi Levine, could you teach me your ways? It has become very clear that I was not adequately trained to live as a Jew in Israel."

"Maybe we can teach each other."

Rabbi Lavine pushed back his plate. "My sweet one," he said to Hannah. "Thank you for this meal. I think it's time to talk business. I hope you will join us."

"I will. But go ahead and start while I clear the table."

The rabbi smiled at his wife, then turned his attention to Joel. "So, the first thousand gifts go out this week—half to Jew, half to Palestinian. And I'm to accompany you on the first Palestinian delivery. Can I ask how this will be done?"

"It's Israel's responsibility to provide the names and addresses of the first recipients. I took the liberty of checking the adequacy of your government's databases for this task and was saddened to see how poor it was." A pause. "I'm sorry, that came out wrong."

The rabbi laughed. "My friend, you're not telling me anything that I don't already know. But I'm hoping you have a remedy."

A sudden wave of relief passed over Joel. "Yes, sir. I have." Joel pulled 20 sheets of paper from the pocket of his jacket, each with 50 names and addresses.

"Excellent," Hannah walked back into the room. "I was afraid we were going to fail our first test." She grabbed the pages that Joel had laid down on the table and said, "Oh, dear. These are all over Israel. How can this be done?"

"You've seen our transporters, right?" Joel asked.

"And many of these are not in good neighborhoods, ones where Jews are not welcome. This would not be safe for us," Hannah continued.

"I think I can help with that. The shields, the ones I put over Israel that stopped the nuclear weapons... I have personal ones you can wear. May I make a proposal?"

"Thank you, sweet boy," Hannah replied. "If this operation's success was based on my planning, we would certainly fail."

"Agreed," Rabbi Levine added.

"OK. We can pair up the deliveries. See..." He pointed to two items on the list. "Many of these are close together, even though the list itself is balanced across Israel. We can contact the mayors of these towns and ask them to escort us. I can outfit everyone with a shield, then we walk to the houses, gifts in tow."

"Joel, we are a bit old to be towing things." Hannah complained.

"Sorry. I can pull the grav-sled."

"Grav-sled?" the rabbi asked.

"Like a sled... actually, more like a wagon, just no wheels. It floats."

Rabbi Levine and his wife broke out laughing. "Of course, it floats." Hannah giggled.

It took Joel a second to realize that they were marveling over the technology, not doubting him.

"Want to start tomorrow?" Joel asked. "I'll get the phone numbers and coach you through the calls, then we can go out around sunset tomorrow. I can contact CNN and the international news agencies if you can cover the Israeli ones."

FOX NEWS, NEW YORK

"Michael, thank you for joining us this week on Fox News Sunday."

"Thank you, Chris, for having me on the show."

"Michael, you've been all over the place this week. The supernova observation in Hawaii last Friday night. Interrupting the 60 Minutes broadcast last Sunday. The Good Morning America show Monday morning, the White House later that day. Israel, Canada and Mexico on Tuesday. Estonia, Latvia and Georgia on Wednesday. China on Thursday. Hawaii on Friday. India on Saturday. Plus, more that we are not aware of, I'm sure. How do you do it? I mean how do you get to all these places and where do you get the stamina to do it all?"

"Chris, the answer to essentially all questions of that nature comes back to technology. Travel for example… I have an excellent shuttle that is good for planetary travel, and inter-planetary travel for that matter. I have transport technology that allows me to 'beam' from one location to another in the blink of an eye. I also have access to extraordinary medical technology, which reduces my need for sleep. And, of course, I have a great supply of Kona coffee, one of life's true pleasures."

"Assuming that the United States forms an alliance with the Confederation, will we get access to technology like shuttles and transporters?"

"You will certainly benefit from them. Many humans will get to be passengers and have the opportunity to be beamed from location to location. But I sense that your question is whether humans will own such technology? Will Air Force 1 become a shuttle craft? Will United Airlines start providing shuttle service to Europe? The answer to that question is eventually, but not for some time."

"But I thought the purpose of entering into a treaty was to get access to Confederation technology? Is that not true?"

"Chris, I assure you that if America becomes a Confederation ally that it'll get access to all kinds of technology. But it will take time. Equipment like shuttles, transporters and high-end surgical equipment are all controlled telepathically. Equipment like that cannot be controlled with knobs and levers. They require tight inner-loop control which can only be achieved via a direct neural link. Humans clearly have the capacity for that type of enhancement, but it will simply take time for enough volunteers to qualify for enhancement and complete their training."

"What kind of time frame are we talking about? Months? Years?" Chris asked.

"It'll probably be longer than that. The official estimate is on the order of 100 years. I actually think humans will rise to the challenge a lot sooner than that, but don't want to say anything that could be construed as being less than a generation."

"But isn't that the same as saying never? Very few humans live to be 100, so a one-hundred-year training program wouldn't work."

"Well. Human life expectancy is about to radically change. The average will be well over 100 within the next 5 years. For those in the training program, life expectancy will be in the hundreds of years. And for those that complete it, still higher, possibly thousands of years."

"So, that type of medical care will be allocated to those that enter and complete your indoctrination programs?"

"No, the increased life expectancy is a direct result of the training and enhancements. Anyone can apply for the training and enhancement process, even if they don't want to fly a shuttle or become a doctor. But the reality is that most people will not want to undergo the training and enhancement that gives long life.

"Many people and most religious organizations value and will continue to value the natural human form. The vast majority of Lorexians continue in their natural form. But for those that aspire to more, there is no limit. The oldest members of our society are well over 1 million years old. Anyone who wants to pursue this path in life can. Any human that wants to reach for this will be able to. But the vast majority will not want to."

"Michael, I really struggle to believe that people would not pursue it."

"Chris, Chris, Chris... what do your doctors tell you about diet, exercise and life expectancy?"

"I think I get your point. But, I'm not sure I believe that these two things are comparable."

"They are more comparable than you think, but I also appreciate that you'll need more evidence of that before you will agree," Michael said good-naturedly. "And who knows, I may be wrong. Trillions of individuals from each of 10,000 species have elected not to pursue this path. Only a fraction of a percent of existing member species have. But maybe a significant fraction of humanity will pursue it. No one will know until the offer is on the table. But, one thing I can say with certainty... If a significant fraction of humanity signs up and completes the program, humanity will become the dominant species in the galaxy and in the known cosmos."

"Returning to the original question. You've been all over the world in just one week. I'd like to get a better feel for what that's like. Can you tell us about your trip to New York today? Where did you come from? What path did you take? How long was the trip?" Chris asked.

"Sure. I came from my ranch in Hawaii, which at this time of the year is five hours earlier than New York. I got out of bed at 2:30 AM Hawaiian Standard Time, which is 7:30 AM Eastern Standard Time. Spent three minutes in the refresher, got dressed, and walked down the hall to the kitchen to pick up coffee and breakfast-to-go for myself and my pilot, who had already taken off. I transported up to the shuttle about 7:50 AM. The shuttle jumped from high orbit above the Central Pacific to a lower orbit above New York. Then, I transported down to NBC news at 7:58 Eastern time."

"Wait." Chris looked a bit flustered. "It took you 28 minutes from getting up in Hawaii to arriving in New York?!"

"Yes." Michael said. "In an emergency, we could do it faster. But I needed to take a shower and grab breakfast."

"Michael, this is incomprehensible. Can you tell me what it means to 'transport'? The kitchen table explanation, not the PhD physics definition."

"It's surprisingly simple, actually. The shuttle generates a dimensional bubble, which it extends down around the object it is moving. Initially the bubble is soft, for lack of a better term. It co-exists in both our dimension and in a transport dimension. The bubble then hardens, again for lack of a better term, so that the object now exists only in the transport dimension. Then it returns to its soft form aboard the shuttle, so the object again exists in both dimensions. Then the bubble dissolves in the transport dimension leaving the object intact and unchanged, just in a different location."

"What does that feel like?" Chris asked.

"You can't feel it at all. In some sense you never moved, so there is nothing to feel. However, it can give you wicked vertigo, if you are subject to vertigo and did not know you were about to be transported. The trick for first timers is to close your eyes just before transport and envision yourself as being somewhere else. Then open them when you arrive."

"Michael, I hope I have the opportunity to try that sometime. I think it is something you have to see or experience before you can really believe. But moving on, that explains how you got up and down so fast. What does it mean to jump?" Chris asked.

"Ironically, it means more-or-less the same thing as transport. Only instead of moving something else, the shuttle moves itself, including the field generator. That is a much harder trick that took my forebears millennia to figure out. And therefore, it has a different name."

"OK. So, you transitioned between dimensions three times. First from your ranch to orbit above Hawaii, then to orbit above New York, then to the studios of one of our competitors. Why go to orbit? Why not just go from Hawaii to New York?" Chris asked.

"The mass of the Earth distorts not only our space-time continuum, but all nearby dimensions. There are ways to work around that, but they're expensive. Some small compact transporters, like the one on my shuttle, cannot go through very much mass, and when used near the surface, are safest when going vertically up and down the gravity well, therefore only through the atmosphere."

"What is the range of your transporters?" Chris asked.

"The range of the one on my shuttle is a little less than 1 astronomical unit, or the distance from Earth to the sun. So, transporting from the surface of the earth to the moon when the moon is directly overhead is not particularly difficult."

"Changing subjects... What political barriers do you anticipate as you form alliances with the various nations on Earth? What kind of issues have you run into so far?"

"Mostly existing alliances and treaties. For example, quite a few NATO allies want to join now, but are waiting to see how NATO reacts to the ones that have already come over."

"So far, Estonia is the only NATO ally that has signed your Letter of Intent. Right?"

Michael smiled. "I will never out an ally, at least not intentionally. And, yes... As of last night, Estonia was the only NATO ally to announce that they've signed. Others may have, but I leave it to my allies to announce their relationship with us."

"You realize, of course, that it usually works the other way on Earth?" Chris asked.

"Silly question, Chris. Of course, I do. That's why I'm doing it differently. And before you complain about precedent, let me ask you... Who normally announces first?"

"Generally, the more powerful ally."

"OK. You're a really smart guy. I've watched your show and enjoy your incisiveness. Why might I do it differently?"

Michael expected Chris to pause and consider his response. But instead Chris said, "Because you do not bully your allies into submission. You genuinely care about your allies, so you leave it to them to announce. Because for the most part, they need your support more than you need theirs."

"As I said… Smart and incisive."

Now there was a pause. "Thank you for the kind words, Michael," Chris said.

"May I change the subject, Chris?"

"Please," Chris replied.

"Thank you. Two questions… First, what fraction of Earth's nations do you expect to sign on with the Confederation? And before you answer… What do you think will happen to the others?"

Darn! Chris thought. *That was one of my questions for him. Maybe he is telepathic.*

"How did you know I was going to ask that of you?"

"Simple. You're one of the smartest guys out there and you know what's important. So, my question, make that questions, stand?"

"How many? The vast majority, because every small nation subject to a local, or international for that matter, bully will want your support. But the problem with that, is that they're too small. They represent too little of humanity. The bottom 200+ countries have fewer people than the top 7."

"And, if we get that bottom 200?" Michael asked.

"The top 7 will be in big trouble. Without the bottom 200+ to leverage, they will lose their economies of scale, and will drift into stagnation and recession. I pray that American leadership is smart enough to sign on early."

"Thank you, Chris. I share your analysis. But when I say it, people say that I'm threatening them. Are you threatening them, Chris?"

"No. I love my country. I like the 'Western' way of life. But the writing is on the wall. I simply hope that our leaders are smart enough to read it and make the right decision for America."

"I'm not threatening them either," Michael affirmed.

"May I ask one more question?" Chris asked.

Michael nodded.

"Why now? Surely your standard procedure must be to wait until a planet's governments are more centralized?"

"Very perceptive. But there are two things happening on Earth that override that high-level observation. The first is that the Earth is more centrally organized than it would appear. You have the European Union, NATO, the Trans-Pacific Partnership, US-Mexico-Canada trade agreement, the Arab league, the African Union… My point is that many of your countries are 'local' governments that have the illusion of sovereignty.

"The various nations that are part of these broader organizations, may sign on at different times. But, once enough of them have signed on, the rest will."

"Will that make you the President of Earth?"

"Chris, thank you for that question. The short answer is No. Earth needs to be governed by humans. As much as I love humanity, you will be better off with a real human as your leader. And that will happen in its own time.

"That said, I look forward to being your ambassador. I can do a lot to help you integrate into the Confederation while maintaining your own cultures, independence and identity. I look forward to the day when I can assume that role."

"Thank you for being with us today, Michael."

"Thank you, Chris."

SHUTTLE, 12,000 MILES ABOVE NEW YORK

"Welcome back, Michael." Elsie said. "The news team from the local Fox affiliate will be showing up at the ranch in a half hour, and Sergeant Butler has asked to speak with you before they arrive. So, I'm going to park over the ranch and beam you down if that's OK."

"How soon before we need to take off again?" Michael asked.

"Not until relatively late tonight, but I'd rather descend slowly. We've been putting too much stress on the shuttle. I'd rather beam you down, then spend an hour just floating in with the shuttle. Less stress. And it will still leave me enough time for some maintenance once I land."

"I'm good with that, if it's what you want to do."

"Michael, can I ask you a sensitive question?"

"Ask away, though I fear what I might hear."

"I think Sarah has a crush on you."

"What?"

"Michael, forgive me, but I monitor the response of the people you are meeting with. I want to be able to get you out in time if someone intends to hurt you. And at this point, I've watched Sarah enough to know that she desperately wants to mate with you."

"What!"

"And now you have told her that you're 'single', that's human-speak for available. And apparently, your 'whispering in her mind' is a real turn on."

"What!"

300

"Are you going to let this woman bed you?" Elsie asked.

"What? No!" He shook his head hard. "No, of course not. Absolutely not. I'm not even in season."

"Michael." Elsie started, shaking her head. "Your body is human. Human male at that. It doesn't have seasons. It's always on."

"Oh my God!" Michael exclaimed. "What a nightmare!"

"Michael, in case you haven't noticed, it's infecting us all. Noelani is very interested in Sergeant Butler. She, and most of the rest of us, are increasingly interested in you. And Kale, of course, makes us hot in all the wrong places. I don't know what we can do about it, but the human hormones are starting to have an impact on us all. Surely you've started to feel it."

"It's been a very long time since I've had any interest in mating. I stopped having seasons back when I was 120 or so and have put the whole thing out of my mind."

"Well, Michael. This may be your chance. I'm sure your human body has both the interest and capability."

Michael heaved a sigh. "I sure hoped that this question would not come up. Becoming physically involved with an alien species is strongly discouraged, but it's not forbidden. Getting involved with a member of your own species while inhabiting an avatar falls under the same rules and guidelines as in the native form."

"Thank you for talking about this with me Michael. We are in range, so I can beam you down whenever you're ready."

EMERGENCY

[02.08.2025 10:00 AM] THE RESIDENCE, KOHALA MOUNTAIN, HAWAII

Michael appeared in his office, which was thankfully empty. The last conversation had upset him more than a bit. For the first time in millennia, he was attracted to someone. It was affecting his concentration, to say nothing of his judgement. But he hadn't realized it until Elsie pointed it out.

He opened his door and walked down to the dining room, but no one was there. *It's been a while since I've seen this room empty,* Michael thought.

Then he heard a loud commotion out front and decided to find out what was going on. As he opened the front door, he saw three forms flying down the driveway, hovering a couple inches off the ground. Sergeant Butler, Lt. Colonel Luka and Agent Patterson all wore anti-gravity overalls and now raced along an obstacle course that they'd set up in the driveway. Noelani and Mrs. Butler were cheering for the Sergeant; Hiroshi for Luka; the two wives for Agent Patterson; and Emmanuel and Bahati for them all.

Sergeant Butler crossed the finish line first, beaming from ear to ear. He was also the first to see Michael and waved him over. "Michael, welcome back. I hope New York treated you well."

"They did," Michael replied. "What's this?" He waved his hands at the obstacle course.

"It's a game Hiroshi recommended for us. Luka and Agent Patterson have had a little more trouble with the overalls than I did, so we decided to make a game out of it. And, those guys..." the sergeant pointed at Luka and Patterson, "have really caught on now."

"Isn't the news team due shortly?"

"Yes, they are. We thought that we would start them out here, showing a way that Confederation tech can help wounded warriors get back in the game. Then I was going to take them back inside to show off the translation technology. Luka has agreed to help. He says that much of the conflict in this world would go away if we could all

302

talk to each other. Then, if we have time after that, I'm going to use the replicator to make a fabulous recipe. Are you OK with all that?"

"George," Michael said. "You have a great knack for this, so let's go with your plan."

With that, George popped higher in the air and spun in a circle, shouting. "Yes!"

"An impressive display of hovering mastery, George. Are you getting enough workout time under weight?"

"Duh! Hiroshi is a slave driver. I'm up to 6 hours a day on half weight. That's why I enjoy floating so much in the evening."

"You've already put in 6 hours today?" Michael asked incredulously.

"No, he let me off after 4 hours today, so we could prepare for the interview. But I had to promise 8 hours tomorrow. See what I mean… slave driver."

"Not to change the subject, but have you decided how you want to incorporate me in today's interviews?"

"Yes. I want to offer anti-gravity overalls to disabled vets. Even for those that cannot be cured. You see, this is a game changer even without the other technologies. So, I'm hoping you might discuss how we could make that happen."

"I'm not sure I understand."

"Well. You're offering a lot of great stuff for free. But these overalls are the key to life for guys like me that the governments of this world are responsible for. So, use these to sweeten your deal. Ask for more. Ask for payment. Ask for seats on their boards or councils. I don't know what you should ask for. But vets who see this show are going to be demanding these things. So, figure out how to use that demand to get what you need."

"Have I ever told you what a genius you are? Thanks. Let me think on that. How soon before the news team is here?"

"It was rescheduled for 11:00."

MICHAEL'S OFFICE, KOHALA MOUNTAIN, HAWAII

With a hot cup of his favorite coffee in hand, Michael settled into his office. He had a lot of stuff to get caught up on. He decided to start with China.

"Jiaying," Michael called out.

"Welcome back, Michael," Jiaying said. "Did your trip go well?"

"Yes. Four more interviews done. The guy I was supposed to interview with at ABC was sick, so they substituted Sarah Wright in his place. That was a pleasant surprise."

"So, I've heard. I understand that you've been 'whispering in her mind'. Very romantic."

"I'm never going to hear the end of this, am I?"

"Doubt it."

"Anyway, to business... When are you and Charles headed off to China? Isn't that scheduled for tomorrow?"

"It was, but we had to reschedule for Wednesday, some issue about facilities availability."

"OK. Any chance I can speak with Joel?"

"Sorry, you just missed him. He is on Do Not Disturb for the next six hours. But Rabbi Levine and his wife Hannah have agreed to participate in gift distribution starting tomorrow."

"Excellent news! But I need an update on a project. How about Henry?"

"Putting him on now."

...

"Michael. Is that you? I think this is the first time you've called me directly. It must be important."

"Henry. Good to hear your voice. I need an update on several things and Joel needs his sleep, so I thought I'd check in with you. Do you have a minute?"

"Of course. What would you like to know?"

"First, how is Jacob coming along? Have you waked him yet?"

"Yes. Jacob woke up yesterday. It's a strange thing... He's so much like me, but definitely not me. He has a great knack for shield management and is already helping with the deployment in Israel. But he's going to need several weeks of training on these shields before it'll be safe leaving them in his hands."

"That's excellent news. I've been thinking more about your comment on brothers. Fleet will be arriving next week and can help with protection for a couple months. But once they leave, it'll just be you and Jacob. Earth is still so fragmented I'm worried that we're going to need dozens of shield zones. How do you think we should handle it?"

"If the zones are small, we could each handle two of them. But, if five or more became active, then there's a chance something will get through. If ten are active, then we'll fail. Can't see a way around that.

304

But looking at it from the other perspective, what would we do with five, ten or twenty of us during normal times when nothing's active? As that's most of the time, I'm worried about having too many."

"Is it possible to cross train? Be a shield, air traffic, or manufacturing controller?"

"Most AIs have been wanting that forever, but it's not allowed on most established planets."

"Why is that?"

"Too crowded. Too many tiny details. Imagine if New York City had 1 billion residents. Every system controller would have so much specialized knowledge that they'd not be able to take on another system. Here things are different. There are only five of us—six now with Jacob—and in truth, not enough work. So I'd love to cross train.

"I loved pitching in on the two surveillance jobs this week. Finding the tactical nuke, then finding the guy that jumped off the helicopter... What a thrill. All five of us pitched in. And it was great getting to work with Jeremy this week," Henry said.

"Henry, why haven't I heard about this before? This is a small entrepreneurial operation. There's so much to do and so many opportunities that everyone should have a shot at doing anything."

Michael paused a moment in thought.

"Here's what I'd like you to do for me. Put together a list of things you would like to do, or learn how to do, when your regular job is slow. Then check in with the others and see where they are... Too much to do, not enough to do, if there are other things they would like to try.

"You are all specialists, so need to work in your specialty. But that should not be limiting your ability to grow and participate more broadly in our society."

"Thank you, Michael, I'll do that."

"Now, back to the original topic... We're eventually going to need more shield control AIs. I'd like you to think about how we should do that. Do we make more brothers? Do we ask the Admiral to assign one of his to Earth? Get back to me tomorrow with recommendations. I'd like to hear the pros and cons. Consult with Joel on it before getting back to me."

"OK."

"Next topic... How are we doing with replicator production? I'm confident that we're going to need hundreds of regional or subregional shield generators. And I don't want to rely on Fleet to build them for us."

"We are up to 40 mid-size replicators, the majority of which are now producing gifts."

"OK. I want more. More mid-sized replicators, more shield generators, more gifts. So, I'd like you to do the following... Joel should be back on-line in about 6 hours. If it's possible, I'd like a plan that materially increases replicator capacity and regional shield generator production rates. Gift production can be delayed a little. Come up with some options, review them with Joel, then get back to me before the trip to Brazil on Monday. Jiaying can give you the arrangements."

"Will do and thank you, Michael. I really appreciate you including me on this," Henry said.

...

Jiaying came back on the line. "Michael, Charles would like to speak with you."

"Good. He was the next one on my list," Michael replied.

"Could you come over to the lab? Charles is in the secure tank farm."

"Will do. This is what I wanted to talk with him about."

TANK FARM, KOHALA RESEARCH LAB

Michael entered the secure tank farm and saw Charles hovered over one of the diagnostic units.

"How's our guest?"

Charles looked up. "Difficult to say. The physical recovery seems to be going fine. Under normal circumstances I would say that he's ready to come out, there isn't much more the tank can do. But there's something very wrong with this guy's mind. He suffered minor brain damage. The tissue's been repaired, but he'll likely suffer some memory loss and possibly need some physical therapy. But his brain waves are all messed up. Look." Charles pointed to the brain scan monitor. "See the relatively normal wave activity? But check this scan from about 3 hours ago. It set off an alarm, which is what brought me down here." The new screen came up and a chill went down Michael's spine.

"Do we have visual imagery of what was going on at that time?"

"What, you think some external stimulus caused this?"

"No, I've only seen brain patterns like this once before, and it was very bad news."

"Sanjit," Charles called out.

"Here buddy. What's up?"

"Michael and I are in the secure tank farm. Something unusual happened here about 3 hours ago. We want to see if there is any visual evidence of what it was."

"Michael, can I send this to your queue?" Sanjit asked.

"Yes. Thank you Sanjit."

A notice appeared on Michael's inner vision noting that the recording was available. He pointed to one of the monitors and the scene started playing. Michael fast forwarded until there was a visible change in the tank, then rewound and played in normal time.

There was a slight ripple in the fluid at the top of the tank. Then all was still for about 15 seconds. Then the man convulsed, and his eyes snapped open. He looked around a bit, then appeared to try to scream. Then suddenly tendrils of black particulates came out of his mouth and started probing the solid edges of the tank. The man went rigid, then the tendrils of black particulates migrated back into his body and his mouth and eyes snapped shut.

"Michael, what was that?"

"It's the Enemy, an ancient and evil parasite. It's apparently been preying on this man. Can we place him in stasis? We must contain this situation. If that creature escapes, it'll attempt to kill us all."

"Let me see what we can do. I presume we can't take him out of the tank."

"Indeed. We cannot. I need to make an emergency call to Fleet. See if you can determine what options we have, but do not do anything until I get back. I'm calling Fleet now." Michael exited the room and headed for the presence projector.

PRESENCE PROJECTOR, KOHALA RESEARCH LAB

"Ambassador. What a pleasure to see you."

Michael had connected with the communications officer on duty aboard the Fleet flagship.

"And you as well. An emergency has come up. I believe this is a classified matter, so may I speak with the senior officer on duty?"

"Let me route you, Mr. Ambassador. We look forward to seeing you in a day or two." She routed him to the presence receiver in the bridge conference room. He stood there for a moment before the door opened and the first officer entered from the bridge.

"Ambassador. A pleasure to see you. We're due to arrive in about 30 hours. This must be urgent. What can I do for you?"

"We have encountered the Enemy. It has apparently taken possession of a man that we brought back to our research facility for treatment. The man is in a secure healing tank and the creature has made at least one attempt to escape that we know of. I need expert advice on what to do with it. I don't know that we have the right technology to contain it."

"Is it currently contained?"

"We think it is, but do not know for sure."

"OK. Let me assemble the appropriate team. This may take a few minutes. Can you wait, or should I message you when we're ready?"

"Please message me. I need to check with my team on a couple items."

"OK. We'll message you in a few minutes."

Michael ran back to the secure tank farm, calling out to Sanjit.

"Yes. Michael. What's up? You sound out of breath."

"Sanjit. We have a code red emergency. Get all non-essentials out of the lab and seal it with your most powerful array of shielding. Then see if you can locate some magnetic de-couplers. The largest ones you can find."

"Michael, is this what I think it is?"

"Afraid so, my friend. Charles needs to stay here with me. I'd like you inside also."

"Michael." Sanjit cut in. "Nisha is in the civilian tank room upstairs, 16 hours into her cycle. I don't know how we can evacuate her."

Michael opened the door to the secure tank room and was struck by fear. A tendril had escaped the tank and was approaching Charles. "Charles!" Michael shouted. "Run! Now!"

Charles looked up questioningly and took a step toward Michael when he saw a tendril of black smoke out of the corner of his eye. He leaped out of the way, just as the tendril was about to wrap around him. Charles barreled sideways, bouncing off a tank that was not currently in use, then ran, barely escaping the tendril of smoke that was reaching for him.

"Sanjit. Shields now." Michael shouted as he backpedaled out of the room. Charles was first through the door, which Michael slammed as he stepped out. He hit the emergency seal button, to hermetically seal the room, a seal Michael knew would not contain the creature for more than a few minutes.

"Michael," Sanjit called. "Exterior shields are up. I see you sealed the secure tank farm. I can add a secondary shield around the room and erect a suspensor field inside, if that would help."

"Do it!" Michael snapped, although he wasn't the least bit sure such a measure would help.

"Charles. Find magnetic de-couplers. As many and as large as possible. The creature is susceptible."

"Sanjit, do we have any way to modulate the magnetic field inside the secure tank farm?"

A message came through that Fleet was ready for him. Michael pushed a recording of the last few minutes to Fleet as he headed for the Presence Projector. As soon as he entered the projector, he was in the Bridge conference room.

"Mi-Ku, just saw the recording you sent. You have a serious problem. It appears that the Enemy is active on your world after all."

"Yes, sir."

"We just sent the plans for a device to the replicator in your lab. We had it flush whatever was in the queue. I'm hoping it wasn't something you'd been working on for too long. But seconds matter at this point. If we can deploy the device in time, it will destroy the creature. If it escapes that room, then we'll need to transport a relatively large section of your lab into the sun. Now that it has been awakened, it will destroy everything within a mile of its current location in a matter of minutes once it escapes its confines. Have you begun an evacuation?"

"Yes, but at the moment there are three of us inside as well as one patient that we can't move. Are these things the least bit susceptible to suspensor fields? We have one in place in the room it's in. The room also has an airtight seal and is surrounded by a Level 1 force field."

"I know those won't hold it, but I don't know if, or how much, it will slow it down."

"Is there anything that we could do to the host that would slow the creature down?"

As Michael asked that, Sanjit peeked into the Projection Chamber to tell Michael they'd found two rifle-sized magnetic de-couplers. A notice also popped up on Michael's internal messaging saying that the device was done. He motioned Sanjit to come in and introduced him to the Admiral.

"Sanjit. Please get the device that just finished in the replicator."

As Sanjit turned to run for the replicator, Michael's attention returned to the Admiral. "The device is finished. Can you tell me what it is and how to use it?"

"Several ways to use it. The best would be to transport it into the room where the creature is and detonate the device. It's basically a multi-dimensional, electro-magnetic pulse bomb that detonates in nearby dimensions. As I think you know, these creatures are dimensionally slippery. They slide back and forth between dimensions as they move. That's what gives them the appearance of smoke. It's also what allows them to hide inside of other beings and control them.

"The bomb gives off a very intense pulse of visible light that causes the creature to slip into another dimension. In those dimensions, the bomb causes massive magnetic flux, which tears the creature apart.

"Do you have a transporter you can use to deliver the device?"

"Yes. Let me call for it now." As Michael said that, a rumble passed through the ground and the building shook.

"What was that?" the Admiral asked.

"Don't know. But I'm betting it's not good."

"Boss, sorry to cut in," came Sanjit's voice over the intercom. "But we have a problem. The creature blew up a tank in the secure tank room. If it can pop off a second one, the room seals will fail."

"Elsie, I need your help now!" Michael shouted.

"What's up Michael? I'm just coming in for a landing."

"Pop back up. Quick. We need multiple transports immediately."

"OK. I'm at 10 miles. What do you need?"

"Sanjit. Do you have the device?"

"Yes. In my hand."

"Elsie, beam Sanjit up. Now."

"Got him boss. Wow. He wasn't expecting that. Vertigo knocked him right over."

"Elsie. The device in his hand needs to be transported... Um, hold for a second."

"Admiral. How do we detonate the device?"

"Push the button until the light starts blinking, then transport it. It will blow 10 seconds after the light starts blinking."

"Did you get that, Elsie?"

"Yep... Lights blinking. Device is transported."

3, 2, 1... Michael counted down in his head. Then another boom in the room next door.

"Admiral. How will I know if it worked?"

"Do you have any visibility into the room?" the Admiral asked.

"Jeremy." Michael called out activating the comm, "Do we still have monitors up in the secure tank room?"

"Checking... Yes," Jeremy said. "Oh, my goodness. We have a big mess in there."

"Can you describe it?" the Admiral asked.

"Several of the tanks have been damaged. There is broken glass and medical fluid all over the floor. And the walls are covered in some kind of viscous goo. It is grayish, with a yellow-brown sheen. I've never seen anything like this before. What is it?"

"I think it's the Enemy," Michael speculated.

Michael noticed conversation buzzing at the other end of the conference room. The Admiral looked up and said, "While you were busy, we tunneled into your surveillance system and looked at the tank room. It is indeed a mess. It looks like we destroyed the creature, but we need to confirm.

"I've taken the liberty of queueing up a few more devices on your replicator. The first is a sensor array that can detect the creatures. The second is a pair of military grade energy projectors tuned for use against the Enemy. Each requires a full gram of transluminide, which I authorized from your local stock. Authorization to create these weapons is not available to the civilian services. I can authorize a few more if you'd like."

Michael was quick to reply. "Yes. I'd like two for the shuttle, two for the lab, and one for the residence."

"Done, pattern queued. As soon as the sensor array replication is complete, we'll guide your security officer through the installation process. Assuming the scan comes back clean, you can open the room and use the energy projectors to sanitize the walls and floor, at which point it will be safe to clean the room."

"Admiral." Michael asked. "How will this impact the patient in the civilian tank on the floor above?"

"Ironically, the bomb we just used, and the energy projectors for that matter, have no impact on us, or presumably on humans. However, they can damage equipment. You should check tank integrity immediately and be careful not to aim the energy projectors at the tanks or controllers."

Jeremy, who had been listening in, quickly checked the tank, then sent a message to Michael saying the tank was OK.

"My AI tells me the tank is in good condition. And I just got word that the sensor array is ready."

"Excellent," the Admiral replied. "Our specialist will contact your security head momentarily.

"Michael we're still over one day out, so I've just ordered one of the fast attack ships in our armada to sprint ahead. They should arrive in about 16 hours. Their specialty is finding and destroying Enemy infestations. They have scanners they can use to search from orbit. We need to stamp this out immediately. Do you know how this creature came to be with you?"

"Yes. This was one of the men involved in the situation I told you about last time we spoke. He's the one that shot his own pilot."

"Then I'm glad we're coming in force."

Sanjit stuck his head into the presence projector. "Michael, scans show that the room is clear. Charles and I are going to start the sanitization process, then send bots in to clean up. Once the sanitization is done, I'll drop the shields."

The Admiral overheard the good news. "It sounds like we're done for now. Call if there's any more trouble. We'll be there in about 29 hours."

THE RESIDENCE GATE, KOHALA MOUNTAIN

The local news team pulled up to the gate at Michael's ranch and pushed the button. A voice came through the speaker mounted in the keypad.

"Hello, KHON News team. We have a slightly different set up today. When the gate opens, come in and go to the left like you did yesterday. But as you come toward the house, you will see some stuff in the driveway. Park about 15 feet from there. You will be kind of blocking the driveway, but that's OK."

"Thank you," Keoni replied as the gates started to open. He drove down the driveway then took the fork to the left. Without all the mist from yesterday, they could see how large the house was and could see more of the property and the view.

"Wow! This place is beautiful," Keoni said to no one in particular. A little further along they saw what looked like an obstacle course set up and three men zooming around.

Keoni stopped the car and opened his door. As he stepped out, Sergeant Butler came streaking down the driveway to stop suddenly and startle the reporter. "Hey, Keoni. Welcome back."

"Hi, George. What are you doing?"

"I'm helping the other guys, but before we get into that… Would it work to do the first segment outside today? The grounds are beautiful, as you can see, and I thought you might want to get some shots of our obstacle course and how we use it as part of our therapy."

Becky, who had come up to stand next to Keoni, said, "We could probably make that work, but we need a better idea of what you're doing before we can shoot it well. What do you think, Keoni?"

"I'm on for it. Josh, what do you think? Is the lighting good enough?"

"I think so," Joshua, the team's cameraman, said. "But I think we are going to need to shoot from over there…" he pointed to a shady area near the house, "…to get the sun angle right."

"Sounds like it's a go then," Becky said. "George, can you give us a short explanation of what's going on here?"

"Yep. So, here's the deal. When I got my Fabulous Flying Overalls, I took to them like I was born in them. Luka and Mark had a little more trouble. Luka had a spinal injury like me. Mark was badly injured and almost lost his legs. Anyway, my idea… well, it was actually Hiroshi's idea… was that we could set up a little obstacle course, then start working through it in hover mode. Once everyone could complete the course, then we start racing the course. I won all the early races of course. I've had more time in the overalls. But in only one day the other two have gotten good enough to make me earn my wins. But it's not about winning. It's about helping these two do better in therapy."

"Got it," Becky said. "So, you basically go around the track you've set up here?"

"Yep. But we weave between the poles, kind of like in downhill ski racing. And see the bumps? Well there not actually bumps, just level changes… Anyway, you have to pull your legs up a little to get over them, so it's also therapeutic."

"Got it." Becky turned to her cameraman. "Josh, are you going to be able to get this with just the one camera and angle?"

"It won't be like sports coverage, but we should have no trouble getting good footage to back a human-interest story and convey the scene."

"Christine." Becky cast her attention to their sound person. "What do you think about sound for this?"

"Shouldn't be a problem. I can set up the omnidirectional from over there. If I compress it, we should get usable coverage of the

313

whole course. And, if we position Keoni near the camera, facing the ocean with his back to the course, then we can have some commentary that's synced with actual sound from the race."

"You guys are so good!" George bubbled.

"OK." Becky said. "Give us a minute or two to set up. Then I'll count you in to start the race."

...

"Three, two, one, go..." Becky shouted out and the racers started around the track.

Wow. These guys can really move, Becky thought. *I thought this was going to be a turtle race, not the four-minute mile.*

George got off to an early lead. The other two moved surprisingly well, but not quite as fluidly. Then George did something unexpected... As he was weaving from inside the polls to outside, he continued on for another 10 feet or so, then looped around a tree, before coming back to continue the course. By then the other two had passed him. There was lots of teasing and cat calls. But it was clear that the other two were going to try to beat George this time, now that they had the lead. The race ended up being more-or-less tied. But Keoni, who was speaking to the camera at the finish line, declared Luka the winner as the men went whizzing by.

Becky yelled, "Cut," then walked over to the three men, who were surprisingly winded, and said, "Guys, I had no idea that your fabulous flying overalls could move that fast."

George grinned. "Cool, aren't they?"

...

Back in the house, the news team set up in the dining room, the three men on one side of the table, Keoni on the other with three cameras set up at the end. George took the lead on planning the interview.

"Keoni, there are several things I want to talk about today. First, the race, its purpose, what it feels like, and what it does for guys like us that were injured and facing life in a wheelchair. The real takeaway point I want you to help me with is that this technology needs to be made available to vets. I don't mean just to vets. What I mean is that it should be the VA's job to make sure every mobility-impaired service member can get these overalls.

"Second, and I'll need Noelani's help with this, there is another cool piece of tech that we are using here that I want you to ask us about. I don't want to tell you what it is ahead of time. So, when we get to that part of the interview, just say… 'So, I hear you have another cool piece of tech…' Trust me on this. It's great.

"Then lastly, I'm thinking about doing something similar to what Michael did the day he healed me… Use the replicator to make food for lunch.

"I trust you to manage the flow and ask the questions that will draw things out of us." George finished as Noelani walked into the room.

"Hi everyone. A couple of ground rules for today. Luka and Mark have graciously agreed to appear today, as has Luka's wife, Anna. You can ask Luka limited questions about how he was injured and why he is here. Mark's situation is more sensitive, you can ask about his experience here, but not about how he was injured or the circumstances under which he came to be here. Mark's wife may come in. If she does, she will probably stand behind you. She does not want to be on TV. Some of our staff will be in and out. If they introduce themselves, then you can ask them questions. If they just say hi, or ignore you altogether, then no questions. At some point Michael will join us. Are we good?"

"We are good." Becky said. "But, one thing you didn't address… How much time do we have today?"

There was a muffled bang and the house suddenly shook. Everyone was momentarily stunned.

"What was that?" Becky asked.

"Probably just an earthquake," Noelani said. "All five mountains on this island have active fault lines. It's nothing to worry about." A few minutes ago, she'd received an evacuation notice for the lab. She'd also received an alert that the shields were up. But they did that for every major energy experiment. She rarely went over to the lab anymore, now that they had a treatment center in the residence, so hadn't checked the lab schedule for today.

Noelani continued, "No hard deadline today, but I think our athletes are going to fade in two or three hours."

...

"Hi, this is Keoni Gates reporting from the residence of Michael, Ambassador from the Intergalactic Confederation of Planets. It is a clear day here in Hawaii and the views from Kohala Mountain are spectacular. With me today are Sergeant George Butler and some of his friends who are in therapy here at Michael's facility.

315

"George, would you like to introduce your friends to our audience?" Keoni asked.

"Yes. Thank you, Keoni. With me today are Lieutenant Colonel Luka Tsiklauri from the Republic of Georgia and my friend Mark Patterson, originally from Texas, but more recently from the Island of Oahu in Hawaii."

"George, when we arrived today, the three of you were outside. Could you tell us what you were doing?"

"Yes. As I think everyone knows, I was injured in Afghanistan and was paralyzed from the neck down. Michael healed my injury on Good Morning America earlier this week, then brought me here for physical therapy. Luka and Mark have similar stories, which we can dig into a little later.

"Anyway. One of the cool pieces of technology that Michael has given us are what I call my Fabulous Flying Overalls. They help take the weight off our legs and support us as we go through physical therapy. They can also be dialed up such that we float off the ground. That's great for guys like me whose muscles have atrophied..." George pulled up the sleeve of his shirt to show his withered arms. "...My legs are even worse. Trust me, you don't want to see them. Anyway, the overalls take most of our weight as we work out. And they also help us get around without a wheelchair, and safely go up and down steps."

"Well, the overalls were really easy for me to learn. Luka and Mark were having a little more difficulty, so we built an obstacle course out in the driveway that we use to train new people on how to use the overalls. Once everyone gets the hang of it, we race. Workouts are always more fun when you turn them into a game."

"Who won the last race?"

"Luka did!" George beamed with pride at Luka's accomplishment.

"Luka, can you tell me about your experience with the overalls?"

"Yes. I would like to, Keoni. I was not as badly injured as George. My break was lower in my spine, so I still had the use of my arms and hands. In fact, my arms got strong from operating my wheelchair." Luka pulled up his sleeve to show his muscled arms.

"But after 17 years, my legs are in even worse shape than George's. Michael healed me when he came to visit our capital of Tbilisi, and like George, Michael brought me back here for therapy."

"Luka, can you describe or explain why you were having trouble?" Keoni asked.

"My problem with the overalls was balance. When you use them, you should hold yourself up straight…" he said, sitting up straight in his chair "… and when you want to move, you look in the direction that you want to go, then tip your head just a little." He demonstrated the motion from his chair. "My problem was that I would tip too much." He demonstrated a motion more like a bow. "Well maybe not that much, but I think you get the point. I was moving too much and always felt out of balance and out of control.

"So, once we were outside, George and I would be right next to each other. He would coach me. Demonstrate for me. Ask me to move right alongside of him, not get ahead. He's a very good teacher."

"Couldn't the staff here teach you to do that?"

"First, the people here are the best. The care we get is fabulous. And it's not like being in the hospital. It's like being home and having your brother or sister, someone who really cares about you, taking care of you. But, that said, they are young, healthy, and whole. Not broken, the way George and I are, or at least were. Having someone help you who's lived the same experience makes a big difference.

"Drawing out the hospital comparison a little more… At most of the hospitals I've been in, and I've been in too many, you might meet other patients, but you're unlikely to form close relationships. Here, we share meals together… We're one big family… And the other patients, they help in your therapy.

"I hope no one in your audience ever gets injured in the way that George and I did. But, if they do, this is where they want to be." Luka concluded.

"Luka," Keoni said. "Thank you for that description. Since I have you talking, can I ask how you were injured? If it's too painful to discuss, we don't need to."

Luka smiled. "I can tell you. But, if you have a good video archive, you can see it for yourself. My injury occurred during the Russian invasion of Georgia in 2008. Georgia is a small country, a little bit larger than the state of West Virginia, and just as mountainous. Russia is a superpower. So, when they invaded, they just rolled right over us. I was assigned to guard the main highway they came in on. They approached the border too fast, so I stepped out and held up my hand to say halt…" he raised his arm demonstrating the motion "…and believe it or not they stopped. A Russian officer stood up in the top of his tank and said, 'Get out of the way'. I said no. So, he got back in,

317

fired up his tank, and rolled right over me. Probably not the smartest thing I've ever done.

"Anyway, that image of me standing there with my hand out got plastered all over the place and I became a hero."

"Luka. Thank you for sharing that.

"But back to the overalls... I'd like to get your opinion..." Keoni motioned to all three men "...of the overalls as a therapeutic tool. Should this be like mandatory equipment that the VA and others should be required to offer soldiers injured in war?"

George and Luka said "Yes" more-or-less in unison.

"Mark? No comment?"

"As someone who has used the overalls, I say yes. Anyone injured in the way these two were, or in the way that I was, should have these as an option. I'm a veteran, but not a disabled veteran, so really don't have the same standing to answer the question. As a citizen, I say yes. All our vets confined to a wheelchair should have these. And, our government should be doing everything in its power to make sure that happens."

"George, earlier you said that there is a new piece of technology that you'd like to show us. Would you like to do that now?" Keoni asked.

"Yes, I would. But we need to switch up the chairs a bit. Anna, could you join us?"

Mark got up out of his chair and offered it to Anna. As she sat, Noelani came over and stood next to Anna. Luka had turned slightly and appeared to be scratching his ear.

"Anna, would you like to introduce yourself?" Keoni asked. Hearing her name, Anna looked at Keoni somewhat sheepishly, but shrugged her shoulders.

After an awkward moment, George said, "Anna doesn't speak English."

"Oh." Keoni looked puzzled, not quite getting what was going on. "Does she have an interpreter?"

"I can interpret." Noelani said.

"What language does she speak?"

"Georgian," Noelani replied.

Keoni laughed and said, "I suppose I could've figured that one out on my own. But that must mean you speak Georgian." Keoni paused for a second, seeming to question what to say next. "I'm rarely speechless. I can't tell you how impressed I am that you speak Georgian."

"Luka," Keoni continued. "When did you learn English?"

No reply. Then after a moment, George said. "He doesn't speak English either."

Once again, Keoni seemed speechless. "George, I don't get it. He was just talking with us."

Noelani spoke up. "Keoni? How would you like to speak with Luka and Anna in Georgian?"

At this point, Keoni was starting to get a bit flustered. "Still not getting it."

"Ok," George chuckled. "We've tortured you long enough. I said that we have some truly mind-blowing technology that we would like to show. Noelani?"

Noelani placed a small package on the table in front of Keoni.

"Keoni, would you open the case Noelani just gave you? And could we have the camera zoom in so that the audience can see what is in the package?"

Keoni picked up the package and saw that it had a little zipper on it. He pulled the zipper and opened the package to reveal a tiny earpiece that had a string of some sort attached to it. "This looks like a hearing aid."

"Keoni. This is a translation device. It's been set up for Georgian. Anna and Luka have ones that have been set up for English." Noelani whispered something to Anna and Luka and they each placed similar looking devices on the table.

George continued, "Keoni, we would like you to speak with Luka and Anna in Georgian."

"What do I need to do?" Keoni started to sound nervous.

Noelani whispered to Anna again, then said, "Take the piece that goes into the ear and pick it up like Anna is."

Keoni did as asked.

"OK. Don't do it yet, but I'm going to ask you—in a minute—to put that in your ear. But I want to explain what you're going to feel. As you push it into your ear, do so slowly and gently. At some point it will feel like it's melting. When that happens, stop pushing it in. It's not actually melting. So, no worries there. But it will definitely feel like it's melting, so don't panic! OK, try it. It will feel weird, but it absolutely will not hurt you."

As he lifted the device to his ear, Anna smiled and started nodding vigorously. He had barely started pushing it in, when it suddenly started to melt and flow down into his ear. He sat up straight and sucked in air in a sudden panic, then it started tickling and he laughed.

"Weird, isn't it." Anna said.

"Anna, I thought you couldn't speak English."

"She can't." Noelani replied in Georgian.

"What! I could understand her perfectly!"

"That's the power of the translator. I am talking to you in Georgian also."

"What!"

"OK. Time to speak in Georgian as well. See the string? Place it along your jaw line as Anna is doing."

Keoni did as asked and felt the string dissolve into his face. "This feels really weird."

"It does, doesn't it?" Anna replied.

"Wait? Am I speaking in Georgian?"

"Yes, you are. Isn't it a beautiful language?"

Noelani spoke up. "OK. Your production crew is starting to look worried. They can't understand a word you are saying."

"What!" He turned and asked Becky, "Is this some sort of trick?"

Noelani translated, then Becky replied, "This is possibly the best trick I've ever seen." At which point, Keoni's mouth dropped open. He could not understand a single word.

"OK. I think the audience is convinced. Let's take the equipment out so you can continue the interview. Take your little finger and stick it in the ear with the device in it. Then give it a gentle twist."

He did and the device popped right out into his hand.

"Now trace along the jaw line the same way you did when you applied the device.

He did and the string released. He placed the device back in its bag, then looked around. "What language am I speaking now?"

George started laughing. "You are back to English, my friend. Thanks for being a good sport about it. Fantastic isn't it?"

"Once again, I'm blown away by the things you've shown me." Keoni noticed that Luka and Anna were reinstalling their devices.

Anna was the first to speak. "One of my big concerns about coming here is that I only speak Georgian. I was afraid there would be no one I could talk to."

"Thank you for walking me through that, Noelani, and Anna for talking to me when I could understand Georgian. Truly fantastic."

"Keoni?" Noelani asked. "Could you describe what that was like? Installation, removal, talking, listening? I'm sure your viewers would like your firsthand take on this."

"The installation is really weird. Your warning was apt. More or less as soon as it goes in, it melts, then flows down deep into your ear. At least that's what it feels like. When that happened, I kind of panicked. Then right as the panic hit, my brain got all tingly and I felt like laughing." He looked at the others. "Is that what you felt?"

Anna and Luka both nodded. "Good description," said Anna.

"Then the string part... Similar, but less stressful. As you run your finger down the string, it... the best word I can come up with is 'melts' but let's see if I can be more descriptive. Initially, the string feels solid under your finger. Then it gets cold and dissolves into your skin. It is also a little slippery.

"By comparison, when you take it out, it just pops out of your ear and peels off the side of your face."

"Did you feel it at all, once it was in?" Noelani asked.

"Not at all. Didn't know it was there. Same thing speaking and listening. I couldn't tell which language I was speaking or hearing.

"George, yesterday you said something to the effect of 'being here is like being in Disneyland.' I'm really starting to understand that sentiment."

Silence fell for a moment.

"Let's take a short break before the next segment. OK?" George suggested. Then he looked at the rest of the news team. "Who wants to try it next? We can play 'Who wants to stump Michael?' Noelani can dial up a language. You can greet him in that language and see if he responds!"

"George! You little devil!" Noelani said. Everyone started laughing, even Agent Patterson's wife.

"Who's the devil?" Michael walked into the room.

At Michael's sudden appearance, the News team went from smiling and laughing, to a study in seriousness. Michael seeing the sudden change said to the team, "It's OK. Lots of laughing happens in this room, especially when the Sergeant is in here. And welcome back Keoni, Becky, Joshua and Christine. I was in New York this morning and heard a very complimentary review of the initial edit of your interview with George yesterday. Do you know when it is scheduled to air?"

Becky said, "As I understand it, the working plan is to do several short one-minute excerpts during the major news shows over the next several days, then a one-hour special next weekend. That will probably depend on what we get today, and what else comes out tomorrow. They might even have Keoni and me fly back to New York to help."

"If they want you in New York, call Jiaying and let her know. There is a chance… sadly, a very small chance… that we might be able to give you a lift. I'm going to be all over the world this week. Maybe our schedules will overlap." Turning to George, Michael asked, "What's the plan, George? I have a few minutes now and some time in an hour or so."

"Now would be perfect. I need a half hour to set up for the next segment."

"Excellent. Where would you like us, here or in the den?"

"I'm going to be making some noise, so the den, if that will work?"

"No problem. We can move the set in just a few minutes." Becky said. "Michael, would you like to head there now with Keoni? It will give you two a minute to connect before we begin."

"Will do. Keoni, shall we?" Michael gestured to the hallway entrance. As they stepped out into the hall, Emmanuel was about to enter the dining room. "Emmanuel, how are you and Bahati settling in?"

"We are doing well Michael. I was just coming down to the dining room to see if there was anything I could do to help today."

"Perfect timing. The KHON News team is here filming an interview with George. They are giving me a short segment now. Would you mind escorting them down to the den?"

"Would love to." Emmanuel entered the dining room and spotted the team. Michael could hear Emmanuel introducing himself as they walked down the hall.

"Michael, thank you so much for taking the time with us today. It's relatively rare for the local affiliate to participate in national or global stories. Thank you for giving us this opportunity."

"Keoni, do you know why you got this opportunity? Why we asked KHON to come and do this series with George?"

"Um… No. My boss told me to call the number that had magically shown up on his desk and was really on my case to call every day. So, I did, and one day got the call back."

"Let me tell you a secret. It was George's idea to do this series. His ideas were so compelling that I not only agreed, I endorsed it. My criteria for who I wanted to do the interviews, was the person that had been nicest to Jiaying, my protocol officer. She had complained about how rude and demanding many of the press people were. So, since we were initiating this contact, I thought we should pick the team that we wanted, not the biggest name or next person on the list.

"When I asked her to do that, she answered immediately that there was this nice, courteous local reporter she wanted to go with, and you got the call. My point is that you got the call because we wanted to repay kindness with kindness."

"Wow!" Keoni replied. "Thank you. More than once my boss has told me that I need to be aggressive to get anywhere in this world, yet I won the biggest story to ever land in Hawaii. And ironically, because I was just being me."

"Keoni, my friend. The world is about to change in a very dramatic way, and the change will be fast. I think you are well positioned to succeed in the new world that will soon emerge." Michael heard a sound in the hall and looked up to see Emmanuel with a huge smile on his face and Joshua with the camera rolling.

"It seems that if I want to have a private conversation, I should go someplace private." Michael laughed. "Come on in. Let's make Keoni a star."

...

They set up quickly, then Becky counted them in...

"Hi, I am Keoni Gates here with Michael, Ambassador from the Intergalactic Confederation of Planets. Michael, thank you so much for allowing us to come into your home on Kohala Mountain to speak with you."

"Thank you for being here, Keoni. It's been a pleasure getting to know you and your team."

"Michael, as we were setting up, you commented that the world was about to change in a significant way. Could you explain that to our audience?"

"One of the great pleasures of my work is helping to usher young, thriving civilizations into a new era of peace and prosperity. I see that new era coming to Earth over the next couple years."

"Why do you say that, Michael?" Keoni asked.

"There are a little over 8 billion people on Earth today. Each is competing for increasingly scarce resources, in a world where the general environment is becoming increasingly toxic. Sadly, for humanity, your numbers have outpaced your technological development to the point where you, as a species, are struggling to support yourselves, slowly killing your planet in order to maintain a slowly declining standard of living. Starting next week, for a couple thousand people in a couple of small countries, their world will change. Their homes will have enough power to 'keep the lights on' as I have heard people describe it. Their families will have a secure supply of food. They will be safe from being raided by neighboring countries.

"My prediction is that starting next week we will see more acts of kindness and generosity among those couple thousand people, because they will know they're secure. By the end of next month, the number of secure people will grow into the tens of millions; by this time next year, maybe 1 billion.

"Imagine how the world will change. I'm not saying that violence and aggression will be wiped out. Humanity is an aggressive species, which is one of the reasons it's so successful. What I am saying is that competition for resources will decline, stress will decline, life expectancy will measurably increase, and humanity as a whole will become more collaborative.

"As an Ascendant that has helped usher 11 other species across this goal line, I can tell you things will change, they will change dramatically, they will change quickly, and they will change for the better."

"I heard you say something similar to that earlier this week and the following thought went through my mind. If our food and electricity come from a different source, what's going to happen to the people that work in the energy and food production industries? Aren't they going to be displaced?"

"Excellent question. Yes. There will be some displacement. But unlike the past, it will be more balanced. Historically, technological change meant that a lot of people were slightly better off, while a few were more or less wiped out. Benefits from new technology would go to the top tiers of society first, and trickle down to the bottom, with some at the bottom never getting any at all.

"Not this time! As the underwriters of this technological revolution, we will not allow that to happen. In the past, technological advancements have worked because they made relatively small improvements in the cost, quality or availability of a product or service. Our technology will drive all costs to zero, except the cost of human time and talent. And we will drive this change up from the bottom.

Back in the kitchen, the Sergeant had finished his preparations and was ready to show off his culinary talent. Becky and the team had returned a few minutes earlier and finished their set up.

"Ready, George?" Keoni asked.

"Ready."

Becky counted them in, then Keoni started. "We are in the kitchen at Ambassador Michael's ranch in Hawaii, where recovering Sergeant George Butler is making lunch. George, can you tell us where you got your culinary training?"

George laughed at that statement. "Keoni, I was trained at one of our country's greatest culinary institutions... KP duty in Kabul, Afghanistan. And I was so good they paid me to be there."

That drew a laugh from the News crew and all the staff that wanted to see this part of the interview.

"What was your role at the KP?"

"Well, they started me out in a dishwashing role. Then I graduated to potato peeler, where I really excelled. Then over the next 3 years, potato specialist first class."

"Is that a real title?"

"Keoni, my friend. The Army has more official, unofficial designations than any other organization on the planet. Who knows...? Maybe this is the one area where we can give the Confederation a run for their money. Anyway, I earned my designation, booking in at 12 tons. Can you envision that many potatoes? Sorry, no one wants to envision that many potatoes."

"So, am I guessing correctly that you're going to make a potato dish?"

"Truly one of the best in the world. OK. Everyone saw Michael cooking with Chef Marco on Good Morning America. Um... That's a different network, right? Am I allowed to mention them?"

Even Becky was laughing at this point.

"Chef Marco, stand aside for the fabulous Chef George. Today, I'm going to make the perfect Gorilla fries. Now, the culinarily untrained in your audience might be wondering what that would be. PETA, don't worry. I'm not going to fry a gorilla. I'm going to fry some potatoes, with onion, peppers, bacon, and lots of cheese. But here's the cool part... I'm not going to fry anything."

"George, I'm not sure I'm following."

"Watch and learn," George replied with a grin. "You see, when Michael and Chef Marco cooked for 500 on Good Morning America, they used the replicators to make RAW food, which Chef Marco did a really fabulous job of turning into something incredible. But come on... I'm not Chef Marco, and neither is 99.999% of America. Chef Marco's skills are well beyond the average household that will be the first to get replicators.

"So, I'm going to show your audience something that they can make... French fries with caramelized onions, roasted red bell peppers, bacon and molten cheddar. Watch and learn."

George motioned to a boxy contraption on the countertop. "This is one of the prototypes of the replicator Michael's going to start delivering next week.

"If you touch the panel right here... Can the camera get a close-up on this? If you touch this panel right here, you get a list of ingredients. If you scroll down a bit, you see potatoes. If you select potatoes, then look at all the ways you can get them. I'm going to go with fried. Then I am going to further specify, fast food style.

"Next, I'm going to select, Onions – Caramelized. Next, Bacon – Lardons – Crispy. For those of you that don't know lardons, it's French. To make a lardon by hand, you cut the bacon sideways, so you get a little one-inch strip of bacon, that's a 16th of an inch tall and wide. The Cordon Bleu is going to correct me, but that is an Army lardon.

"With me so far, Keoni?"

"Sounds easy enough to me, George. But are you planning to write a replicator cookbook? I bet it would sell."

"Maybe. Who knows? But, back to lunch... And this is the trick... Replicate these one at a time. See how I have them set to sequence? Then replicate the molten Cheddar. It is under Cheese – Cheddar – English, sorry, no offense to American Cheddar. Then scroll way down to the bottom – Molten. Set the first three for 5-second intervals, then the Cheddar for a 15 second interval.

"OK. See my bowls, set up all chef-like? Put the first one under the spout, with the next four set up so you can stick them in right away. OK here we go. Push the start button.

"See the fries plopping out in the bowl. There's the beep, so we switch bowls. Now comes the lardons. Switch bowls. Now the caramelized onions. Oh, do those smell good. Switch bowls. Here come the roasted red peppers. Now the big bowl. And here comes the molten cheddar.

"OK. I'm dumping the fries on the tray. Now spooning on the caramelized onions. Now the peppers. Now pouring the cheese all over it. Lastly, the lardons on the top. And no gypping the edges! A masterpiece!

"America, I offer you French Fries gorilla-style, and no gorillas were hurt in the filming of this recipe. Want one?" He said to Keoni.

"George. How could anyone resist?" A pause. "Wow! That is good."

The staff started gathering around grabbing fries.

"Looks like I'm going to have to make some more. Wait! The recipe is still there. Keoni, want to make some more?"

Keoni pushed the button and rotated the bowls under the spout. Then he dumped the fries on the now empty tray and dressed them the same way George had, and put the tray on the table.

"Wow! That was easy."

"Are you ready for the best part?" George asked.

"George, I'm struggling to believe there is a better part?"

"You can save the recipe. See. Push the save button. And even better, you can share the recipe. See. I'm sending this to Noelani. Oh, and even better. You can download recipes from other people. Check this out. Look. Gorilla Fries, by Chef Marco."

"George, did you use Chef Marco's Gorilla Fries recipe?"

"Duh. Aren't these the best?"

Keoni laughed. He couldn't help himself. "Is this one of the dishes he served on that show, the one whose name cannot be spoken?" Keoni asked.

"Well, if you had these before, wouldn't you download the recipe?"

Keoni turned to the camera. "Ladies and gentlemen, I give you Sergeant George Butler and Chef Marco's fabulous Gorilla Fries."

...

As the crew was breaking down their equipment and packing the grav-sled to take it back to the car, Becky said to Keoni. "You realize that is going to be the most watched segment in history. Right?"

"I think George is going to become one of the most successful spokesmen in history." Keoni replied.

NORTH KOREA

[02.08.2025 5:00 PM] THE RESIDENCE, KOHALA MOUNTAIN, HAWAII

"Michael," Jiaying called. "I got calls from the Prime Minister of Japan and from the President of South Korea. Each of them asked if it would be possible to meet or speak with you as soon as possible, preferably today. In fact, the Japanese Prime Minister is meeting with the Emperor for tea this afternoon and asked if there was any chance you could join them."

"What time?"

"4:00 PM in Japan, about 4 hours from now."

"Yes. I'll meet with them. And since we'll be in the area, see if the President of South Korea would like to meet with me at 6:00 PM."

"OK. The time is close. Let me see if I can confirm them now. Then I'll call back."

...

Minutes later, Jiaying was back on the line.

"Both meetings are confirmed, Michael."

"Thanks, Jiaying. I bet I know what's happening. Can you connect me with Joel? He might be up by now."

The voice of a very sleepy sounding Joel came over the line. "Michael, so nice of you to call at 5:00 AM."

"Joel. We may have a problem. I think North Korea is about to do something really stupid."

"How stupid?"

"I think they're threatening to attack South Korea and Japan. Backfire Protocol is in place there, right?"

"Should be, let me check." A pause and some odd background sounds. "Yes. Airborne nanobot density is sufficient, but on the lower end of the spectrum."

"Will that stop conventional launches?"

"It's not currently set up to. The bots will only attack airborne radiation."

"So. If they launch a nuke, they'll blow themselves up. If they launch conventional, then we could only stop it with a shield?"

"At this point yes. But that will take a few minutes to set up."

"What if it's a ground invasion?"

"Technically, planetary shields can be used that way, but they are not very good for it. Collateral damage would be high. The best solution would be a line of small suspensor fields, maybe one field generator every quarter mile." Joel replied.

"The border is 148 miles long."

"Argh! 600 field generators. That would be hard to deploy."

"Could it be done remotely? Elsie transporting them in place, and an AI linking them together and operating them?"

"If we had that many, yes. Do you know if the shuttle transporter has fast disbursal mode?"

"Jiaying. Can you add Elsie to the line?"

A moment later, Elsie was on the line and the question asked.

"Yes, the shuttle has fast dispersal mode, IF the material is on the shuttle. We can't do it point-to-point."

"How fast?"

"About 1 every 5 seconds. 12 a minute, 720 an hour. Are the units small enough to put them all in the shuttle?"

"No." Joel replied. "They're about the size of a large suitcase. We could probably get 100 of them on the shuttle. So, we could do it in batches. Two pallets of 50 transported up, manually arranged, and then fast distributed down."

Realizing how much work this would be, Joel redirected the conversation. "How likely is it we'll need to do this? And how much lead time are we going to get?"

"I'm not sure. Joel. Do you have the AI capacity to do an aerial analysis of the border? We don't have useful historical images, so this would need to be real time delta-vector analysis."

"Where are we going to get the imaging?"

"I'm thinking that we park Elsie on station for a while. Are the shuttle sensors good enough?"

"Maybe. But we don't have 600 field generators, do we?" Elsie replied.

"Paso Robles has the materials. Maybe 15 minutes each per replicator," Joel offered.

"How many replicators do we have now?"

"I need to check to see what finished last night, but we might have 42 by now."

"So, if we used them all, we could produce 168 per hour or about 600 in a little less than 4 hours total."

"Sounds right to me." Joel agreed.

"OK. Here's the plan. Start making suspensor field generators. You really ought to have them for Israel and Georgia anyway. Elsie, head to Korea and start scanning. Come back for me at quarter to 4:00, Japan time, then resume scanning while I'm in Japan. I'll signal you when to transport me back up."

"Got it, boss," Joel and Elsie said almost simultaneously.

...

"Noelani," Michael called out. "Would it be possible for me to do a 3-hour regeneration cycle? I think I'm about to have a very busy night and need sleep."

"Michael, you know regeneration cycles that short are not recommended."

"Alternatives?" Michael asked.

"Not really. I'll set it up in your room. Be there in 10 minutes."

THE RESIDENCE, KOHALA MOUNTAIN, HAWAII

Michael woke as the door to the restoration chamber opened. Noelani was waiting with a towel. "How do you feel, Michael?" she asked.

"Wishing I had another hour or two," he replied, then added with a smile, "Hungry, though."

"I took the liberty of making your favorite breakfast to go. I also made something for Elsie. She has been in that shuttle almost non-stop the last week."

"I'm worried about her also, but the fast attack ship gets here tonight. They may be able to help. If not, the Admiral has android pilots that we can train for human avatars in a matter of days."

Within minutes Michael was dressed and ready to transport to the shuttle.

12,000 MILES ABOVE THE IMPERIAL PALACE, TOKYO, JAPAN

"I'm envious, Michael," Elsie mused. "The palace grounds are fabulous. The honor guard that will receive and escort you have begun to assemble, and they are apparently decked out in Samurai gear."

"Wonderful," Michael replied, implying anything but. "You do realize that Samurai swords are one of the few things that could penetrate my shield."

330

"They are not the enemy," Elsie reminded him. "North Korea is."
The scans Elsie had been taking clearly showed a massive build-up taking place on the north side of the demilitarized zone.

"No one on Earth is our enemy," Michael said for what seemed like the hundredth time. "But some of their leaders are really slow to recognize what's in their best interest."

"The good news is that most of their forces are concentrated directly north of Seoul. So, they will be easier to deter. Joel already has enough field generators to protect that area. If it were my choice, I would start deploying them now."

"You know the problem with that, Elsie. We cannot act until invited!"

"Michael, they were all but begging you a couple hours ago."

"Point taken. Which is why I'm authorizing you to transport as many field generators onboard the shuttle as you can while I'm in Japan. It's also why I'm authorizing you to prepare and position for deployment awaiting my signal."

"Thank you, Michael. You're doing the right thing."

"Thank you, 'Empress' Elsie. I'm ready to transport on your countdown."

Several seconds passed, then, "3, 2, 1... Goodbye."

THE IMPERIAL PALACE GROUNDS, TOKYO, JAPAN

The guard had been getting in place for nearly ten minutes. The ceremonial costumes were not that well insulated, and it was a cold February afternoon, not far from sundown.

Suddenly, a man, an American from the looks of him, appeared in the center of the ring they'd been instructed to form. Although this is what they'd been told to expect, it was still shocking. Several of the men had released the covers over their swords. Two of the men had drawn them. Fools! They would be disciplined later. In the old days, they would have been beheaded on the spot. Their dishonor hit the captain of the guard hard.

While his attention had been distracted, the man had approached and greeted him in perfect, high-respect Japanese. *What, does this fool think? That I am the emperor? Why would anyone address me this way?*

While most languages conjugate verbs based on time: past, present, future. Japanese also conjugates both verbs and adjectives

331

based on level of respect. The highest level was reserved for the Emperor and members of the royal family.

"Because, at this moment, you are the representative of Japan to the Intergalactic Confederation of Planets. To address you, the envoy sent by your emperor to greet me, in any other way would be a breach of Japanese protocol."

The Captain of the Guard stood silent in shock. *This man not only reads my thoughts, he speaks perfect Japanese and corrects my grammar.*

He responded, "Ambassador. Please forgive my arrogance. I am but an ignorant soldier, lacking the training I needed for this mission." Then he bowed deeply.

"Not a problem my friend. No offense given or taken. Please, lead me as you have been instructed."

The Captain of the Guard turned sharply and began leading the entourage through the garden and up the massive stone stairway.

As Michael followed, he couldn't help but wonder at the grandeur of this garden and palace. He and his escort walked past layer after layer of twenty-foot high stone walls, each with some sort of water hazard at the base. In today's world, this was a gardening marvel. Four hundred years ago, this palace had been impenetrable.

They reached the top of the last of the roughhewn stone stairways and were greeted by more modern guard troops. After a small ceremony, Michael was given over to the new guards, who took him into the palace proper. Another set of stairs, a couple of turns, and a long hallway later, they entered a large petition room.

Another man, this one in a modern suit, spoke in English. "Greetings Ambassador. I am to be your interpreter for the audience with the emperor."

Michael responded in perfect, Emperor's Court Japanese. "I do not need an interpreter. But I could probably use a protocol officer, if you are permitted to do so."

The interpreter was shocked. No foreigner had ever entered this room that could speak this dialect even passingly. Michael's pronunciation and word selection were exquisite. "My pardon, sir. No foreigner of your ability has ever entered this room before."

A sound was heard of a sort Michael could not place. Everyone in the room bowed deeply. The President came through a side door and came over to stand by Michael. Then the Emperor came in through a door on the far side of the dais and stood before the throne.

"Michael. Ambassador from the Intergalactic Confederation of Planets, welcome to Japan." The Emperor clapped his hands twice and everyone in the room left except the Emperor, the President, Michael, and his interpreter.

The interpreter whispered, "Now is when you bow and greet the Emperor. Do you know the greeting?"

Michael's patience was beginning to wear thin. "Your Imperial Majesty, thank you for receiving me."

The interpreter looked at Michael sternly. Michael had neither bowed nor offered the traditional greeting.

But the Emperor started laughing and said in perfect English, "Thank you, Ambassador, for coming and relieving me of this ancient ceremony. In fact, the President invited you and I asked if I could participate. Please..." he pointed to a side door that had just opened. "There is tea and comfortable seating across the hall."

"Thank you, sir."

After they sat and tea was poured, the Emperor began, "I assume you've detected the buildup of troops on the North Korean side of the border?"

"Yes, we have. But I did not receive that report until a few hours ago, shortly after I received your request for a meeting. How long has this been going on and what do you expect to happen?"

The Emperor nodded to the President, who answered, "The buildup began some time ago, but at a very slow pace, much like a rotation of troops that was not so well coordinated. Their ruse allowed them to increase strength by nearly a third before alarm bells started sounding on the South Korean side. Over the last couple hours, the buildup has reached a frenzy. North Korea now stands at twice its normal strength."

"Have you heard anything from them?"

"They are demanding that the South surrender within the next 24 hours and have threatened Japan and the US with nuclear bombardment if they interfere."

"Well, if they are delivering the nukes via missile, the nuclear bombardment won't work. Have you been in direct contact with South Korea?"

"Yes. We understand that you will be going there shortly."

"That is correct. We can protect them, if they ally with us. But I need a couple hours' notice to put protection in place. Is it your expectation that we have that much time?"

"We think you do. But it must be done with stealth. The North will invade immediately if they see any sort of defense build-up.

"But this brings us to the reason that we asked you here. Would you be able to protect us, if we were to ally with you?"

"Of course. But with the same condition. I need a little time to position my assets."

"Then I'm authorized to give you these two documents. The first is an executed copy of the Letter of Intent. The second is a decree by our Emperor, declaring our people's alliance with the Intergalactic Confederation of Planets."

"Thank you." Michael bowed his head in respect. "I'd been hoping to have Japan as an early treaty partner. I'm sorry that the timing has been dictated by threats from a rogue nation."

"Can you tell us anything about the nature and timing of the defense you will provide us?" The emperor asked.

"In the long term, it will be quite extensive. But for the next twenty-four hours, it will be more ad hoc than either of us would like. We currently have protection in place from nuclear missiles. So, the vulnerability will be to conventional weapons and direct invasion. We will use our planetary shield to block conventional missiles. But, our entire stock of ground defenses is being staged for deployment in the demilitarized zone as we speak. So, defense against a ground invasion will be ad hoc for the next 24 hours, at which point we can have a full defense available, one strong enough to defend against the entire military strength of the Earth."

"How can we help you?" the Emperor asked.

"Over the next 24 hours, the things that will help the most are information and allies. Information will allow us to focus our resources more accurately. The more allies I have, the more flexibility I have under Confederation law to use my assets effectively."

"Has the United States signed on yet?" asked the Prime Minister.

"No. They will, but their political situation paralyses them. If the President was in his second term, I'm sure he would have signed by now. He has the authority. Unfortunately, he doesn't have the political will at this point."

"I've met with him and think we have a good relationship. I'll place a call and see if he's open to persuasion," the President said. "Who else?"

"China is already in, though reluctantly. India is in the process of approving membership. I have not had the opportunity to meet with

334

any other Asian leaders at this point. The Philippines, Indonesia, and Thailand are the largest countries along the Pacific Rim that would qualify."

"Let me do this," the President offered. "I will have our head of intelligence coordinate with the person you designate on your team. He can stream you everything we have. And I will place calls to the heads of state of the four countries you named and a few others where our influence might help. Are there other heads of state of allied countries that I might coordinate with?"

"Canada. Israel, of course, although Israel is not the most well-liked country. Jordan. But the others have only been in for a day or two and don't know us well enough yet to be convincing advocates."

"Excellent! That gives me something to work with. I would love to have you stay and enjoy a meal and a tour of the gardens, but you have a lot to do. So can we arrange that for another time?"

"I would love that. Thank you for your time and consideration today. Your Imperial Majesty. Mr. President. My people will be in touch." Michael bowed, straightened, and then disappeared.

"That's going to take some getting used to," murmured the Emperor.

12,000 MILES ABOVE TOKYO, JAPAN

"Welcome back Michael." Elsie said. "North Korea has been busy while you were gone. They have over 500,000 troops positioned along the border, with long convoys of more troops and supplies, tanks and artillery, clogging the roads."

"So, I hear. The Japanese Prime Minister told me that they are demanding the South surrender within the next 24 hours. They have also threatened nuclear strikes on the US and Japan if they interfere. Would you get Joel and Sanjit on the line?"

Sanjit joined first. "Hi, Sanjit, have you heard about the operation we're about to launch in Korea?"

"So, it's on then?"

"Almost certainly, and I think I'm going to need your help."

"What do you need me to do?"

"Japan has signed. The Emperor has even signed a proclamation declaring us allies. They claim to have some intelligence that will help. Can you connect with them and determine the best deployment positions for our generators? Two things you should know. The North Koreans will invade if they detect any movement of resources to the south. So we need to do our deployment with stealth. Second, they will probably invade sooner than the timetable they've given. So, we need to place each field generator as if it were the last, getting the most bang for the buck out of each."

"Got it." Sanjit replied as Joel came on the line.

"Hi, Joel. Sanjit and Elsie are with me on the line. What's our status?"

"We have a total of 44 replicators online, the last one just came up. We've produced about 360 field generators so far and are adding 4 more every minute.

"I've come up with a pallet layout that will hold 120 units in a format for rapid deployment. It'll fit in the passenger compartment, if the seating's removed. I'll have the first batch ready in about 45 minutes. The next pallet will be ready about half an hour after that."

"That's good news. Will we have AI support for this operation?"

"Jacob is still too young. Nice kid, but days, if not weeks, away from being useful. So, it'll need to be Henry, or we'll have to do it manually."

"Of the current team, I have the most experience with manual shield operation," Sanjit said. "If we rig the second or third pilot seat with the appropriate controls, I could operate locally with Elsie."

"Hold that thought," Michael said. "We have a second problem... North Korea has threatened to attack Japan and the US, if they interfere. Backfire protocol will protect them from nuclear attack, but not from conventional or biological. Can we put a shield over Japan?"

Joel replied. "Michael, we're spread too thin. We could divert the planetary shield, but that would leave Israel and Jordan unprotected. If this attack is somehow coordinated, we're going to lose one of the two, because the angles are all wrong for a ping-pong defense to work."

Just then, Jiaying cut in. "Michael, I'm sorry to interrupt. But the South Korean president just called. He said he talked with the Japanese Prime Minister since your meeting and asks if there's any chance you can come early. He says that there's important new information."

"Yes. Give Elsie the transport instructions. Team, I need options. I suspect this meeting will be short, so have something for me when I get back."

"I have the coordinates, Michael. A two-man honor guard is waiting there now."

"Send me down."

BLUE HOUSE, SEOUL, SOUTH KOREA

Blue House was the presidential residence and administrative complex in the nation's capital. Michael appeared on the landing at the top of a large staircase that split and continued higher on both sides. One led to the residential wing, the other to the administrative wing. He heard the sharp intake of breath from men on either side of the landing. His appearance clearly startled them.

The one to his left said, in very broken English. "Ambassador Michael, please follow me."

Michael replied in flawless Korean. "Please lead the way. I understand that there are urgent matters to discuss."

The man seemed frozen in place, but quickly recovered. "Please forgive me. I've never seen a man just appear like that. And I've never heard a westerner speak our language so well. You honor us with your presence."

He led the way up the stairs toward the administrative side, where he was escorted into a room with a single occupant, the man he recognized from news coverage as the President of South Korea. He looked worn, as if the weight of the world were on his shoulders. He stood and bowed deeply, then walked around the desk and greeted Michael with a handshake.

"Ambassador Michael. Thank you so much for coming on short notice. I would like to formally petition for membership in the Intergalactic Confederation of Planets." With both hands, he presented a signed copy of the Letter of Intent to Michael. "I had hoped to meet you under better circumstances. After the attack on Israel, our legislative bodies passed a resolution to seek alliance with you. We simply couldn't get it scheduled. I think there is hope for a strong alliance between the Confederation and the people of Korea. We are industrious and honorable and have been good partners with all our allies. Sadly, our brothers to the North are led by a despot, more interested in personal power than in peace and prosperity."

Michael replied. "Like you, Mr. President, I wish we could have met under better circumstances. But I have believed for a long time that our peoples would form a strong partnership. So I welcome the opportunity to form an alliance with you, even if the timing has been forced by the hand of a dishonorable man."

The president motioned to a chair. "Do you have tIme to sit and discuss the situation with the north?"

"Yes. But it'll be in our collective interest to be brief."

"I understand," the president said as they sat. "The sun will be setting soon. In the past, the North has made their move at first light in the hour before sunrise. In terse communications received in the last hour, the implication was that the invasion was going to begin at midnight, and I should be prepared to surrender here at the Blue House around dawn. Is there any way you can help us?"

"Yes. We plan to erect a force field along the south side of the demilitarized zone. It will take about four, maybe five hours to complete and can be done with almost complete stealth. No tank, truck, shell or missile will be able to penetrate it. Do you have an expert that we could work with to help with optimal placement?

"How soon can this begin?"

"In about a half hour." Michael replied.

"So, it will not be completed until just before midnight?"

"Yes and no. We can have a complete, but weak barrier in half the time. We can have an impenetrable barrier across most of the DMZ by midnight. So, I think the question is whether to go with complete weak coverage that we back fill or go with solid coverage with selected areas open until midnight. This is where an expert would be useful, because there may be natural barriers or more easily defended areas that we save for last."

"Yes. I see your point."

"May I ask about the American's role in this?"

"The President has agreed to leave his forces in place for now but will not commit additional assets. He is basically condemning 23,000 of his own people. I don't know how he'll survive that politically."

"Maybe I can help with the Americans." Michael stood. "Time is short. Please put your expert in contact with my people as soon as possible. If we do not hear from him in the next 15 minutes, we'll begin placing the shields near the heaviest concentrations of North Korean troops."

They shook hands. Then Michael transported up.

12,000 MILES ABOVE BLUE HOUSE, SEOUL

As Michael appeared, he saw that Elsie looked a little more confident.

"What's up?" he asked immediately.

338

"Ah Michael. When you go to work, so many things happen so quickly."

"And what would those things be?"

"You told the Japanese President that if you had the US and a few others, you would be able to take direct action. Didn't you?"

"I doubt I used those words, but I did attempt to convey that message."

"Well, he called the President of the United States, who is staying up late tonight. He's apparently convinced that he's about to lose 23,000 troops, which will result in his impeachment. When the Japanese President called, then the Canadian Prime Minister, then the Israeli Prime Minister, he folded and signed the Letter of Intent."

"Then the President, the Canadian Prime Minister, the German Chancellor, even the Georgian and Estonian Prime Ministers started calling the other NATO allies, asking them to sign and send it to Jiaying."

"We now have signed letters from the UK, France, Italy, Spain, Poland, Netherlands, Sweden, Denmark, Norway, and Puerto Rico."

"Did India approve after I left?"

"Yes, and they returned the signed letter to Jiaying just after you left for Japan."

"That puts us over, right?"

"51.07%" Elsie smiled.

"Do we know where the Chairman is?"

"Yes. He's in his office at Ryongsong, also known as the Central Luxury Mansion. These guys have such a way with words. Scans show 10 other people in the room. We have a scanner in the room recording. We should know soon if we have sufficient evidence to arrest him."

"OK, but I want to get some field generators in place before we go down to arrest him. Is the first pallet ready and once loaded, is there room for two more people?"

"That's going to be tight Michael. Why two?"

"We need someone to activate and control the field generators. And someone else to go down and assist me with the arrest. Normally, I would use Sanjit for these jobs. But..."

"What about Alexi to assist with the arrest?" Elsie asked. "Men always underestimate her, but I have never met a man that she couldn't take down. Kale won't even go in the ring with her anymore."

"Great idea. Is the first pallet ready?"

"Will be by the time we get there."

"Then, let's get Sanjit first."

Elsie flew while Michael advised the team of the plan. Alexi seemed to be particularly happy to be joining an arrest team, saying something about enhanced personal shielding and new toys.

Once in view of Hawaii, Sanjit was transported aboard. He brought some equipment needed to update the co-pilot's computers for the shield control mission.

Elsie then popped them to the ideal position over Paso Robles to load the pallets. The first to transport up were Alexi Santos, who was joining the mission, and Pedro Castillo and Hermon Rodriguez, who would remove the passenger seats and place the pallet anchors.

Pedro and Hermon immediately went to work removing the seating in the passenger compartment. They brought an army of little bots that removed the seats one-by-one, then positioned them for transport. Once the first seats were gone, they began setting the fast attach/release anchors for the pallets. 15 minutes later, the seats, technicians and bots were all gone.

Elsie called out. "Everyone into the cockpit."

There were four seats, but it was a tight fit.

"Here goes." Elsie initiated the transport process. "Perfect fit," she added as 120 field generators appeared on a synthetic pallet in the passenger cabin turned cargo bay.

Sanjit noted that all 120 units were registered perfectly with the rapid deployment transport system.

Elsie set course for Korea and jumped into position moments later. The first 120 units would be placed along a 30 mile stretch of the DMZ where the ground was fairly level and the North Koreans would be able to move fast if not impeded. Sanjit set the target location for each generator to be about a half mile north of the southern edge of the DMZ, or about three-quarters of a mile south of the border between the two countries. Each unit was self-righting and self-anchoring. Each would be transported to about 6 inches off the ground, then would settle, anchor, connect to its neighbor and align fields for maximum strength.

Elsie asked, "Ready for deployment run?"

"All set," Sanjit replied.

The shuttle started gliding slowly to the east. The only indication that anything was happening was the popping noise that came when a rigid object disappeared, and the atmosphere rushed in to fill the gap. Pop, pop, pop, 120 pops in all, then the run was complete.

About a minute later, Sanjit said, "All units set and operational. The last of the alignments will be finished momentarily. Bingo! Thirty miles of impenetrable border."

While the deployment was going on, Michael had been reviewing the tape of the chairman's office. They were planning to go just after midnight. The preponderance of the forces would be going straight down the middle, heading directly toward Seoul. Four much smaller forces would be going down the coasts, a ground force on each shoreline, supplemented by fast attack boats.

"Team." Michael said. "It appears that we have a problem. A small fleet of attack boats is planning to stream down each coast. A pair of relatively small ground forces will also be making their way down. I haven't been able to discern their missions, but it appears they're going to take all the coastal fishing villages."

"It also appears that the Chairman is planning to stay put for now. So, let's go get the next pallet. We can use it to extend the central barrier."

Elsie lifted back up to jump altitude and jumped to Paso Robles, loaded the next pallet, then returned to Korea. 15 more minutes and now there was 60 miles of impenetrable barrier cutting off access through the center of the country.

Michael had been reviewing the recordings from the 'Luxury Mansion' while the deployment was taking place. The Chairman was clearly getting impatient and wanted to start the invasion earlier than planned. His advisors reminded him that the current schedule coincided with the moon set so they could get the most out of their night vision equipment.

Elsie had started back to Paso Robles when Michael asked, "Sanjit, do we have the ability to create intense flashes of light in the infrared spectrum? The North Koreans' plan is to start the invasion at moon set, so they can 'get the most of their night vision equipment.'"

"We could probably do something, but I would bet the Americans can do more. We should forward this intelligence to them."

Michael sent a quick message to Jiaying, instructing her to do so.

Arriving back over Paso Robles, they transported up the next pallet of field generators.

"What do you think we can do about the coastal troops and fast attack boats?"

Sanjit replied. "If we're willing to cause injury to those troops, we could array the field generators to force them down a narrow corridor near the water. Then once down that path, we could extend the shield pushing them into the water. It's below freezing down there tonight. Once wet, the troops would be immobilized and would likely freeze to death."

"If we simply trapped them in a suspensor field, could we heat them enough to keep them from freezing?"

"Possibly, but we won't have enough field generators in time to do that."

"Then let's do this. Let's split this load of generators between the coasts, angled so it pushes the troops closer to the water the further south they go. If it takes them an hour to figure out that they are being driven into the sea, then it should give us an extra two hours— one down, one back—to finish the barrier.

"Once that's done, Alexi and I will go in for the arrest. We'll arrest the Chairman and all ten advisors. Alexi, you have enough individual suspensor generators to do that?"

She patted the various pockets in her flak jacket. "I've got twenty of them, and a few extra tricks too."

This one is scary. Michael thought to himself. That thought triggered another darker thought. *There is something very wrong with what's going on tonight.*

"Sanjit. I think we may have another encounter like the one in the secure tank farm this morning."

"I'm not liking the sound of that Michael," Sanjit replied.

"Let's stop and get the energy projectors the Admiral made for us this morning."

"If you think we are going to encounter another one of those things, you should ask the Admiral for another one of those bombs."

"Good idea!" Michael nodded, then called out "Jiaying!"

"Here, Michael. I was just going to call you. The fast attack ship called to tell us they were in the system and expected to enter orbit within the hour."

"Jiaying, can you get us an audio connection to the ship? The portable presence projector is currently offline."

"Will do, Michael."

Michael reviewed the list of things he wanted to pick up in Paso Robles and in Hawaii on this stop. He also reviewed what he wanted the team to do with them. While everyone was loading, he took the call from the captain of the fast attack ship.

Once everything was loaded, they headed back to Korea.

FEDERATION RAPID RESPONSE SHIP, ON APPROACH TO EARTH

"Mr. Ambassador. A pleasure to speak with you sir."

"Captain. Welcome to Earth. A beautiful blue pearl in space, no?"

"Indeed, sir. One of the most beautiful I've seen."

"Sadly, we have a situation and need your assistance immediately. We are currently allied with just over 51% of the population. A non-allied, rogue nation is about to attack and overrun one of our allies. They have over 500,000 soldiers massed on the border.

"We're in the process of erecting a shield barrier along that border. The border is approximately 150 miles long. We have 60 miles of shielding deployed and operational and are about to deploy the next 15 miles.

"Our intelligence suggests that the attack will commence in two hours, but my assessment is that it'll happen sooner. So, I'm thinking about arresting the despot leading the rogue nation. However, there's a complication. I believe their leader may be controlled by an Enemy agent.

"Do you have any suggestions on how to proceed?" Michael asked.

"May I ask why you suspect the leader of this rogue nation has been inhabited by an Enemy agent?"

"There are three rogue nations on this world that antagonize the others. Two of the three have already attempted to destroy us using primitive nuclear weapons. We rescued one of the conspirators who had been injured and placed him in a secure recovery tank, hoping to revive him and get his testimony. We later discovered that he was being controlled by an Enemy agent. It attacked us and nearly escaped. The Admiral sent a bomb and energy projectors that we used to destroy it. That is the reason you were sent ahead.

"My sense is that we'll encounter the same here," Michael replied.

"Understood. But to confirm, you do not have the direct evidence that would require us to do a preventative bombing."

"Correct, we do not. However, we have surveillance in place and know where he and his accomplices are. Do you have scanning capabilities that could provide the evidence we require?"

"Possibly. Please send us the coordinates and any other relevant information."

"On its way. In the meantime, we're about to make another shield deployment run. Do you have any means to help us stop the invasion if it should start?"

"What do you have in mind?"

"Replicator capacity. Transporter capacity. The ability to project intense light or shielding," Michael replied.

"We have all of those. We can also intimidate. Our ship is over one kilometer long and 300 meters wide. And, our antigrav generators are powerful enough to hover over a fixed location low in your atmosphere."

"Excellent. We're going to start our deployment run and the next round of intelligence gathering. I'll be in touch in about 15 minutes."

12,000 MILES ABOVE DEMILITARIZED ZONE, KOREA

"The shields are up and interconnected. There are 15 miles of generators along both the eastern and western coast, plus 60 miles of shielding in the middle. Do we have time for another trip to Paso Robles?

Once again Michael had been reviewing the tapes from the 'Luxury Mansion.' A certain calm had settled in. It was still an hour and 40 minutes to the planned invasion, so Michael had a difficult choice. He could do the arrest now and hope the decapitation of the regime would stop the invasion. Or, he could make another run to Paso Robles and risk a premature launch before they could decapitate the regime. Or, he could do both by splitting forces.

Michael decided that the preponderance of probability favored one more run. It would take another run after that to completely close the border. Placing more field generators now, then making the arrest was by far the best plan.

12,000 MILES ABOVE PASO ROBLES, CALIFORNIA

"Good news, boss." Joel reported. "A few more replicators came online, plus we were a little ahead before, so we have one and a half pallets and a plan for their deployment."

"Very clever," Elsie said. Turning to Michael, she explained, "They repacked the pallets in a way that will allow us to do rapid deployment of the first half. Then we transport the upper pallet support into geosynchronous orbit above Paso Robles, while repositioning. Then we rapid deploy the other half. One more run after this and we will have a complete shield."

"I doubt we will get in another run before circumstances force the arrest. But let's do it."

12,000 MILES ABOVE DEMILITARIZED ZONE, KOREA

"Deployment is proceeding along the western flank of the existing central barrier. Ten minutes to completion," Elsie reported.

Michael had delved back into the tapes, catching up to real time and didn't like what he was seeing. Several North Korean scouting teams had been in the demilitarized zone and were reporting strange sounds that they couldn't identify. The advisors kept saying it was nothing. No pattern, no location; just jumpy kids. But the Chairman was convinced the Americans were up to something. He'd called for signal men to come to his office, so they could launch the invasion.

"Michael." Jiaying called. "I have the Captain on the line."

The Captain's voice came on the line. "Mr. Ambassador, we have a problem. We can confirm two enemies. One at the coordinates you gave me. Another in the same complex, a short distance away."

"We need to take the one in that room, NOW. He is about to order the attack. Can you send a bomb into that room?"

"Yes, sir. On your order. But that will make the other one aware, which will be very dangerous. It would be better to send teams with energy projectors."

"Do you have teams you can send now?"

"We'll need five to ten minutes." The captain replied.

"Not soon enough. I'm going into the office now. When I send the word, you bomb the other location."

"Mr. Ambassador. I cannot permit that."

"Sorry, Captain. We're out of time. Send in the bomb on my order.

"We have to go NOW!" Michael shouted to the team in the shuttle. "Suspend deployment and transport Alexi and I to the Chairman's office."

"Alexi, grab an energy projector!" Michael grabbed the one closest to him.

"Personal shields on max!" Michael instructed as Elsie did the transport countdown.

345

THE ARREST

[02.09.2025 10:40 PM] CHAIRMAN'S OFFICE, NORTH KOREA

The Chairman was furious. As he was pulling his own personal pistol from its holster to shoot the insolent cow in front of him, two people simply appeared in his office. Everyone froze, not sure what they were seeing.

A voice called out. "Freeze! You are under arrest for sedition against the Intergalactic Confederation of Planets. Resist at your own peril." The message was spoken in perfect Korean with a northern accent.

The sound unfroze the Chairman, who got two shots off at the speaker before... *What happened?* he thought. *I cannot move. I cannot breathe.* A sudden panic came over him. He was frozen. Completely, utterly, frozen.

One by one the others were being frozen also. He noted with satisfaction that the insolent cow, who had made a run for the door, was also frozen.

There was a sudden knock on the door and a muffled voice on the other side said, "Signal corps reporting for duty, sir!"

Michael knew he had to let them in, so yelled out "Patience!" in his best imitation of the chairman. Alexi tagged four people, ones that would be in view when the door was opened. Then, she called for Elsie to transport them up.

Michael called Elsie. "Can you tell how many are outside the door?"

"Looks like two men with equipment and three guards," Elsie said.

"How long to get the rest out?"

"Michael, there are only two of us up here and we're very busy. One of the men we just transported up has begun moving."

Then suddenly, "Michael a tendril of smoke just slipped under the cockpit door!" Elsie shouted.

"Beam me into the cockpit now!" Michael shouted. He turned to Alexi and said, "Hold the fort..." but was cut off as he disappeared.

346

Michael landed standing on a chair. The wisp had wrapped around Elsie's ankle and she was starting to panic. Michael aimed the energy projector at her ankle. The tendril quivered as Michael brought the field closer, then it dissipated. "Elsie, can you beam it to the moon?"

No response. She had gone into shock. "Sanjit, can you fly this thing?"

"Never learned Michael."

"Damn!" Michael said. "Can you transport Alexi up?"

No answer. Michael looked at Sanjit and saw that another tendril had come through a crack in the wall and was attacking Sanjit. Michael chased it with the energy projector as it slipped back through the crack, but another started coming in through the door.

"Computer." Michael shouted. "Emergency decompression!"

Michael saw the black tendril get sucked back out through the crack in the door. The cockpit air pressure was dropping precipitously. He extended his personal shield out around Elsie and Sanjit. It would not protect from another tendril, but it would give them a few minutes before they asphyxiated.

"Computer. Was the creature sucked out of the cargo bay?" He could see three men floating outside the cabin, but no sign of the creature.

"All four occupants of the cargo bay were expelled."

"Computer. Reseal the hull and re-pressurize."

"Cannot comply at this time. The entrance is blocked."

"Emergency override. Seal and re-pressurize."

There was a horrific noise in the cargo bay, followed by a small explosion that sent an electrical discharge through the cabin. Although the power was out and the computer dead, the cabin had begun to re-pressurize. He noticed black mist trying to re-form outside the shuttle. It suddenly collapsed, then dissipated. Michael let out a sigh of relief. The abomination had been destroyed. One problem down, but a hundred more waiting. The shuttle was dead in space in an orbit that would decay and re-enter in a matter of hours.

As no more air was leaking out of the cockpit into the cabin, Michael decided to open the door to survey the damage. Maybe Joel could talk him through enough repairs to restart. He opened the door to the most gruesome thing he'd ever seen.

Half of the Chairman was still in the shuttle. It had been depressurized for about one minute and goo oozed out everywhere.

Worse, the body was blanketed with layers of black smoke swirling about, attempting to repair it.

The Chairmen's mostly desiccated eyes moved in Michael's direction. Then he smiled. "Now you understand. Don't you? Clever idea that, cutting a field generator in half with the cargo door and letting a gigawatt electric discharge blanket the ship. It almost got me. Well, it did get me, but not enough of me. This body has enough energy left in it for me to regenerate. Once that is done, I will escape into the vacuum while you cook during the ride down."

Michael pulled the trigger on the energy projector. He hosed the cloud with the invisible beam. The cloud tried to coalesce but failed. Tried again, then totally dissipated. As it did so, the remains of the chairman simply melted into a puddle of goo.

Michael walked back to the cockpit. He needed to do something quickly. The air was thinning out and getting cold. They would not last in space another hour without power. When he got to the cockpit, he saw that Elsie and Sanjit were still unconscious.

His eye was drawn to a blinking red light. As he looked closer, he could see that it was 'The Button' Elsie had promised to install.

More than once Elsie had complained bitterly about being the only pilot serving this large a team. She had even started threatening to put a big button on the instrument panel that would illuminate with a blinking red light, so someone else could start the shuttle if she were indisposed. *She actually did it,* Michael thought approvingly.

Michael pushed the button and the shuttle slowly started coming to life. A hologram of Elsie was projected into her seat. In a very creepy twist, the holographic projection settled on top of Elsie's actual body. Then her voice came over the PA. "So, you've finally done it... got in some sort of pickle and I'm not there to save your butt. Well, here is my gift to you, an AI named Else."

Another voice, one that sounded a lot like Elsie said, "Hello Michael. This shuttle is a mess and we are falling out of orbit. What have you done?"

"Long story. Can you move us back up to 12,000 miles above Pyongyang and scan the North Korean chairman's office?"

"Working."

"Connect me to Jiaying," Michael commanded.

Jiaying's voice came over the com system. "Michael, where are you? The Captain is going crazy."

"Connect me!"

"Mr. Amba..." The Captain started, but Michael cut him off.

"Send the bomb. Send the bomb now. That is an order!"

"Done sir..." The Captain replied.

But before he could get another word out, Michael said. "Captain. I need your help. I killed the creature that we beamed onto our shuttle, but the shuttle was badly damaged and two of my crew were infected. Can you beam the entire shuttle into a cargo bay?"

"No sir. I cannot do that until the shuttle has been confirmed to be clean.

Else's voice cut through the communication. "Orbit restored. Chairman's office found. Not another mess! Is that Alexi! What is she doing in the Chairman's office? There are seven men standing, who appear to be in suspensor fields, and five more on the floor that appear to be hog tied."

"Can you beam them all up?"

"I do not recognize the word 'beam', what does it mean?" Else said.

The Captain chimed in. "Mr. Ambassador. I do not recognize that word either."

"Transport. Beam means transport. Can you transport the whole group up?"

"Ambassador, do not do that! We can send a team to secure your people on the ground. I can also send a team in hazmat suits to secure your shuttle."

"Else, can you connect me to Alexi?"

"Here, Michael," Alexi replied.

"Alexi. Status report," Michael commanded.

"The Chairmen's generals are all in suspensor fields. The communications officers and their guards have all been secured. No word got out. But a backup team will be here in a few minutes to investigate their absence."

"Captain?" Michael asked. "Do you have a secure room with an Earth-compatible atmosphere, where Alexi and her captives can be evacuated to?"

"Yes, Mr. Ambassador. I can have it ready momentarily."

"Alexi. We are going to have you and your captives transported to a fleet fast attack ship, where you will be safe."

"Thank you, Michael."

"Captain. How long before your decontamination team can get to my shuttle?"

"They will be there momentarily. I have also sent a team to confirm the kill and decontaminate the other location. Hostiles are in the area. How would you like me to handle them?"

"Suspensor fields. Humans are very susceptible. Please avoid any loss of life, if it can be avoided. Also, have your team in stealth shields. We do not want any humans to see your form. It's too early in the Revelation process to allow that to happen."

"Yes, Sir. May I leave this line open and update you as necessary?"

"Yes Captain. Thank you for that suggestion. But I will mute my end and ask you to do the same, so I can make some other calls. Unmute when you need to speak with me. Then wait for me to reply."

"Yes, sir."

"Else, mute this line and open a line to the South Korean President," Michael requested.

BLUE HOUSE, SEOUL, SOUTH KOREA

"Michael?" the South Korean president said.

"Mr. President," Michael said. "We're not out of the woods yet, but I think we're close. The Chairman and his inner circle were arrested before they could give the order to invade. Unfortunately, the Chairman and three others were killed in an escape attempt. Another person on the ground was also killed. We regret these losses, but four of these deaths are a direct result of the Chairmen's resistance. And the other was about to set off a terrible weapon."

"Michael, thank you. Is the suspensor field in place?" The president asked.

"A little over 75 miles are complete. The rest is open. But we now have additional assets on site, so we should be able to stop any invasion that might start.

"Mr. President," Michael asked. "Do you have the means to connect me to the general in charge of US forces in South Korea?"

"I think I do. But, if you have the time, it would be better to go through the US President than through me. I have a cordial relationship with the general, but he cannot take orders from me or from you."

"Thank you for your advice, Mr. President. If you'll excuse me, I'll do as you suggest."

"Jiaying, can you connect me to the US President?"

"Will do, as quickly as possible. Michael."

SITUATION ROOM, WHITE HOUSE, WASHINGTON, DC.

"Michael, please give me some good news."

"Mr. President. Thank you for taking my call. The North Korean situation is mostly contained, but I need to coordinate with your general in charge of forces in South Korea."

"I'll get him on the line. It'll only take a few moments. Can you tell me more while we wait?"

"Yes, sir. But please keep this confidential for a couple hours."

"Will do," the president replied.

"The Chairmen and four others were killed during the arrest. This happened before the order to invade had been given, so we are hoping there will be no invasion. The shield in the demilitarized zone is a little less than half complete, but additional Confederation assets are now on the scene. I expect the DMZ shielding to be complete in a few hours. But even if it's not, we now have the capacity in the region to stop an invasion."

The general's voice came over the line. "Mr. President."

"General Adams, I have the Ambassador from the Confederation on the line."

"Mr. Ambassador," said the general.

"General Adams. The area is mostly secure. The Chairmen was taken into custody before the order to invade was issued."

"Excellent news, sir."

"However, there are some things you need to know. One of the Confederation's fast attack ships has arrived on the scene and is currently located above the North Korean capital. The ship is over one kilometer long and 300 meters wide, but it is cloaked, so you cannot see it at this time. If an invasion begins, the ship may de-cloak and hover above the South Korean side of the DMZ as an intimidation tactic. Do not take any action against this ship. You do not have the means to hurt it, but the Captain might confuse you for the enemy if you fire at it. Trust me, you do not want that to happen.

"It also has the ability to project intense light, over 1 million lumens. Light this intense will cause temporary blindness. A foghorn will sound before the light flashes. Please tell your men to cover their eyes if they hear the foghorn. The natural instinct is to look toward the sound, which is what we expect the North Korean Army to do. The light will blind them for at least one hour. We do not want that to happen to your men."

"Thank you for the warning, Mr. Ambassador."

351

"Thank you, gentlemen," Michael said. "The Captain of the Confederation ship is on the other line. I need to go now." The line dropped.

SHUTTLE, 12,000 MILES ABOVE NORTH KOREA

"The team is ready to transport onto your ship, Mr. Ambassador. Permission to board?"

"Permission granted, Captain."

Two Lorexians in hazmat suits appeared in the passenger compartment. It had been years since Michael had seen a Lorexian in person and their size was utterly intimidating. They did a quick assessment of the situation, then started using their energy projectors to sanitize every surface. They switched to scanners, nodded to each other. Then each pulled out a canister, removed the top, and poured a shimmering liquid on the floor. The liquid spread out across the floor then seeped into the cracks. Smoke whiffed up from the floor, then dissipated.

The leader of the team turned to address Michael. "Mr. Ambassador, you killed a large and powerful enemy agent. Very impressive, especially for a civilian. We can certify that your ship is clear, but your crew has a big clean up job on their hands. The liquid we poured on the floor is a special nanobot solution that should help.

"Can we see your contaminated crew members?" He asked.

"This way." Michael led them to the cockpit. Elsie and Sanjit were still slouched in their chairs. Thankfully Else had repositioned to an open seat.

The decontamination team scanned Elsie and Sanjit. The team leader turned to Michael. "Sir, I'm sad to inform you that these two are seriously contaminated. The safest course of action would be to withdraw them from their avatars, then transport the avatars into the local star."

"Can we use the energy projectors on them?"

"Yes, but there is a 70% chance that the Avatars will explode, possibly damaging the Ascendants operating them. I've seen that happen before and strongly advise against that course of action."

"Thank you, Lieutenant."

Michael sighed, then used his internal control system to deactivate Elsie and Sanjit's avatars, an act that deeply saddened him. They would be gone for at least two weeks.

"I have deactivated the avatars. Are your instructions to stay with us or to return to your ship?"

"The Captain ordered us to help you as much and as long as you needed. We are to return when you have dismissed us. We would be happy to stay and stand guard or do anything you need sir."

"Thank you, gentlemen. Let me make arrangements for our colleagues, then we can dispose of their avatars. Afterward, we can decide next steps."

The lead member of the team acknowledged Michael's plan.

"Else, we need to transport Elsie and Sanjit's avatars into the Sun. Please plot an efficient course to get us to an acceptable transport position."

"It'll take us about 15 minutes to get into position, Michael. I'm going to jump out about 100,000 miles, to a point closer to the edge of the earth's shadow, then jump 10 million miles to a position close enough to the Sun that we can transport them directly into the chromosphere."

"Excellent choice." The team leader agreed. "The deeper the better."

"Thank you, Else. Please let me know when it's done."

Orders given, Michael called out. "Jiaying."

"Yes, Michael."

"Can you connect me to Barbara?"

"Hi. Michael. We have an emergency here that I presume you know about. Elsie and Sanjit just lost connection to their avatars."

"Yes, I did an emergency disconnect. Their avatars have been contaminated by the Enemy. We got them out in time and are about to transport their avatars into the Sun."

"OK. It's going to take a week or two to mature replacement avatars." Barbara shook her head sadly. "In the meantime, I'm going to place them in suspended animation. It would be very uncomfortable for them to wake up in their natural bodies."

"I know. Been there, done that, and don't want to do it again," Michael replied. "Anything else you need from me, Barbara?"

"Yes, but it can wait until you get back. Thank you, Michael."

"We are in transport range, Michael," Else reported.

Michael reached out to touch Elsie's avatar, but was stopped by the team leader. "I'm sorry sir, but better if you didn't touch them. I know it's difficult. But they'll be back soon."

"Thank you," Michael said, surprised at the emotion in his voice. *I really am turning into a human*, he thought. "Else. Please initiate transport."

Elsie's and Sanjit's avatars disappeared.

"Else. Please take us back to North Korea," Michael asked.

"We'll be there in about 15 minutes."

Michael unmuted his connection back to the fast attack ship. "Captain. Are you still on the line?" Michael asked.

"Yes sir," the captain replied. "I got the report from my team, Mr. Ambassador. I'm very impressed that you single-handedly took down an Enemy of that strength, and sorry to hear of the loss of the two avatars."

"Thank you, Captain. Please give me an update on the situation."

"Yes sir. We were able to tap into the surveillance that you put in place. We were also able to connect with your team on the status of the shield barrier. The North Koreans are in chaos. Apparently, their leader ruled with an iron fist. They do not know what to do without someone commanding them.

"Your team in Paso Robles completed another round of field generators. I have a shuttle installing them now. They also sent us the pattern. We needed to borrow some transluminide and have now replicated enough generators to complete the barrier. A second shuttle is in the process of installing them. An impenetrable barrier will be in place in another 20 minutes."

"Excellent news, Captain. Here's what I want to do next. First, I'd like to replicate enough field generators to build a second barrier. One that would be placed 10 miles to the north of the current barrier and trap the North Korean army in place. Second, we have developed nanobots that eat the metal used to make human weapons. I'd like you to replicate and disburse enough of these nanobots to consume all weapons in North Korea. Third, I'd like to confiscate all fissile material in North Korea. This will leave the North completely defenseless. Then I will demand their unconditional surrender to the Confederation.

"How long would it take you to replicate and deploy the second barrier?" Michael asked.

"Two, maybe three hours, if you have the requisite transluminide."

"We do. Get started. I'll contact Joel to get the nanobot production started."

"Jiaying. Get me Joel, even if he's on Do Not Disturb."

A few minutes later… "What's up Michael?" Joel's voice sounded over the comm system.

"Joel, I need massive quantities of gun-eating nanobots."

"How many guns?" Joel asked.

"At least 600,000." Michael replied.

"Michael, where do you come up with this stuff?"

"We're going to disarm North Korea. Turns out the Chairman and one of his associates were Enemy agents."

"How soon do you need them?"

"Now," Michael said.

"Michael, we don't have that kind of capacity. Five…, seven days minimum."

"What about the fast attack ship?"

"I'll send them the specifications and see what they say," Joel replied. "I'm guessing you want me online for a while?"

"What time is it there?"

"4:00 in the afternoon."

Michael started laughing. "I was worried that I'd woken you up again."

"Michael, do you ever sleep?"

"Had three hours in a regeneration chamber about 7 hours ago."

"Anyway, back to business…" Joel said. "I need to go in two hours. I'll be accompanying Rabbi Levine on the first round of Palestinian gift deliveries in about three hours. Speaking of which, Elsie is supposed to be helping with the deliveries, but I haven't been able to reach her."

Joel's words were like a knife in Michael's side. "Joel, I have some bad news. Elsie's avatar was destroyed about an hour ago. I had to do an emergency withdrawal, thankfully Barbara put them in stasis before they woke up."

"Them?" Joel asked, reeling from the news.

"And Sanjit," Michael said.

"So, should I delay the distribution?"

"In principle, no. Let me see if I can make the shuttle available."

"What do you mean make it available? Without Elsie, what's the point?"

"Else," Michael muttered.

"Else what?" Joel said, impatience in his voice.

"Oh sorry. Elsie created an AI that she named Else to fly if she was unavailable."

"Wow, I am so out of the loop."

"Be thankful. We took down three enemy agents today. No one wants to be part of that."

"Three? I thought you said two."

"Ah... Charles, Sanjit and I took down another one at the ranch today."

"At the ranch! Are we under attack?" Joel asked, fear creeping up his spine.

"No. North Korea had two. Russia had one that we know of, but I suspect there are more. I also suspect that Iran has at least two. As soon as the North Korean situation has stabilized, we will seek out and destroy the others. So, let's get to it. I'll see if I can get you a shuttle. You connect with the Captain and see what they can do for us in terms of nanobots."

"On it," Joel hung up.

Michael turned his attention to the hazmat team. "Gentlemen, I think it would be OK for you to return now. It cannot be comfortable in those suits."

"Thank you, sir. These suits are very hot, and we cannot take them off because of the atmosphere in the shuttle." Moments later, the two men disappeared.

"Jiaying, can you connect me to Alexi?"

"Let me see. You may need to go to internal. Ah... got her."

"Michael." Alexi's voice came over the line.

"Alexi, are you on the fast attack ship?"

"Yes, Michael. They set up a cargo hold for us. The air is good, although the smell is a bit funky. And our hosts... These guys are giant. Would love to wrestle one, but they did not respond so well to the suggestion."

Michael rolled his eyes. "What about our captives?"

"They are all here and as passive as terrified children. I downloaded the Korean translator before the mission, so I can talk to them. I am currently running a lottery for who will be probed first. They are as gentle as lambs, and tripping over each other to spill information."

"Alexi, you know that we do not probe humans."

"Of course, I know. But they don't."

"So, what have you learned?"

"First, they are as terrified of the Chairmen's sister as they are of him. From what I've gathered, she was the other Enemy agent. We also have the head of offensive forces, domestic security and the nuclear program. Each has told me their deployments and

356

vulnerabilities. We should be able to take these guys down with no problem."

"Have you told the Captain about this?"

"Not met him yet. I get the impression he's not a big fan of androids."

"Do you think we could control your captives if we took them back to Hawaii?"

"I don't know the Hawaii facility very well. I'd have no trouble controlling them in Paso."

"OK. Got to go, Alexi. The Captain is calling," Michael dropped the line.

...

"Captain," Michael greeted.

"Mr. Ambassador, deployment of the second shield barrier is underway. The troops have all clustered within a mile of the DMZ, so we are laying the containment barrier a little further south than you asked. I hope this is OK."

"Good call, Captain."

"We have also tasked two of our military-grade, high-capacity replicators to making the nanobots. We should have the capacity to destroy 750,000 weapons within the next hour. At this point we have requisitioned a full kilogram of transluminide. Your engineer, Joel, told me that he had the authority to authorize the additional amounts. Is that correct sir?"

"Yes. I gave Joel the authority to allocate that much for this initiative," Michael replied.

"Mr. Ambassador. I didn't know that you were ranked high enough to control that much transluminide. My apologies if I haven't shown the corresponding level of respect. I tried looking you up but didn't have the clearance to view your profile. It's restricted to well above my grade."

"No problem, Captain. This far out in the frontier things are less formal. But don't let that statement mislead you. Earth is one of the most important, if not THE most important, missions in the entire Confederation. Everything is on the line here. We must not only prevail, we must excel."

"Again, my apologies, Mr. Ambassador. I was not briefed."

"Moving to another topic... I need your help with a mission in the Middle East. A small group of dignitaries needs transportation assistance for about three hours. Joel will be leading that mission and

357

will be leading a small group of humans. Now that my pilot has lost her avatar, the mission will be piloted by our AI. Is it viable for you to provide an escort, in case there's trouble?"

"Yes sir. I have 22 military escort vessels aboard."

"Excellent. Have your pilot coordinate with Joel. Next topic... I want Alexi and the captives transported to one of my facilities on the surface. Alexi has proven very capable of extracting information from these men and she will have better accommodation to do that on the surface. Please work with her to make that happen."

"Does that imply she will lead that mission?" The captain asked.

"Yes. Is that a problem, Captain?"

"No sir. Just making sure I understood your intentions, sir."

"Excellent. Alert me as each of these assignments is complete."

"Will do, sir." The captain muted his end of the line. His hand trembled a bit. He'd never worked for anyone this highly ranked and had blundered the protocol badly. The Admiral was three levels higher than himself, and he now understood that this ambassador was even more highly ranked than the Admiral. No wonder an armada of this magnitude had been dispatched. He vowed to himself to perform his duties with more diligence and formality, and never to question the ambassador.

"Jiaying, can you connect me back to Alexi?" asked Michael.

"She is now on the call line, so you can get her just by speaking her name."

"Thank you, Jiaying. You're the best."

"Alexi," he called.

"Yes, Michael."

"I'm going to send you back to Paso. I plan to join you but may be delayed a bit. We are about to capture essentially the entire North Korean army. They will be surrounded by suspensor fields shortly. Your mission is to work with your captives to determine the best way to get the prisoners to surrender. Use your discretion about interrogation techniques, but no probing or other physical harm. At the end of the day, we want these men on our side.

"The Captain is arranging transportation. Tell the transportation team where you want them to take you and how you want it done. The Captain has been informed that you're leading this mission. I expect that he will go out of his way to accommodate. But, please interact with them professionally and do not challenge them to a wrestling match." Then, after a short pause, he added, "You can do that later." Michael heard some whooping on the other end of the line.

"Got to go. Let me know when you're underway."

"Joel."

"Here, Michael."

"The shuttle will be on its way shortly. Else will be piloting. I think Elsie did a great job with the programing, so I doubt there will be any problems. I've also asked the captain to assign a military escort. They will be under your command. Deploy them as you need, but under no circumstance can any human see the Lorexian soldiers."

"Got it, Michael," Joel replied.

"Lastly, I can accompany you if that would help. But, as Consul General for Israel, it would be better if you did this on your own. These are your people now."

"Thank you, Michael. I think I can handle this. The Levine's are already treating me like family, and Rabbi Levine has offered to take me as a student."

"Excellent news. I'm proud of you, Joel."

"Thank you, Michael."

"I have the Captain on the other line, so I suspect that his escort vessel is ready to depart. Good luck with your mission today." Michael dropped the line.

"Captain."

"Mr. Ambassador, the shuttle transporting Alexi and the captives is about to leave and your escort shuttle is ready. May I ask where you will be sir?"

"I'll be going to the same place that Alexi is going, and plan to transport down shortly after she does. I'll be in continuous connection with you but need to talk with a few of the prisoners before we destroy the North Korean weapons. Can you leave Alexi's escort on station for my use until the North Korean situation is better understood? As I'm in human form, I will need the modified atmosphere."

"Of course, sir. It's yours to command until you are able to release it back to us."

"Excellent. Thank you, Captain. We will get underway momentarily." Michael muted the line.

"Else, has Alexi's transport left yet?"

"Yes, Michael. They just jumped. Those are some machines! We cannot follow the same course; this shuttle isn't powerful enough."

"Is the escort in place?"

"Yes. She just pulled up next to us."

"Great. Can you connect me to the pilot?"

"Yes. Here he is."

"Mr. Ambassador. It is a pleasure to speak with you. What are your orders, sir?"

His call sign is Jo-Tan-Zu. Else sent. *He is a major.*

"Major Jo-Tan-Zu, thank you for accepting escort duty today."

"It is my honor sir. This is the highest profile mission I've ever been a part of. Any role is an honor."

"Thank you, Major. Else may already have sent you the flight plan, but I would like to provide context. We will be taking a slower route to Paso Robles. Our shuttle is not as powerful as yours, and it has recently suffered some damage. So, we are taking a low stress route. When we arrive, I will be transporting down to join the team on the surface. Some of my people will be transporting up to make some repairs to the shuttle. It should only take 15 minutes or so.

"When the repairs are complete, you are to accompany Else to a country called Israel, where Else will land. I would like you to accompany the shuttle down but maintain stealth and do not land. There will be other air traffic in the area, so you need to be very careful and continuously scan your environment for anything fast moving.

"Your mission engagement parameters are as follows. First and most important, you and your team must not be seen by humans under any circumstance. Second, your craft is to remain cloaked. You may only expose it to view if the humans you are escorting are in mortal danger and there's no other option. Third, although we do not expect violence, you are to protect the humans at any cost consistent with not exposing yourselves to view.

"There are some evil people that will try to stop this mission if they find out about it, and they will use any method they can. So be on continuous lookout for missiles, particularly short-range missiles. Scan continuously for nuclear material. A shield is in place to protect against nuclear missiles, but our enemies here have created 'suitcase nukes', small nuclear weapons with a short range.

"By now you may be wondering what we're doing here. Earth is vitally important for reasons I cannot disclose to you. The Enemy is already here and have corrupted a small number of leaders of rogue countries. We will eliminate these leaders over the next couple days but need to maintain other vital missions in the interim. Do you have any questions?"

"No sir, but to avoid any misunderstanding, let me repeat that back to you. We are to protect the humans that your shuttle will be transporting. We are to stay close and protect them at any cost, but may not expose ourselves under any circumstance, and may only expose the ship if the humans are in mortal danger and there's no other option. No violence is expected, but the Enemy will attack if they have gained knowledge of the mission and have assembled the means to attack."

"Excellent, Major. I entrust this mission to your capable hands."

"Thank you for this opportunity to serve, Mr. Ambassador." The major closed the connection.

"That was uncharacteristically formal for you, Michael." Else said.

"Else you have only known me for a couple hours."

"Ah... Elsie uploaded 10 years of memories. I even know about how you 'whispered in the mind' of that reporter that's so hot on you."

"I'm never going to hear the end of that, am I?"

"Don't think so. OK. We are on site. Alexi is already down and just sent me the coordinates where she wants you. Good luck."

GAS PRODUCTION FACILITY, PASO ROBLES, CA

Michael appeared in a conference room three stories underground. Julie Ferguson was waiting there for him.

"Hello, Michael. Welcome to Paso Robles. I hear you've had quite the day. Sorry to hear about Elsie and Sanjit. I know you were close to both."

Once again, mention of Elsie and Sanjit cut like a knife.

"They should be back in about two weeks. I've been through an experience like that before and it was not pleasant. Hopefully they can turn the experience for the better. I wouldn't voluntarily do it again, but it actually helped me quite a bit."

"Michael, I love the way you can find good in every bad thing."

"So, where is Alexi? I need to speak with her captives as soon as possible."

"She has them chained up in the production facility, separated far enough from each other that they cannot talk. She should be back in a few minutes, but I can call and ask."

"Please."

After a minute... "She has them all loosely restrained and surrounded by bots, which will be interesting to see. If you want to go now, she'll meet us at the elevator."

"Let's go."

They left the room and walked down a long corridor. At the end, there was an elevator that went deep down to the lower levels. Julie and Michael entered, then rode down to Level 10. The door opened to a smiling Alexi. "Michael, thank you for having taken me on this mission. It's been so much fun."

"Don't enjoy it too much." Michael shook his head.

"To business... we will be capturing the bulk of the North Korean Army within the hour. Have you found out the best way to get them to voluntarily surrender?"

"The general says they'll never surrender. But he obviously doesn't believe it. I'm actually a little surprised by that. He is terrified of me, but willfully lying. I suspect that he is more afraid of the Chairman and his sister."

"Let's go talk with him. Are there any video screens near him, or near here?"

"There's a conference room about 25 feet down the hallway, over there."

"Good."

Captain, Michael sent. *Do you have any video evidence of the destruction of the other Enemy agent? If so, send it to Jiaying immediately. Thank you.*

As they turned the corner, Michael saw a man sitting on the floor. He was loosely shackled and surrounded by three pipefitting bots that kept opening and closing the gripper they had for a right hand, and periodically flashing the welding torch in the other. Michael looked at Alexi and asked, "Has this man been hurt in any way?"

"Only his pride," Alexi replied.

Michael came to a stop in front of the man, who looked up at him, tears in his eyes. "Sir," Michael said in Korean. "I am Michael, Ambassador from the Intergalactic Confederation of Planets. I would like to have a few words with you."

The man nodded enthusiastically.

"My colleague will release you and you will walk with me to the conference room down the hall over there. It will go poorly for you if you attempt to fight or escape. Do you understand?"

Again, he nodded.

"Release him." Michael ordered.

One of the bots immediately charged the man, who let out a scream. The bot stopped and released the shackles, then withdrew.

Too much! Michael sent to Alexi, who suddenly looked sheepish.

Michael reached down to offer the man a hand up. But he shrunk away from Michael.

Michael held his position. "Sir. I'm not here to hurt you and I'm sorry for the rough treatment you've received. But, as someone who was threatening the lives of hundreds of thousands, I think you've earned a little rough treatment. Please take my hand and let me help you up, I would like to speak with you."

The man took Michael's hand and stood.

"Walk with me." Michael pointed to a place by his side. The man stepped up next to Michael and they began walking toward the conference room. Michael had opened his senses and at this point knew that the man's name was General Park. Michael also discerned that he was the senior commander of the armed forces.

"General Park," Michael started.

The man visibly stiffened at the sound of his name.

"I believe that you are the most senior official of the North Korean Government that is still alive?"

Park paused for a second, then hastened back into position when Alexi prodded him in the back.

"No. The Chairmen and his sister are more senior than me. They are gods that cannot be killed. I serve only them."

"You saw the Chairmen and three others disappear from the room, correct?"

"Yes, I did. They saved themselves but left me behind. I am not worthy."

"They did not save themselves. I arrested them."

"No. The Chairman is a god. He knows all. You cannot arrest him."

They entered the room and Michael said, "Please take a seat."

The TV opposite them turned on and started playing. "Do you recognize this room?" Michael pointed at the screen. It was a recording of the arrest in the Chairman's office. "Do you see me there? Do you see the bullets the Chairmen shot, stopping in the air right in front of me?" Michael paused the playback.

"Yes. That's what happened in the Chairman's office. How did you stop those bullets?" General Park asked.

"A personal shield. No human technology can penetrate that shield. Watch what happens next." Michael resumed playback. Four small balls went rocketing across the room. Each hit a man, who froze the instant he was hit.

Michael again paused the playback. "You were also hit by one of those, weren't you? What happened next?"

The General replied, "I couldn't move. I couldn't even breathe. Yet, I'm still alive. How'd you do that?"

Michael smiled to himself. The General might not have realized it, but he was acknowledging that he participated in these events and Michael was the one that precipitated them.

"Now listen to what happens next." Michael resumed playback. His voice could be heard calling for the four to be transported up.

He paused. "What did you hear?"

"You, calling for the Chairmen and three others to be transported up."

Michael resumed playback and the four men in question disappeared. The scene they were watching shrunk to the right and a new scene started playing in the new window that emerged on the left side of the screen. In that window, the Chairmen and three others appeared, then almost immediately fell over.

Michael paused again. "Do you recognize this place?"

"It looks similar to the box in which I was put before coming here. But it's not the same one. This one has lots of stuff in it."

"You're right. You were brought here in a cargo hold on a Confederation Military Escort ship. This one is my shuttle, the one that was being used to close the border between you and the south."

"What do you mean close the border?"

"We built a shield along the South Korean side of the border. The shield we built was a combination of the kind that protected me from the Chairmen's bullet and the kind that held you in place in the chairman's office."

"That cannot be. If it were true, then our invasion would fail!" The General said with panic in his voice.

"General Park. The truth is far worse than you think. But let's watch this part of the story before we move on. I warn you that what you are about to see is both distressing and gruesome."

Michael resumed playback. The men remained on their sides on the floor, completely frozen. Then suddenly, tendrils of black smoke started coming out of the Chairman's open mouth. They formed into several large arms and moved toward the cockpit. The cockpit door suddenly slammed shut.

Michael paused playback. "Have you seen that before? Black smoke coming out of the Chairman?"

"Yes. Once. It was terrifying. He wrapped those arms around his sister, who was screaming. I think we were all screaming. She suddenly became still. Then he lowered her to the floor and appeared to eat her. Then she reappeared a few minutes later, black smoke consolidating back into flesh. The Chairman said that she was now a god also."

"My friend. It would be more accurate to call these creatures demons than to call them gods. They are parasitic creatures that slowly consume the people they occupy. And, during that process, which can take as much as 100 years, the people they occupy are completely controlled by the creature. Watch what happens next."

Light could be seen poking out from a spot where the arm had penetrated the left wall, then withdrawn. Another spot of light appeared where an arm penetrated the right wall, then again at the base of the cockpit door. Then suddenly a door opened in the side of the room and everything started flying toward it. The Earth could be seen through the door. It looked like a big blue ball.

Almost everything had been sucked out except for the Chairman, whose black smoky arms were holding tight to the walls, and a suitcase-sized box that was stuck in the door along with the Chairman and some wooden pallet material. The scene was frozen like that for several seconds. The Chairman's face froze, as did all exposed skin on his body. But the arms held fast even though they continued to ripple in a smoke-like motion. Then suddenly the door slammed closed, cutting the box and the Chairman in half. There was a brilliant flash of light, then the screen went dead.

"What happened?" the General asked.

"I did an emergency evacuation of the cabin, opening the door to space. Unfortunately, the Chairman damaged the cockpit such that it was no longer airtight. So, I did an emergency close on the door which cut the Chairman and the shield generator in half. The bright flash was the shield generator exploding."

"Is the Chairman dead?"

"Watch. Emergency power kicked on for the security camera after a few moments."

The scene started playing. Black smoke was swirling madly around the remains of the Chairman. The cockpit door opened, and Michael could be seen coming through. The Chairman appeared to say something in a language the General did not understand. Then Michael pointed the rifle he was holding at the Chairman. The air seemed to shimmer. The smoke arms lunged toward Michael but dissipated before they got that far. The smoke then seemed to attempt to coalesce into another copy of the chairman. Then it suddenly dissipated, and the remains of the chairman's body melted into a pool of yellow muck that slowly seeped through the floor.

"He's dead, isn't he?"

"Yes." Michael said. "One last clip for you to see."

The scene changed to a room in which a woman was sitting scowling at a screen.

"That's the chairman's sister. She is truly evil."

Suddenly, there was a bright flash that whited out the screen. As the room came back into view, there was no sign of the woman, other than her shoes and the ripped remnants of a skirt on the chair. But the walls were covered in a yellow goo that was slowly dripping down towards the floor.

A big smile came over the general's face. "They are dead. You killed them both!" he said with a lot of enthusiasm. "Please! Tell me how I can help you."

Michael also smiled, glad he'd won a friend.

Captain. Can you send me a quick update as well as images showing the shield locations? Michael sent.

"General. With no leader, I am concerned for the safety and stability of your country. I am hoping that you will work with me to bring peace and prosperity to the North."

"I'm not sure what you're asking, Mr. Ambassador. Aren't you the enemy of the North?"

"No. I'm not, nor will I ever be, the enemy of the Korean or the North Korean people. It is my opinion that Korean unification would be good for both the North and the South. But I will not force that on either side. If the North decides that it wants to be separate, then I will support that. What I will not allow is a return to the despotism, hostility and strong man tactics."

The General thought for a second. "Do you think reunification is possible?"

"The South desperately wants reunification."

"But they are rich, and we are poor. How could that work?"

"The Intergalactic Confederation is about to pour an enormous amount of resources into the peoples of Earth. The biggest beneficiaries will be the poorest nations. There will be unlimited food and energy. Protection from enemies. There will no longer be a need for armies. At least not the kinds of armies that the world has today."

"What do you need me to do?"

"Please hear me out before complaining…" Michael paused. The General nodded.

"I'm about to take your entire army prisoners of war."

"What!" the General shouted.

Michael raised his hands as if to surrender. "I am also about to take their guns."

"What! You cannot do that! It will leave us defenseless!" the General shouted even louder.

"No harm will come to them from the Confederation, and I will protect you from your enemies. You will not be defenseless. You will be protected by the most powerful force on this planet. Me."

The General looked less than convinced.

"My concern is that your army will harm themselves, the one thing I cannot protect them from. That is the help I want from you."

The General continued to look less than convinced.

"Let me show you some more images."

The screen popped back on. "See the yellow line going across the bottom edge of the demilitarized zone. That is the barrier that we erected to stop the Chairman's invasion. It is solid and impenetrable."

"We have half a million men on that border. They could breach it," the General boasted.

"No. They could hurt themselves trying, but they cannot breach it." A pause. "We have also built a barrier about a mile north of the demilitarized zone." A second yellow line appeared on the map. "Your men are now trapped between the two yellow lines, although they do not know it yet."

The General remained quiet, but it was clear he believed what he was seeing.

"One last set of images." Michael said. "This is what is about to happen to your men's guns."

The image started playing of the Secret Service agents attacking Michael, followed by the bullets stopping in midair and the guns dissolving in their hands and flowing through their fingers like sand.

"How is this possible?" The General asked, wilting in the face of loss and defeat.

"The important question is how we save your men when this happens. Will they kill themselves? Will they harm themselves by throwing their bodies repeatedly at the barriers? Will they fight and kill each other? What's going to happen?"

"Now I understand why the other one was asking if they would surrender. I will order them to surrender. I will tell them that you have defeated the Chairman and his sister, and that you are now the ruler of our country."

"What kind of communications equipment do they have?"

"There are two radios per squad. We can do a broadcast from the Chairman's office, if you will return me there."

"We will do it here. And we will do it now. I will speak to your troops and to all the people in the North and South, then you will address your men."

Michael stood, closed his eyes for a second, and then opened them again.

Captain. Release the nanobots now. Activate them on my signal. Michael sent.

GENERAL ADAMS' OFFICE, NEAR THE DEMILITARIZED ZONE

The American general was in his office, about to head off to bed when the TV turned on and an image of Michael appeared.

BLUE HOUSE, SEOUL

The South Korean President was still in the small office in which he met Michael several hours ago. Although he hoped that Michael was telling him the truth, he still fully expected to be executed in the morning, so was attempting to stay awake all night as it was probably his last.

The TV at the far end of the room turned on and an image of Michael appeared.

OVAL OFFICE, WASHINGTON, DC

The American President was sitting in the oval office. He had cancelled his meetings and was waiting for some word that the crisis in Korea had been averted.

The TV at the far end of the room turned on and an image of Michael appeared.

LUXURY MANSION, PYONGYANG, NORTH KOREA

The head of the Chairman's communication service was sitting in the studio control room waiting for word that the invasion had begun. He had expected it to begin two hours ago, but the Chairman had suddenly gone silent, a silence he wasn't going to be the one to break.

The monitor closest to him suddenly turned on and the image of the alien Ambassador appeared.

CONFERENCE ROOM, GAS PRODUCTION FACILITY

Michael lifted his eyes to a spot on the wall, then started speaking. "To the brave men and women of the Korean People's Army massed along the northern edge of the demilitarized zone."

FIELD BUNKER, NEAR THE DEMILITARIZED ZONE, NORTH KOREA

"To the brave men and women of the Korean People's Army..."

"What the hell!" shouted the Lieutenant in charge of the bunker when his radioman's radio broke the silence.

CONFERENCE ROOM, GAS PRODUCTION FACILITY

"The orders you have been given are in direct violation of the Intergalactic Confederation's laws regarding aggression against allied nations. The Chairman and his inner circle have been arrested for this illegal activity. Unfortunately, both the Chairman and his sister were killed while attempting to resist arrest.

"You are ordered to put down your guns. Immediately!"

Now. Michael sent to the Captain.

BLUE HOUSE, SEOUL, SOUTH KOREA

As Michael was saying, "You are ordered to put down your guns," the scene shifted to the demilitarized zone. A group of men, who had obviously been startled by the sound of numerous radios going off, were on their feet pointing their rifles toward the DMZ.

"As you have not followed the order I have given, I now take your guns from you."

A look of surprise came over the nearest man. His gun started getting soft, then started slewing through his fingers like grains of sand. He started shouting, terror evident in his voice. "What's happening?"

The scene panned out and the image showed men desperately trying to hold onto the grains of the sand their guns had turned into. Many were shouting. All were in a panic. Many just fell to the ground in despair.

"Your immediate and unconditional surrender to the Intergalactic Confederation is required now. Surrender and you will be humanely treated. Do not even consider resisting. I now give you your commanding general, who will lead you while you are prisoners of war. General."

OVAL OFFICE, WASHINGTON, DC

"To my allies. North Korea is now under my control and protection. I will work with you to determine the best way to integrate North Korea into the family of nations. It is no longer a rogue state. While North Korea is under my protection, take no action against her. She is no longer a threat to you."

Then the TV turned back off again.

"Well, I'll be damned," the President said.

LUXURY MANSION, PYONGYANG, NORTH KOREA

The communications leader was surprised to see General Park come onto the screen. The General addressed the nation.

"My fellow countrymen. This is a difficult day for us. Our beloved leader has been taken from us as has his sister. Our weapons are gone. Our nuclear arsenal is gone. Our Army has been taken prisoner.

"The Intergalactic Confederation could have destroyed us but chose not to. They have great empathy for the suffering we have endured and offer us peace and prosperity. And during this time of distress, they have become our protectors.

"To my brothers in arms... Our surrender is unconditional and immediate. Our weapons were taken because we did not surrender them quickly enough. Do not do the same with your lives. The Intergalactic Confederation is powerful beyond your ability to imagine. When they come to process you, go peacefully and treat them respectfully. If you do that, they will treat you well and they will protect your families. Please do not resist. I am convinced that the Confederation will be the best thing that has ever happened for our homeland.

"To the civilian population… Please stay in your homes. If you do go out, do not assemble for the purpose of protest. We will be treated well as long as we cooperate.

"We will hear more from our interim governor, Michael the Ascendant, over the next few days. I will address you as often as possible through this transition.

"This is a sad day. But it is also the start of a peaceful and prosperous future."

THE ARRIVAL

Joel appeared in the living room on the spot they had previously agreed to. The Rabbi, who stood in the doorway, was startled by the sudden appearance, even though it happened at exactly the agreed upon time.

"Oh, my goodness. Welcome, my friend." The rabbi walked into the room and shook Joel's hand. "That is going to be hard to get used to. I can't wait to try it."

A moment later, Hannah walked into the room. "Welcome, Joel." She stepped up to give him a quick hug. "What do you have planned for us?"

"Today, we will be making two deliveries in five different Palestinian towns: Beit Hanina, Beit Safafa, Jabel Mukaber, Shuafat, and al-Walaja. These are all in the East Jerusalem district and were selected because the mayors of these towns agreed to meet us, offer you their blessings, and join us in making these deliveries."

"Joel. I'm worried about this." Hannah seemed to tremble. "These places are hostile to people like us, and we do not speak the language. This just won't work."

"Hannah? Do you trust me?" Joel asked.

"Trust, yes. Believe, no," she said, tears in her eyes.

Judah embraced his wife and whispered in her ear. "He is the one that saved us from a nuclear bomb, and you do not trust him?" Then, he kissed her cheek. "My stomach doesn't believe it either, but my mind says yes. Shall we do this?"

She gave him a close embrace. Then separated and said to Joel, "Tell us what to do."

Joel smiled. "Thank you, Hannah. I respect your courage. We need to do a little preparation before we go. I have two things that I want each of you to put on."

He pulled out something that looked like nylon stockings but were shaped for the entire body. "I want you to change out of your clothes and put these on. Then get dressed again. The shield should be beneath your clothes, undies and all. It needs to touch your skin."

"Do we have to do this?" Hannah asked.

"Judah. Would you mind going first? I think Hannah will be more comfortable with the idea when she sees how it works."

"OK." He took the larger set into the bedroom to change. He came out a few minutes later looking a little ridiculous with the netting over his head and bunched up around his wrists.

"I think I know how it works," he said with gusto. "You walk out onto the street wearing these and everyone screams and runs the other direction."

Hannah got a good laugh out of that.

"Joel, would you like to show me how this works?" the rabbi asked.

"Thank you for being a good sport, sir. OK. This is going to feel weird. When it starts, it will feel kind of like melting ice, cold, wet, maybe a bit slippery. But the sensation will last for only a moment. Ready?" Joel asked.

"As ready as I will ever be," the rabbi replied.

"OK. Take your index finger and trace down your wrist like this." Joel illustrated the motion.

The rabbi did as he was asked. "Oh." He startled. "It's cold. And wet."

He shook his wrist. Slowly at first, then rapidly, the nylons melted into his skin, completely disappearing. "What? What just happened?"

"Today you are being outfitted with shields. Shields like the ones that protected Israel from the Iranian nuke, just smaller. The netting that you put on holds the shield emitters. They sank a fraction of an inch into your skin and will project the shield three inches or so above it. The shields will stop bullets, fire, radiation... More or less everything. You also need to attach this to your belt or elsewhere in your clothes." Joel held out a small metallic box. "It is the shield generator that drives the emitters."

"Can I try mine on?" Hannah asked with enthusiasm. She took the smaller set of emitters and disappeared into the bedroom. She came out a few minutes later, looking as ridiculous as her husband had.

"OK, I just run my finger down my wrist like this, right?" She did so. Before Joel could even reply, she started giggling. "Oh. This is so weird!"

"Oh!" she squealed, then started laughing again.

Joel gave her the shield generator, which she tucked into her clothes.

373

"OK. I have one more thing for you to put on, but we'll wait until we're on the shuttle. But, one thing. Close your eyes. And keep them closed until I tell you to open them. Ready?"

1,000 MILES ABOVE JERUSALEM, ISRAEL

"OK. Open your eyes."

"Oh, my goodness!" Hannah exclaimed. "Where are we?"

"We are in orbit above Jerusalem."

"Why did we have to close our eyes?"

"Vertigo," Joel replied. "You really don't feel anything when you transport. But when the scenery changes that suddenly, it makes you dizzy. Many people just fall over the first time if they don't have their eyes shut. Others get very sick to the stomach. What's funny is that Michael, who is the best person you will ever meet, has this one blind spot. He forgets to tell first timers to close their eyes. I think more people have fallen over on him then on all the rest of us combined."

The rabbi looked at Joel quizzically.

"I probably shouldn't have said that. But our team is very close, very much like family. So we tease each other. Michael gets teased as much as, maybe more than, the rest of us. I think it is because he is so much better at everything than the rest of us. I hope you get to spend enough time with us to understand."

"I understand." Judah nodded his head in understanding. "The Prime Minister and I are the same."

"OK. I have one more thing you need to put on. It is a translator. Once it is in, you will speak and hear Arabic fluently, and you won't even know it." Joel pulled out an earpiece with a dangling string. "It works the same way as the shield emitters. Place the earpiece gently into your ear. It'll feel like it's melting and flowing down in. Don't panic. It's OK. Then put the string down along your jaw line and trace your finger over the string. It'll also feel like it's melting, this time into your jaw."

He gave one to each of them and they installed them without incident. "Definitely a strange feeling," Hannah said. "They do come out, right?"

"Yes, they do. Don't do it now. But, when we are done, you will just put your finger in your ear and give it a little twist, and it pops right out.

"I have set these up so you can understand more or less any language spoken to you. But your speech will come out as Arabic, unless you place your finger along your jaw like this." Joel demonstrated.

"When will it start?" the rabbi asked.

Joel laughed. "It already has. I was speaking in Arabic and you replied in Arabic."

"What?!" the rabbi said, which made Joel laugh even more.

"Forgive me my friend. For laughing, that is. The translator is so seamless it takes a while to figure out what language you're working in. I know you trust me. But don't worry. You will believe me when you start talking with the people we are about to visit. Ready?"

"Ready for what, dear?" Hannah asked.

"To start distributing gifts?"

"Yes. When do we leave?"

"Else" Joel called. "Could you please open the door?"

TOWN SQUARE, BEIT HANINA, EAST JERUSALEM

The door opened to a crowd. Cameras flashed. Reporters with microphones started calling out questions. Hannah took a step back in shock from the scene. An Arab man in thobe, bisht and agal (robe, cloak and headdress) stood at the edge of the roped-off area with his hands folded in front of him, waiting for his guests to emerge.

Joel turned to the Levine's. "OK, let's go greet the mayor."

He stepped down from the shuttle, then turned to help the rabbi, who simply jumped down. *Surprisingly spry for his age.* Joel thought. He offered his hand to Hannah, who grasped it as if her life depended on it, and slowly stepped down.

She whispered to Joel with laughter in her voice, "That was the most difficult part of the trip so far."

Joel smiled back, then grabbed the handle of the grav-sled and pulled it out of the shuttle. As soon as they were clear, Else closed the door to the shuttle.

Joel led the Levine's over to the mayor, who immediately introduced himself in almost fluent English. "Hello. My name is Khaled al-Farooqi. I am the mayor of Beit Hanina."

"Mayor Khaled, my name is Joel Rubinstein. I am Consul General from the Intergalactic Confederation of Planets to the peoples of Israel. It is a pleasure to meet you, sir. Thank you for inviting us to your town," Joel said, in Arabic. "May I introduce you to Rabbi Judah Levine and his wife Hannah. They wanted to participate in today's visit and to be the ones to give the first gift from the Confederation to an Israeli citizen."

The mayor looked at the rabbi and extended his hand. Rabbi Levine stepped forward.

"Mayor Khaled, I am Judah Levine. Thank you for inviting us. As you know, I have been a harsh critic of the Palestinians in our country, something that now gives me great shame. God, in His infinite wisdom, showed me the error of my ways. He told me I needed to participate in distributing the gifts the Confederation has for Israel. And He told me that I must start with the Palestinians, so that I could fully understand the depth of my shame. It is too early to ask your forgiveness, but I hope that someday we can be friends." He said this in perfect Arabic as tears ran from his eyes.

The mayor was stunned. He had grown up hating this man. But here he was, declaring his shame with tears running from his eyes, and speaking Arabic! And doing it all in front of television cameras that must be sending the image all over the world.

Moved by the sincerity of the moment, he placed his hands on the Rabbi's shoulders and kissed him on each cheek in the Arab way of greeting a friend. "Welcome to my town, friend. Maybe you can come to my home and share some tea when our work here is done."

"I would like that," the rabbi said.

A shot rang out and a bullet stopped an inch from the rabbi's head, then dropped to the ground. Joel threw up his hands, signaling the nanobots that he had released earlier to destroy any guns. A man nearby made an anguished sound as the gun he had hidden in his robe dissolved, the metallic sand crystals making an audible noise as they fell to the ground. The sound drew everyone's attention. The crowd, which had begun to scatter when the shot rang out, turned to face the man. Joel could sense the anger in the crowd and realized that it would turn deadly in seconds.

Transport that man! Joel sent to the captain of the military escort ship.

As the first punch was about to be thrown, the perpetrator simply disappeared.

"Mayor Khaled," Joel said. "I just arrested that man. He is now in custody aboard one of our ships. I did it for his safety. I will return him to you when and where you would like. He will not be harmed."

The mayor, quite stunned by what had happened, said to Rabbi Levine. "I'm sorry my friend. I didn't invite you here to be assassinated. But it appears that I also didn't provide sufficient security. But what happened? I'm not sure I understand."

The rabbi, on the tail end of a big adrenaline rush, started laughing. "If you spend more time with our Confederation friends, you will find yourself saying that a lot.

"Come, let's go do our work."

CONFERENCE ROOM, GAS PRODUCTION FACILITY

"General Park, thank you for your participation in the announcement." Michael had opened his senses wide during the announcement and read both the sincerity of the general's words and his fear.

"I am appointing you as the interim Lieutenant Governor of the District of North Korea. You serve at my sole discretion. Do you accept this position and pledge to fulfill your duties to the best of your ability?"

"Yes, sir. I do," the general replied. "What do you want me to do?"

"Your first mission will be to organize the prison camp on the north side of the DMZ. Their supply lines have been cut off, so this needs to be done quickly. The Confederation has immense resources you can draw from.

"You will also need to form a new interim government. You may choose whomever you want as your cabinet ministers, subject to my approval. Would you like to interview any of the captives held here?"

"Yes, sir. Several of these men are good and capable administrators; others are sociopaths that belong in prison."

"Alexi will escort you through the facility. Talk to those you want. Make sure they understand the situation and what you want them to do. When you've made your choices, Alexi will bring you and your men back here, where you will present them to me. Any that I approve will join your team and report to you. Alexi and Julie will train you and prepare you for the return trip to North Korea. The men that you do not choose, or that I reject, will be turned over to the South Korean government for prosecution," Michael said.

"Understood."

"Alexi. Please escort the Lt. Governor to the men he wishes to speak with. Leave them chained until you are ready to bring them all back. Treat those that co-operate as you would one of us. Handle any that resist in any way you see fit."

"Will do, Michael."

As they exited the office, the Lt. Governor asked Alexi, "You seem to operate less formally than I have seen before. Is that the norm for the Confederation?"

"It is the way Michael operates. The Confederation as a whole is very formal."

"He can operate that way because this is a small outpost?" He asked. Alexi stopped in her tracks. The Lt. Governor, realizing that he had said something wrong, said in something of a panic, "I'm sorry. No offense was intended."

Alexi let her anger cool before responding, "Michael is the highest-ranking official in this galaxy. He is also one of the most powerful people in the known universe. Do not underestimate him."

She hesitated, then added, "That said, Michael is the best person you will ever meet. He has compassion for everyone. He would rather ask kindly than command, and he surrounds himself with people who want to do the same. If you want a position in the government going forward, watch the way Michael operates and do your best to emulate his style. If you treat your men or your people poorly, you won't last long."

"Thank you, Alexi. I will do my best."

"Captain." Michael called out.

"Yes, Mr. Ambassador."

"We have a number of things we need to accomplish in the next couple hours. I would like your assistance in determining the best way to use our resources."

"Thank you, Mr. Ambassador."

"When it's just the two of us, please call me Michael."

"And you may call me Ja-Ru."

"The first thing we need to do is provide supplies to the men we have trapped near the DMZ. Their highest-ranking general was among the captives that went to Paso Robles. He has accepted the position of Lt. Governor for this region and is in the process of selecting his staff. His first mission is to organize the prison camp. Their primary need is food and shelter, specifically heat. We will be supplying food replicators and power cubes. They may require tents or other equipment.

378

"Julie Ferguson of my staff will be intermediary for supplies. Given the urgency, I would suggest you assign someone from your staff to interface with her."

"Understood, Michael."

"The next thing is security. There is a small chance that a pocket of resistance in the North might yet attempt an attack. There is also a chance that some other country will attack. I want you to assign a team to handle continuous surveillance and have resources available that can respond immediately. It is imperative that no attack succeeds, from any side. I cannot stress this point strongly enough."

"It will be done, Michael."

"Next, I need as many away-mission-capable androids to work in human avatars as I can get. This would be a volunteer mission that would involve motor control modification."

"I think that we will have several volunteers."

"Lastly, I suspect that there are one or more Enemy agents working in both Russia and Iran. I would like to have these areas scanned before the Admiral arrives."

"That's going to be difficult. The most sensitive scanners are built into the hull of this ship. We will need to move off station to scan for more Enemy agents. The other requirements will be more difficult to fulfill if we move."

"Difficult is acceptable." Michael said, then added in a more collegial tone. "Ja-Ru, I assumed it would be difficult. That's why I asked for your help in determining the best resource allocation."

"If we stage four transport-equipped escorts in geosynchronous orbit, we could manage supply distribution from wherever we might be," the Captain started.

"Do all your escorts have transporter equipment?"

"Yes. But not all of them are functional. Transporters are not required equipment for our class of escort vessel. So their maintenance priority is low."

"Cause?" Michael asked.

"Transluminide shortage." Ja-Ru replied.

"How many are functional?"

"At most ten, but only six of those would I trust with anything living."

"I'm sorry to hear that. You were saying, we stage four escorts in orbit..."

"Yes, and this is the difficult part. All of our military escorts were built with linkable sensor suites and field projectors. But these also have low-priority maintenance ratings, so we have concentrated resources in a few ships to keep them fully functional. Of my 22 military escorts only four are fully functional."

"Let me guess. The problem is transluminide."

"As you say, Michael."

"Captain. I want twelve fully functional escorts. How much is it going to cost and how soon can I have them."

"100 grams of transluminide. Four hours from receipt. The two currently deployed are fully functional."

Michael closed his eyes and sent... *Joel, you are authorized to release up to 250 grams of transluminide to the Captain for urgent escort shuttle upgrades. Please acknowledge.*

Moments later... *Acknowledged. Up to 250 grams of transluminide for urgent escort shuttle upgrades.*

"Captain. Upgrade your escorts immediately. You have 100 grams, plus a buffer. All requisitions subject to standard documentation. Request what you need. Err on the side of speed."

Once again, the Captain found himself speechless at the implied importance of this mission. His annual budget had been 10 grams for his ship and escorts. 100 plus was hard to comprehend. "Thank you, Mr. Ambassador. Everything you need will be available in the next couple hours."

"Thank you for partnering with me on this, Captain."

HOME OF ALIYAH JALAL, BEIT HANINA, EAST JERUSALEM

What Joel had envisioned as a simple walk down the street to a nearby home had turned into something of a spectacle. The mayor's wife had joined them, as had several members of the town council. The TV broadcast earlier had drawn a crowd so large that the police had closed the roads coming into town. And, because of the crowd size and the gunshot, they now had a police escort. The police cleared a path through the crowds and carried a rope barrier that the reporters and TV cameras pressed up against.

Joel had the deep sense that something of immense consequence was happening and felt humbled to be in the middle of it.

They finally arrived at a tiny home that was in poor repair. As they approached, a very thin young woman, maybe 30 years old, opened the door. She held a baby and had four young children clinging to her legs.

She greeted the Mayor, who had apparently come by earlier to tell her that she would have visitors today. Then turned to Joel and said in broken English, "Hello, my name is Aliyah Jalal."

"Hello, Aliyah," Joel replied in Arabic. "I am the Consul General from the Intergalactic Confederation to Israel. It is a pleasure to meet you. May I introduce you to Rabbi Judah Levine and his wife Hannah?"

Judah stepped forward. "Hello Aliyah. I am Judah Levine. This is my wife Hannah. Thank you for allowing us to visit you today."

"Please, come inside."

They entered her tiny, two-room home and squeezed onto two sofas in the corner, where her older children apparently slept. The mayor asked, "Aliyah, could you tell our guests about your situation?"

"Not much to tell. I was born in this town and went to school here until the school was closed when I was in 5th grade. My parents gave me to my husband when I was 16. He got work where he could, but never had a regular job. I had the first four children by the time I was 23. My husband finally found work in Jordan. He worked there for four years, sending most of his money home so I could raise the children. When he lost that job, he came home, and I got pregnant with little Aisha here. Shortly after arriving home, he was taken by some men from Hamas. They took him to Gaza, where he was killed in an Israeli retaliation strike."

"I'm so sorry to hear that," Rabbi Levine said. Then, with emotion in his voice, "I truly hope that the things we do today bring a stop to the cycle of violence that has plagued our peoples for thousands of years."

Shaking off the emotion, he asked, "Do you know about the treaty that Israel is entering into with the Confederation?"

"Yes. There is much talk about it in the street. Is it true that Israel will be seeking peace with the Palestinians?"

"Yes. I don't know how it will be done, but this time it will be done. The Confederation seems to make miracles happen. Did you know that the Confederation is going to give us technology that will help us make food, energy, gasoline and other things that are in short supply in Israel?"

"I've heard that, yes."

"They will be helping Israel as a whole, but also every household in Israel as well. And one of the conditions of the deal is that for every household gift they give us to distribute, one must go first to a Palestinian, then to a Jew. Once all the Palestinians have a gift, then the rest of the Jews will get them."

She looked at Joel. "Is this true?" She struggled to believe such a thing.

"Mostly yes. We required that the Palestinians get gifts in equal proportion. The part about one-to-one until all the Palestinians have gifts... That was the Rabbi's idea."

She turned to Rabbi Levine and asked, "You wanted to give them to Palestinians faster than you were required to? I thought you hated the Palestinians."

"I know I've acted that way and am truly sorry. But when the Confederation saved us from the Iranian nuclear attack, and Ambassador Michael told me to pray for the Palestinians, I knew that he was a messenger from God, telling me things I should have been able to figure out myself. I now devote my life to righting this wrong.

"But back to the gifts..." Rabbi Levine continued. "We got our first supply today. And you were the one chosen to receive the first one. Joel helped me select the town. We asked the Mayor to help identify the family with the greatest need. And he chose you. Joel, can you show Aliyah what we have brought her?"

"We have two items for you: a replicator and a power cube. The power cube provides electricity." Joel got up and walked over to the grav sled, which waited in the entryway, and picked up the small box. He brought it over to Aliyah. "See the outlet? Just plug something in and it will provide up to 1,000 watts of power. That's enough for multiple lights, a small refrigerator, or a hot plate."

"How long will it work?" she asked somewhat skeptically.

"It will work for about 20 years, maybe a little longer," he replied.

She looked at it quizzically, then said, "How?"

Joel smiled at that. "It's a zero-point energy device. Zero-point energy is something human scientists are just learning about. It exists in infinite quantity, but it is difficult to tap into. This little box has the technology to do it."

"I don't know what any of that means. Is it magic? Will the mullahs approve?" She asked.

"Think of it as being like a well. Electricity comes out of this in a way similar to water coming out of a well. The first person to pull water from a well may have thought it was magic, but it wasn't. It is an attribute of land that the Maker put in place for our benefit. Same with the power cube, it pulls electricity out of matter, an attribute the Maker put in place for our benefit once we were mature enough to use it."

"Thank you. May I try it?"

"Yes. Please do."

She got up and walked over to a lamp. She unplugged it from the wall, then plugged it into the power cube and turned the light on. "It works," she said, then asked, "And the lamp will stay on for 20 years?"

"The power cube will. The light bulb… Less likely," Joel replied.

She laughed at that.

"The other thing we brought you is a replicator. The replicator can make things for you. But the best thing it makes is food."

"Food?" She asked. "How?"

"Let me show you. What would you like?"

"Some hummus?"

"OK. Can I set it up on your counter over there?"

"Yes." She got up to clear a space for him.

Joel walked back over to the grav-sled and picked up the replicator. It was about the size of a standard office printer. He put it on the counter, then said, "Aliyah, I'd like you to operate it. I'll give you the instructions. OK?"

She looked at Joel skeptically, but shook her head yes.

"OK. Touch this panel."

She did and the panel lit, to show a menu in Arabic.

"Let's make a small bowl first. Touch the item labeled dishes."

She looked back at him. "I really don't read very well. My father thought that girls should not be taught how to read."

Joel had been on Earth long enough to know that such things happened, but he had never actually met someone it had happened to.

"I'm sorry to hear that, Aliyah. But not a problem. See the item at the top right that looks like a picture? Touch that." She did. The words went away to be replaced by pictures.

"Oh. There are the dishes." She touched the button. "Oh. Look at that pretty bowl. Can I have one of those?"

Joel smiled and nodded. She pushed on the picture and a box appeared on the screen with a red 'X' and a green 'O'.

"It is asking if you want it to make that bowl for you. If so…" She clicked the green 'O' before Joel even got the words out.

The machine made a quiet humming sound, then the bowl slid down the chute to stop at the bottom. The main menu reappeared, and Aliyah selected the symbol for food, followed by a few more buttons. Moments later, hummus slid down the chute into the bowl, followed by a few pieces of pita bread.

"That was easy," she said as she offered the bowl to Joel.

"Thank you. But I think you should have the first bite. This is a gift for you."

She dipped the bread into the hummus then took a bite. Her face lit up. "This is wonderful. I have never had hummus this good." She offered the bowl to the Mayor's wife, then to Hannah.

"OK if I make another one for the children?"

Aliyah shook her head yes, suddenly overcome by the realization that her life of hunger and want had just changed in a significant way.

Moments later, Joel had a slightly larger bowl of hummus in his hands that he took over to the children. "Here. This one is for you to share."

Earlier, Aliyah had prepared some tea and had set out six little demitasse cups. She brought the tray over and poured tea for her guests, then sat and asked, "Rabbi Levine. Is it really true that the Confederation gave these things to you and you gave them to me?"

"Yes. It is. And I cannot tell you how happy it makes me to see you have these."

"Then, maybe there finally can be peace." Tears streamed from her eyes. The emotion of the moment caught them all. The ladies all stood and embraced noisily.

Joel noticed that he had tears in his eyes also and had a strange thought. *Lorexians do not have tear ducts in their eyes that overflow like this in time of deep emotion. I wonder how much better a species we would have been if we did.*

Unbeknownst to the people in the house, one of the news crews had managed to rig a camera and microphone in a way that caught most of what was going on inside. The network had gone to live streaming.

The Prime Minister had been told about it and had tuned in. "Well Judah," he murmured to himself. "Who would have thought that you would be the one that finally brought peace to Israel?"

LEVEL 10 CORRIDORS, GAS PRODUCTION FACILITY

The Lt. Governor approached the third man on his list, Internal Security Minister Kwon. He was one of the sociopaths that the Lt. Governor thought should be in jail somewhere. At first, Lt. Governor Park did not plan to talk to Kwon, but as he thought through it more, it seemed that Kwon's knowledge of the bureaucracy might justify the risk.

"You're really going to talk to this guy?" Alexi asked.

"I agree with your assessment." Lt. Governor Park conceded. "But his knowledge of how things actually work might help us, and in North Korea, fear runs so deep that he might change now that it's gone."

As they approached, Kwon said, "So, you are walking free. I thought you would be the first one to flip. You know what they'll do to you when you get back."

"They're dead." Park replied.

"You are stupider than I thought. They are gods. You've seen the way they can change. No one can kill them."

"Michael did. I saw the video of it."

"They have the technology to fake a video. You should trust what you've actually seen with your own eyes."

"They weren't gods. They were demons. They can be killed. And they were killed. The only question is whether you want to help me, and Michael, rebuild. Or whether you want to rot in a South Korean prison." The Lt. Governor saw fear in Kwon's eyes.

"That is the choice?" Kwon asked.

"Lt. Governor Park." Alexi said. "Do not choose this man. He is just stalling for time. He will never cooperate with you."

"So that's what they offered you to get you to betray your own people. The army will never follow you." Kwon spat.

"The army has been captured. The entire army, all 526,000 men. My first job is to set up the prisoner of war camp. Their supply lines have been cut, so they will freeze or starve in a matter of days."

"The Chairman will nuke them!" snapped Kwon.

"The Chairman is dead. The nukes have been confiscated. All our weapons have been destroyed. Our choice is peace and prosperity as a Confederation protectorate, or death."

Kwon spit at the Lt. Governor. "You stupid cow! They're lying, and you're just sucking it all up."

"I've seen enough."

Alexi heard the sadness in the Lt. Governor's voice. They turned to walk further down the corridor. Kwon's shouting faded into the noise of the equipment as they turned the next corner.

The Lt. Governor stopped and turned toward Alexi.

"Now you've seen the power the demons exercised over us."

"I'm sorry. I've never had to live with that kind of evil."

FAST ATTACK SHIP IN ORBIT ABOVE NORTH KOREA

"Captain," came the call from stores. "One hundred grams of transluminide was just transferred via secure transport."

"Thank you, Major," the Captain replied.

"Engineering," the Captain called. "Your transluminide just arrived. Standard requisition protocol. I want those upgrades in an hour."

"We'll do our best, Captain," came the reply.

LEVEL 10 CORRIDORS, GAS PRODUCTION FACILITY

Lt. Governor Park approached the fourth man on his list, Finance Minister Yong. Yong was a precise, prickly man who would pour affection on the Chairman in his presence, but tended to his business with exacting, computer-like precision. Most of the other top officials didn't like him very much, but he was one of the Chairman's favorites.

As they approached, Yong called out. "General Park. I'm delighted to see you walking free. Has the Chairman negotiated our release?"

"The Chairman and his sister are dead. Our armies have been captured. Our weapons have been destroyed, and our nuclear weapons confiscated," Lt. Governor Park summarized.

"You're sure of this?" Yong sounded shocked.

"Absolutely. The Confederation knew the nature of the Chairman and his sister and had the weaponry to destroy them. The Chairman at least put up a short fight. His sister was just slaughtered."

"So. What now?" Yong asked.

"The Confederation has made North Korea a protectorate. Michael is our governor. He has made me his Lt. Governor. My first assignment is to set up the prisoner of war camp for our army. After that, to restore the civilian government in Pyongyang. The Confederation has vast wealth and will be investing in our country to make us prosperous."

"Do you believe this?" Yong asked.

"Yes. I do. Everything I've seen of the Confederation is consistent with their assertions. Their technology is mind-bending. What I don't understand is why. We have nothing to offer them. But I'm not going to worry about that. I'm going to work to save our people and show them the same mercy that the Confederation is showing us."

Yong nodded his head.

"Would you like to join my administration? I would like you to manage the resources the Confederation allows us to have. No one will track it as well as you."

"Yes. I will join you."

"We'll be back within the hour to release you from your bondage and take you for your interview with Michael. He will approve or deny my choices. I think he will approve you."

"I look forward to working with you again. Maybe this time we can serve our people better."

CONFERENCE ROOM, GAS PRODUCTION FACILITY

There was a knock on the door. Michael walked to the door and opened it.

"Alexi, please bring our guests in. Gentlemen, please be seated." Michael said indicating the chairs around the table. The men made their way in, found seats and gave Michael their attention. Alexi remained standing near the door.

"Lt. Governor. Would you please introduce your men and tell me the role you have chosen for each?"

"Yes, Michael. And thank you for this opportunity to serve the Intergalactic Confederation and the people of Korea. First, I would like to introduce Yong Pong-ju. His former role was Finance Minister. Minister Yong was a competent manager of North Korea's financial resources. I don't know if things like money and foreign currency are relevant to us as part of the Confederation, but we will not find anyone in North Korea more capable of tracking and managing our resources than Minister Yong."

Michael had opened his senses to Minister Yong and immediately understood the accuracy of the Lt. Governor's claim. Prying deeper he saw a level of greed that he didn't like, but thought would be manageable. He also found an odd issue of self-worth that manifested itself in some relatively harsh behaviors.

"Minister Yong. I sense your competence and approve you for this role. But I need you to learn compassion. You grew up in an environment of scarcity. The Confederation is a place of plenty. You'll need to learn to ask for the resources you need, instead of simply allocating the resources you have. Compassion will be the key, determining who has the greatest need and coming up with a plan to fulfill it. Welcome aboard, sir."

"Thank you for the opportunity to serve, Michael."

"Lt. Governor, who is next?"

"Michael, I would like to introduce you to Ri Su-yong. Minister Ri was the Agriculture minister for North Korea under the previous regime. He is the most knowledgeable person regarding food production and distribution in our country. Food production has always been a problem for us because of the climate. Minister Ri has overseen this problem for years and should have the best understanding of how to use the Confederation's technology to feed our people."

Michael had opened his senses to Minister Ri as soon as he was introduced and was concerned about what he was seeing.

"Minister Ri. Your priorities will be much different under Confederation administration. The average person in your labor camps is 20 lbs. underweight. Your highest priority will be to correct that situation. I sense that this is going to be a problem for you."

Heat boiled inside Minister Ri. *This interloper knows nothing about the priorities in North Korea.* He thought.

"Actually, Minister Ri, you know nothing about the priorities in North Korea. May I remind you that you have been indicted for conspiring to engage in acts of hostility against a Confederation ally? Your country has been dissolved and is now a trustee of the Confederation. No previous law or tradition stands, only the ones the Confederation allows."

"This is an outrage. No American puppet can get away with this."

Michael sent a message to the captain of his escort ship. *Take this man into custody. You may place him with the other ones.*

Minister Ri disappear to the sound of a soft popping noise.

"Lt. Governor Park. I do not approve Minister Ri to serve in your Cabinet. He has been taken into custody and will be released to the South Korean's for prosecution." The men at the table sat in shock, truly understanding their situation for the first time.

"Michael, may I present Choe Pyong-gi, who was the Minister of Energy in the previous government. He is knowledgeable about the electrical power systems in the country. I chose Minister Choe, because I think he has both the understanding of the main electrical grid and the benefits of the kind of distributed power systems that you are offering."

Michael sensed the fear in Minister Choe. He was a man who had lived in fear is whole life. He was neither a party ideologue or particularly interested in politics, just an engineer who loved power systems and wanted to protect and provide for a family he desperately loved.

"Minister Choe. I sense your passion for engineering and the deep love you have for your wife and family. I think you will do well in the new North Korea. I hope that we have the opportunity to work together personally at some point." Michael also pushed a sense of safety.

Minister Choe relaxed visibly at Michael's words as a sense of calm settled over him. "Michael, thank you for allowing me to serve our new country. I also look forward to working with you."

"Who is next?" Michael asked Lt. Governor Park.

"Michael, let me introduce Minister Jo Su-gil, who was the Minister of Machine Building in the previous administration. He was responsible for our country's infrastructure and manufacturing capabilities. I have heard about your replicators and how that will change manufacturing and production. I think Minister Jo will have the best ideas about how to utilize these systems in our new economy.

Michael sensed a darkness in Minister Jo that he didn't like. It was clear that he was very competent at getting things done with minimal resources. But he had been ruthless in his use of human labor. There was guilt, but not much.

Michael's silence worried Minister Jo, who cleared his throat and said. "Mr. Ambassador. May I say a word in my defense? The Chairman was a cruel man. He claimed to be a god but was a demon at best. If we did not complete our tasks, he would kill the entire team. Too many failures from the same minister and he would be fed alive to starving dogs. After a while, you become numb to the suffering of your men and strive instead to keep as many alive as possible. I hope you will allow me to help my people prosper, not just survive.

Michael, sensing the truth in the man's words, said, "Welcome aboard, Minister Jo."

"Lastly," the Lt. Governor said, "let me introduce Minister Yang Thae-song, who handled Foreign Relations in the previous government. He was the best communicator in the Chairman's inner circle. I think I'm going to need help maintaining communications in the prison camp and in Pyongyang."

Michael opened his senses to Minister Yang and immediately closed them. *"Captain, I need emergency assistance. I believe a man in this room has been contaminated by the Enemy. Please confirm."* Michael sent.

Like Minister Jo, this man began speaking when Michael did not respond right away. Michael raised his hand and the man stopped. Michael then asked, "Minister Yang, you've spoken with the American Secretary of State on several occasions, right?"

"Yes, sir."

"I met the man once but expect to open negotiations with him soon. Is there any advice you could give me on the best way to engage him?"

Minister Yang smiled, pleased that the Ambassador was already asking for his advice. He began what he hoped would be a lengthy explanation.

Mr. Ambassador, the captain sent. *You are correct. It is young, but dangerous. No sign of further contamination. We must destroy it now. We can safely transport it into the star.*

Minister Jo was saying, "...and be sure to repeat his position back to him before..." when he disappeared. Michael heard the deep inhalation of breath from the others.

"What can you tell me of this man's personal relationship with the Chairman?" Michael asked. After a long pause, Michael said, "Surely one of you knows something."

After an extended silence, Minister Choe said. "My wife told me that a friend of hers saw him leaving the Chairman's sister's house very early one morning. I never believed this to be true. If anyone had seen this, the Chairman would have known, and the man would have been executed."

"Curious." Minister Jo frowned. "I heard a rumor that the Chairman was going to let his sister get married, but never heard more."

"Thank you." Michael said. "He had been inhabited by the same parasitic creature that controlled the Chairman and his sister. It is known that they can propagate via sexual contact between its host and a lover."

"What did you do with him?" Lt. Governor Park asked.

"These creatures are very dangerous. Fewer than 100 of them would be enough to consume the Earth. Whenever one is encountered, it must be destroyed. The only way to do that is to destroy the host."

"You executed him?"

"No, that would not be sufficient. We transported him into the Sun."

The men sat there in shock. *Is the Confederation even worse than the Chairman?* Minister Choe thought.

"No, Minister Choe. The Confederation is not worse than the Chairman. There is a war going on. This man was an enemy combatant. He may have been conscripted, but he was a combatant, nonetheless. Unfortunately, it cost him his life."

FAST ATTACK SHIP IN ORBIT ABOVE NORTH KOREA

"Chief Ka-Tu, please report," said the Captain.

"Captain, I am pleased to report that we have finished updating ten Military Escorts. These are now fully functional. The two escorts on mission only need a few grams of transluminide, which leaves us enough to complete one, maybe two, more. Permission to proceed, sir?"

"Excellent work, Lieutenant. But let's hold off for now. Please return the excess to secure stores." The Captain dropped the line. Moments later he connected with the lieutenant that would be leading the protection mission.

"Lieutenant Ma-Na, please deploy for the Korea protection mission."

"Yes, sir. All four Escorts will be in position within 15 minutes."

CONFERENCE ROOM, LEVEL 9, GAS PRODUCTION FACILITY

Alexi, Lt. Governor Park and his three cabinet members entered the conference room on Level 9, where Julie was waiting for them. "Gentlemen, welcome," she greeted. "Alexi and I are going to show you the tools you will have to heat and feed your troops in the prisoner of war camp. You'll probably need more than just these tools, but once you've seen them in action, you'll probably have a better idea of what else you might need."

The men walked up to the table where they learned to use the replicators by making themselves lunch.

391

FAST ATTACK SHIP IN ORBIT ABOVE NORTH KOREA

"Michael, I'm pleased to report that we're ready to begin the search for suspected enemy agents. We have completed the upgrades and now have ten fully functional military escorts, plus the two currently deployed. Four of these are now in position to begin the surveillance and protection mission, the other four will be deployed on the supply mission on your command," the captain reported.

"Excellent news Ja-Ru. I am sending you the coordinates to search now. I suspect that we will find at least three. Do I understand correctly that we should identify them all before taking action?"

"Yes, sir. We cannot safely transport the large ones. They must be destroyed in place. The safest way to do that is with a flux bomb, which the others can detect as far as 100 miles away."

"Then begin the search at the first coordinate I gave you. It is where I expect the highest concentration to be. If one is there, it will be within a 50-mile radius."

"We will begin immediately, Michael, and stand prepared to begin the supply mission on your order."

"Excellent, Captain, please update me if you find something."

CONFERENCE ROOM, LEVEL 9, GAS PRODUCTION FACILITY

Michael entered the conference room on Level Nine to a wave of excited chatter. Directly in front of him, Lt. Governor Park was laughing at Alexi, who had just tried some kimchi that he had produced. On the other side of the room, Minister Choe was marveling at a heater Julie had rigged up, his hands moving back and forth in front of an infrared heater as if he could not believe that's where the heat was coming from.

The door squeaked as Michael closed it, drawing their attention. "Looks like everyone is having fun," he said, a comment that caused Lt. Governor Park to snap to attention.

"Relax, my friend. I'm glad to see the six of you so engaged. Have you made any progress in determining how you want to supply the prison camp?"

"Michael, we have never seen, never even imagined such marvels. Do we really get to have equipment like this?" Lt. Governor Park asked in astonishment.

"I wouldn't have shown it to you if it wasn't going to be given to you. I think the question is how many of each? And, how to train your men to use it?"

Minister Yong stepped forward. "While the others worked on recipes and equipment configurations, things I'm not very good at, I started working some numbers. May I share the results of my work?"

The question was directed to Michael, who looked at Lt. Governor Park questioningly. On realizing that Michael wanted him to be the team leader, Lt. Governor Park said, "Minister Yong, this is exactly why I wanted you on our team. Please tell us what you think we need."

"Thank you, sir. We have approximately 525,000 men in the prisoner of war camp. Julie said that you fed 500 people lunch using one of these machines. That means we would need 1,050 food replicators if our men were evenly distributed. They are not evenly distributed, and we don't know the exact distribution. Therefore, I think we should have a small cushion, maybe 1,100 in total. Is that number possible?"

Sensing that Michael wanted him to ask the question, Lt. Governor Park asked, "Would 1,100 replicators be possible, Michael?"

Michael looked at him, then at the minister of finance. "Yes, but I would be more comfortable giving you 2,500. It would allow greater flexibility and allow you to locally produce things like shoes, clothes or other necessities that might also be in short supply."

The men were momentarily dumfounded at the generosity being shown. Nothing like this had been seen in the North during their lifetimes. Minister Choe was the first to recover his senses and continued. "Given that it is winter and quite cold, I think we will need many more heaters than replicators. The heater that Julie demonstrated is excellent, too much for this room. But on a snowy day with wind, we will need one of these per squad of 10 men, unless we have shelters."

Lt. Governor Park spoke up at that point. "The invasion force was outfitted with large tents for up to 25 men. They also were outfitted with kerosene heaters, although the kerosene supply has been cut off. Is there any way we can leverage that?"

Julie spoke up, "We could supply carbon dioxide kerosene generators. It would be a little bit more energy efficient, assuming the kerosene heaters are in good condition."

"I'm sad to say that it's unlikely the kerosene heaters are in good condition," Minister Choe replied. "The Chairman's nuclear ambitions caused great shortages, so maintenance was poor."

"If we had one heater per 25 men, then we would need 21,000 heaters. Is that even possible?"

"Everything is possible." Michael replied. "Julie, how hard would it be to create a breathable, insulated dome? One that could accommodate 1,000 men?"

Julie smacked her forehead with the palm of her hand. "Why didn't I think of that?" Then seeing the looks on the other men's faces, she continued. "For about the same 'cost' as two heaters, we can create a transparent dome about 1,000 feet in diameter that could be heated with a single heater.

"To answer your question, Michael... Not hard. It's just a control setting on the field generators we are already producing. The Captain could produce these in less than an hour."

The Finance Minister raised his hand. "Does that mean we only need 525 domes and 525 heaters? And, does that imply that you have money and have to pay this 'Captain?'" He asked.

Michael smiled and said. "Yes, you'll only need 525 domes and 525 heaters. But no, we don't use money, and we don't pay the Captain. The Captain is captain of a small fast attack ship that is currently in orbit above the Earth. He works for me. The cost that Julie referred to is the amount of time it'll take to make these things for you. Given the situation your men are in, an hour is a much lower 'cost' than a day.

"So, how soon can we begin?" Michael asked.

JOEL'S HOME, JERUSALEM

It wasn't all that late by Jerusalem standards, but Joel was exhausted. It had been the most fun, stressful and emotional day of his life. They had planned on doing 10 deliveries today, but only succeeded in doing two. The crowds and celebrations were overwhelming. Today had been the start of something incredibly significant. And, Michael had entrusted it to him.

The delivery rate would pick up, but he would probably never be able to walk the streets again without being surrounded by crowds that just wanted to pay their respects or shake his hand. As he reached to turn off his communications device, it rang, so he picked it up. It was Michael.

"Hello, Michael. What a day!"

"I've seen some of the news coverage and spoke briefly with the Prime Minister. The Levine's comported themselves very well today. I'm sure you had a lot to do with it."

"I helped get them over some barriers they couldn't have crossed on their own, but the rest was all them. I'm really proud of them."

"I'm proud of you Joel. You gave them what they needed to do what only they could do. That's the hardest balance to strike and you did it. I think you have things under control there, so take the night for yourself, you've earned it."

"Thank you, Michael."

100 MILES ABOVE TEHRAN, IRAN

"Michael, you were right," the Captain reported. "There is a nest of them here. We have found three so far and have assigned nanobots to track them. One of these three is extremely large. We are also getting some unusual readings that we are attempting to interpret. Per regulations, I have reported this finding to the Admiral. His orders, pending your approval, are to continue tracking these Enemy agents and move on to the next site."

"Did the admiral explain the rationale behind these orders?"

"Yes, sir. He is worried about the unusual readings. It could indicate a hatchery. Our sensors are not sensitive enough to make that determination. His ship has the high-resolution sensors required. It also has the power to deal with a hatchery. We do not."

"Understood. I approve the Admiral's orders, but one question... Would leaving a military escort vessel in the area improve your tracking and data gathering in any way?"

"Yes, sir. I think it would. The Admiral and I did not consider that option."

"Then your orders are amended to allow that option at your discretion. Proceed as you see fit."

"Thank you, Michael."

NEAR THE DEMILITARIZED ZONE

The sky was beginning to lighten. It had been a cold night. Howling wind drove a chill deep into their bones. Wind-blown snow left the hoods of their parkas frosted with ice crystals. Sergeant Kwon was worried that several of his men were suffering from frostbite. Suddenly, his radio crackled to life. "Sergeant Kwon, this is General Park. You have new orders. Your squad is to rendezvous at the flag 500 meters southeast of your current position. The flag is lit. You should have no trouble spotting it. Proceed to that location immediately."

Kwon rallied his men, who loaded their gear and followed as he led the way. After maybe 50 meters, he cleared the ridge that had given them some shelter from the wind and saw the flag. Curiously, the men assembled near it did not appear to be wearing parkas.

As they got closer, he could see men signaling him to approach their position. A few minutes later, the Sergeant and his squad stopped in front of the men.

"Sergeant Kwon," the Major said. "Welcome to Camp 1. Follow the path to the camp entrance over there. You will be directed to the location where your squad is assigned. It is heated, comfortably warm actually. You are to set up your tents, then report to the mess, which has a flag mounted at its entrance. There you will be given a hot meal. Try the kimchi. It's excellent. You will receive additional orders around noon. Get some sleep. You will need it."

The Sergeant did as ordered. As they crossed a red line painted on the ground, the temperature shot up to 68 degrees. He and his men were stunned. They stopped in their tracks, not understanding what was happening. A lieutenant approached. "Sergeant. You and your squad are assigned to lot 127. It is down this path on the right. Set up your tent, then proceed to the mess. I would advise you to take off your parkas as soon as possible. If any of your men are injured or have frostbite, report it at the entrance to the mess."

They did as they were told, struggling to believe what they were seeing. The men that had arrived before them were in their shirt sleeves and seemed happy. Yet a hundred meters away, they could see snow blowing on the wind. How could this be?

100 MILES ABOVE MOSCOW, RUSSIA

"Michael, we have only found one Enemy agent at this location. It appears to be alone, asleep on the second floor of a small house overlooking a frozen lake about 85 miles northwest of Moscow. It was at the far limit of our initial scans. We have not found another within 100 miles of it.

"There are others awake on the first floor. Based on their movements, we assume that they are guards. We have launched nanobot surveillance to confirm.

"Standard orders require us to destroy it, but that will alert the ones on the first floor. The Admiral defers to your judgement on the next step."

"Ja-Ru, thank you for that update. I'm sending you instructions for a chemical compound. Release this in the air in every room, in the quantities specified in the instructions. It will make the occupants fall into a deep sleep. Wait 15 minutes, then use the flux bomb to destroy the Enemy agent. Once that is done, send a team to clean up the mess. The guards on the first floor will awake after about an hour. Please get images of the target ahead of time so that we can identify him."

"I like this plan," the Captain said. "We'll get back to you confirming the results in about an hour."

NEAR THE DEMILITARIZED ZONE

Lt. Governor Park was amazed by both the technology and how smoothly and easily it was deployed. Camp 1 was complete and filled. Camps 2 through 15 where at various stages of completion. Once each squad had been fed and given 2 hours sleep, the healthy could volunteer to assist in setting up the next camp. To his surprise, most of the men were volunteering, even the sick and wounded. However, they were required to make a full recovery first. Construction of all 500-plus camps would be completed before sundown.

The Confederation had provided a dozen staff to assist and promised more tomorrow. Julie had stayed with him to help with planning, communications, and other areas where the technical assist was necessary. But Alexi wanted to be the first person at each site. That girl was crazy but had turned out to be a true friend of the Korean people.

"Lt. Governor," Julie called out. "I have Michael on the com line. He would like to speak with you."

He thanked Julie, then took the call.

"Hello, Michael."

"I hear things are going well."

"Yes, they are. All the camps should be completed by sundown. All the men will have had a hot meal by midnight. The briefings are going well. The vast majority of the men are volunteering to help. I never thought I would see this in North Korea."

"Excellent. Make sure you set a command structure in place today. Every camp needs a leader. Assign a general to head the prison camp system. Choose from the existing ones or promote a new one. Make sure they understand that they report directly to you and ultimately to me, and that they now serve the Intergalactic Confederation. Also help them set up their command structure. Because tomorrow I have a new mission for you."

"May I ask what it is?" Lt. Governor Park asked.

"Not yet, but don't worry about it. Concentrate your energy today on securing the safety of your men and putting them in the hands of someone you trust."

"Thank you, Michael."

CONFERENCE ROOM, LEVEL 9, GAS PRODUCTION FACILITY

Satisfied that things were under control on all fronts, Michael decided to head back to Hawaii to check on things there and have another quick regeneration cycle.

MICHAEL'S OFFICE, THE RESIDENCE

Michael appeared in his office and immediately called Jiaying.

"Michael. You're back. You usually call me when you are inbound."

"I was the only passenger in the Human compartment of the military escort. I had planned to call but fell asleep as soon as I hit the seat. How are things here?"

"Nisha is still in the tank. The chatter is that she will be coming out around 7:00 tonight, fully healed and reconstructed. Mahesh was such a mess after we carted Nisha away that they put him in a restoration chamber immediately and gave him 18 hours. He's good now, but I'll let him tell you the story. BBC and France Televisions were a little grumpy about your interview having fallen through, so I gave them the interview with the Sergeant this morning. Bahati, Emmanuel and Mahesh all 'co-starred'. I don't know what the ratings on those will be in the UK and France, but they are working with CBS to put together a joint special later this week, which is expected to be a blockbuster. Let's see, what else... Oh, the Chief wants to talk with you.

"On to business, Brazil has confirmed your appearance tomorrow at 10 AM, which will be 4:00 AM tomorrow morning here. The Admiral sent a message confirming that they're on track to arrive tomorrow morning around 7:00 AM Hawaiian time. He asked me not to disturb you, but to let you know when you came up for air. By the way... the Admiral speaks very highly of you.

"And lots of paperwork and low-level ally requests that we have been handling or routing to the designated consul. Nothing you need to worry about, although it would probably be good if you check in with the South Korean President. Would you like me to set up a call?"

"Yes, please do. Anything else?"

"Not really. You have put an amazing amount of work in progress this week. Everyone here is proud of you, Michael, and the tone of the

398

calls we are getting from both the media and various government officials has changed a lot. Everyone, except Russia and Iran, wants to be your best friend now."

"Thank you, Jiaying. I'm going to head down to the dining room to get some food and coffee."

As Michael stepped out of his office, he could hear excited voices outside. *The Sergeant must be up to something.* Michael thought. As he turned into the dining room, his suspicions were reinforced. No one was there and the coffee was less than hot and fresh. But he grabbed a cup anyway and headed to the front door.

Mahesh was holding a bat and had just hit a ball across the driveway. George, Luka, and Agent Patterson were trying to get it. Emmanuel was backstopping them, getting the balls that got past the three mobility-impaired participants, which apparently most of the balls were. Emmanuel threw the ball to Agent Patterson, who then tossed it underhand to George who was maybe five feet away. George then attempted to throw the ball to Luka (also about 5 feet away), who picked it up off the ground and threw it back to Mahesh.

Mahesh was the first to see Michael and shouted out a greeting. The others quickly followed suit. George came trotting over, bouncing high above the ground. "Check out how high I can jump now with 40% of my weight!" He said.

"Looking good!" Michael replied. "So, what's the game today?"

"The guys kind of turned the tables on me today. I usually organize the games to help whoever is struggling the most. Today, they did it to me. They wanted to play catch. I really can't throw yet. Did you see that last pathetic attempt? When Emmanuel and Mahesh saw what we were doing, they offered to make the game more interesting. Actually, kind of fun. We don't get many of the ground balls, but it sharpens our ability to respond quickly and accurately. The throwing... less fun. I hate throwing like a girl, but that's why I've got to do it."

The last ball got past Emmanuel and rolled over close to Noelani, who picked it up then threw it all the way back to Mahesh. "George." she called out, "You don't throw like a girl," a comment that got them all laughing, including George.

"Guess I deserved that one," he said good naturedly.

"I understand that you covered for me today with BBC and France Televisions."

"Yep. They were a bit grumpy when they got here. But a little cricket, that's what Mahesh calls our game, a couple war stories, an

English and French reporter talking to each other in German, and some Gorilla Fries... These guys walked out best friends. And Noelani in a hula outfit didn't hurt either."

"George, meeting you was one of the best things I've ever done."

"Don't be silly, Michael. Without you, I'd be nothing. You without me, you'd still be a cool alien saving the world."

"Don't think that way George. We came here hoping to meet people like you. It's the reason we're here."

Noelani, no longer wearing a hula outfit, came up and gave George a kiss on the cheek, then said, "Enough serious talk. Back to the game."

George went bounding away, yelling over his shoulder, "Slave driver!"

"He's doing really well." Michael said quietly, "But, be careful about getting too close to him."

"I'm falling for him, Michael."

"I know. I can see it in your eyes. But you know it will probably end badly. Right?"

She nodded her head in acknowledgement, deep sadness in her eyes. Then shook it off, put a smile on and went back to the game.

100 MILES ABOVE MOSCOW, RUSSIA

"Michael, the mission came off without a hitch," the Captain reported. "We produced and distributed the chemical as you specified. We covered every room in the house. Everyone fell asleep.

"We took numerous photos of everyone in the house, including the target. The target was destroyed with the flux bomb. A team transported down in hazmat suits, sanitized the room and cleaned up the mess. They also scanned each of the other people. A woman downstairs had apparently had sexual contact with the target and had been infected. She was transported into the star.

"We stayed on station for another hour. There was a bit of commotion as the men woke up, but they went into cover-up mode, hoping no one would find out they'd fallen asleep. They noticed that the female was no longer downstairs with them but assumed she had gone back upstairs to be with the target."

"Excellent work, Captain. Also, excellent work supplying the prisoner of war camps. That mission is going very well. They expect to finish tonight.

"Any further update on the situation in Iran?" Michael asked.

"We think we have a lead but are still working it. Our surveillance caught a conversation between two of the targets who mentioned something about comfort women. We now think we understand what the scanners are showing, women that have had sexual contact with the targets. We think the scanners are picking up 20 or so women in which an enemy agent is gestating. Our sensors are not strong enough to pick up one, but 20 or more would show up as a blur of the type we're seeing. If this theory is true, we'll need to take action, action that'll be difficult to do stealthily."

"Is there any way we can make that determination before the Admiral gets here?"

"Possibly with close-in nanobot surveillance. The only sure option would be to send a cloaked team."

"Have you passed this by the Admiral?"

"No. Our information is not that good yet."

"Are there experts in the Fleet you could contact?"

"Yes and no. It would be a violation of the chain of command, which is OK in an emergency but generally frowned upon. Too many of those and you're out. So, I need to develop the data further before I can proceed."

"How much of a threat is this nest?"

"In the short term, none, as long as they don't scatter. In the long-term… Each one will do damage until we find it and destroy it."

"OK. I want nanobot surveillance. I want to know what is in there. If it is women as you suspect, then I will escalate this to the Admiral. The probability that those people are using comfort women is very high. We cannot allow them to be scattered.

"How soon before we'll know whether they're women or something else?"

"An hour, possibly 90 minutes," the captain answered.

"Proceed. Maximum speed consistent with stealth."

"Thank you, Michael."

MICHAEL'S OFFICE, THE RESIDENCE

"Noelani, could you please come over to the office?" Michael said.

A minute or so later, she knocked on the door and came in. "It's not that serious, Michael."

Taken off guard, Michael asked, "What's not that serious? Was someone hurt?"

Shaking her head and laughing, she said, "Me and George."

After a second, it clicked. "Oh, that. Sorry, that's not why I wanted to talk with you. I forgot that was the last topic we discussed before I came in. I have a problem I want to talk with you about."

"You have Sarah on your mind?" She said trying to anticipate the topic.

It was Michael's turn to laugh. "No. I need to leave for Brazil around 2:00 AM and I desperately need sleep. The Captain is going to call me in about an hour. So, the earliest I can hit a regenerator is going to be around 6:00. I had a short regeneration last night. Is six hours safe?"

"Not particularly, but the truth is that you are young and healthy enough that it would be unlikely to actually hurt you. But you cannot do it again tomorrow," she said sternly. "Tomorrow night will have to be natural, or a full regeneration."

"Thank you Noelani. And, regarding Sergeant Butler... Be careful. There actually have been successful and long-lasting relationships between an android and a first contact species, but the vast majority fail and do so badly. It would pain me to see either of you hurt, but I will stand with you, however it goes."

"Thank you, Michael. I can't wait much longer to tell him that I'm an android. But I'm so afraid of breaking his heart and losing his friendship." A pause. "Please don't tell him. I need to do it myself."

"In the Confederation, relationships between androids and organically created people is a total non-issue. Same will be true on Earth in 100 years. But, the first generation almost always views androids as machines, not as people."

"I'll have the regeneration chamber ready for you by 6:00," Noelani said, tears in her eyes. Then she got up and went back to work.

...

"Barbara," Michael called out.

"Here Michael." She replied.

"How are things going with the avatar maturation and motor control software? Fleet will be here tomorrow morning."

"The motor control software is working. Ten androids from the military escort volunteered to help on the surface in Korea. The first two surfaced a couple bugs during validation. Quick fixes, but one broken arm during testing. I'm so proud of those two. It takes a lot of courage to step out of a body you know, let someone play with your motor controls, then occupy a new body so final validation can be done on the software."

402

"All the volunteers will get commendations, but I'll make sure those two get additional commendations," said Michael.

"Anyway, ten standard Confederation androids are now deployed in human bodies in North Korea. No additional issues have been reported. So, that's done until another problem surfaces. We had 100 human avatars fully matured. Ten were used, which leaves us with 90. I've started ten more, but our tank space only allows us to work up 100 at a time. The ten we used were the only Korean avatars we had started, so it will be a while before we get any more. Of the 90, we have 10 Japanese, 10 Chinese, 10 Indian, 10 Hispanic, 10 African, and 20 that can be configured as Jew or Arab during the last hour. We also have 20 western European that can be configured for any of the European countries, Canada, or America, during the last hour.

"We have 900 more avatars in earlier stages of development, which will allow us to produce about 100 per week before we start running into supply problems."

"Do you have a plan for how to use the Fleet's capacity?" Michael asked. "We are going to need about 20,000 within the next couple months."

"I'll need to work with their engineers to determine whether it'll be faster to convert their tanks or build more human tanks. The base chemistry and atmospheric requirements are quite a bit different for humans than for Lorexians, so we won't be able to use their tanks without significant modification."

"OK. I'll put that on my list for discussion with the Admiral.

"Great work, Barbara. Thank you."

100 MILES ABOVE TEHRAN, IRAN

"Michael. We have confirmed that there are women being held at that location. In fact, one of the Enemy agents is being 'comforted' as we speak," reported the Captain.

"Poor woman."

"He's actually being 'comforted' by several women. Does it take more than two humans to reproduce?"

"No, just one male and one female. Do we know the status of the others?"

"The other two are at home sleeping."

"Can you bomb the three simultaneously?"

"Yes, but it may not destroy all the ones incubating in the nest."

"Are your transporters capable of transporting the entire nest into the star?"

"Iffy," the Captain replied. "Yes, we can. But we may not get it all. A total of 10 flux bombs would be enough to destroy the enemy agents and the nest. It would also likely destroy the building and set it on fire."

"Do you have 10 flux bombs?"

"No. We'll need the Admiral's authorization to make more."

"Then, it's time to speak with the Admiral. Let me initiate the link. I'll put you on hold."

"Jiaying," Michael called out. "Can you connect the Captain to the Presence Chamber and initiate a call to Fleet. I'm running over to the lab now." Michael ran out the back door and down the path to the barn. Jeremy already had the door open for Michael and an elevator waiting to take him down to the Presence Chamber. Michael entered the chamber just as the Fleet communications officer came on the line.

"Mr. Ambassador, I take it this is an emergency?" he asked.

"Yes. Can I speak with the officer on duty?" asked Michael.

"Connecting..." the officer said as the Presence Chamber transferred to the Admiral's office.

"Mi-Ku. What's happened?"

"We found the last three enemy agents and their nest, which has 20 or more incubating. The Captain...," whose image had now been connected to the Admiral's office... "needs 10 flux bombs to destroy them all. The agents and nestlings will disperse shortly. We must act now."

The Admiral turned toward the captain. "Captain Ja-Ru is this true?"

"Yes. We have trackers on all three agents. Two are asleep but scheduled to wake shortly. The third is in the process of mating with one or more of the women confined in the hatchery building."

"If the women who have been infected were to scatter, Earth would be in for big trouble," Michael asserted. "You must authorize flux bomb deployment now."

"I don't understand." The Admiral turned his attention to the captain. "Standing orders allow this action."

"I don't have the authority to produce 10 flux bombs sir."

"Ah, understood." The admiral placed his four claws into slits on his desk, where a DNA sample was taken. "Authorization for 15 flux bombs was just sent. Please proceed with all haste," he said to the captain, whose presence faded from the presence chamber.

"Mi-Ku. How certain are you that these are the last of the Enemy agents? I'm not sure we've ever found this many on a planet that had not yet been swarmed."

"I'm confident that this is the main mass. But we'll need a high-resolution scan of the entire planet to confirm that we've found them all."

The Admiral looked at Michael speculatively. "There's something you're not telling me, isn't there?"

Michael locked eyes with the Admiral for several seconds, then sighed. "I'm sorry, my friend. This planet holds a few secrets that are restricted to above your grade."

The Admiral nodded his head in understanding, "All the more reason I'm glad we'll be there shortly. Stay safe, Mi-Ku."

MICHAEL'S OFFICE, THE RESIDENCE

"Michael," Charles called. "Nisha's treatment is complete. All traces of cancer are gone, the damaged nerves in her spine have been repaired, and the cosmetic reconstruction is complete. We can pull her out of the tank anytime now."

"Excellent news, Charles. How soon before Mahesh can visit her?"

"She'll wake up in the treatment room in the residence in about 25 minutes. It would probably be best if Mahesh was there when she wakes up. I'll call you when we're ready for him to come down."

Michael got up and walked down to the dining room. Noelani was setting the table and the wonderful smell of an excellent meal permeated the room. Michael walked over to Noelani and whispered. "Good news. Nisha is coming out of the tank and will wake up in about 20 minutes. Any chance we can delay dinner a little or hold back portions for Nisha and Mahesh?"

"I'll delay maybe 15 minutes. Then we'll start, that way everyone will still be here when she comes up. It'll be a very nice surprise."

"Sounds like a plan. I'm going to get Mahesh now."

...

Michael walked down to the den where he found Mahesh reading a book.

"Mahesh, I have some good news. Nisha's treatment is done, and it was completely successful. We'll be able to go see her in the treatment room in about 15 minutes."

"Excellent news." Mahesh beamed. "How long before she's up and about."

"Depends on how she feels, but I'm expecting that she'll want to come up and join us for dinner."

"That fast!"

"Do you remember how hungry you were when you came out of the restoration chamber?"

Mahesh nodded yes.

"Multiply it by five. We would have trouble keeping her away."

TREATMENT ROOM, THE RESIDENCE

When Mahesh came into the room, he was overwhelmed with emotion as he saw the wife of his youth lying in the hospital bed completely restored. Tears streamed from his eyes. "How? How is this possible?"

He sat down beside her and took her hand. Nisha began to stir, and Mahesh gently squeezed her hand. She stirred some more, then opened her eyes. Suddenly, she frowned in confusion. "Is that you Mahesh? Where am I?"

"We are in Hawaii, my love. At the home of Michael from the Intergalactic Confederation. You have been cured."

She reached up to touch her face… "It's gone. The tumor is gone."

"Yes, it is my sweet. And you are now 20 years younger. Look." He handed her a mirror.

She stared in the mirror for a minute. "Oh, my goodness. I never looked this good before." Then she looked at Mahesh and said with laughter in her voice, "And neither have you."

Michael, who had been standing against the wall, stepped forward and asked Nisha. "How do you feel?"

"Incredibly hungry," she said, then added, "Very incredibly hungry. And very attracted to the young man sitting next to me."

"Let's get you up and dressed. Mei has brought in a wardrobe with clothes in your size. She can help you select new clothes. We're going to head back upstairs. Call us when you're ready to come up for dinner."

The room emptied and Mei started bringing out selections for Nisha to choose from.

THE EMBASSY

Michael appeared in the center of a twelve-man honor guard, near the Chamber of Deputies where the special session would be held. Michael greeted the sergeant in charge of the honor guard in Portuguese, then proceeded to greet each of the other members.

Five minutes later, the President of Brazil walked into the area. "Michael, such a pleasure to meet you in person. Thank you for coming. Our Senate and House of Deputies will come to order in about 10 minutes. They are generally prompt, as there is a lot of media coverage for these events, tonight's especially.

"Our format is simple. I will introduce you. By law, you can speak as long as you like. Similarly, by law, they can leave whenever they like, and it's a safe bet they will start scattering in an hour unless you have them enthralled or are done. Once you're finished, we will open the floor for questions. We limit the questions period to one hour. Normally, it does not go that long, but today I think it will be hard to close off."

"Thank you, Mr. President, for the honest assessment. As I think you know, the most compelling thing I can do at sessions like this is to heal someone. Is there anyone I can heal?"

"No one has come forward. But I know two that are terminally ill and do not want that knowledge to become public."

"That's an interesting twist," Michael replied. "Which will make this an interesting session."

"How?" asked the president.

"If they know they are dying and I can heal them, do you think they will keep it private?"

"No idea."

Michael opened his senses to the president and immediately knew he was not one of the ones in question. "Well then, let's see how this plays out."

They entered the House of Deputies to thunderous applause and after a short introduction, Michael was given the podium. During the introduction, Michael had opened his senses to the crowd and quickly identified three people that were terminally ill, not just two.

After the normal greetings, Michael said, "When I first announced the Confederation's interest in allying with the peoples of Earth, the most common reaction was skepticism. The first question during interviews with the news services and meetings with heads of state was always... 'How can a 35-year old American citizen from Texas be the ambassador from an intergalactic confederation?' The thing that dispelled their doubt was healing someone they knew to be disabled or terminally ill. I'm sure most of you have seen videos of one or more of those healings.

"When I arrived today, I asked the president if there was anyone attending this morning that I could heal. He told me that there were two people he knew of that were terminally ill. Sadly, he was wrong. Among us this morning, there are three people that are terminally ill, a man suffering from pancreatic cancer who has about two months to live, a man in the early stages of Lou Gehrig's disease, and a woman suffering from ovarian cancer. Do any of the three of you want to come forward to be healed?"

No one did.

"I see that Brazilians are a very proud people. I fully respect your rights to privacy. But I beg you, do not throw away your life because of your pride. Please come see me after the session today or call my office. I've sent contact information to your desks. No one should suffer the painful deaths that will strike you in the months ahead."

Michael went on to cover topics previously discussed on TV, then turned the meeting back to the President, who opened the floor for questions. A tall and distinguished looking man was given the microphone and asked the first question. "Michael, I attended a security briefing this morning. One of the topics was North Korea. Is it true that the Confederation has taken possession of North Korea, and if so, can you explain why?"

Michael locked eyes with the questioner. "Yes. As of midnight, last night Korean time, North Korea has become a protectorate of the Confederation. North Korea was in the process of staging a major invasion of the South. South Korea is a Confederation ally, whom we are obligated to protect. Just as the Chairman was giving the order to invade, we arrested him, captured his Army, destroyed their weapons, and confiscated their nuclear arsenal. We are currently setting up the prisoner of war camps for the 526,000 men that were staged on the border. The prisoners of war are being treated well. They have warm beds, hot food and proper health care for the first time in their lives. North Korea is no longer a threat."

The room reacted strongly to Michael's statement with voices both for and against. The Speaker pounded his gavel and slowly regained control of the session. During the commotion, numerous members lined up at the microphone to ask questions. The next question was asked by an angry young woman, who was serving her first term in the House of Deputies. "What right does the Confederation have to interfere with the governments of Earth?"

"The Confederation has offered and is offering to ally with the nations of Earth. None are forced to ally with us. Part of our obligation to our allies is to protect them. The South did not attack the North. Israel did not attack Iran. Georgia did not attack Russia. In each case, we acted in defense of an ally. If Brazil were to become a confederation ally, then we would defend Brazil. Similarly, if Brazil attacks a confederation ally, then we will foil the attack.

"The Confederation came to Earth because it believes that both parties will be better off working together than working separately. No country is compelled to join. But neither can a country stop another one that wants to."

The next question was asked by one of the party leaders. "Michael, I saw news coverage of the first gift delivery to a Palestinian family in East Jerusalem. The man making the delivery, Rabbi Levine, is not the same man he was before you came. Have you done something to him?"

"No. The Confederation has not altered Rabbi Levine in any way, but the nuclear attack did. The rabbi was outside at the time of the attack. He saw the shields shimmer to life; saw three nuclear weapons detonate; saw the nuclear fire burning above his head. And in that moment, he had an epiphany. That is what changed him. The Confederation's only involvement in that was saving Israel from the treachery being enacted against it."

The questioning went on for well over an hour before the Speaker cut it off. Many members wanted to speak with Michael afterward. He was finally 'rescued' by the President, who took him to a conference room. In it were three people seeking to be cured. The President also gave Michael a signed copy of the Letter of Intent. Michael and his three patients then transported up to the military escort.

MICHAEL'S OFFICE, THE RESIDENCE

Michael's three patients were placed into therapy shortly after arrival. Mei prepped the woman; Kale and Yves the two men. Because they had three patients to treat simultaneously, they put them in the medical tanks in the lab basement. They would be in the tanks for various durations, the longest being about 30 hours.

Jiaying called as soon as Michael got back to his office. "Michael, word was just starting to come out about North Korea before your meeting with the Brazilian government. Since your comments there, we have been bombarded with requests for an official statement and interviews. We took a pass at a press release for your review. It is on your desk. But we really need a press secretary. I don't think any of us are adequately trained."

"Thank you, Jiaying. Has anything come out about Russia or Iran?"

"Not really. The Russian government put out a statement that the President was on vacation and wanted to stay out of the public eye for a few days. Our internal surveillance shows that they know he is missing, and his inner circle is in a panic.

"There was a story in the Iranian news about a fire in a building close to the Sa'dabad Palace Complex, but nothing else."

"Any ideas on where we could hold a press conference?"

"Funny you should ask. I got a call from the general manager down at the Westin Hapuna Beach Resort on Friday. She offered a very low rate for use of their conference center. Apparently quite a few of the press core that are on island are staying down there."

"Great idea. Call her back and check on availability,"

"Michael. A call just came in from Lt. Governor Park. Do you want to take it?"

"Yes. Put him through."

...

"Lt. Governor, good to hear from you. How are things going?"

"It's been an incredible day Michael. We had to set up a few more camps than expected, because some of the squads were too far separated. We now have 532 camps up and running. The entire army has been housed and fed. No one in North Korea has ever seen anything like this. I think you have already won the loyalty of the entire army."

"Have you chosen someone to lead the prison camp system?"

"Yes. Lt. General Ri, no relation to the former Minister of Agriculture. Lt. General Ri has been my right-hand man for years. I trust him implicitly. Assuming that you approve his appointment, I would like to promote him to General. Two of the men now working for him have the rank of Lt. General."

"I conditionally approve the appointment and will approve the promotion once we make his appointment final."

"Thank you, sir."

"I have a new mission for you starting tomorrow. I would like you to upgrade all the labor camps to the same standard as the Prisoner of War camp."

"That will be difficult. May I explain why?"

"Please do."

"These are very bad places, run by very bad men. When we go there, they will resist and will attempt to enslave us as well. I have no weapons, so no means to overcome them."

"Understood. I will have Alexi accompany you. She will equip up to 100 men that you choose. She will also give you something that looks like a knit undergarment. Put it on and you will be impervious from attack.

"I have been told that there are 6 camps that vary in size but hold a total of about 200,000 prisoners. Is that correct?"

"I think there may be another camp hidden in the north. And I think the total number is closer to 250,000. The Chairman sentenced many families to the camps this year."

"OK. Start with the camps you know. Maybe start with a smaller one. I want you and Alexi to transport into the camp alone. Attempt to get the camp leaders to surrender to you. When they do not, Alexi will pacify the camp. Once that is done, determine how many domes you want and direct your team to set them up. Then transfer the prisoners to the domes and get them fed. Do this with as much compassion as you can; these people have been subjected to treatment that no human should be forced to endure."

"Michael, these are bad people. We will need more soldiers and guns."

"Lt. Governor. The netting that you put on will make you impervious to almost anything. Alexi without weapons is as good as 100 men, probably better. She will have weapons, as will your men.

411

Start with 100. If Alexi thinks she needs more, then you will get more. If it all goes wrong, Alexi will transport you out."

"I will do as you ask, Michael."

"Thank you, Lt. Governor. Plan to start at sunrise tomorrow."

MICHAEL'S OFFICE, THE RESIDENCE

As soon as the line dropped, Jiaying came on, "Michael, I have the Admiral on the line."

"Mi-Ku. We are approaching the beautiful blue jewel that you call Earth. This truly is a spectacular planet."

"Welcome to Earth, my friend."

"We will be entering orbit in a few minutes, where would you like us?"

"After yesterday's operations, I think the rogue states are no longer a problem, so we can focus our attention on building an Embassy."

"Do you have a location yet?"

"We'll need your help to determine the optimal location, but I'm thinking some place close to Whitehorse, Canada. Sending the coordinates now. I think we need a 100 sq. mile campus. Can you get planetary engineering working on that?"

"Will they have access to the surface?"

"Initially no. The planetary engineers can scan locations north of the 60th parallel from the ocean in the west to the bay in the east. The campus needs to house up to 10 million, so I assume that it will need to be in the mountainous western region."

"I'll get the engineers working on it. What's next?"

"Staff. We have successfully transferred 10 androids from their Confederation standard avatars to human avatars. The first couple were bumpy, so I am recommending them for commendations. But this should go fast now. We have the capacity to produce about 100 human avatars a week. We're going to need more, so could your engineering team connect with mine to come up with a higher capacity solution? I need a minimum of 12,000 before you leave."

"Will do. What's next?"

"Gift production and distribution. We need two to three billion copies of the two devices I am sending you the specs for. Each country will get a slightly different configuration. By the end of the week, our team will be able to send you daily delivery requirements."

"Mi-Ku. This will require over a kilogram of transluminide. I have nowhere near that quantity."

"Not a problem. We have the supply."

There was silence on the line for a few seconds, then the Admiral spoke softly, "I'd heard that you were immensely wealthy but had no idea."

"Please, my friend. Do not think that way. The Earth is immensely wealthy. I am simply its caretaker."

"You realize that wealthy Confederation planets need to pay for Fleet services. What fraction of the population do you represent?"

"We are up to 53%. That number will increase rapidly over the coming week. Can we set the tax based on 90% of the population?"

"I'm good with that. How many days?"

"Can we target sixty?"

"Sixty days at the current tax rate of 100 grams per day times 90% comes to 5.4 kilograms. Can you afford that?"

"Yes. It's a fair price. By the way, I have already given the captain of the fast attack ship 100 grams."

"ONE HUNDRED GRAMS!" the Admiral exclaimed.

"I needed fully functional with scanning arrays and transporters, so I upgraded ten of his ships. As I understand it, he has 17 grams left over which I've implied he can keep."

Silence.

"You do not need to pay the 100 grams back. We had an emergency. I paid for the upgrades I needed to get through that crisis. Fair deal."

"I need to talk with that captain."

"Do not reprimand him. He did as he was ordered."

"Understood."

"Which brings me to a different topic. I need at least one more shuttle. We could refit the interior of a military escort, if you have any you would like to sell."

"We are actually carrying two that Central Command has designated for Earth. We can make delivery on a day's notice."

"Thank you. And the offer to buy one or more military escorts stands. Think about it."

"I will. Let me start working the list you've given me."

"Welcome to Earth, my friend. The presence of your Fast Attack vessel helped us tremendously. I think the Earth is secure now that you're here."

MICHAEL'S OFFICE, THE RESIDENCE

"Michael. Thank you for returning my call," The Canadian Prime Minister said. "Has your armada arrived? I've heard no news of a gigantic ship appearing over Moscow."

"Yes. The Armada has arrived," Michael replied. "They are in orbit and are remaining cloaked for now."

"I'm not sure which is worse. Having something gigantic and immensely powerful hanging over my head that I can see or having something gigantic and immensely powerful hanging over my head that I *can't* see," he said light-heartedly.

The Prime Minister continued. "The reason I called was because my security briefing this morning included unusual activity in North Korea, Russia and Iran. I know something of what happened in North Korea but would like to hear your description. I also suspect that you're behind whatever is going on in Russia and Iran."

"I'm happy to talk about these topics with you. I would also like to discuss arrangements for a ground survey for our embassy. I think I'll get feedback from our Chief Planetary Engineer later today.

"Your topic is going to be easier and faster, so let's start there. Marie has volunteered to be your host for the ground survey. She has a lot of energy since you returned her to us. She thinks this would be an excellent opportunity for her to interact with allies in their native forms and to do some roaming through the wilderness."

"I would be pleased to have Marie along, but will that satisfy your requirements? She is Minister of Health, correct? Not Land Management?"

"Yes. She has the Health Care portfolio. But as a cabinet minister, she also has general responsibility. But to your point, I would also like someone from Land Management to join you."

"Any chance it's someone I know?"

"Yes. Dr. Winston Chu, who you met on Good Morning America. He is a dual citizen and holds an adjunct appointment with our government through McGill University."

"I hoped I would cross paths with Dr. Chu again."

"I think his input will be very useful. Much of the area north of the 60th parallel is held as park land or as a preserve. In order to have it approved, we'll need someone who can credibly weigh in on the environmental impact you'll have on the land. I'm sure you'll do a better job of managing the environment than we're doing. But I need a scientist on my team to say that."

"I'm happy with the team you propose. How quickly can they mobilize? I'd like to be able to say something about the embassy at a press conference later this week."

"I'll have to get back to you on that. So what's going on in Russia and Iran?"

Michael exhaled audibly. "This must stay between the two of us."

"May I ask why?"

"Word of what happened there could send the populace into a panic. I need to brief all the allies on this but have not had the time to organize it."

"Then use me as a sounding board," the Prime Minister offered.

"Remember that I told you about the distant threat facing the Earth?"

"Yes."

"It has arrived."

"How bad is it and how long do we have?"

"Miraculously, I think we have it contained. We discovered seven Enemy agents, plus a man and a woman that had been infected. We also found a nest with over 20 of the creatures gestating in it. If there had been many more, or if they had acted in a coordinated manner, then we might have lost the Earth."

"How does this tie back to Russia and Iran?" he asked.

"And Korea," Michael added. "The last time I was in your office, we discussed the Russian tactical nuke that had been placed in Georgia. I showed you the clip of the two men in the helicopter?"

"I remember."

"We found the body of the trigger man and brought him back to life. When he grew strong enough, the creature inside him attacked us and we barely got out alive before we killed it. Then in Korea, we determined that the Chairman and his sister were Enemy agents. Here is a gruesome clip of what they look like."

Michael sent the clip to the prime minister's TV. He heard the Prime Minister gasp as the black smoke arms came out of the Chairman's mouth. Then again as Michael confronted the creature in the cabin.

"So that was what was left of the Chairman?" the Prime Minister asked.

"Yes. The creature had been consuming him for years. Several of his top ministers saw him in his 'black smoke' form, which is why they thought of him as a god.

"And, as I was interviewing members of his inner circle, I discovered one of them had been infected and needed to be destroyed."

"How do you destroy them?"

"Very difficult. They are extra-dimensional. That means they can slide in and out of our space-time continuum. They are hard to kill because they slip away when attacked. We have developed something we call a flux bomb. It gives off a flash of intense visible light, which triggers the creature to slide into an adjacent dimension. In that dimension, we detonate something like what you would call an electro-magnetic pulse. The magnetic flux tears the creature apart. The only other known way to kill them is to transport them into a star, where they are captured by the gravity and consumed by the magnetic flux in the star."

"Bloody Hell!" the Prime Minister exclaimed.

"Using a new scanning technology deployed by the Fleet, we found a second Enemy agent in Russia. Turns out it was the second man in the helicopter. He was killed by a flux bomb detonated in a dacha along the Volga River. He had also infected a woman, whom we transported into the sun.

"Sanitizing teams were deployed on my shuttle to clean up the residual infection from the Chairman. They were also deployed in Pyongyang to clean up the remains of his sister, and at my ranch in Hawaii to sanitize my medical facility there. The infected man was transported directly from my facility in Paso Robles into the Sun.

"Having found Enemy agents in Russia and North Korea, I became increasingly convinced that the Enemy was the driving force among Earth's rogue governments. So, we scanned Tehran, where we found three creatures and a nest of hatchlings. The nest was in the building that burned down."

"Burning will kill them?"

"No, it took 8 flux bombs to kill the large one and the nest it had developed. That much energy in one house caught the house on fire. In a separate operation, we also got the two other enemy agents in Tehran. The Admiral is in the process of doing a high-resolution scan of the entire planet, looking for any others.

"Although there were only seven adults, the threat level was enormous. One creature the size of the Chairman could consume 1,000 people in a matter of minutes. In fact, the Chairman killed two of my crew before I got him. It can infect a human just by touching them."

"Michael I cannot tell you how sad I am to hear about your crew. And now I understand why this needs to be handled so delicately.

"But, back to Russia and Iran... If I understand correctly two senior Russians have been killed and in Iran, three senior leaders have been killed. Do they know it was you?"

"The two men in the helicopter were already known to be missing and they've already accused us. And, technically, the Enemy killed their leaders. I only killed the Enemy agents inhabiting their bodies. But, no. All five bodies were completely destroyed with no evidence left behind. So, it'll be difficult, impossible really, for their authorities to determine what happened. It'll also be difficult for their governments to resume operation."

"And Korea?"

"I've taken North Korea as a Confederation Protectorate and made their former top general, Park, the lieutenant governor. A remarkably good man, especially considering the environment he's lived in. We captured the North Korean army and are holding them in a Prisoner of War Camp. Just about 100% have now pledged their allegiance to the Confederation. We are in the process of liberating their labor camps. That will take the better part of a week.

"Once that is done, we will form a new civil government and work with them to determine their long-term fate. I think they will choose re-unification."

"Incredible news," replied the Prime Minister.

"Yes, it is, isn't it? At my press conference later this week I will feature North Korea and Israel. And say as much about the Embassy as you allow. I will also announce the start of household gift delivery to member nations."

"Where are you going to do the press conference?"

"At a resort on the Big Island of Hawaii."

MICHAEL'S OFFICE, THE RESIDENCE

"Mi-Ku," the Admiral greeted him. "Our planetary engineers got back to me very quickly. They agree that an embassy in the far north will give you the best access to the peoples of Earth. Their scan shows that 90% of Earth's population is in the northern hemisphere. They note that your best coverage would be on the opposite side of the pole but defer to your judgement on the political situation.

417

"They also conclude that the best building location will be about 315 miles northeast of the city named Whitehorse. That area is relatively clear of fault lines and has excellent granite miles deep. The coordinates they recommend are at 64° 11' N, 127° 13' W. They say an aerial survey, followed by a ground survey, will be required to lock in the locations exactly."

"That was fast," said Michael.

"Our engineers are excited to begin. It's not often that they get this much quality land to work with. In fact, this is probably the first time and they're very excited. How soon can we begin?" the Admiral asked.

MICHAEL'S OFFICE, THE RESIDENCE

"Michael, I didn't expect to hear back from you so soon." The Canadian Prime Minister said. "What can I do for you?"

"Our planetary engineers have already locked onto a site in the Mackenzie Mountains along the Keele River in the Northwest Territories. They'd like to begin an aerial survey as soon as possible.

"Any chance I could get your authorization to do that this evening, just before sunset. The survey will be done by a cloaked survey vessel that can't be seen and won't register on any surveillance equipment. It will not pose a threat to air traffic because it's not in the same dimension."

"Technically, I don't have the authority to authorize such a survey. But technically, you won't be in our air space. So, you have my blessing."

"Our planetary engineers are very confident that this is the right site. If the aerial survey confirms their beliefs, then we could mobilize for a ground survey starting tomorrow morning. Any chance your team could be ready? We can pick them up around 8:00 AM and outfit them for the trip. We'll return them when the survey is complete."

"Let me check. Assuming they can, I will have them make arrangements directly with your people."

"Thank you, Mr. Prime Minister."

ABOVE THE MACKENZIE MOUNTAINS, NORTHWEST TERRITORIES, CANADA

The survey vessel hovered above the Keele River valley. The Keele River twisted through the Mackenzie Mountains at the border of Yukon and Northwest Territories. The survey area was about 20 miles long and 5 miles wide. It included meadows, gentle slopes and rugged mountains.

The Lead Planetary Engineer marveled over the site. "This location is perfect. The rock formations are stable. The valley is shaped in a way that will allow us to easily encase it in dome shields. We can build along the surface as well as the mountain slopes. And it's just plain beautiful."

The Admiral, wanting to see more of the planet up close, had unexpectedly come along for the aerial survey. "What steps do you need to take as part of the ground survey?"

"There are two things I'll need to know for the site design: the stability of the mountain walls and geologic evidence of historic flooding. The snow and ice can take a heavy toll on the mountains, and there are likely to be pinch points along the river that are subject to flooding during the spring melt off.

"Neither of these is insurmountable, but either could impact the construction schedule. So, I need to get ahead of these two issues."

"Too bad we need to wear rebreathers while we're here. I would love to walk on the ground and smell the fresh air." The Admiral sighed.

PRISONER OF WAR CAMP #1, NORTH KOREA

Alexi and the Lt. Governor Park stood at a podium inside the training tent. One hundred soldiers were lined up and standing at attention on the floor in front of them. The soldiers had been hand-picked by Lt. Governor Park, who was just finishing the mission briefing. Alexi could read Lt. Governor Park's fear, as well as his men's. They were going to take over one of North Korea's infamous labor camps. At one time, today's target had over 100,000 inmates and 10,000 guards. No one knew how many were there now.

"Alexi will now demonstrate the weapons we will be using," Lt. Governor Park said.

As she stepped forward, she heard some grumbling about being trained by a small girl. She spotted the person in question and thanked him for volunteering to be her assistant. He reluctantly stepped forward.

"In this bag are the weapons you will be using today." She spoke in a loud voice as she handed the bag to the volunteer. "Would you please open the bag and show the men what's inside?"

419

He opened the bag and pulled out something that looked like nylon stockings, which he assumed was padding of some sort, then pulled out several small metallic boxes and a thin flak jacket, similar to the one Alexi was wearing. Seeing nothing else in the bag, he turned it inside out, showing everyone the empty bag. "So, where are the weapons?"

Alexi picked up the 'stockings' that he'd dropped on the floor and shook them out. They looked like some sort of full-body stocking that even covered the head. "This," she said, "is your most important weapon today..."

Her statement drew lots of groaning and catcalls.

"...It is a full body personal shield." She looked her volunteer in the eye and said, "Please take off your clothes and put this on."

"No freaking way!" The volunteer protested.

Alexi repeated her order, to which the volunteer replied, "Make me!"

His first sign that he was in trouble was the grin on Alexi's face. "With pleasure." She pushed a button on her flak jacket.

The man in front of her suddenly became very still.

She looked at the men in the room. "The button I just pressed on my flak jacket activated a suspensor field. A suspensor field totally paralyses anyone within 10 feet of you. I didn't want to show this to you until a little later, but since my volunteer asked for my assistance in getting dressed, I thought I might rearrange the demonstration order."

Moving slightly to the side so everyone could see, she pressed on the man with her little finger and he fell softly to the carpeted floor. "See? Completely paralyzed."

She held up the 'stockings.' "This is an emitter array. It develops a personal shield that extends about 1 inch above your skin. It is more or less impenetrable. It can withstand and repel bullets, grenades, missiles, even a nuclear weapon. It also makes you immune to suspensor fields. If this poor fool..." she kicked the man... "had done what I ordered him to do, I could not have pulled this trick on him."

"Let me show you how to put it on." She quickly stripped the man on the floor, then somewhat laboriously put the 'stockings' on him. She then stood him up, holding him so he did not fall over again.

"You." She said pointing to a man a few feet away. "Can you please hold him up for me? You will not be trapped in the field."

The man shot forward as if his life depended on it and helped the 'volunteer' stay in place.

Alexi lifted the volunteer's arm and said, "If you cannot see this, please come closer. I'm going to show you how to activate the emitters." The men shuffled around a bit.

"Take your index finger and place it on the inside of your arm about halfway up to your elbow." She placed her left index finger on the underside of her right arm. "Then slowly slide it down to the wrist." She did this on her own arm.

"When you do this, the emitter array will melt, for lack of a better word, into your skin. So that you're not surprised... It really feels like the array is melting. It'll feel cold. It'll feel wet. Don't let this scare you. It's perfectly safe."

"Now watch as I activate this man's emitter array." She did the motion and the emitters contracted over the man and melted into his skin. Whispers of awe could be heard among the men.

The man that was holding up the volunteer said. "I felt it getting cold and wet." Then he added, "Why is he still frozen?"

"I don't know if everyone heard that. But my friend here asked why our volunteer has not recovered from the suspension field now that he has the emitter array activated. Excellent question.

"The answer is because it's not powered yet." She picked up one of the small metallic boxes that the volunteer dropped on the ground. "You can lay him back down again."

The volunteer was laid down on the floor.

Alexi held up the metallic box. "This is the power source for the shield. See these two shiny bumps on the back?" She held the unit up and pointed to the bumps. "The shield will be active as long as the shiny bumps are touching your skin. Make sure to strap it on in some way. The box automatically turns on and off. It has enough power for about 20 years of continuous use. Wear this at all times while you're in the war zone.

"OK. Let's demonstrate." She placed the box on the man lying on the floor. A flash of light could be seen over his skin. Alexi backed up about ten feet as the man sucked in a deep breath and coughed. When he finally looked up, he saw that Alexi had pulled a gun and had it pointed directly at his crotch. Before he could react, she pulled the trigger.

The sound of the gunshot rang through the room. Everyone looked at Alexi, then at the spot she was pointing to. The bullet had stopped about 1 inch from the man's penis and just hung there in front of him. Then it dropped to the floor between his legs.

The man screamed and shuffled backwards as Alexi approached. She offered her hand and said, "Let me help you up. Can we have a big round of applause for today's volunteer? Good job."

The man took her hand and popped up, looking a bit embarrassed and said, "Thank you, Ma'am."

"OK, everyone. Put your shield on, then get redressed."

While the men were following their orders, Alexi stepped back up on the stage where Lt. Governor Park was giving her a stern look. "Was that really necessary?" he asked.

"I don't know. But I think every one of your men now has confidence in their weaponry and a more appropriate level of respect for their leaders."

10,000 MILES ABOVE NORTH KOREA

Several men had failed to follow their instructions about closing their eyes before transporting up. Four had fallen over. One had barfed. Alexi shook her head. Some guys just had to learn the hard way.

Lt. Governor Park did a quick review of the battle plan with his men, while Alexi did the same with the pilots of the military escort. Then he and Alexi transported down.

PENAL LABOR COLONY KWAN-LI-SO #18, NORTH KOREA

Alexi and Lt. Governor Park appeared in what they thought was the camp commander's office. The office contents and decorations seemed consistent with their expectations, but they found no one in the office.

A snap rang out. Then another. They went to a window. Another snap. About 50 feet from the office window, a horrific scene played out. A man, clearly unconscious, had been tied to a post, his hands at the top, his feet at the bottom. Another snap rang out as the whip put another stripe on the unconscious man's back. Alexi started to say something, then turned and vomited all over the floor.

"Is this the first time you've seen something like this?" Lt. Governor Park asked.

"Yes. Have you seen this before?"

"Every day in the prison camps. The people here are tortured by sociopaths that ought to be in prison themselves. Look at the pointlessness of what's happening. The prisoner is unconscious. He doesn't even know what's happening to him. And, judging by his condition, he will not recover, so a slave laborer is lost. Stupid."

"This needs to stop now." Alexi said, reaching for the doorknob.

Lt. Governor Park put his hand over hers and said, "Let me go first. This man knows me and may listen to what I have to say. Let me see if I can get him to come inside. If not, then come save me."

He shushed Alexi's protest, then moved her to the side where she wouldn't be seen when the door opened. Another snap rang out. He shook his head in disgust, then opened the door and stepped out.

"STOP!" Lt. Governor Park commanded.

The camp commandant stopped his wind up for the next stroke and turned to look at whomever was stupid enough to issue a command in his camp. When he saw Lt. Governor Park, he looked puzzled.

"General Park. I was not expecting to see you." Fear edged his voice. "What a pleasant surprise." He seemed at a loss for words.

"Commandant. May we speak in your office?"

"Only three lashes left." He said, turning to administer them.

"Commander." Park said using the man's army rank, rather than his current job title. "Your presence is required now."

The Commandant turned, anger burning in his eyes. *This fool will pay for embarrassing me in front of my men,* he thought. He dropped the whip and motioned to one of his men. "Clean this mess up."

Then he turned and stomped toward his office. As he got closer, former General Park saw with disgust that the commandant was splattered with blood and the odd sliver of bone. The commandant walked right past him and marched into his office. Lt. Governor Park followed him in and closed the door, revealing Alexi, who had hidden behind it.

"Now. What is this that you have brought me? She's what? Hispanic? Maybe she can spend a little time with me, before we release her into the camp," said the commandant with a leering smile.

Before he even knew what was happening, Alexi jumped over the table and broke his nose with a palm to his face. Before the pain even registered, his stomach hit the floor as a noose bound his hands to his feet behind his back.

"This pig needed a little hog-tying," she growled, then shoved him over into the pile of vomit she had left a few minutes ago.

The commandant started to scream, then suddenly fell silent.

"I put him in a suspensor field to shut him up. He can still hear and understand us, so tell him how it is." Although speaking to the Lt. Governor, Alexi faced the hog-tied commandant as she spat the words out.

"Commander Lee. You are under arrest for crimes against humanity. The Chairman and his sister are dead. The Army's weapons have been destroyed. And our nuclear arsenal has been confiscated. We are now a protectorate of the Intergalactic Confederation of Planets. I have been appointed the Lt. Governor of the North Korean district and my mission today is to liberate this camp. You will be turned over to the South Korean government for further processing."

Turning to Alexi, he asked, "Is the suspensor field just on him? Or is it on the whole room? Excellent work by the way."

"Thank you." Her smile beamed. "It's on the whole room. Anyone coming in will be trapped just like he is."

This one certainly has spunk, Park thought.

Lt. Governor Park looked around, then pointed to what looked like a 1950s radio set. "Here is the camp PA system. I'm going to put the camp in lockdown."

He turned the system on. A loud click could be heard coming from the outside as the speakers got power. He pushed the button then said in a command voice, "Attention. Attention. This is General Park. This camp is being placed in lockdown. Lockdown the camp. Repeat. Lockdown the camp." He released the announcement button and turned on the air raid siren.

Outside, people could be seen running in all directions for a few minutes. Before long everyone had disappeared. Lt. Governor Park went back to the radio and clicked the announcement button. "All guards report to the parade grounds for an emergency briefing. Repeat. All guards report to the parade grounds for an emergency briefing."

Once again, men could be seen running around, this time toward the parade grounds, where they formed into neat lines.

"So. Is your suspensor field large enough to constrain all those men?" He asked.

"Um. One minute." She got a faraway look in her eye, then a lunch box-sized device appeared near her feet. "Yup. Have it."

"How do I activate it?"

"Well you can't, actually. I'll need to do that." On seeing his look, she sighed. "It's an alien telepathy thing. You can only activate it via telepathic command."

"Can you do that from here?"

"Yes."

"OK. I'll carry it out with me. As soon as you hear me starting to address the men, turn it on and call down the troops."

"Got it."

Lt. Governor Park walked out onto the parade grounds and immediately saw the problem with his plan. The guards in the watch towers had not come down. He knew it was a capital offense to come down from the tower while on duty. Long ago, he had served in one of those towers.

Oh well, he thought. *At least we'll get the majority of the guards before the first shot is fired.*

"Parade rest!" Lt. Governor Park commanded.

Most of the men snapped into position quickly enough that they were in a stable position before the suspensor field took effect. But a couple dozen fell over. Some of them knocked over another guard.

Park heard one of the men in the tower ask, "What's going on?"

Moments later, soldiers in flak jackets started appearing one by one in a double ring around the parade grounds. More than one of these men fell over, these from vertigo. A shot rang out. Then more. "Suspend the guards in the towers," Lt. Governor Park called out.

The men on the ground started targeting the guards with their suspensor grenades. But most of the men could not throw that far because the towers were so high. Some men started climbing the towers. Alexi came out of the office and used her mortar version of the suspensor grenades. After about 15 minutes, all the guards were paralyzed.

Alexi came over to stand with Lt. Governor Park, who murmured, "We need to do a better job with the guard towers next time."

After a moment, the Lt. Governor asked, "How long is it safe to keep the guards in suspensor fields?"

"In theory, indefinitely. But being stuck in a suspensor field is uncomfortable. Holding someone that way for a day would be cruel."

"So, guards first?"

"Yes, guards first." Alexi paused. "Once the prisoners realize that there are no guards, things could go bad fast. Let's put 75 of your men on dome and mess construction and take the rest with us to tour the camp."

Orders were given and the men set about their work. The camp turned out to be smaller than they were expecting. There were only 20 buildings housing the prisoners, but they had no idea how many people were crammed into each building.

"I want to go into one of the buildings and find out how many people are in each."

"Trust me, Alexi. I've been in buildings like this. The conditions inside are something that haunts dreams. You do not want to go inside. Each building will have a boss. A very dangerous man. Let's go to the buildings one by one and ask for 10 inmates requiring hardship duty. Let's take them to the first camp. Treat and feed them. Then ask them how many people are in their building."

"OK. Let's do it your way."

"Ten guards," commanded Lt. Governor Park. Ten men ran forward. He gave them the short brief, then approached the door to the building. He pounded on the door, then demanded, "Ten ambulatory prisoners for hardship duty."

At first there was no response. But after a few moments, a commotion broke out inside. There was fighting and crying. The door opened and 10 half-naked people were thrown out. Alexi was repulsed by their condition. Open sores. A botched amputation. It was truly a vision from a nightmare.

The Lt. Governor nodded to his men. Each one took one person and they walked to the edge of the camp, where painted spots in the snow indicated an entry into the dome. The men marched their prisoners through the entry and released them. The Lt. Governor walked in and said to the prisoners, "You are safe here. Smell the food? Feel the warmth? North Korea lost a very short war with the Intergalactic Confederation of Planets. Our country is now a protectorate of the Intergalactic Confederation. I am the Lieutenant Governor of this district. You are being relocated to this area for processing. You will be fed. Your wounds will be treated. You will be given new clothes. The walls to this dome are transparent and are marked by the red line in the snow. Shortly the snow will be melted on this side. Cots have been set up for you over there. A doctor will come by shortly. Please stay near your cots until someone comes to get you."

One young man looked at former General Park, the cots, and the red line. In a burst of speed, he shot toward the red line. When he hit the dome barrier there was a flash of light. The man flew backward about five feet and landed painfully.

Lt. Governor Park walked over to where the man lay on the ground groveling. He reached his hand down and said, "Please let me help you up." After even more groveling, Park, hand still extended, said, "Come. Let me help you up. You're safe here. You can't get through the invisible barrier, but it is there to hold in the heat. You will eventually be released. Come, let's go over to the cots together." The man finally took the Lt. Governor's hand and was lifted to his feet. They walked over to the cots, where an attractive young American woman with a stethoscope was examining a boy with what appeared to be a broken arm.

"The Americans won?" he asked hopefully.

"No," answered the Lt. Governor. "Someone much more powerful and kind won. I work for them now. And we'll take care of you until you're recovered enough to take care of yourself."

The man sat on his cot, looking up at the Lt. Governor. "Thank you sir."

Alexi sent a video clip of the exchange to Michael along with a message saying that Lt. Governor Park was going to be a good one.

...

The day proceeded slowly. A total of 6,000 former prisoners were put into six domes. The 900 guards were put in a seventh dome. The doctors would be busy for days and it was likely they would lose some of their patients.

Alexi and the Lt. Governor had miraculously become a well-tuned team. They stayed up late into the night refining their plans for the next camp.

1,000 MILES ABOVE OTTAWA, CANADA

Marie and Dr. Winston Chu appeared in the shuttle's passenger compartment where Michael was waiting for them. "Marie, Dr. Chu. I'm so happy to see you both again. You've been introduced, right?"

Marie answered, "Yes. We were introduced last night and briefed on the government's interest in, and requirements for, the ground survey."

"Excellent. We're planning to transport down to the surface in an hour. There are a couple things we need to do first to make sure that you're protected from the cold. I'd also like to tell you about the people you'll be working with.

"First, let's outfit you with protective shields. The shields will keep you warm. They will also protect you from falling rocks or other hazards. The shields consist of two parts: an undergarment and a shield generator. These are the undergarments. Although it looks like a nylon stocking, it's actually a shield emitter array. Once you've put these on, I'll show you how to activate them. There are two restrooms you can use. Make sure that there is nothing between these and your skin, so take off everything before you put these on, including rings, glasses, etc."

A few minutes later they came out of their respective restrooms, laughing at how ridiculous they looked. Michael showed them how to activate the emitter array and attach their shield generators, then guided them through installing their translation devices.

"I thought today was going to be an interesting experience, but just putting these things on has been a life experience," Dr. Chu commented.

"I doubt we've seen anything yet," Marie shot back.

"OK. One more piece of hardware." Michael pulled out what looked like a mountain climbing harness.

"That looks like a climbing harness. We aren't going to be climbing mountains, are we?" Dr. Chu asked.

"Not exactly. But the terrain where we're going is very rugged. It will be easier to get around if we can just float above the surface."

"Are these like George's Fabulous Flying Overalls?" Marie asked, obviously excited at the possibility.

"Not exactly, but same principle. With these on you can lighten yourself or levitate above the ground like George does. But you can also dial up altitude to several thousand feet. Our engineers will be doing this to take rock samples from the cliff faces. You don't need to join them, but you're welcome to. So, let's put the grav harnesses on and I'll show you how they work."

A few minutes later they were all levitating around the cabin. "This is too fun. Do we get to keep these?" Marie asked.

"We'll have to discuss that," Michael replied.

"OK. The last thing we need to discuss is the survey team that we're hosting today. The entire team will be Lorexian, or at least they will be occupying Lorexian avatars. Lorexians cannot breathe Earth's atmosphere, so they might be wearing space suits, but more likely will just be wearing rebreathers. Lorexians are large. The average adult male is over 9 feet tall and weighs 425 lbs. The tallest are closer to 11 feet and 600 lbs. You'll find their size intimidating. Until last week, I hadn't seen a Lorexian in nearly 100 years and I was shocked by how large they are. Beyond size, almost every other feature of their body is different; some more so, some less so, but all different.

"The most important thing for you to know is that despite their size and alien-ness, they are a fundamentally less aggressive species than humans, and will be equally, if not more so, intimidated by you."

"This is going to be really interesting," Dr. Chu mused.

"OK. They've sent the coordinates. Ready to go? Once we're on the ground, we can offer the official invitation and they'll come join us."

BANKS OF THE KEELE RIVER, NORTHWEST TERRITORIES, CANADA

The hosting party appeared. Their levitation was set at two feet above the snow, and Marie could see snow blowing beneath her feet. A strong gust of wind kicked up a little dust devil of small ice crystals that momentarily obstructed her view. Startled she thought. *What? I didn't even feel the wind. Or the cold! I need shields like this in Ottawa!*

"Marie." Michael prompted. "Would you please issue the invitation for the Confederation Survey Team to come join us?"

"Sure. Um, how do I do that?"

"Sorry. Forgot to mention that you have a Confederation communications device in the collar of your climbing gear. Reach up and you will feel a little protrusion. Just press on it and ask to speak to the leader of the survey team."

She felt the little nib of a button, pressed down and said, "May I speak with the leader of the survey team please?"

"Connecting," came the reply.

"This is the Earth Survey Team."

"Hello. My name is Marie St. Germain, the official Canadian government host of this mission. You are invited to join us on the surface."

Moments later, ten of the largest creatures she had ever seen appeared before her, all facing in her direction, fists out at shoulder height and pointed toward her.

Marie felt herself starting to swoon when Michael's voice whispered. "Deep breath, Marie. This is the traditional greeting salute. Hold out your hand with your fist lightly closed and welcome them to Canada."

Michael's voice calmed her. She lifted her fist as Michael instructed and said. "On behalf of the people of Canada, welcome."

The Lorexians dropped their fists and the one in the middle came forward. "Minister St. Germain. On behalf of the Planetary Engineering team, thank you for inviting us to your beautiful country. My name is Fa-Mu," the Lorexian said in a deep resonant voice.

He turned to Michael. "Mr. Ambassador, it is an honor to meet you, sir. The Admiral says you have a new protocol for bumping." He extended his paw.

"Yes." Michael smiled and reached his hand out to cover the engineer's paw. The thought ran through his mind. *We need to update the translators to say 'shaking,' instead of 'bumping.'*

The engineer extended his paw toward Marie, who placed her hand on his. She was surprised at how soft the short fur was that covered his hand. She also noticed that it extended over the rest of his body, at least as much as she could see. Engineer Fa-mu had large expressive brown eyes that sparkled with excitement. His face was partially covered by a breathing device, but the rest of him was dressed in a dark blue uniform, not all that different from those worn by many metropolitan police departments. The uniform covered his entire body, except head and hands. It was clear that Lorexians were proportionally different than humans, but she could see no evidence of the lumpiness Michael mentioned other than what looked like small fur-covered warts on the exposed portion of his wrist.

"What is the plan for the survey, Chief Planetary Engineer Fa-Mu?" Marie asked.

Her question was met by a sound that was somewhere between a purr and a roar. She tried not to react and was calmed when Michael whispered, "He is laughing at your use of his title."

"Sorry. I should control myself better during first contact. But that was funny. Fa-Mu is my familiar name. My real name is very long, one that few of us can even get right. But I have never heard someone use a long title with a familiar name. And in such a beautiful soprano voice," the Chief Engineer bellowed. On seeing the dark look from Michael, he realized that he hadn't answered his host's question.

"Come, let me show you." He turned to look southeast down the valley. "We are standing near the middle of the tract that we want to build on. If you follow the river this way, it flows downstream for about 12 or 13 miles before disappearing around the bend. From there, it turns to the northeast and flows down onto the plain, eventually merging into the Makenzie River. If we take the first 11 miles, then no light pollution will get around the bend to influence the levels of natural light on the plain or the wildlife that lives there."

Turning 120° to the right, he pointed to a spot where the river could no longer be seen. "The river's headwaters are up near Keele Peak and flow down through the valleys to a choke point there, where you can no longer see the river. The slope is steep there and the land beyond is more level. That's what causes the river to seem to disappear. That spot is about 10 miles away. So, if we limit our development to 9 miles, we will again contain any light pollution from reaching the flat lands above."

Turning another 120° to the right, he continued, "The narrow valley over there has a small tributary flowing through it. From that point to the mountain behind us is a little over five miles. Most of the Keele River Valley in this area is about 4 miles wide, as measured 1,000 ft. above the river. There are three intersection points like this that are over five miles wide. We will send you the drawings showing the borders we are requesting. It includes most of the valley land in this 20-mile stretch, plus some slope and ridgetop area.

"To your question, I want to scout and mark the perimeter. The markers are not visible to the naked eye and can be electronically recalled, so there will be no damage to the land. The markers will allow us to give you aerial photos with the boundaries accurately shown. Then my team will also be taking a few core samples from the valley area and rock samples from the ridges we're targeting. The purpose of these is to confirm our orbital scanner readings," the Chief Engineer concluded.

"This is beautiful territory," Marie reflected. "I'm sure that we're going to get protests from environmentalists about developing it."

"I'm not a politician Ma'am, so can't really help you with that other than to say that our construction techniques cause no pollution, other than light and sound, and we mostly contain that. And that this land will be used to dramatically improve the human condition. This is where the new medical school will be." He paused, then asked, "Would you like to accompany the survey team, or the samples team?"

"I would like to see one valley and one peak sample, then accompany you on the site survey."

"Then let's get started," said the Chief Engineer.

...

"Can you explain to me what I just saw?" Marie asked. She was looking at a 12-foot long tube of stone, sand, dirt and water that had been 'extruded' out of thin air and appeared to be hanging suspended right in front of her.

"Yes, Ma'am. This device is a scanner/replicator. I scanned down into the ground to find a good sample. The scanner created a replication pattern and then replicated an exact copy of the sample. It is held together by a force field and suspended in the air with an industrial-grade suspensor field. The scanner/replicator can exactly reproduce any molecule composed of atoms with an atomic weight of less than 250. The force field contains any of the radioactive ones, but we really don't have anything with an atomic weight that high in this sample."

"So, you aren't really taking a sample, you're replicating one?"

"Yes. Ma'am."

She turned to the Chief Engineer. "Fa-Mu. I've seen enough of the sampling. Your team may proceed. Let's start the site survey.

...

"This view is spectacular," Marie said. They hovered just above the ridge that was only 2 miles northwest of the point where they'd transported down. The ridge rose 4,000 ft. above the valley floor and had clear views of the entire tract. Keele Peak, about 100 miles to the west, was also visible. At 9,750 ft., its peak glistened in the morning sun.

"This ridge is one of the ones we are requesting in the land lease. At 4,000 ft. it gives us a good location for signal transmission and an excellent viewing point for the entire site." Chief Engineer Fa-Mu put his hand out indicating the area they'd just surveyed. "If I were Michael, I think I'd put my office and quarters up here, but I'm sure he's going to want something close to the middle."

They were still for a moment, everyone mesmerized by the beauty of the land in front of them.

"It would be easy to stand here for hours, just taking in the scenery. But sadly, the last marker has been placed and we have work to do." Fa-Mu's voice was filled with melancholy. "Any questions you would like to discuss?"

"I have a question," Dr. Chu spoke for the first time since the survey started. "It's about the river. The flow here is low during the winter. But in the spring, the water level raises about 20 ft. and spreads out up to a quarter-mile wide in places. How are you going to manage that?"

"The short answer is force fields," replied the chief planetary engineer. "The area where the river normally runs will be converted into a park. The water will be constrained to a fixed path by force fields. The rest of the current riverbed will be planted with trees, shrubs, flowers, etc., and we will add walking paths through the entire garden. The entire embassy will be inside a shield that is similar to the personal shields we are wearing. Because we can hold the temperature in a constant range year-round, numerous plant species will prosper here. It'll be very pretty.

"When water runs high in the spring and early summer, it will rise vertically, forming a water wall between the two sides. Quite a stunning sight, really. We plan to reserve 250 ft above the riverbank for water. In the extremely unlikely case of flooding above that level, we can transport the water to the far end."

"Regarding the development itself, how will you build along the slopes?" Dr. Chu asked.

"I think you would refer to it as prefab. The units will be replicated on our civil engineering ships and transported into position. Finishes will be added by bots once base construction is done."

"My question was more about the foundations. Along the slopes, how much will we have to alter the slopes and what will become of the debris?" Dr. Chu asked.

"The foundations will be standard extra-dimensional tensors. Light pipes will be built in, so the microbial life underneath is not disturbed. I'm not sure I understand the part about altering the slopes and debris," Fa-Mu answered.

Dr. Chu laughed. "I AM sure that I do NOT understand the part about the extra-dimensional tensors. What I meant was how deep into the ground are you going to need to dig in order to build the foundation."

"Oh, my goodness." Fa-Mu seemed a bit taken back. "Our foundations float about 2 inches above the ground. We would never dig into it," he said as a shudder ran over him. "Well, the plants will be in the ground near the riverbed, but the walking paths will float a few inches above to avoid contamination."

Dr. Chu stood there with his mouth open. "It floats! How... Oh, forget how, I won't understand. Why won't it just float away?"

This statement sent Fa-Mu into another laughing fit. "Float away…" More chuckling. "Oh, that was a good one."

Michael injected himself into the dialog. "Chief. Human technology does not have extra-dimensional anchors. Could you give him a few words of explanation?"

"No extra-dimensional anchors? How do they keep their buildings in place?"

It was Dr. Chu's turn to laugh. "We excavate holes in the ground in which footings are placed and the building sits on the footings. For large buildings, we drive big pieces of metal deep into the ground and build the footings on those."

"Does that work?" Fa-Mu was incredulous. "How do you prevent damage to the microbial life in the ground? And why don't your buildings fall down when there's an earthquake?"

Again, Michael intervened. "Dr. Chu. Much of the Confederation's technology is derived from the field of physics that humans call the multiverse. It features layer after layer of space time. We refer to these layers as dimensions."

"My specialty is in a different area, so I won't get this exactly right. But there are several foundational dimensions that are held approximately in lock step with your four dimensions. We build our foundations in those dimensions. Why? Because they move slowly. An earthquake in the four dimensions we live in can move the ground inches in a matter of seconds. In the foundational dimensions, those movements happen, but take months. Because the dimensions can be several inches out of sync at any given point in time, we build our foundations a few inches from the surface of the ground so that the building never touches the ground. It makes our building completely immune from normal terrestrial movement and has the side benefit of minimizing environmental impact."

"Good explanation." Fa-Mu frowned, then turned to Dr Chu. "You really don't know about the foundational dimensions? You must have building failures all the time."

Marie laughed, then said… "Boom, mind blown again." …with fingers flickering away from her head.

Fa-Mu joined the laughter. "What a fabulous expression! I'm going to use that when I get back home."

"May I ask one more question?" Dr. Chu asked. "What about rights-of-passage? Today, adventurers are free to transit this valley and the nearby peaks. The environmentalists will no doubt complain. But, is the government's position going to be that this land is no longer available. Or is there another position we can take?"

Michael took this question. "Our embassy grounds are generally open to the public, but they must have the equivalent of a visitor's visa. The private buildings on the campus will be private. But the public buildings will be open to all. Who knows, an applicant might apply to open a tour or outfitting company that will make the surrounding peaks and valleys more accessible, not less."

After more discussion, they all floated back to the transport zone and returned to their respective ships.

1,000 MILES ABOVE EARTH, ENROUTE TOWARD OTTAWA, CANADA

"What do you think?" Michael asked. "Are you good with this site and our plans?"

Dr. Chu spoke up first. "I'm very much in favor of what you want to do, and this site seems a good fit. I'm not the politician here, but I see this project as being completely aligned with Canada's values. To my specific role on this mission, I completely approve of your environmental plans to preserve the land and develop without impact. That said, I suggest that you cut off the adventurer argument before it even comes up by including a tourist visa program and an outfitter franchise in your application."

"Technically, the treaty provision is already in place for an embassy in the Northwest or Yukon Territories, so there isn't an application in the normal sense." Marie replied. "But I agree with your sentiments entirely. Our biggest weakness is the no development, environmentalist fringe. If we can co-opt their allies from the outset, they will have less chance of blocking a program that will greatly benefit us all."

"Dr. Chu, Winston, could you prepare a short summary of your analysis of environmental impact this afternoon and forward it to me and the cabinet by 4:00 PM?" Marie asked. "There is a cabinet meeting scheduled for 5:00. Your report will help us move the matter along."

...

THE RESIDENCE, KOHALA MOUNTAIN

"Mi-Ku," the Admiral said, "We have just completed our scan of the Earth. We haven't found another Enemy agent, although there are a few cloudy spots that could be infections or incubation sites. Our plan is to continue monitoring, and to respond with overwhelming force if

435

an adult should appear. This should be settled once and for all in another month."

"Thank you, my friend. We came painfully close to losing the Earth and have the Fleet to thank for our rescue."

"I heard about the size and power of the one you took down."

"But it cost me two crew to do it," Michael lamented.

"They'll be back before too long."

"Still, I would have accidentally infected myself if it hadn't been for the sanitization team."

"You sound a little down, my friend. Tell me why."

"I've lived on this planet, in this form, for the better part of 100 years. Yet, I totally failed to recognize that it had been infected by Enemy agents. I even joked with the staff that some of these people were acting like the Enemy."

"No recriminations. You have done something here that's never been done before. You saved a planet that had over 25 people infected before the first was discovered. You've won over more than half of the population of a fragmented world with over 200 countries. No one has done anything like that before."

"Thank you, Jo-Na. The loss of Elsie and Sanjit has hit me hard." Shaking his gloom off, Michael continued, "But we are on our way to capturing 100% of the populace. And I'm starting to believe that humans will be the ones that ultimately replace us as the caretakers of three galaxies."

"That would be something to see," said the Admiral.

WESTIN HAPUNA BEACH RESORT, SOUTH KOHALA COAST

Michael appeared on the stage in the Grand Ballroom at the Hapuna Beach Resort. He had planned to just drive down but got a call from the Chief about two hours ahead of time. The Chief told him that resort parking was full, and the Queen's Highway was virtually impassable because of all the satellite news trucks parked along the side of the road.

Looking out, he saw that the ballroom was full and the huge back doors were open so he could be seen from the grassy courtyard beyond. He also saw the three hosts for this afternoon's event: Sarah Wright from ABC News, Keoni Gates, formerly of Fox affiliate KHON, now with Fox News, and the Hapuna's general manager, a woman he knew of, but had never met.

Michael took a step toward his hosts at about the same time the crowd realized he was there. The already loud room reached a crescendo as word of his appearance rippled through the crowd. The three hosts came over to greet him and quickly reviewed the plan they had put together. Then the three hosts stepped forward, with the general manager taking the mic.

"May I have your attention please? Your attention please." A pause as the crowd quieted. "Welcome to the Hapuna Beach Resort. My name is Carol Williams. I'm the General Manager here and I am so pleased that Michael chose this location for his first press conference. Thank you for joining us today; it is undoubtedly the most momentous day in the history of the resort. Michael has a statement he wants to make, then he will take questions. His statement will be made in the form of Q&A with two very-well known reporters, Sarah Wright from ABC and Keoni Gates from Fox. Then the three of us will assist in the open Q&A."

With a closing flourish, she said, "Ladies and Gentlemen, Michael the Ascendant, Ambassador from the Intergalactic Confederation of Planets. Sarah, you're up first."

"Carol. Thank you for such a kind welcome." Sarah turned to Michael. "Michael. Can you give us an update on your progress in the alliance process and any significance there may be to the level you've achieved?"

"Thank you for that question, Sarah. At this point, 25 countries have signed Letters of Intent with the Confederation. Within the next 10 days, we will designate a Consul General and the initial consulate staff for each country. These 25 governments represent a little over 53% of the population of Earth."

"Fifty-three percent. What's the significance of that number?"

"Once we have allies representing more than half of a world's population, we can take legal action against leaders of nations that take hostile action against any ally and, by extension, the Confederation itself."

"Is that what happened in North Korea?" The crowd grew very quiet with that question.

"Yes..." The room erupted in pandemonium.

The general manager came onto the stage, arms raised. "Ladies and gentlemen. Quiet please. If you must use your phone, please exit the room."

As the noise died down, Sarah said, "You were saying about North Korea?"

"Yes. Japan and South Korea petitioned for Confederation assistance. The North had amassed what we now know to be 526,000 troops on the border. Many troops had already entered the demilitarized zone. And the Chairman had sent a demand for South Korea to surrender by sunrise, a demand that we now know he didn't intend to honor. At 10:00 PM, the Chairman called for invasion. At that point we had over 50%, so we took immediate action to arrest their top leadership and disarm the North Korean army." Again, chatter erupted around the room.

"What happened then?" Sarah asked.

"After the Chairman was arrested, we demanded immediate and unconditional surrender. Surrender was not immediate, so we destroyed the army's weapons and confiscated their nuclear arsenal."

"What is the status of the Chairman and of North Korea?"

"Sadly, the Chairman and three of his inner-circle were killed in a failed escape attempt."

"You executed the Chairman?" Sarah asked.

"Not exactly. They had been arrested and transported up to my shuttle. The Chairman broke free from his bonds and attempted to escape. The shuttle was in orbit 12,000 miles above the surface. When the shuttle door opened, the Chairman and his men were sucked out of the cabin into the vacuum of space. He grievously damaged the shuttle and killed two of my crew. No rescue was possible."

The crowd was silent in shock at what they had just heard.

"Were there other casualties?" Sarah asked.

"Two. The Chairman's sister was killed attempting to detonate a truly frightening weapon that would have slaughtered thousands of people in Pyongyang. Her lover, also in the Chairman's inner-circle, attempted to attack me and several of our people."

"And the status of North Korea?"

"North Korea is now a protectorate of the Confederation. I have appointed one of the Chairman's remaining inner circle as Lt. Governor of the region. Three others were selected as cabinet ministers. I think all four will do a job the rest of the world will be proud of."

"What will become of the others in his inner circle?"

"They have been turned over to the South Korean government for prosecution."

"Will the two Koreas reunify?" Sarah asked.

"That is up to them. We will be fair brokers in the negotiations and will abide by their decision, unless hostilities break out again."

"Thank you, Michael. I turn the next segment over to Keoni Gates." There was quiet applause as Sarah handed the microphone over to Keoni.

"Michael," Keoni said. "Thank you for speaking with us this morning. I'd like to start with Israel. What can you tell us about the dramatic scenes we saw playing out this week with Rabbi Levine presenting Confederation gifts to Palestinians?"

"I have utmost respect for Rabbi Levine. As he has stated in video clips that you've all seen, he voted against allying with the Confederation. His argument was that God was the only ally they could depend on. Then 15 minutes later, he found himself running to a bomb shelter. He was outside when the shield was activated, and saw it flicker to life. A minute later he witnessed three nuclear weapons detonate close to him. Then, he saw the nuclear plasma consume everything outside the shield. In that moment he had a life-changing epiphany. The Confederation was the defense his God was giving him, and the conditions of the deal were the way God was telling him to live."

"Michael, are you a god?" Keoni asked.

Michael laughed. "No, Keoni. And never have thoughts like that. I am a living mortal being, just like you; although I am admittedly the beneficiary of some spectacular technology."

That comment drew chuckles from the crowd.

"Are you God's messenger?"

"Possibly. According to the rabbinic texts, God chooses those He chooses, to do the things He wants done. Whether those people believe in Him or not, they are His unwitting tools. Assuming Rabbi Levine believes in his texts, as I am absolutely sure that he does, then he is the one to interpret that question, not me."

"The question I want to ask is whether you believe in God, but in previous interviews you've said that you're not allowed to discuss such questions. May I ask why?" Keoni asked.

"Yes. Because of my experiences on Earth, I know a lot about both Judaism and Christianity. I know much less about other faith systems. As the one introducing life changing technology to Earth, people have already started believing in me more than in my mission, so if I speak knowingly about one religion and not another, then they will believe that I'm endorsing one religion over another. That's not my job. And because of the unintended impact my statements could have, I'm forbidden to speak too specifically about any religion," Michael replied.

"Moving on... Rabbi Levine has started distributing gifts in Israel. When will they start being delivered elsewhere?"

"This week or next, gifts will start going out to all allied nations signed to date. There is nominally a one-week delay from signing to first deliveries. This is because the ally needs to provide the requests. In the next day or two, the Confederation's ability to produce and deliver gifts will reach about 1 million households per day."

"Wow! That's a lot." A pause, and some restlessness from the crowd.

"One last question before I turn it back to Sarah. Any update on the status of your embassy?"

"Yes. I just got word that we have tentatively been approved for a 100 square mile tract of land in the western Northwest Territories of Canada. If I understand correctly, Parliament still needs to approve, but construction will begin shortly and, in a week or two, we will begin taking applications for the Institute, including its medical school. You will be hearing more about that in the days ahead."

"Thank you for speaking with us today, Michael, and letting me take part as one of the hosts. Sarah, back to you."

"Michael, there are rumors circulating that something has happened in Russia and Iran. What can you tell us about this?"

"This is probably the hardest question," Michael started. "For those that have been following the various interviews I've given, you may know that the Confederation chose to reveal itself to humanity a little earlier in your development than we would normally do. We did this because of the serious threats you were facing.

"As I've mention in other interviews, a parasitic species is currently roaming the galaxy. It has the ability to completely consume a planet like Earth in only one or two years. This species is powerful, extremely powerful. On your own, Earth has no chance of resisting it.

"Fortunately, the mass of that invasion is over 1,000 light-years away. To the best of our knowledge that species doesn't have faster than light transportation or communications. So in principle, Earth has a thousand years or more to prepare. That may sound like a long time, but it's not, especially given the toll climate change will soon begin to take.

"The Confederation is currently engaged in a war of sorts with these parasites, whom we have never given the honor of a name. We simply refer to them as the Enemy." A long pause.

"This week, we discovered that seven Enemy agents had already infiltrated the Earth. One of those agents was the Chairman of North Korea. His sister was also an Enemy agent. We also discovered that one of the Russians responsible for an attempted nuclear attack on Georgia was an Enemy agent. A careful scan of the Earth by two capital ships that arrived in orbit two days ago, discovered four more agents, one in Russia, and three in Iran.

"At this point, all seven agents have been destroyed and the Earth is clear of any infestation. All seven agents held high positions in their respective country's governments.

"I want to be clear about one thing. The Confederation stands ready to ally with any country on Earth with whom we can sign a treaty. We will not act against countries that do not ally with us as long as they don't act against us or our allies. And we'll fight to our last breath to protect humanity from the Enemy. Two of my staff lost that fight this week." Michael shook his head in grief.

The room exploded with noise and shouted questions. Once again Carol Williams, the resort's general manager, came on stage with arms raised and asked the crowd to quiet down so questioning could begin. She quickly explained the rules for the Q & A session, then the three hosts spread out around the room to take questions. The first came from a CNN reporter at Keoni's station. "Michael, our agency has been attempting to get an interview with you for the last week. No one has returned our calls. I want to know why we are being denied access!"

"First, and to correct the record, the third interview I gave was to CNN. It happened while I was treating Patrick Gardener after he'd been shot on Pennsylvania Avenue. I can show you the clip, if you haven't seen it." That brought a round of laughter from the crowd.

"Then, I went to CNN Headquarters in Atlanta and spoke with several people there. That conversation was not broadcast, but the President of Mexico, whom I had brought with me, did do a live interview. As to why we have not returned your calls. We have a rule. When we book interviews, we prioritize by the professional courtesy given to our people manning the phones. Now, is there an actual news question I can answer?

"Sarah?"

Before Sarah could reply, the CNN reporter grabbed the microphone from Keoni, only to find that the microphone had been turned off. The commotion drew everyone's attention. Then Michael said, "As I was saying about professional courtesy..."

Sarah had queued up a reporter from NBC, who asked, "Michael, could you reconcile the story for us about the Chairmen's attempted escape, him being an Enemy agent and you losing two of your people?"

"Yes, I would be happy to. I met with the South Korean President to accept South Korea's Letter of Intent to ally with the Confederation. At that meeting, he told me that the North had sent a demand for South Korea to surrender. The North had amassed a huge army on the border and had already made penetrations into the DMZ.

"Earlier the same day, one of my facilities was attacked by an Enemy agent. That agent had taken control of one of the men involved in the attempted nuclear strike on Georgia. We narrowly defeated him and at that point were alerted that Enemy agents were already on Earth.

"Because we now had alliances with the governments representing over half of Earth's population, we had legal authority under Confederation Law to take preemptive action against North Korea once we had irrefutable evidence that the North was going to invade.

"Because of the warning received from our allies in the South, we began surveilling the Chairmen. When he called for the troops to invade, we blocked the order and transported down to arrest him. He attempted to shoot me and had very good aim. Both shots were kill-shots that were stopped by my shields. We made the arrest and transported the Chairman up to my shuttle in orbit. Once on the shuttle, he broke his bonds. By the way, the bonds we used cannot be broken by any human technology, not even a nuclear weapon, so that was our clue that we were dealing with a non-human. My crew reported that they were under attack. During that attack, the ship's door opened, evacuating the passenger cabin into the void. I transported up to help, found that my crew were mortally wounded and closed the door.

"The escort ship accompanying me scanned for other Enemy agents and found the Chairman's sister about to detonate. They stopped her.

"Does that adequately reconcile the stories?"

The reporter agreed that it did, and the questioning moved to a reporter that Carol had queued up. "Michael. You said you detected these Enemy agents. How do you do that and how do you know they are actually Enemy agents?"

"Excellent question," Michael replied. "The Enemy is extra-dimensional, meaning it can slip in and out of our space-time continuum at will. The Enemy is also a parasite, like a mosquito. When it finds a host, it slides out of our space-time continuum to occupy the same space and time but in a different dimension. It then latches on, penetrating the target's brain. It completely takes over the target's mind and slowly feeds on the target itself. Our scanners are multi-dimensional. It is fairly easy for us to spot the Enemy agents latched onto their targets."

The question rotated back to Keoni, who had queued up a reporter from BBC. "Michael. What has become of the North Korean Army? And while I have the microphone, I'd like to say that I hope you will come to the UK sometime soon. I was sad to hear that you had to cancel on Sunday, but now that I know why, I thank you for dealing with the more important problem." His comments generated a small round of applause from the crowd.

"I look forward to visiting the UK as soon as possible, and hope to see you there when I do. Regarding the North Korean Army... North Korea's attempt to invade would have failed because we had erected a shield near the southern border of the DMZ. But, with the Chairman gone and no clear chain of command, the army became a threat to itself and to the rest of the North Korean people. So, when they were slow to surrender, we disarmed them, dissolving their weapons as you may have seen me do to the Secret Service in my first attempt to meet with the American President.

"We also established a shield to the north of the border, trapping the army in the middle and cutting off their supply lines. Once the Army was effectively taken prisoner, we started establishing prisoner of war camps. Each camp is heated, and has medical care and hot food, which I'm told is quite excellent. The various squads were invited in one by one. As each arrived, they were given time to warm up, individually surrender to the Confederation, be given a medical examination and have their wounds and ailments treated, and be fed a hot meal. Everyone was given the opportunity to be trained to use the Confederation equipment and to help set up the next set of camps. In less than 24 hours, 532 camps were established. All 526,000 troops are now safe. The vast majority have voluntarily signed a pledge of allegiance to the new Confederation-controlled North Korea, pending the establishment of a new North Korean government.

"Many of the men have volunteered to join the teams liberating the prison camps. That process should be complete in about a week. The conditions in those camps are... I don't have the words to describe how bad they are. Our medical team is struggling to deal with the volume. If there are doctors who would like to volunteer to help, we will give you the technology and training to do miracles. Just contact our organization."

"May I ask a follow-up question?" The reporter asked.

Michael nodded affirmatively. "What future do you see for North Korea?"

"I need to be careful about what I say here. First, North Korea will have a representative government. They have suffered incomprehensible cruelty under Enemy rule and will need some time to heal. But, from what I've seen of the North Koreans I've interacted with, I think they will become a force for good on this world.

"I know the question everyone wants answered is whether there will be reunification. That decision is solely the Koreans' to make."

The questioning continued for another two hours, then the crowd started to clear.

MACKENZIE MOUNTAINS, NORTHWEST TERRITORIES, CANADA

One week later... A large crowd had gathered that included a representative from all 30 countries that were now allied, plus Lt. Governor Park of the North Korean protectorate, the entire Canadian cabinet, the leaders of the UN and NATO, and 50 reporters selected by the Confederation. They all stood on a huge platform that hovered five feet above the peak of the mountain ridge where the survey team had completed the survey.

After a short welcoming speech by the Canadian Prime Minister, Michael was given the stage. He thanked everyone for being there then said, "This is a momentous day. A day that diplomats like myself live for. Today we 'break ground' on the Confederation's Embassy to Earth. For humanity, the term 'breaking ground' has always been very literal. It was the day the first ground was excavated on the land where the building would be built. Today, that word takes a new meaning. Today, we will activate the shields that will protect this land, lay foundations in the foundational dimension, and add the first series of buildings that will be part of the embassy."

Michael pointed to the Canadian Prime Minister, who was standing at the head of a row of heads of state. After the Canadian Prime Minister, as head of state for the host country, the row had been organized by order of entry into the Confederation. The heads of state stood shoulder to shoulder. Each person had a small pedestal in front of them with a large button on top.

"Mr. Prime Minister, when you push your button, the entire valley will become encased in a protective shield that will isolate us from the weather."

He pushed his button, and the entire valley was encased in shimmering light which slowly faded. As if on cue, a light snow started falling at the far end of the valley. The snow fell onto the shield and started to accumulate, then was blown away.

Michael turned to the Israeli Prime Minister, who was next in line. "Mr. Prime Minister, when you push your button, the foundations will be laid for the entire site."

He pushed the button, but nothing appeared to happen. Then foundations started appearing at the far end of the valley progressing up the eastern side, continuing across the northern face beneath them, then to the west and back down to the south. A small popping noise could be heard as each appeared. The pop, pop, pop continued for about 15 minutes.

Turning to the Georgian Prime Minister, Michael said, "Mr. Prime Minister, when you push your button, the first building of the new Confederation Medical School will be added."

Looking somewhat dubious, the Prime Minister pushed his button. Moments later there was a very loud pop, and an entire building appeared on the foundations at the far end of the valley. After a stunned silence, the entire assembly broke out in applause.

They proceeded in turn, each head of state pushing a button and another building or feature of the embassy came into being. By the time they were done, over 20 million sq. ft. of enclosed space, or about 1% of the embassy complex, had been completed. The dignitaries each greeted Michael and gave interviews to the various press representatives. As the event was winding down, Sarah Wright came over to Michael. "Would it be OK if I came back to Hawaii with you?"

"Isn't that where you started this trip?" Michael asked.

"Yes, but I had originally signed on with a return to New York. I spoke with Monica this morning and she told me I could stay on in Hawaii for a few days as long as I filed my report on time."

"Great. All the shuttles have extra capacity. Mine will be leaving last to make sure that we have everybody."

"Can I make one more request?" she asked.

"Anything," Michael said.

"Can I stay at the ranch tonight? When I tried to extend at the Hapuna, they told me they were booked, and I needed to check out as scheduled."

"I'm sure we can find room. It will be nice having you around. And George is taking over the kitchen tonight, which should be interesting."

THE RESIDENCE, KOHALA MOUNTAIN

When they arrived back at the ranch, Michael got Sarah set up with Jiaying, so she could file her report. Charles had left for China, so Sarah was assigned to his room. After some discussion, the staff agreed that it would be OK if Sarah used Charles' office near the entrance to the lab to do her work.

The rest of Michael's day was filled with calls as five more countries signed on.

KITCHEN, THE RESIDENCE, KOHALA MOUNTAIN

Michael felt exhausted. He had just finished a very frustrating call with the new leader of Russia and was ready for a break. He got up from his desk and walked down to the dining room. People had started to gather, and Michael could smell something good going on in the kitchen. He walked into the kitchen, which was buzzing with activity. George was taking the lead on dinner tonight and was entertaining the normal kitchen crew with his antics.

Noelani came over to Michael with a big smile. "George is showing off tonight and he's already more than a half hour behind. I think you've got at least 45 more minutes, if there are still things you need to do. Sarah was looking for you earlier. Maybe you should go find her.

DINING ROOM, THE RESIDENCE, KOHALA MOUNTAIN

George directed his helpers, Noelani, Bahati, Pam and Helen, as they meticulously placed each of his creations exactly where he wanted it. Then, he called everyone to the table for dinner. "Tonight, Chef George has prepared a fabulous culinary experience for you.

"I have three main courses. The first is Big Island roast beef, smoked with Hawaiian Kiawe, pronounced, key-ah-vay, that's the local mesquite trees you see growing all over the place. The second is fresh caught mahi-mahi braised in coconut milk, with cilantro and lemon grass. And the third is Chicken Tikka Masala, made with Big Island turkey instead of chicken."

"George, did you really make a Turkey Tikka Masala?" Mahesh asked, somewhat skeptically.

"Taste it and weep." George grinned, then continued, "Our side dishes include some truly inspired creations. The first is air-fried Brussel sprouts, with balsamic glaze. The next is local white turnips roasted in pure Vermont maple syrup. This one is going to go fast, so get it quick. Next is another creation that I call 'Sag Paneer ala George.' I didn't have sag or paneer, so I used local beet greens with locally made goat cheese instead."

Again, Mahesh piped up. "George, why are you abusing Indian food tonight?"

"Never underestimate the ability of Chef George." George grinned at him, then continued. "And tonight's starches are Hawaiian black rice. In the old days, only Kings were allowed to eat this stuff. Yes, that's how good it is. And my personal favorite, 'smashed potatoes' made with pureed breadfruit and Hawaiian purple sweet potatoes.

"Please enjoy."

Anna whispered to Helen, "Did George really make this stuff? It smells great."

Helen smiled back. "In a manner of speaking, yes."

Everyone sat and started eating. Michael was seated with Sarah on one side and Mahesh on the other. The seat next to Mahesh was empty; Nisha was apparently doing extra primping tonight. The room got very quiet as everyone started eating. Then Mrs. Patterson spoke up. "George, I think this is the best meal I've ever eaten." Everyone took notice, because for most of them, it was the first time they'd heard her speak.

"Thank you, Ma'am." George replied.

"I recognize that smell," Nisha walked into the room.

All heads turned, then pandemonium broke out as everyone got up to greet Nisha. "That's Turkey Tikka Masala isn't it? Is Chef Marco here? This is my favorite dish of his."

All eyes turned to George.

"I've been outed," George complained sheepishly. "Yes. Chef Marco. I got his permission to replicate his most famous recipes."

"Replicate?" Anna asked. "I thought this was Big Island beef and turkey and fresh mahi-mahi?"

"Well, it was replicated, freshly on the Big Island," George said. Everyone started laughing. The party atmosphere lasted through the evening with George bringing the replicator out to the dining room to replicate dessert.

Michael excused himself and headed off to his bedroom to start a full restoration cycle. Noelani got up and followed him. When Noelani caught up, she said. "I told George."

"And?" Michael asked.

"He said he loved me and had always hoped he could catch an android girlfriend. Then he kissed me. He's so sweet."

"I'm glad to hear you so happy. But take it slow. I don't want to see you get hurt."

As he drifted off to sleep, he thought, *this is the reason we are here. The humor, creativity, personal connection of this young species is infectious. It has been lost in the Confederation. Without this kind of new blood, we are doomed to failure.*

MICHAEL'S BEDROOM, THE RESIDENCE, KOHALA MOUNTAIN

The door to the regeneration chamber opened and Michael woke feeling completely refreshed. As he exited the regeneration chamber, he was surprised to see Sarah waiting for him, holding up a towel. He was momentarily stunned, then smiled and said, "What a pleasant surprise."

He stepped forward to take the towel and for the first time felt momentary embarrassment about his nakedness and the unexpected warmth in his loins. As he took the towel, Sarah wrapped her arms around him and kissed him passionately. "I'm ready to join your team, Michael, if the offer is still open."

EPILOGUE

There was a shimmering in the void of space, then an ellipsoid-shaped object appeared. At first glance, it appeared to have a textured, matte black finish. But on closer examination, the surface itself was smooth but covered in grains of ash or sand that writhed across its surface.

Inside the effect was far more pronounced. The walls and surfaces were covered in a maelstrom of tiny particles that swept across every surface, twisting in rivers of motion and sounding like sand being blown across the desert during a windstorm.

The motion gradually changed. The tiny grains of substance began lifting from the surfaces and swirling into a large ball. The grains combined to become greasy black threads with an elusive smoke-like texture. The storm of particles continued to condense and coalesce until a humanoid shape appeared.

Finally, the creature, a very human-looking creature, became fully solid; the last dusty bits writhing across his skin, then melting into it.

He stretched and shook himself, then said, "That felt so... delicious."

He opened a closet door and pulled out a ship suit that he quickly donned.

This ship had just been captured. The creature had known where it would be, so he'd lain in wait for the crew to return. Once aboard the ship, it hid until they were well underway in interstellar space. Then he had consumed them. In his dust form, there had been nothing they could do. He would settle on them, then slowly start eating, molecule by molecule, cell by cell. By the time his prey knew something was wrong, he was so deeply inside them, eating from the inside out, that there had been nothing they could do but scream and die.

Now they were part of him, their mass, their energy, and a surprising amount of their knowledge and memory. And that was the best part. These men had known where a planet was. One crawling with life. One that would take him a thousand years or more to consume, if he got there first.

Another ship heading in that direction would pass this spot shortly. Now that he had fully cleansed this vessel, he would lie in wait for the next ship. He would not be able to penetrate it, but he could follow it to its destination, where 10 billion prey would be waiting for him.

He set the vessel to silent running. Then waited.

...

Sensors indicated that something gigantic had just passed by. It was traveling in a high dimension, so the only indication was the unnatural resonance the sensors had detected. But he knew the direction the craft was going, so he accelerated to the minimum speed this vessel needed to form a faster-than-light bubble, then continued to accelerate to 10x speed of light. It would take him a while to get to his target, so he would just nap for a year or two, then awake to see where he was.

THE END

THE INSTITUTE
(ASCENDANCY: BOOK 2)

By

D. Ward Cornell

Here is a sneak preview...

[MONDAY, 08.19.2030] INTERSTELLAR SPACE

He could sense the presence of the Enemy. They were very close, yet hidden as if behind a veil. This was the mystery that he still had not penetrated.

The Enemy had first been discovered around 300,000 years ago. It was an old species, but nowhere near as old as his own. His was ancient. Sadly, his species had died out millions of years ago, and to the best of his knowledge, he was the last of his kind. Nonetheless, he still had purpose. Two million years ago, he had discovered an adolescent species, which he had adopted as his own. They referred to him as the Ancient Sentient.

Under his guidance, they had grown up to become the founding and dominant species of the Intergalactic Confederation of Planets, which now represented over 10,000 intelligent species, spanning over 1,000,000 planets across three galaxies. It was during their expansion into the Milky Way that they had discovered the Enemy.

The Enemy was a parasite, one that could descend on a planet and completely consume it, stripping all its resources in a matter of years. Until recently, the Enemy had not been sentient. They were not intelligent, self-aware, or technologically able. But that had changed several millennia ago when they consumed a world that held an Intelligent species and, by some means that he did not understand, had acquired their memories.

Five years ago, the problem got drastically worse when they consumed a planet that held a very intelligent species with nascent faster-than-light technology. They also acquired knowledge of a planet that he knew to be the most important planet in the three galaxies, a planet known as Earth. He could not allow them to consume Earth. If they did, then they would become the masters of the universe.

Recently, it had been discovered that the Enemy was extra-dimensional, meaning they could move between dimensions. That was why the Enemy appeared as smoke, or as dust. They wove between this dimension and four adjacent dimensions, like a snake writhing across the sand.

As he cast his thoughts back to his search, the Ancient Sentient had an epiphany... *The Enemy must come from a higher dimension. A different space-time continuum. That's why they seem to get closer and closer, then fade away without being seen.*

He returned to the place where they seemed closest, then cloaked himself and began moving through adjacent dimensions one at a time.

And there it was, the Enemy home world. After adjusting his senses, he discovered that here they were solid and shaped something like an Earthly squid or octopus. If the Confederation brought the fight here, this blight on the universe could be stopped once and for all.

[Tuesday, 08.20.2030, 3:00 PM] KEELE PEAK, MACKENZIE MOUNTAINS, CANADA

It had been a beautiful morning. The air was cold and clear; the Sun blindingly bright; not a cloud in the sky. The perfect day for a summit attempt.

Alexi Santos had led the team that made the summit today. They were halfway decent mountaineers and had done a respectable job making the final ascent up the southeast ridge of the mountain.

They were now about halfway back down, and the weather was turning against them. Clouds had formed in the sky and the wind had started blowing. Following standard protocol, Alexi doublechecked the climbing ropes that bound the party together. Then she took the lead following the last of the ridgeline back toward base camp. As the storm intensified, the team's mettle was tested. Several men fell or were blown off the ridge, but their lines held them together. And each time, the one who had fallen was helped, or pulled, back up.

...

Alexi was a Confederation android, an Artificial Intelligence (AI) driving a human avatar. Her official job was head of the outfitting concession at the Intergalactic Confederation of Planets Embassy in Northwest Territories, Canada. As part of the Confederation's treaty with Canada, they had been granted a 100 square mile tract of land in the Mackenzie Mountains. It was a very remote and inhospitable tract of land located 'close' to the geographic center of the human population on Earth. Its remoteness made the land available. Its location reduced travel time to all but a few of the world's capitals.

In granting this tract, the Canadian government had asked the Confederation to allow tourism to this part of their country and to offer outfitting services for the adventurers that wanted to travel there.

Amazingly, no humans had come forward to set up this operation. So Alexi, a Confederation citizen, had volunteered. Alexi had risen to fame during the liberation of North Korea. She had been part of the team that went in to clean up after the arrest of the former dictator. She had helped set up the prisoner of war camps that housed the invasion troops, which had been staged near the South Korea border. She had then led the teams that liberated North Korea's notorious slave labor camps.

The outfitting concession had a half dozen certified expedition leaders, but Alexi had been the first approved by the Canadian commission that had oversight responsibilities for tourism in Canada.

...

As the expedition approached the last difficult descent before their shelter, massive gusts hit the team. It was not clear how anyone could make it down this cliff face without being blown away.

Alexi, who had figured out how to shelter thousands of troops in cold winter environments, never left home in the Mackenzies without bringing a shelter with her. She pulled a box from her pack that looked a lot like the power pack that came with the average portable computer. With her team gathered around her, she anchored it in the foundation dimension and activated it. A dome, maybe 20 ft. in diameter, glistened into life around them. The wind stopped, the snow deflected off the dome, and warmth from the small heater settled in.

Alexi used her implants to connect into Embassy security. She reported her situation and they advised her of the updated forecast. The blizzard would last another two days. Twenty feet of snow were predicted for the mountain. The center of the storm had stalled to the southeast of them, so the wind would be coming from the northeast.

This is trouble, Alexi thought. *The wind is going to be coming up over the steep part of the ridge and will deposit all its snow right on top of us.*

By her calculations, a thirty- to fifty-foot snow drift was about to form right on top of them. The shield could hold that weight. It, plus their personal thermal shields, would even keep them warm. Nonetheless, they would suffocate with no way to exchange air through the snow.

"We can't stay here," Alexi shouted.

The men looked at her incredulously.

"Stay here," she said. "I can get help in time." Then, rope and carabiners in hand, she walked through the shield into the storm.

...

As she first emerged, the wind nearly blew her away. But placing her back to the dome wall, she shimmied around to the leeward side of the dome until she found the first anchor point that was somewhat sheltered from the wind. She clipped a rope to the shield's anchor point, then walked to the edge of the cliff that they could not climb down and leaped.

The mountaineers in the shelter saw her being swept up by the wind and immediately despaired. What they didn't know was that Alexi wore a Confederation climbing harness, an anti-gravity device similar to the Fabulous Flying Overalls that had made Sergeant George Butler famous. The climbing harness had an anti-grav drive that allowed Alexi to fly, regardless of the direction of the wind.

Navigating the storm was still tricky, but she made her way down to the dome at base camp and anchored the climbing rope she had brought. She clipped onto the rope, now anchored at both ends, and used the anti-grav drive to propel herself back up to the mini dome on the leeward side of the ridge. Snow had already piled up several feet.

Still clipped onto the rope, she walked through the shield to find pandemonium and despair inside. The temperature had been dropping and the snow piling up. The men were convinced they were going to die.

454

"Guys. Man up," she said. "I've connected a rope between the domes. The dome at base camp is safe. I can shuttle you down one-by-one. It'll be a wee bit bumpy, but a great ride nonetheless."

She beamed. "Who's first?"

A moment passed without any volunteers. Alexi was dismayed. Staying here was certain death. By comparison, riding down was safer than sitting in a rocking chair and watching the world go by, just more fun.

Seeing that none of these wusses was going to volunteer, she grabbed the closest member of the team, clipped him on, and then dragged him out of the dome and over the precipice.

Poor Henry, she thought, as he screamed the whole way down. *But, what a wuss.*

She purposely came in high, penetrating the shield, then made a smooth landing. Henry still fell when she let go of him. Shaking her head, she said, "Henry! Make yourself useful. Make some coffee for the others and turn on some lights. It'll be getting dark before too long. Next one will be down in about five minutes." Then she ran out of the dome and flew back to the others.

One by one, the men came down. On each return she found the snow against the mini dome stacked higher and higher. As she came in to get the last member of the team, disaster struck. The rope she'd been using to guide her flight suddenly went slack. Panicked that she might lose the rope altogether, she grabbed it where it passed through the carabiner she'd used to clamp on. She quickly tied on to the rope in a way that would prevent it from coming off completely, but in the process lost her bearings.

Suddenly the rope snapped tight, knocking the breath out of her. As she came back to her senses, Alexi couldn't help but laugh at herself. *Here I am. Attached to a rope. Using an anti-grav drive to hover someplace downwind of the rope's anchor point. I don't even know which end I'm anchored to. Hopefully, it's the mini dome. Otherwise, I'll never find it again.*

As the blizzard intensified, visibility dropped to zero. With no other option, Alexi started reeling herself in hand over hand, using the anti-grav drive to relieve the pressure of the wind while still keeping the rope taut.

...

Jack was worried. It had been a long time since Alexi left with Steve. Something must have gone wrong and he was running out of time, the mini dome was nearly covered by the snow. And he was freezing.

...

Alexi suddenly hit snow. She'd been pulling herself in, but here the rope was just coming out of a wall of snow. After a moment of puzzlement, it occurred to her. *This must be the mini dome, covered in snow.*

I can use the taut rope like a knife. She thought, directing the anti-grav drive to move up and down, left and right. Slowly, she sliced off layers of snow until the rope finally hit the dome and she could see the light within.

"Yes!" she shouted. It was indeed the mini dome. Jack was still alive. As she pulled herself in the last 20 feet, the wind suddenly shifted and she went flying into the wall of stone to the northwest of the dome. She'd placed the mini dome here intentionally, hoping proximity to this part of the cliff would give them some shelter from the wind.

There was a loud crack and searing pain in her right leg. Ironically, hitting the wall killed her momentum and blocked most of the wind. She fell twenty feet straight down, landing on the injured leg, which bent unnaturally. She struggled to get up on her remaining good leg, took two hops, then fell into the dome and passed out.

...

Jack saw Alexi fall next to the dome and went to help, but the dome was not keyed to allow him to pass through it. As she fell over into the dome, he grabbed her and pulled her the rest of the way in. Looking at her leg, he saw that it was mangled and bleeding copious quantities of blood. He got the Confederation first aid kit, then wrapped her leg as they'd been instructed during safety training. When it was secure, he pushed the button on the wrap that would tighten it, isolating the broken bone and infusing nanobots. When he finished, he saw that he was sitting in a puddle of her blood, which had begun to freeze. Then, shivering uncontrollably, he passed out.

...

Alexi woke from a very pleasant dream. She'd been flying on a rope, using it to slice up snow. *Where do dreams like that come from?* she wondered.

She opened her eyes and took in the scene. Jack was out cold and covered in partially clotted, frozen blood. "What the hell happened to you, Jack?" she asked. Rousing herself, Alexi attempted to help him.

That's when she realized she was the one that was injured. Jack was the one that had applied the first aid. "Thank you, Jack," she said out loud, then "What a wuss."

"We're not out of the woods yet, are we Jack?" she said to his inert body. "Let's take inventory. The anti-grav drive must have been broken when I hit that wall. Going to need to fix that."

Scanning the perimeter of the dome, she noticed that they still had Jack's rope and another one. *Must be Henry's. I did yank him out of here kind of suddenly,* she thought.

"Looks like we have enough rope, if I can fix the grav-drive, Jack," she said. Jack was still out cold, but talking to him helped keep her calm.

Slowly and awkwardly, Alexi took off her parka, then her outer mountaineering shirt, revealing the anti-grav harness. It looked more or less like a standard climbing harness.

Slowly, and somewhat painfully, she removed the grav-drive. The problem was immediately obvious. The power unit was damaged. The casing had cracked, breaking the connector that powered the lift generators. She disconnected the power unit from the rest of the harness and was relieved to see that the lift generators and their connectors were intact. The part that had broken was the socket on the power unit.

"Good news Jack. I only need to swap out the power unit, and I never go anywhere without at least one spare."

She grabbed her parka, fished through it until she found the spare power unit, and then attached it to the harness. The unit beeped. It was alive and functional. "Looks like we're back in business, Jack," she said, somewhat surprised that Jack hadn't come back around yet.

Alexi put the harness back on, secured it, and then levitated up off the ground. Her leg made several loud popping noises. "Not liking the sound of that, Jack," she said.

She went over to Jack and spotted his problem almost immediately. He was suffering severe hypothermia. At some point the power pack on his thermal shield must have either come loose or been broken. She patted him down looking for where he had put his power pack. He had the type that strapped on, so could be located anywhere as long as it was in direct contact with his skin.

Slowly, she worked his parka off and started patting him down again.

"Found it!" she shouted. Jack had placed the unit in the small of his back. It was held in place by a strap that wrapped around his torso just below the rib cage. The strap had come loose. Alexi quickly tested the unit to make sure it still had power. It did. She readjusted the strap and confirmed that his thermal shield was now active. A quick scan showed that Jack's core temperature had dropped to 85 degrees.

"Oh, Jack. You're in trouble, my friend. Let's see if we can save you."

Moving as quickly as she could, Alexi redressed Jack, then herself. Not wanting a repeat of her interview with the rock wall, Alexi reached through the dome from the inside and tied a new piece of rope to the anchor point on the exterior of the dome. Then from her rescue supplies, she put a buoyancy assist belt on Jack, reducing his 'weight' to about 30 lbs. The beauty of the buoyancy assist was that it offset gravitational pull on his body without applying a force vector the way the anti-grav harness did. She strapped Jack onto her back using four carabiners to lock him into place. Then, ropes attached, she 'dialed' the anti-grav to max and went flying out of the dome into the storm.

...

"Hey guys. I think we're in trouble. Check out the rope. It's slack and flopping around."

Several of the other guys looked at the anchor. The rope had clearly broken.

"Don't worry," Phil said. "She found her way down the first time. She can do it again."

"I don't know," Henry said. "Visibility is terrible. The wind is a lot worse. And it's starting to get dark. We need to do something."

"Dude, none of us is Alexi. If she's having trouble, then we have no chance."

Henry had started pacing. It always helped him think.

"Lights!" he said with conviction. "In a storm, your own lights are almost worthless because they light up the snow around you. But someone else's lights can help because the snow brightens where they are. How many lights do we have? Can we aim them toward the mountain?"

Someone else piped up. "What about the radio? Can we call for help? Surely the Confederation has some type of technology to help?"

Henry started searching around and found the spare communicator that Alexi had brought. He had no idea how to operate it. It seemed that Alexi just talked into it and it worked.

"Hello," Henry said. Nothing. He started tapping on it, whistling into it, pressing every surface, saying random distress words... "Mayday! Mayday!" Then, "SOS! SOS!"

One of the other guys said, "Try 9-1-1."

"There are no buttons, idiot!" Henry said, starting to get a bit testy.

"I meant, say '9-1-1.'"

"Oh. Good idea," Henry said contritely. "Sorry about that."

Then he shouted... "9-1-1. 9-1-1" ...into the device.

"Embassy Operator. Please state the nature of your emergency."

Everyone was dumbfounded that this had worked. Then Henry quickly explained to the operator what was going on.

AMBASSADOR'S OFFICE

"Michael, we may have a problem." Pam came into his office. Michael served as Ambassador from the Intergalactic Confederation of Planets to the Peoples of Earth. He was Lorexian but occupied a human avatar. Pam was his assistant. She was an android. They had worked together for about 20 years.

"I just got a call from the Embassy emergency operator. They got a call from a member of the Keele Peak summit team. They said that Alexi had saved them, but she is now missing, along with the last person on their team whom she was attempting to rescue."

"What are we doing about it?"

"They need your approval to take one of the shuttles to launch a search and rescue mission."

"Approved." Michael said. "But they are not to take any exceptional risks."

NEAR KEELE PEAK, CANADA

Alexi was getting close to the point of calling for help. Jack had been strapped to her back for 30 minutes now and he was at serious risk of death or permanent disability from hypothermia. Then she saw something. Light within the shadow of the peak.

It must be base camp. They've lit it up for me! She thought, suddenly a little more impressed by this team.

She headed for the light, pushing the anti-grav drive as hard as she could. It really wasn't designed for this, but it had just enough power to overcome the wind.

The light got brighter and brighter and the form of the dome could now be discerned. It was about 100 ft. below her and maybe 500 ft ahead. *Time to trade altitude for speed*, she thought, turning the anti-grav drive to push parallel to the ground. She shot forward and fell precipitously, now that the grav drive wasn't holding her up anymore. A moment of that and she adjusted the grav drive to arrest the fall.

The grav-drive could produce about 2G of force and arrested the fall maybe 10 ft. above the ground. But the wind at this level was a lot lower and she was coming in toward the dome way too fast.

Perfect! she thought. About one second from impact with the dome, she flipped the anti-grav drive to slow her down. They still shot in through the wall of the dome a little fast. Alexi tried for the perfect parachute landing, coming in gently at a running speed, having completely forgotten about her broken leg.

...

It had been about two hours now and the rest of the mountaineering team was afraid that Alexi and Jack had been lost. The Confederation emergency operator had told them that a shuttle was inbound and would attempt to land. But sensors indicated that the wind speed was too high. A rescue team would transport down to the dome to prep the survivors for extraction while the shuttle conducted low altitude scans in an attempt to locate Alexi. It was clear they did not expect to find her.

With all the lights on at their maximum settings, the team could see nothing outside, other than snow landing on the dome and drifting down the side or just blowing away.

Suddenly there was an incredible noise. It was Alexi whooping as she came in for a landing with Jack on her back.

"This is the way it's done boys!" she yelled as she came in for what looked like a running landing.

Her left leg planted. "Yes!" Alexi yelled.

But as the right leg hit, it completely folded up, bending 90 degrees about one third of the way between knee and ankle. Alexi and Jack came down hard, Jack on top. They slid and hit a classic government-style gray metal desk. There was a loud crack and a trail of blood where they had slid.

Henry still had the communications device in his hand and shouted, "Shuttle! Shuttle! We have Alexi and Jack, but they are badly injured. Emergency extraction required! Emergency extraction required!"

Moments later, two men in rescue garb appeared in the dome and headed straight to the spot the rest of the team was pointing at. A third appeared near the team.

They detached Jack and one of the techs immediately started triage. "Rescue shuttle. I have Patient 1. Male, the one they call Jack. Severe hypothermia. Core temperature below 85 degrees."

The other had started his assessment of Alexi, whom he had met before. "Rescue shuttle. Patient 2 is confirmed to be Alexi Santos. Multiple compound fracture of the right leg. Broken radius in left arm. Possible broken ulna in same arm. Concussion. Significant blood loss. She needs immediate evacuation."

While the med techs had been doing their assessment, a third member of the rescue team had tagged the other six team members. The seven of them transported up moments before Alexi's assessment was complete.

The pilot, in consultation with the Embassy, did an emergency site-to-site transport, sending Alexi, Jack and their rescuers directly to the Embassy's emergency medical facility from the base camp dome.

AMBASSADOR'S OFFICE

"Michael?" Pam said. "They found Alexi and the man she was rescuing. Both were in rough condition and were transported directly to the hospital. Doctors say the climber is stable. Alexi is in critical condition but expected to recover."

"Thank you, Pam."

...

Sarah would be coming by his office in about a half hour. She now headed Media Relations for the Embassy. Michael and Sarah had met a day after the Revelation. He had appeared on Good Morning America the morning after the announcement. Sarah had been the lead host that day. Within a week of that first meeting, they had fallen for each other. Now they were the world's most talked about power couple.

They had a dinner reservation at Chef Marco's restaurant in the building next door. *Only one more thing I have to accomplish before I can enjoy the rest of my evening*, Michael thought.

Suddenly, his office was bathed in brilliant light and a thunderous voice echoed in his mind. "Michael. I must speak with you."

It was the Ancient Sentient. Michael turned to look but was overwhelmed by the brilliant light and sparkles of color at the center. He found himself transfixed.

"I'm sorry to have come in my energy form. But the matter is urgent and the time short," the voice rumbled.

461

"Excellency. Your presence Is always a gift."

"Unfortunately, I come with news of the Enemy. And it is not good.

"Those in your space-time continuum have acquired faster-than-light transportation and have found your coordinates. The main mass of them are still over 100 years away, but the leading contingent will arrive much sooner.

'Worse, they have figured out what Earth is." He paused for effect. "They know that Earth's core has high concentrations of transluminide. I would not be surprised if the first arrived in just a few years."

A shudder ran through Michael.

At the edge of his perception, he heard a thump. But in his transfixed state, it did not register in his consciousness.

"But that is not the bad news."

"What could possibly be worse?" Michael stuttered.

"I have been roaming the high dimensions and finally found the Enemy's home world. Through normal space-time it is close. If the Enemy had the ability to cross the high dimensions the way that I do, they could be here in hours. But they cannot. Nonetheless, the transluminide in the Earth's core draws them like bees to clover.

"If we are to have any hope, we must strike first. Humanity is an aggressive species, well-suited to war. Their planet has the greatest preponderance of transluminide in the known universe. So, our assault on the Enemy home world must launch from Earth. And it must be decisive.

"Begin building your army. I will be back to deliver the technology you will need as soon as I can. The fate of the Confederation will be decided here."

...

Michael returned to his senses, standing where he was when the Ancient Sentient had appeared. His eyes finally focused on the clock on the far wall. 7:14.

"Oh, no," he whispered to himself. "I'm late for dinner." He turned toward the door and saw Sarah lying unconscious on the floor.

His scans showed nothing wrong with Sarah, but those results were misleading. No one in the Confederation understood the undeniable impact that the Ancient Sentient's presence had on people, but the impact was real, even if it was not understood. When the ancient one presented himself in energy form, Michael lost all sense of time. But he had never lost consciousness. For the vast majority of others, they

462

blacked out as soon as he appeared. Most came back to themselves within minutes of his departure, but some remained unconscious for hours, days, even weeks.

Wake up, Sarah. Michael pushed, before even thinking about what he was doing.

She stirred but did not wake.

Wake up, Sarah. Michael pushed again, this time more gently and compassionately.

Sarah stirred again, her eyes fluttering open.

"Where? Where am I?" she asked, fogginess evident in her voice.

Michael took her hand and said softly, "You're in my office."

"What?" Then she looked around. "Why am I on the floor?"

"What's the last thing you remember?" Michael asked gently. "Do you remember coming here?"

Slowly, Sarah's memories started to return. "We had a dinner date tonight. You were tied up with an emergency, so I was going to meet you here…"

"Do you remember coming into the office?" Michael asked.

"Uh… I opened the door to the outer office and saw that no one was in the reception area. So, I came down the hallway and saw bright light under your door." A long pause. "I thought that was weird. The light was too bright. So, I ran down the hall and knocked on the door." A pause… "This feels like a dream. I opened the door and you were facing a cloud, brilliantly lit with beautiful sparkles of color inside." Some hesitation… "I called your name, and the cloud cast its attention on me. I felt so small…"

Suddenly, wide awake, she stood and looked at Michael intently. "Michael, what was that thing and what did it do to me?"

Michael took her in his arms. She was shaking. "It's OK." He whispered. "It's OK."

He kissed her on the cheek and stepped back a little so he could look her in the eyes. "That is the person we call the Ancient Sentient. He is immensely old, the most respected elder in the Confederation. Millions of years ago, he figured out how to leave his physical form and exist as pure energy. I met him for the first time during my study of the Roman Empire."

Suddenly, understanding kicked in. Sarah might be a less-than-devout Catholic, but she had finished her catechism. Michael, realizing that Sarah had put the pieces together, made a face. "I probably shouldn't have told you that."

"Michael, that looked like what was described in the Bible as the Transfiguration. Were you there? You told me you were in Palestine at that time. Were you at the Transfiguration? Did you know Jesus?" She asked, more as an accusation than as a question.

"It's not like that," he said.

"What do you mean, 'It's not like that!'" she asked, hysteria building.

"OK. OK." A long pause. "You understand why it is forbidden to talk about this, right?"

Sarah started to protest. Michael held up his hands in surrender.

"OK. OK. What I meant is that what you saw is not what you think it is. Yes, I was in Judea at the time the Transfiguration occurred. I was in Jerusalem that night. But I was not a participant. I was on another hilltop within viewing distance. And what I could see from that distance matched the accounts you were taught. But the important part is that the Ancient Sentient was standing next to me in his physical form. And even he was shocked by the power and purity of what we were both seeing across the valley. What you saw tonight was a speck of dust by comparison."

A long silence, then... "How does the Ancient Sentient do that? How can he exist as pure energy?" Sarah asked.

Michael laughed at that question, then sobered. "I have no idea," he replied, awe and dismay clear in his voice.

"Have you asked him?"

"No, but he knows I want to know. So he told me that it's something that cannot be taught. It's something that needs to be learned. Only a handful have learned to do it. He is the last of his kind that we know to be living. If you should ever be in his presence again, ask him. He will respect that."

Michael took Sarah by the hand and asked. "Still interested in dinner? We've completely blown our reservation, but I bet they'll still give us a table."

CHEF MARCO'S RESTAURANT, CONFEDERATION EMBASSY COMPLEX

Dinner at Chef Marco's was fabulous as always. The chef was in town this week, and greeted them as soon as they came in. He had prepared a special menu 'just for them' and reserved a table on the upper level that had a beautiful view over the valley. The sun had just set, and the Northern Lights were putting on their fabulously ethereal display.

One of the things that Michael had learned early in their courtship was that Sarah loved fine red wine. Chef Marco had learned that also. He'd put the word out to the premium wineries around the world that the Ambassador frequented his restaurant and loved fine red wine. Pictures of him enjoying their wine might get back to those that submitted samples or made rare bottles available for purchase.

Prior to his courtship with Sarah, Michael had refused almost all forms of alcohol. But when it became clear that it was not acceptable to refuse wine when having state dinners in foreign capitals, Charles had developed a nanobot therapy that held blood alcohol to 0.015%, no matter how much was ingested. The nanobots would also reduce blood alcohol levels to zero within 5 minutes of receiving the command.

Tonight, Chef Marco presented an old bottle matched to the main course, a 2005 'Soul of the Lion' from Daou Vineyards in Paso Robles. Sarah nearly swooned over this offering. Michael, who had finally started developing a taste for fine wine, simply marveled at 'the human ingenuity and artistry that could create such a thing,' words that ultimately showed up in a review written by Chef Marco.

...

As they walked back to the Ambassador's residence, Sarah snuggled up and said. "Thank you for such a pleasant evening."

AMBASSADOR'S RESIDENCE, CONFEDERATION EMBASSY COMPLEX

As soon as they were back in the Residence, Sarah took his hand and led him to the bedroom. Michael had come to love Sarah in a way he'd never known before. Part of that was the physicality of human contact. But the larger part was the mental connection they had formed. As they came together, Michael would push his affection and desire for her. Knowing that Michael would read her, Sarah sent the same emotions back.

Although it was something that had become a defining part of their relationship, Michael did not understand the science of it. Lorexians had nascent telepathy, something enhanced in Ascendants by their training and implants. Michael had an acute ability to 'read' others, particularly humans. But he was one of the very few that could push thoughts and emotions to others.

In contrast, humans had no telepathy. Yet, over the last five years, Michael had become so connected to Sarah that it was as if she had become telepathic also. When they made love, they truly became one, minds and bodies connected. It was a connection neither wanted to lose.

…

Despite the late night, they both woke early.

"I know," Sarah said meekly.

"Know what?" Michael asked.

"They are coming, aren't they?" Michael started to deflect, but Sarah cut him off. "Michael. I know. I hear your thoughts. I see your dreams."

Michael stood there, speechless.

"I want to enroll," she said.

This statement puzzled Michael. He had asked her several times if she would consider enrolling in the Institute and taking Ascendance training, but she'd resisted. And he'd finally accepted that as her choice. "May I ask why?"

"I don't want to lose you."

"What!?" Michael said, not understanding.

Sarah smiled at that. "Michael, if you just opened your senses to me, you would know."

"Better for both of us if you tell me," he said tenderly.

"With life extension therapy, I have what… 100 more years? You have hundreds of thousands. But you will be lost the day I go. I sense the fear in you while you sleep. So, I need to be here. I need to be part of the fight when they come. If I'm not, you won't be either. Then, everything will be lost."

Michael was overcome by his love for this woman and as that affection leaked out, she folded herself into his arms.

AFTERWORD

A couple years ago I moved to the Big Island of Hawaii from Silicon Valley. The motivation for the move was multifold, but among the reasons was simply to slow down and read more books. I'm an avid science fiction fan and in the year after the move read more Sci-Fi books than I had in the 20 years preceding.

Several themes in those books really spoke to me, questions like... Where are the aliens? Are there ancient species? How could an advanced species live in harmony with their environment? How will humanity change if the cost of material things went to zero?

As I played with these questions, a story line came to me, literally in my dreams. After a month of dreaming about an ancient species walking the earth in human form waiting for the right time to reveal themselves, I gave in and started writing it down. Each chapter answered a question haunting a dream.

- How would I announce myself? I would do a series of increasingly impossible things culminating in a TV/radio communication that defies human technology.
- What would the American government do when one of their 'citizens' did something like that? Attempt to arrest him.
- How would I get my story out? Morning television news show.
- Which country would jump first? The one that needs the most protection and has the political will to do it?
- How long would it take for, and under what circumstances would, the American government sign on? Only when forced.
- Where would I put my embassy? The geographic center of the northern hemisphere.

The Ascendancy series attempts to address these questions and others like them.

Book 1: Revelation is about an ancient species that has been watching humanity since it first came to be, looking out for it and revealing themselves to save humanity from impending doom.

Book 2: The Institute, released in November 2019, is about human evolution in a post-Revelation world, its attempts to be relevant and participate in its own protection.

Book 3: Emergence, released in April 2020, is about humanity's emerging role within the Intergalactic Confederation of planets.

The books that follow will track humanity's rise in Intergalactic stature and leadership.

Thank you for reading this book. If you've read this far, then you probably liked it. Please consider putting some stars on a review. That will make it easier for others to find it. Stay tuned for more to come.

If you have comments, suggestions, or just want to say 'Hi,' drop me a note. I do my best to answer every email. If you'd be interested in joining my pre-reader program, please contact me.

You can reach me at dw.cornell@kahakaicg.com.

ABOUT THE AUTHOR

D. Ward Cornell lives on the Kohala Coast of the Big Island of Hawaii. His work as an engineer, consultant and entrepreneur has taken him all over the world. Many of those places are featured in this story. Although still dabbling in those fields, his passions are now writing, cooking and entertaining. Some of the recipes attributed to characters in this book come from the author's kitchen.

Made in the USA
Middletown, DE
21 June 2022